TRUE 2 LIFE
PUBLICATION

AL-SAADIQ BANKS

CAUGHT 'EM SLIPPIN'

Al- SAADIQ BANKS

TRUE 2 LIFE PRODUCTIONS

Caught 'Em Slippin'

For information contact:
True 2 Life Productions
P.O. Box 8722
Newark, N.J. 07108
E-mail: *True2lifeproductions@verizon.net*
Website: *www.True2LifeProductions.com*
Author's E-mail: *Alsaadiqbanks@aol.com*

ISBN: 0-974-0610-3-4

This book is dedicated to everyone who said I couldn't do it. When will you finally realize that your hate and negative energy only motivates me? Love is love.

July 1, 2004

Today is the hottest day of the summer, so far. It's a record breaking 101 sticky and muggy degrees. The sun beams on the heads of Miranda and her long time boyfriend Sha-Rock, as they cruise through the blocks in the candy apple red convertible Porsche Boxter. They're catching the attention of everyone they pass.

They slow down as they approach an intersection. Directly across the street, ten young boys crowd the corner of the small sandwich shop.

As they near the corner, Sha-Rock steers the car toward the right as to pull over. The crowd of boys watches attentively. Not only are they admiring the vehicle and the beautiful passenger, they're also paying close attention to the out of state license plates.

The car comes to a complete stop. Sha-Rock slams the gear into park and hops out of the car.

He has a lot of nerve to jump out on one of Newark's roughest streets, without knowing a soul on the block.

As he steps toward the store, he looks into the eyes of everyone individually. They all exchange long, hard, cold looks. They want to test him, but his confidence makes them unsure. Not to mention his size. His demeanor is threatening to most. He stands six feet four inches tall and weighs a solid 225 pounds.

His tight wife beater is glued to his torso. His body resembles the body of a boxer. He has a tiny waistline and very broad shoulders. His wide chest bounces with every step. Beads of sweat cover his shiny bald head. His pitch-black skin glistens flawlessly. His sleepy half opened eyes give him a distinctive look.

The spectators pay close attention to his swagger. He almost drags his right leg due to a slight limp. Every three steps he takes he has to pull his velour Rocawear sweats back on his waist. The sweatpants appear to be at least two sizes too big. His upper body is about three times the size of his lower half.

Once he disappears into the sandwich shop, the chattering begins. "Who the fuck this nigga think he is?" shouts one of the younger boys.

"Word is bond! This nigga disrespecting the block. This ain't

Pennsylvania. A motherfucker can't be pulling up on our set, leaving his shit running like we won't jump in and take that shit."

"No bullshit! Take the car and the pretty bitch with it," says another youngster. "Shit ain't sweet."

Miranda can hear the chatter clearly, but never once does she acknowledge it.

"What up, Mommy?" shouts the eldest male of the bunch.

Miranda continues to look straight ahead as if she doesn't hear him.

"Psst, Mommy," he calls again.

Miranda keeps her head facing straight ahead but she peeks through the side of her sunglasses. There he stands to the right of her. Judging by the dress code, he appears to be the boss. He's the only one who isn't wearing a long oversized T-shirt down to the knees of dirty saggy jeans. Miranda notices that the T-shirt thing must be a fad because she has noticed it on every street corner that they have passed. He's also the only one on the corner who isn't wearing his hair in dreadlocks. He sticks out like a sore thumb. He's wearing a pink and sky blue striped button-up shirt, and nicely fitted jeans. He's wearing Gucci sneakers, while the others are wearing dogged out Gore-Tex boots on their feet. He has dark wavy hair, with a thin mustache and beard. His thick, bushy eyebrows peek over his Gucci Aviator shades.

After realizing that she's not paying attention to him, he finally walks off. He walks in the direction of a beautiful white Range Rover with snow-white interior. Just as he gets within a few steps of the truck, he hits the alarm and the trunk pops open.

He fumbles around in the trunk as if he's looking for something, but Miranda knows he just wants her to see his truck.

Just as he's closing the trunk, Miranda opens the door and steps out of the car. Everyone stops what they're doing just to focus on her. The first thing they notice is the pretty feet inside four-inch stilettos that extend from her long slender leg.

They can't believe their eyes. None of them has ever seen a woman this beautiful in person. Sure they have seen girls like this in music videos, but to see her right here in the physical form is a whole different story.

She stands five feet ten inches tall. She has long beautiful legs, which are extremely bowed. She walks like she has an invisible horse

7

in between her legs. Her tiny coochie cutter denim shorts hug her thighs and her perfectly rounded onion. It's just perfect, not too big and not too small. It's just a handful. Her huge breasts always seem to be the focal point of everyone. Her thin spaghetti strapped top can barely hold them. The top of her blouse is cut low, exposing cleavage in abundance. Her long jet-black, silky hair falls to the bottom of her buttocks. Her complexion is dark yet rich.

She walks over to the phone booth and grabs hold of the receiver. As she's dialing the numbers, the kid makes his way back to the corner. She presses her back onto the phone booth and watches the car, just in case one of the little wise guys decides to jump in the car and take off.

As she's whispering into the phone, he walks past her and leans on the opposite side of the phone booth. The smell of his cologne smacks her in the face. She's no stranger to his fragrance. He's wearing Chrome by Azzuro.

She examines him from head to toe, paying close attention to the small details, like his diamond encrusted Breitling, his diamond charmed bracelet, and his pinkie ring which appears to be at least six karats. His manicured nails shows that he's polished. The word "Major" pops into her head.

She slides her Vera Wang sunglasses to the tip of her nose, exposing her chinky, hazel colored eyes. "Excuse me, can I get a little privacy?" she barks. "I'm trying to talk on the phone."

"Privacy?" he asks. "This is my place of business. This is where I work. This ain't Pennsylvania. You and your little boyfriend got the game fucked up. Jumping out of the car, leaving it running. If I wasn't out here y'all would be walking home. My young boys would have jumped in and took that shit."

"My man?" she asks. "How do you know that's my man?"

"I don't. I'm trying to get you to tell me," he says following up with a big smile.

She turns away from him.

"Well is he?"

"Something like that," she admits.

"What do you mean, something like that?"

"I mean something like that," she snaps while peeking into the store to make sure her dude isn't coming out of the store. "It's on and off with us. He doesn't know what he wants. Sometimes he wants me and sometimes he don't."

He looks her over and asks himself, how the fuck could someone not want her? He peeks into the store and notices that her guy is next in line to pay for his food. "Listen, take my number and give me a call. You said y'all are on and off. Call me when y'all off, so I can get on. I can be your long distance lover, feel me?"

She cracks a smile, and peeks into the store before pulling a pen and pad from her purse. She scribbles his number down in a nick of time. Just as she tucks it away, he struts out of the store.

He looks to the car and realizes that she's not sitting there. He then looks to his right. "What the fuck you doing? Get yo ass in the car!" he yells as he races toward her. She drops the phone and backs away from him. Fear is written all over her face. She covers her head like she knows he's about to strike her. Instead he grabs the back of her neck and lifts her a few inches off of the ground. She manages to plant the tips of her toes onto the ground as he pushes her to the car. He snatches the door open. "Get the fuck in the car. I didn't tell yo goofy ass to get out!" he shouts as he shoves her into the car. He glances around at all the spectators as he slams the door. He stares into the eyes of the boss. "What the fuck you looking at?" he asks as he steps around to the driver's side of the car.

The kid just smiles and shakes his head nonchalantly. All the young boys form around the boss as if he's the president. Through the commotion one kid has already managed to escape to the yard across the street. They're all waiting for the boss to give them the word so they can attack the out-of-towner and teach him a lesson. Instead, he continues to laugh. He spares him. Besides, he has a better way to get even with him. He'll hurt him by bagging his chick, he thinks to himself.

"Oh, I thought so!" Sha-Rock yells as he gets into his car. He's so busy being tough that he doesn't even see the kid standing behind him in the alleyway with the "Rachet" gripped tightly in the palm of his hand.

He pulls off slowly, not even realizing the trouble he could have easily gotten himself into. Had this been any other street corner in Newark, he would have been lying splattered across the asphalt. "Leave 'em Stinking" is the phrase used in Newark.

They all watch him cruise up the block. The young boys are so disappointed. They would have loved to tear him apart. Lucky him?

Sha-Rock and his man, Jimmy, sit in Dunkin' Donuts waiting for a phone call. The connect told them he would be there in approximately thirty minutes. He's already twenty minutes late. This will be their first time doing business together.

They just met him the other day when the connect drove through Jimmy's set, without a referral or anything. The Spanish boy jumped out of his silver S-Class Mercedes and introduced himself. He introduced himself as Chulo, which means pretty boy in Spanish. He told them some long drawn out story about how he's just coming home and he's been gone for six years. He also told them that he lost all his clientele while he was away. Now he's forced to hit the street to rebuild his connects. He admitted that he's only the middleman who has access to a lot of work, but he has to prove that he's worthy of moving it.

Normally Jimmy would never trust anyone like this but he sort of believes the guy. After speaking to him over the phone, Jimmy was convinced. Usually he has a good judge of character. Maybe it's his desperateness that's forcing him to believe the new guy. His main connect has been selling pure garbage lately. Hopefully this guy is who he says he is. The last thing Sha-Rock and Jimmy need is to make a deal with a Fed.

Just as Sha-Rock lights his fifth cigarette, the white minivan cruises through the parking lot. The New York plates catch everyone's attention.

Jimmy dashes out of the store and hops into the backseat of the van, while Sha-Rock walks out of the door, and jumps into Jimmy's green Ford Taurus with the dark tinted windows. He lets them exit the parking lot before following them. He doesn't want to draw too much attention to the van.

"What up, Pa?" Chulo asks from the passenger's seat.

"Nothing much, Player," Jimmy replies. Jimmy admires his style. He carries himself with class. Jimmy can tell by his persona that if he doesn't have money right now, he must have had some at one particular time. His confidence shows that.

He's what the hood calls a "Rico Suave." In other words he's the pretty boy type. He doesn't have the typical Latin grade of hair. His coarse Afro gives him a distinguished look. He's wearing a tight short-sleeved muscle shirt and white linen pants.

Leaning back in his seat, he has his feet propped up on the dashboard, showing off his Dolce and Gabbana flip-flops. The sun beams on his diamond fluttered watch, which has so many diamonds on it, it's impossible to see the face.

Chulo notices Jimmy peeking at the watch. This makes him feel uncomfortable, so he sneakily places his hand under his thigh.

"Nice watch," Jimmy compliments, trying to break the tension and ease the boy's mind.

"Thanks, Pa. Me sorry me took so long, but my peoples hold me up. He no want to put the material in my hand without the money first. He ask me why you no come to New York with the money. He make me feel like he no trust me. Me know he for long time, but me leave for too many years. I tell you, I gone for long time, Pa. I tell my peoples listen, my friend he no need me, I need he. He have to trust me or we go nowhere. We can't make a business."

"I feel you," Jimmy interrupts, trying to stop him from chattering. Chulo's accent and broken English is driving Jimmy crazy. "Now, this is the same work, like the samples you gave me, right? No bullshit?"

"Pa, I no bullshit. Before me go away, me have lot of money. You no get rich doing bullshit. I deal a straight up. Ten years much problem. While me gone, me mother sick. Me send me mother and father back to Santo Domingo. Me buy big house for them. Hospital take $300,000 to take care of me mother, and she still die. Two years later, me father die in car crash. He drinka too much. Me lose everything, me house, and everything. Me cousins take more than $200,000, Pa. Now me start from the bottom. All me hard work for nothing. Pa, we do good business, we get rich together. Me need you. You help me, I no forget. Right now, me got nothing. Together we make something."

"So, nineteen is the best price you can do, huh?" Jimmy asks, trying desperately to change the subject. He has never been one for small talk. He likes to get straight to the point.

"Yeah, Pa. That's the best me can do. Me only make half a point. That's nothing. You buy more, maybe me peoples number come down."

Jimmy hands over the money and the connect fumbles through the stacks, before passing the brick to him.

Jimmy examines it closely before speaking. "Yeah, she official.

You gotta keep it like that. Don't switch up on me. I cop heavy. This is nothing. I'm major. You keep it right, I buy six or seven at a time. My clientele is up to the roof."

Chulo's eyes almost pop over the top of his silver aviator shades. "Yeah?"

"Yeah, it's like that. I do twelve or thirteen bricks a week."

"On the street me meet you on?"

"Nah, I don't play the streets. All weight. You give me a better number; I can move a lot more. The ball is in your court. If you treat me right, you don't have to do nothing. If I move forty to fifty birds a week, you won't have to leave your house. You can just sit home, eat, fuck and get fat, feel me? It's like that!" Jimmy is pouring it on thick. He's telling Chulo exactly what he wants to hear. Sure he can move a few kilos a week, but he has never had fifty-bird-a-week clientele. At the top of his game he can move about fifteen birds a week, but lately things have been going downhill for him. Besides his connect having bullshit, he has acquired a terrible gambling habit. In the course of one month, he lost approximately $60,000 in local gambling halls.

The past two years has been the worst years of his hustling career. On top of the gambling losses, he got pinched in Patterson. He got nabbed in the middle of a transaction consisting of two kilos. He's awaiting trial. His lawyer charged him fifty grand on top of the fifty grand he paid for bail. His money hasn't been flowing right since.

He's truly sick and tired of all the hard luck. He's used to being on top. He hasn't done this bad in years. He's been fortunate enough to be on top ever since he first hit the streets. He's been getting lots of money for years. Luckily throughout all the dirt he's done, he's managed to get away with doing only one bid. He served a year in Northern State Prison for a gun charge. That is where he met Sha-Rock, who had already been down there for 1 year prior to meeting Jimmy. In prison, the two developed a tight bond. Sha-Rock was just released about two months ago, while Jimmy has been home for a little over a year now.

Being on the bottom is starting to frustrate him. He's really banking on Chulo, hoping that he'll be his ticket back to the top of the game. Right now, all his faith is riding on Chulo. He sure hopes he can deliver.

Miranda sits at a small table of a cozy little restaurant on South Street in Philly, not too far from her and Sha-Rock's home.

She's eating by her lonesome tonight on the count of Sha-Rock being up in Jersey. Normally she would be tagging along with him but he told her he had business to handle and it would be better if she remained home. She hates to be without him. Those three years away from him was hell. Ever since he's been home, she's been glued to his side. They have so much lost time to make up for.

Miranda will be twenty-two in a few short months. She and Sha-Rock have officially been together for five years, but they crept around for an entire year prior to that. At that time, Sha-Rock was twenty-four years old. Miranda was only fifteen, which is way too young to be dealing with a grown man. She was the talk of the school, coming to school with $1,000 pocketbooks and $500 shoes. Not to mention her extensive fur coat collection. Sha-Rock kept her laced to the max. He even allowed her to push his 1998 white BMW 740iL to school. That's when all hell broke loose. She wasn't even old enough to attain her learner's permit. All the students were sweating her crazily. A couple of girls got so jealous that they told the teacher on her. The teacher questioned her but they didn't have proof. She believed Miranda because Miranda was one of her top students. Then one cold winter day, Miranda was pulling out of the school parking lot and the principal saw her behind the wheel. That almost got Sha-Rock into a lot of trouble. The principal called the police and held her there until they arrived. Miranda held her ground. She never admitted that she and Sha-Rock were dating. She stood by her man just like she was supposed to do. The principal tried to force Miranda's mother to press charges on Sha-Rock and get him locked up for statutory rape. Maybe that would have worked on somebody else's mother but not Miranda's.

Sha-Rock and Miranda's mother (R.I.P.) were so close. No one could get between them, not even Miranda. Whenever he bought something for Miranda, he bought something for her mom too. She really loved him like a son. She was so impressed with his gifts that she allowed him to date her teen-age daughter.

Everything was fine up until Sha-Rock got into big trouble in Atlantic City, and ended up doing a bid in Northern State. Miranda and her mom visited faithfully. They held him down to the fullest. They didn't allow him to want for anything. Miranda was completely faithful to him. Her mother made sure of that. She tried to have a few male friends keep her company while Sha-Rock was gone but her mom would scare them away. She told them that Sha-Rock would kill anyone who came anywhere near Miranda. How true she was. Sha-Rock does not play when it comes to Miranda. He's well aware of what he has. On several occasions he has referred to her as his "dream girl."

It broke Sha-Rock's heart when he received the shocking news that Miranda's mom had died. She died from lupus two days before Miranda's twentieth birthday, a year after being diagnosed. Her body rests in Miami, Florida, where she moved a few months before she died.

Luckily, Miranda's mom had prepared for her death. She left Miranda more than enough money to take care of herself. With her lavish lifestyle and crazy shoe fetish, Miranda ran through the money like it was nothing. Not to mention her buying herself a brand new car. It was then that Sha-Rock instructed his sister to turn the little money he had left over to her. She spent that money a little more wisely after learning the value of a dollar. Once Sha-Rock was released she still had a couple of dollars left over for him.

Miranda's cell phone rings as she consumes the last bit of her Caesar salad. This is always her meal of choice. She has to maintain her beautiful figure.

"Hello," she answers.

"What's the deal, Ma?" the caller replies.

"Who is this?" she asks.

"This that nigga Dollar, baby."

"Dollar?" she asks in a confused tone.

"Yeah. Dollar, from Jersey!"

"Oh, that Dollar." This is the kid she met on the street corner in Newark. "Hello. You're just returning my call?" she asks. "I called you days ago. You must be a busy man?"

"Nah, it ain't like that. I been running hard as hell, that's it. You know, grinding?" he adds. "It ain't like you cared if I called or not?" he says, trying to test her.

"I wouldn't say that I cared, but I did wonder why you haven't called me? That never happens to me," she replies arrogantly.

"Oh, I see. You're used to motherfuckers chasing you around. I feel you, but I'm a different kind of dude, Ma," he says confidently.

"Ooh, I respect your arrogance," she claims.

"Not arrogance, confidence. I mean you bad as hell, but I ain't got time to chase you. Either you feeling me or you not. My motto is, either you with me or you against me. You rolling or you strolling? It's on you!"

"Boy, you're a mess. I can see that already."

"Not hardly, Ma," he replies.

"Dear, you're starting off on the right track. Let's get this straight right now. I'm not you're mother. Delete the Ma, please. I hate that. No Ma, no Mommy, none of that. That's a total turn off."

"My bad, I thought that was a Spanish thing," he explains. "You are Spanish, right?"

"I'm half Cuban and half African American. Yes, Ma or Mommy is a Spanish thing, but when an American says it, it sounds like mockery," she explains.

"Well, what am I supposed to call you, then?"

"How about calling me by my name?'

"I don't know your name. You never told me."

"That's because you never asked. Well anyway, my name is Unique."

"Damn, that's different."

"Yeah, that's what it means, different. That, I am," she replies sarcastically.

He laughs before speaking. "I hear that. That name fits you perfectly. So, Unique where's your dude?"

"He's somewhere doing what he do," she replies.

"What does he do?"

"What do you mean?" she asks.

"I mean, what does he do?"

"He does what he do," she says sarcastically.

"And what is that?"

"Hold up, hold up, are you interested in me or are you interested in my dude?" she snaps.

"I'm interested in you, Ma. I mean Unique. Later for your dude.

If you ain't worried about him than neither am I."

"Well, to be honest, I am a little worried about him," she admits. "He's crazy. You saw how he performed on me that day?"

"Yeah, I saw it. Only a punk would treat a lady like that. My young boys was ready to give him the business."

"I really don't think it would have been that simple. That's what he lives for."

"Yeah, I hear you, but y'all were a long way from home. This is a different kind of town," he explains. "What were y'all doing up here anyway?"

"I had a business meeting in New York."

"What kind of meeting? What do you do?" he asks.

"Nosey, aren't we?" she asks in a playful manner. "I'm a model. I had to meet with my agent."

"What do you model?"

"Everything," she replies. "I've modeled underwear and clothes. I've been in hair commercials, too. You name it, I done it. My portfolio is extensive," she boasts.

"I feel you."

"Enough of me. What do you do?"

"Whatever it takes," he replies quickly.

"And what does that consist of?"

"Whatever it takes," he repeats.

"Ok, I see I won't get a straight answer from you. As nosey as you are you want to keep secrets. How crazy is that?" she jokes. "So tell me a little about yourself, being that you won't answer the questions I asked you," she suggests.

"What do you want to know?"

"Whatever you want to tell me. What are your hobbies? What do you do for fun? What do you enjoy doing?"

"My hobby? I collect money. What do I like to do? Make money. I enjoy going to the bank and making large deposits."

She laughs. "That's cute. Cocky, but cute," she adds.

"Nah, I ain't cocky," he denies. "You asked me what I like to do."

"You sound like a stingy one," she replies, trying to feel him out.

"Stingy?" he asks. "Nah, never that! I show love. If you take care of me, I take care of you. You don't look like you needy, though. I peeped you. Y'all look like y'all doing it big. Is that homeboy's car?"

"There you go asking about him again," she snaps. "Are you checking for me or him?"

"Damn, you get touchy about that subject."

"No, it's not that. It's bad enough; I even took your number. I shouldn't have done that. Every time you mention him, I feel guilty," she claims.

"Ok, I'll leave it alone. I don't want you to feel guilty and change your mind," he jokes. "When can we hook up?" he asks. "I'm dying to see you. Are you familiar with the Bricks?"

"The Bricks?" she asks. "What the hell is the Bricks?"

"Newark."

"Oh, New-ark," she repeats, breaking the word into two syllables. Out-of-towners tend to pronounce it like that. "Is that where we were? We were lost. No, I'm not familiar with it at all."

"Well, when can I give you a tour of our lovely city?"

"Soon, real soon," she replies.

"Soon, like a few hours? Tomorrow? When?"

"No, not that soon. As soon as I can get away from him. That's going to be hard though. He's up my ass with a microscope."

"Why is that? He don't trust you?"

"He don't trust nobody," she relies. "I'll find a way, though. He hates to shop with me. Maybe I'll tell him I'm going shopping or something. I'll figure it out."

"Alright, that's what it is then! Just give me a call whenever you get a chance. I'll be waiting, alright?"

"Ok."

"Alright then, later Ma. I mean Unique. Stay beautiful, alright?"

"I'll try," she laughs, before hanging up the phone.

As soon as the phone hangs up it begins ringing again. "Hello," she answers.

"What's happening, baby?" Sha-Rock yells.

"Nothing much," she replies.

"You miss me?"

"You know I do," she replies.

"Where you at?" he asks.

"On South Street, eating dinner, by myself again," she replies sarcastically.

17

"Here we go with this shit again!"

"It's alright though. I told you, you gone make me find myself a little friend," she teases.

"Go ahead," he threatens. "You gone fuck around and get somebody killed!"

She laughs but deep inside she knows he means exactly what he's saying. He's insanely jealous of her and she knows it.

"I should be home in a few days. Hold it down. Don't be the cause of somebody getting murdered, feel me?'

"Boy please!"

"I love you lady, remember that."

"I love you, too."

Today marks the third meeting with Jimmy, Sha-Rock and Chulo. Three scores in one week. Today they're purchasing two birds instead of one.

They had to switch meeting locations. The last meeting was suspect. Sha-Rock saw too many stragglers sitting idle in their vehicles. That made him extremely uncomfortable.

"Chulo, that last one wasn't all that," Jimmy claims. "It was compressed."

"Compressed? Pa, I no play games with the material. The way me get it, the way me sell it."

"Well, they must have gave it to you compressed then. I know blow. You can tell that thing was put back together. She was hard as cement. I had to bang it with a hammer just to crack her open. And my customers that cook said it lost. Matter of fact, I cooked two hundred grams myself, and I lost about forty grams.

"Pa, you shoulda bring it back. Everything me sell is guarantee. Why you no bring it back?"

"I'm a hustler. If I can move it, I will. No need in bringing it back and leaving you stuck with it. We're a team. I need you and you need me. Just keep it real with me. If you get something that's not that good, just let me know, so I'll know what to expect. You can't put my name on the line like that. At least if you tell me it's so-so, I'll know who to sell it to. Don't let me sell a half a bird of bullshit to my main people. Then we both get jammed up. Please, no more compressed. I hope these are better."

"These just come in. Take a look at 'em. Shiny and white, no hard."

Jimmy grabs hold of the two bricks and passes over the bag of money, which consists of $38,000. While Chulo skims through the money, his driver makes the right turn into the mini-mall, where Sha-Rock is waiting patiently.

"Chulo listen, I told you before about a plug I had from the dirty south. Well he called me yesterday and told me he's coming up in about

19

two weeks. He cops heavy. I hope you can cover the order. Sometimes he buys six or seven at a time."

"Pa, just call me a day before he come, and I be ready."

"I'll do better than that. I'll call like three days before he comes up, ok?"

"Good!"

Meanwhile Sha-Rock waits in the car, while talking to Miranda on the phone.

"When are you coming home?" she asks.

"Give me a few days."

"A few days? You already been gone for two weeks," she barks.

"Please don't start," he begs. "When I get home, I'm staying for at least three weeks. How does that sound?"

"I'll believe it when I see it. Your side of the bed is cold," she laughs.

"It better stay cold, too!" he snaps sarcastically.

Jimmy is walking toward the car.

"Let me hit you right back," Sha-Rock insists.

"Why are you rushing off of the phone?"

"I gotta handle something! Smooches," he says before hanging up in her ear.

Jimmy hops into the car and they exit the parking lot. They have several customers waiting. It's time to make the donuts.

"Excuse me, sir, can you tell me how to get to Twelfth Avenue?" Miranda asks the gas station attendant.

"About six blocks over. What are you looking for, Twelfth Avenue and what?"

"Twelfth Avenue and Littleton Avenue?"

"That's about one block up and six blocks over. You'll run right into it," he claims.

Miranda exits the Exxon station and makes a left followed by a quick right. She drives around clueless until she finally locates Littleton Avenue. She then makes a right turn and proceeds until she sees the Twelfth Avenue sign. She recognizes the block, but she can't spot Dollar. What she does see is about two dozen white T-shirts flaming the corner. She pulls over at the intersection and pulls out her cellular phone.

"Yo!" one filthy little boy calls to her. She ignores him as if he hasn't said a word. It's always the brokest, filthiest one of the bunch who has the nerve to speak, she thinks to herself.

"Hello, Dollar? Where are you?" she shouts into the phone, while looking straight ahead.

"Where are you?" he asks.

"I'm here, where you told me to come to. You're strip as you call it."

The honking of a horn startles her. She looks to the left, and there he is sitting in his Rover wearing the biggest Kool-Aid smile. She was so busy trying to ignore the youngster that she didn't even notice Dollar creep up beside her.

"Damn Ma, you looking good as hell," he says while still on the phone.

"Boy stop." She's blushing from ear to ear. She hangs up the phone, and rolls her window down. His passenger's side window rolls down automatically.

"What's the deal?" he asks while examining her car. She never mentioned that she had her own car. Her black convertible Nissan 350Z matches her style. The bloody red interior complements her complexion.

"Damn, that's a hell of a whip you got, Ma."

21

"Unique, Unique!" she corrects in a frustrated tone. "It's alright. Nothing but a car note. Another bill, that's it."

"Park your car right here, and jump in with me," he suggests.

"Ah, ah! I ain't leaving my car here."

"Oh, I thought it was just another bill?" he asks sarcastically. "It will be alright here."

"No, if somebody steal my shit, my man will want to know what the hell I was doing in New-ark."

"Newark," he corrects. "It's only one syllable."

"Whatever. I heard about Newark." She tries to pronounce it correctly, but it still sounds funny. "I saw the movie, *New Jersey Drive*."

"Listen Ma, *New Jersey Drive* was a poor representation of our town. First of all the movie was filmed in New York. That alone should have shot the credibility of it. They named the streets wrong and everything. They confused major streets with avenues. Sure a lot of kids used to steal cars, but not all of us. When *New Jersey Drive* came out, I was already ghetto rich. What *New Jersey Drive* didn't tell you is, a lot of heavy hitters come from this town. Don't get it fucked up! This town breeds hustlers. Motherfuckers quick to talk about the car thieves. We got some True 2 Life bread- winners. New York has Nicky Barnes. In Philly, y'all got y'all Junior Black Mafia niggas, and we got our Akbar Prey."

"Damn, take it easy. I'm sorry. Don't take it so personal," she begs. "Whoa, you're ready to kill me."

He calms down slightly. "Nah, I'm just tired of being connected with car theft every time I mention that I'm from the Bricks. I never stole a car in my life. I always been a money getter," he claims.

"Sorry, damn. Don't be so defensive. I don't know Nicky Barnes, or Akbar Pray. And the only reason I even heard of JBM is because my guy knows them."

"Oh yeah?" Dollar questions. This strikes a bell in his head. "Yeah right," he challenges. "Your dude don't know them," he says trying to get information out of her. Hopefully she'll fall for his trap.

"Know them?" she asks with a cocky look on her face. He doesn't just know of them. They know him too. He used to be tight with some of them," she claims.

She fell for the trap. If he hung out with those guys, he must be a money getter too.

She can tell he's still pissed off at her. "Can you forgive me?" she asks. "What can I do to make you forget, that I said that?" she asks in a baby voice.

This breaks the tension. He smiles from ear to ear. "I'll come up with something. You can count on that."

"I know you will. One more thing. I need some rims. Do you think someone can steal some off of another car and sell them to me," she teases.

He looks at her with a straight face. "Whatever. I see you got jokes. Hold up for a minute," he shouts as he slams the gear into reverse and backs up a half a block. After parking, he stands in the middle of the street and gestures her to come pick him up. She busts a U-turn and proceeds toward him.

She admires his style. She loves a man with style. That's one of the things that she loves the most about Sha-Rock. He can dress his ass off. She loves to see him put it on. Miranda loves the attention she and Sha-Rock receive when they're out. They look like someone tore them straight out of a magazine.

Dollar is not bad though. He doesn't look like he's too far behind. He looks stunning in his white linen Capri pants, with the drawstring waist, and his white linen pull-over shirt. He has on white Gucci slip-on loafers. There is one thing she would have to change. He's wearing short ankle socks. That sort of throws the entire outfit off. She thinks he shouldn't have worn any socks at all. All that white bouncing off of his caramel colored skin makes him look so pure. Miranda is such a detail freak that she notices he isn't wearing the same watch he had on when she first met him. Today he has on a white band, big-faced Jacob, which is fluttered with diamonds.

He hops into the car. "Doing the all white thing today, huh?" she asks. "What's up with that?"

"Nah, not all white," he replies. Hopefully, I'm going to mix a little Cuban and Black somewhere in there," he jokes.

"Sounds good to me," she replies.

"Pull to the corner," he instructs. She follows his instructions. "Stop right here. I'll be back in a little while," he shouts to the crowd of boys who are standing on the corner. You can pull off now," he says to her. "What is it that you want to do?"

"It doesn't matter. I'm with you. You're the host. You said you would take me for a tour of the town."

"It ain't too much in this city."

"Well, whatever then. It's on you."

"You don't have anything in mind?" he asks.

"No, not really."

"Did you eat yet?"

"Nope," she answers quickly.

"Alright, make the left," he instructs.

As they're cruising up Twelfth Avenue, he constantly takes sneak peeks at her while she's not looking. She's one beautiful chick, he thinks to himself. He can only imagine how upset her dude would be if he found out she was up here with him. Dollar knows how mad he would be if she were his girl. He's no sucker for love, but chicks like her don't come a dime a dozen. When you find one this bad you have to hold onto her. Unfortunately she's taken, so he has to deal with reality. She can never be his, unless of course she was willing to leave her man. Until then, maybe they can just get to know each other, maybe have a little erotic sex every now and then, if he's lucky. He sure hopes she has the same thoughts he does.

Her Seven jeans are glued to her thighs, and her pink T-shirt that reads, "I'm a Virgin" across the front, is revealing her voluptuous ta-tas. Today she isn't wearing shades, allowing him to appreciate her hazel colored eyes. Her long eyelashes flutter at least four times every second.

As they near the parkway sign, Dollar instructs her to make another left. She blasts her radio, as she merges onto the Parkway. The song "Emotional Roller Coaster," by Vivian Green, blares through the speakers.

She must really be going through something, he thinks to himself. He leans his head back and enjoys the ride.

Neither of them is talking. They're both entertaining their own private thoughts.

Bitches ain't shit, Dollar thinks to himself, as they're zipping up Route 78. Just to think, homeboy has spent his hard-earned money on buying this car for this chick, and she doesn't even respect dude enough not to let another nigga ride in it. Look at me; I'm all leaned back, feet on the dashboard, like I bought this shit. Girls are dirty as hell, he thinks to himself.

"Hold up, get off right here," he shouts as they near the mall entrance. The valet attendant hustles his way over to the driver's side and helps her from the car. All the other attendants watch in awe as she walks toward the door. She grabs hold of Dollar's hand as a form of flattery. They slowly walk through the doors of Neiman Marcus.

"What mall is this?" she questions.

"Short Hills. Have you ever heard of it?"

"Yeah, everybody has heard of Short Hills. I have never been here though. I always wanted to come here, but I never made it."

"Well, you are here now, finally. Look, I made your dream come true," he teases.

She catches the attention of all onlookers as they're walking through the mall. They can't deny her beauty. The hate is evident on damn near every woman's face that they pass. The more they hate, the harder Dollar, diddy bops. At this moment he's on top of the world. You can't tell him anything.

She begins her shopping spree in Saks Fifth Avenue. Shortly after, her curiosity leads her into the Chanel store. Her shoe fetish leads her into Jimmy Choo and Gucci. Finally her greed drags her into Nordstrom. Dollar sits back in the cut as she tears the mall up. "Tricking off" is what he likes to call it.

Although she is spending hard, she's actually taking it easy on him. She doesn't want to seem too greedy.

Two hours later and $3,500 lighter, Dollar walks about seven steps behind her as she walks into Victoria's Secret. She fumbles through the racks and locates the raunchiest lingerie she could find. She picks up five pieces to be exact.

While walking toward the counter, Dollar digs into his pocket to pay for the items. To his surprise she already has her American Express Platinum card drawn. He's impressed.

"It comes to $320," the clerk whispers.

"Yo, I got it!" he shouts.

She grabs him by the arm and pulls him close to her. The smell of sweet baby milk exits her mouth. Her lip gloss almost sticks to his earlobe as she whispers into his ear. "I got it, baby. This is my gift to you. You took care of me, and I'm going to take care of you. Not right now, but one day," she adds.

Dollar gets an instant hard-on just thinking about it.

25

After the shopping spree, they end up eating at Legal Seafood inside of the mall.

Their date ends with her dropping him off to his truck. As bad as he wanted her to stay, he still didn't ask. He realizes that she does belong to someone else. The last thing he would want to do is get her into trouble. That will ruin his chances of seeing her again. He'll never blow his chances of smashing her out. Deep down inside, he knows she's a freak, he just can't wait for her to prove him right.

After about ten passionate goodbye kisses, Dollar finally dragged himself out of her car. She then passed the Vickie Secrets bag to him and told him to hold onto it until she comes back to "New-ark." She told him the lingerie belongs to him. She bought the items solely for him.

That alone is enough to keep him good and thirsty for his next drink of Unique.

-6-

Two Weeks Later

Miranda/ Unique manages to get away for a night while Sha-Rock is away on another one of his many business trips, as he calls them. He's been in Virginia Beach with his crew for three days already.

Dollar and Unique spent the entire night partying in Manhattan until 4 A.M. She drank so much that Dollar had to carry her into his apartment. She was so drunk there was no way they could top the night off with hot, steamy sex. Besides, she probably wouldn't have remembered it anyway. He was tempted to make the attempt but he had to force himself not to. He doesn't want to sex her while she's drunk. He wants her sober, so the memory will be impressionable.

She wakes up at 11 A.M. with the worst hangover of her life. She looks to her right only to lock eyes with Dollar, who has been watching her sleep for the past hour.

He's fully dressed and ready to go. He's rocking away in the rocking chair that sits directly parallel to his canopy bed, which Unique happens to adore.

"Damn baby, how long have you been up?" she asks.

"Since six. I get up early. I done been to the block and everything already."

"You should have woke me up. I don't want to hold you up."

"Nah, I'm good. I was just enjoying the view."

"Damn, look at me," she cries. "I look a hot mess," she says while looking down at her wrinkled clothes. She's fully clothed. She even has her stilettos still on her feet. "Ah, my head is pounding. Do you have anything for headaches?"

"Yeah, me. Tender loving care," he laughs.

"Besides that!" she shouts. "How about," she manages to blurt out before her cellular phone interrupts her, leaving the words in her mouth. She looks at the display. "Oh shit, that's him! He's home. Damn! He was supposed to come home Monday. Shhh," she whispers to Dollar. "Hello," she answers, trying to sound fully awake. "At Tish house. I swear. Listen, we went to a club last night and I had too much to drink. Please, listen. I tried to call you last night, but my phone went dead. I swear to God on my life. Listen!" she begs before he hangs up in her ear.

"Damn," she shouts as she looks at her receiver and closes it shut. "Now what the fuck am I going to do? He's going to kick my ass."

"Yeah?"

"Yeah, fucking with you. I knew I shouldn't have come the fuck up here. I can't go home like this, clothes all wrinkled. Looking like I been rolling around with some nigga all night. I hope your cologne didn't rub off on me!" She begins sniffing her clothes. "I have to go!" she shouts as she runs to the door.

Dollar pulls a small duffle bag from his closet and follows close behind her. Once they're inside the car, he instructs her on which way to go. As they're riding she gets the courage to finally question him. "I know you don't have drugs in my car?"

"Drugs? Hell no! I would never put you in a position like that. Turn right here," he advises.

"What is it then?"

"Make a left at the corner. Not drugs," he replies before changing the subject. "Yo, what do you think he gone do to you? You can stay here for a couple of days until he calms down."

"That will make it worse. I'm going home, to get this ass whipping over with. The longer I wait the worse it's going to be. Damn! He better not give me no black eyes. I got a photo shoot in three days. Maybe I should stay here until the shoot is over. This shoot is important." She gets quiet as if she's debating with herself. "Nah, I don't want to get you into any trouble."

"Trouble," he repeats in a high-pitched voice, like she just offended him. "I ain't getting in no trouble. I ain't scared of your dude. You are. I don't give a fuck about him!" he snaps. "Damn, do you like living in fear like that?"

"I have been doing it so long that I'm used to it. I can't imagine it any other way. The beatings don't even hurt anymore. I just cry so he'll stop," she claims.

Dollar can't believe what he's hearing. How can someone treat her like that? Only a sucker would beat her and make her be with him. "Do you love him?" he asks. "Honestly?"

She hesitates before replying. "I love him, but I'm not in love with him," she admits.

"Well, you need to break out. That nigga gone fuck around and kill you."

"You know, I think about that all the time. You just don't know how crazy he is. If I try to leave he'll kill me."

"If you stay, he'll kill you. It's a catch-22."

As the tears drip down her face, Dollar wipes them one by one. "Don't cry, Ma. I'll hold you down. You have to get out of this situation you in. He can't love you, if he beating on you like that. You too pretty for that shit."

Finally, she pulls up parallel to his truck. He hops out. "Listen, if you need me, holler! I'm an hour and a half away. I'll come scoop you with no problem. You hear me?" he asks.

"Yeah, I hear you, but I started it. I have to finish it. I'll call you."

"When?"

"When he finishes fucking me up." She cracks a stupid looking grin. "That's if I'm still conscious," she adds foolishly.

"Yo, you laughing but shit ain't funny," he says in a concerned tone.

"I know. I'll hit you probably the day after tomorrow 'cause he's not going to leave my side for at least two days. After the beating comes the panty sniffing, then twenty-one questions. Then I'll have to fuck him just to prove to him that I haven't fucked anyone else." She shakes her head from side to side. "Hmpphh," she sighs. "I'll call you," she says as she pulls off.

Dollar is pissed. He can't understand how a woman would put herself through that. She's touched a weak spot in his heart.

Three Days Later

It's 8:30 A.M. Chulo and Jimmy have just met up again. This time, there's no work involved. This is a preliminary meeting in reference to the big score.

Jimmy hops into the backseat of the minivan. "What's up?" he shouts.

"Nothing much, Pa. How you doing?"

"Good, Chulo. Dig, I told you my man was on his way? Well, he's ready, but I need to kick it first. What's the best price you can give me? I might want like ten joints. I can't pay nineteen! Fuck that, I gotta eat!"

"Ten," he repeats in a shocked tone. "Are you sure, Pa?"

"Depending on the price. I ain't trying to break you, but if you can give them to me for seventeen, I could work with that."

"Seventeen? I don't even get it at seventeen. For real Pa, the most me make is one point. Me no lie. Me pay eighteen. No way me can sell it for seventeen," he explains.

"If you take ten, he won't bring the price down none? I know two is nothing, but ten is a whole different ball game."

Chulo pulls out his calculator and begins punching numbers. "The best price me can do is eighteen. Hopefully he bring me number down half a point. Me make only $5,000 from the deal."

"Damn man!" Jimmy shouts. "Let me see that calculator." He begins adding aloud. "I need my normal two, that's $36,000. I'm charging him twenty a pop. Seven is $140,000. Two times seven equals $14,000 profit for me. Fourteen thousand plus 36,000 is 50,000. 50,000 divided by 18,000 is two birds and 777 grams. Look, I'm trying to get ten. Ten bricks cost $180,000. I'll have $176,000. Let me owe you $4,000. I'm good for it, Chulo. No bullshit. Come on man," he begs.

"Listen Pa, me almost no make nothing off you. Me only make $5,000. If me get lock up, $5,000 no even pay me bail. If me let you owe me $4,000, me do all the work and take chance for $1,000."

"Don't look at it like that. The next day, you'll have your $4,000.

Matter of fact, I'll give you another grand or two on top of the $4,000, alright?"

"Me can't, Pa. Let me eat a food too?" he begs.

"Pssst," Jimmy sucks his teeth in frustration. "Damn man! Alright, I feel you. You can still bring the ten. By that time, I'll have the other $4,000. It's official. We can work it."

"Are you sure?" Chulo asks.

"I'm positive. I wouldn't do you like that. I'll have it. He said he'd be here in three days. You have to be ready. We can't blow this one. Once this one pops off, we got him. Especially with the flavor you got. He'll be on my dick!"

Chulo smiles in flattery.

"Yo, I'm out. Friday, alright?" Jimmy asks. "You sure, right? No bullshit?"

"Psst, Pa? I no bullshit you. Friday!"

Jimmy races out of the van like a madman.

Meanwhile, a couple of hundred miles away, Miranda/ Unique is yelling hysterically while on the phone with Dollar.

"Where are you?" she asks. "Are you outside?"

"Nah, why? I'm back in the house. Are you crying? What the fuck is wrong with you? Did he hit you?" Dollar is getting more and more furious by the second.

"Fuck this shit! I'm tired. I can't keep going through this. Either he's going to kill me in here, or I'm going to kill his ass!"

"Calm down, lady," says Dollar.

"Calm down my ass. I don't deserve this shit. If he would spend some time with me, we wouldn't be going through this. He found your number earlier."

"What did he say?"

"He's been beating my ass ever since. He's going crazy. I have to get out of here."

"Leave, come up here," Dollar suggests.

"I can't. He took my car somewhere. Him and his boy took both cars. He took the house keys, my money, and all my clothes. I can't go nowhere with this busted shit I got on."

What a bitch ass nigga, he is, Dollar tells himself. "Do you want me to come get you?"

"No, I think he's probably somewhere watching the house to see if I'll try to leave."

"So! Fuck him! I'll round my young boys up, and we'll come down there and scoop you up."

"Ah ah, I can't do it like that," she claims.

"Well, call the cops then."

"I don't want to do it like that either." She goes silent for a few seconds. "Can I catch the train up there? I don't have to stay. I'll get my agent to come pick me up. I don't want to inconvenience you, but I have to get out of here," she cries.

"It ain't no inconvenience. You can stay as long as you need to." Silence fills the air. "Unique, what up? What you gone do?"

She hesitates before replying. "I don't know what to do. I don't even know how to catch the train," she admits.

"I'll come get you then."

"No, ah ah! Where do I catch the train to?" she asks.

"To Newark Penn Station," Dollar replies.

"Alright. Will you be home? Don't leave me stranded. I don't have any money. I barely got enough for the train. I guess I can scrape that up."

"Nah, I ain't gone leave you stranded. Hit me when you get here. I ain't going out. I'm tired as hell. I was out all night. I'm about to catch up on some zzzzs."

"Make sure you listen for the phone," she orders.

"It's right here by the bed. I'll hear it."

"Alright, I'll call you when I get there."

"Alright one!"

Three Hours Later

The ringing of Dollar's phone awakens him. "Hello," he answers groggily.

"Dollar, I'm here. Come get me."

He's so tired that he dozes off while she's talking.

"Dollar do you hear me?" she asks. "Wake up!"

"Hello? Yeah, I hear you. Where you at?"

"New-ark Penn Station! Come get me!"

"Just catch a cab."

"No, come and get me," she demands.

"Ma, I'm tired as hell. Please catch a cab," he begs.

"I don't know how to get there."

"Just tell the man my address. He'll get you here."

"Please Dollar. Please come and get me," she begs.

"Listen, my address is 1978 Compton Place in Hillside. He'll get you here in about twenty minutes."

She realizes that she's fighting a losing battle. "What is it again?"

"1978 Compton."

"What did you say, Hillside?"

"Yeah, Hillside," he shouts before dozing off again.

Thirty minutes later, the phone awakens him again. "Hello?"

"Dollar, I'm out front. Come pay for the cab. I told you I don't have any money."

He manages to get himself together. He walks out front to pay for the cab. As she's climbing out of the cab, Dollar examines her carefully. Her hair is pinned up in a doobie wrap. She's wearing a tight-fitted, pink velour J.Lo sweat suit and some pink and white Nike Boings. Busted, he thinks to himself. What she considers to be busted is really well above average. She hugs him tightly before walking up the steps of the two family house.

As soon as he enters the apartment he walks straight to his bedroom and collapses onto the bed. Just as he dozes off, a tapping on the door awakens him. "Damn, I can't get no sleep for shit!" He stomps to the doorway like a baby having a temper tantrum. Just as he reaches for the doorknob, something tells him to check the peephole. Her boyfriend may have followed her here.

"Check the peephole," she whispers, as if she read his mind.

"Who?" he asks, while peeking through the hole. He recognizes the face of the older woman who lives upstairs. He silently exhales before opening the door. "Hello, Mrs. Jones?" Mrs. Jones is an elderly woman well into her eighties.

"Son, my toilet is stopped up again!" she yells at the top of her lungs. She's hard of hearing, so not only does she scream when talking, you have to scream even louder for her to hear you.

"Ok, I'll be right up," he yells.

"Huh?" she asks.

"I said, I'll be right up!"

"Ok, the door will be open!"

Dollar slams the door. "Damn!" He then storms to the back of the house. He returns shortly with a plumber's snake.

"I didn't know you were a plumber," she teases.

"Ha, ha, ha. Real fucking funny," he replies sarcastically. "I'll be right back."

Two hours later, Dollar finally returns, only to find Unique stretched out across the bed sleep. The creaking of the door wakes her. "Damn, what time is it?" she asks.

"Two o'clock."

"Damn, how long have you been up there?"

"Almost two hours! Fucking toilet full of shit. I don't know what the fuck she be eating. She's always stopping the toilet up."

Unique smiles. "That's good that you look after her like that. She doesn't have kids?"

"Yeah, she lives with her daughter, but her daughter is always away."

"So you look after her while she's gone?"

"Nah, not really. I'm barely here, but when I am, I check on her though," he claims.

"That's good. You'll get blessings for that, but I don't think I would be able to clean up nobody else's shit."

"Shit, I have to. Either that or pay a plumber $300 to fix it."

"Why do you have to pay?"

"It's my house. I rent the apartment to them."

"Oh yeah?" she asks. "How long have you had it?"

"Almost five years."

"Oh, that's nice. You didn't tell me you own a house."

"It didn't come up. I have this one and a little raggedy apartment building down the hill. I'll show it you to you later on today. It's a little eight-unit building. It's raggedy than a motherfucker but I do alright with it business wise."

Her eyes show amazement. "It's good to see a black brother doing something positive."

"What did you think I was? Just another street nigga?"

"I didn't know what to think."

"Nah, I got my head on right. I mean, don't get me wrong, I do my thing but I do the right thing with my money. If this big deal goes through for me, I'm straight. The streets can kiss my ass. I won't need them anymore. I'm just waiting for the credit to go through, that's it!" he shouts with enthusiasm. "I just hope this shit go through. I put up everything for this one. I might be broke for a minute, but when that paper starts coming in, it's over!"

"Broke, my ass," she challenges.

"Yeah broke, no bullshit. I put up damn near every dollar I had for this piece of property. It's worth it though. It's a thirty-unit building. If I get it, I'm turning it into an old folks home. I'm charging $800 a unit. No hassle with the tenants, because the state will pay me on the first of every month. You do the math, that's $24,000, direct deposit every month. So, I'll be starving for a minute. All I have to do is maintain until it goes through. Then it's on!"

Damn, $24,000 a month, she says to herself. She doesn't know anything about the real estate game, but she does have common sense, and that tells her he must have put down a pretty penny in order to attain a property that brings in $24,000 a month. Jackpot is the word that comes to her mind instantly. "Can I ask you a question?"

"Go ahead."

"Why don't you have a girlfriend, or do you?"

"Do it matter?" Before she has a chance to reply, he answers her. "Nah, I'm dolo. I ain't got time right now. In between the streets and the real estate, I ain't got time for nothing else."

"Not even me?"

"Nah, I'm definitely gone make time for you."

"Yeah right."

"No bullshit. You here right?" he asks. "Later for homeboy. You ain't never gotta go back to Philly. You got a new home right here in Jersey. You don't have to go through that shit no more. I mean, you don't have to stay with me. Maybe you ain't feeling me like that? I'll get you a little apartment somewhere and you can do you. How does that sound?"

"You act like it's really that simple."

"It is that simple. I'll call this realtor I know and he'll have a spot for you today."

"Why can't I stay here?" she jokes. "Oh, I'll cramp your style, huh? Can't get no more butt in here, huh? I don't mind, just tell them I'm your roommate," she laughs.

"Ain't no butt coming in here," he says defensively.

"Why?"

"I don't trust them."

"So why did you bring me here? I'm butt," she says seductively. "It's a little butt, but it's still butt," she laughs.

"You alright. Your butt is alright with me," he compliments. "To tell you the truth, I don't know why I brought you here. You different, plus you ain't from around here."

"And, what does that mean?" she asks. "Tell the truth. You brought me here because you want some butt right?"

"Knock it off. It ain't even about the butt. Anyway, I could have taken you to a motel, if that was the case."

"Oh know you wouldn't have! You wouldn't have taken me to no cheesy ass motel."

"Cheesy? Look at me, do it look like I do anything cheesy? Everything I do, I do big," he says arrogantly. "But back to the subject, do you want me to call the realtor or what?"

"It's not that simple. I know he's a fucked-up person, but I just can't get up and leave like that. I have been with him almost ten years."

"Ten years, damn?"

"Yeah, our anniversary is coming up in a few months."

"Yeah?" he questions. "I wonder what he's going to give you? Maybe a broken ribcage?" he asks sarcastically.

Her mouth stretches wide open in shock. She can't believe he just took her there. She leans back on the bed with her eyes closed.

"I'm sorry," he apologizes. "I just can't believe you're putting up with that shit! Leave that nigga! I got you, Ma," he says while hugging her tightly.

————◆◆◆————

The Next Morning

It's eight in the morning. Unique is still sound asleep. Dollar is on his way out the door to start his day.

They spent last night watching old gangster movies. That's all they could do on the count of her little visitor. She was so frisky that he was almost ready to take it like that, until he thought about how disgusting it would be. Anyway, she may be staying here full-time. That means he can get it whenever he wants. He drilled her for so many hours about moving here. She sounds like she's maybe considering it.

"Yo," he whispers in her ear. His voice startles her.

"Huh?"

"I'm out. I'll be back in about two hours. I have to handle something."

"Ok. When you come back, bring me something to eat."

"Alright, give me a few hours. When I come back, we gone hit the mall and get you a couple of outfits, alright?"

"Uh, huh," she replies. "Take your time. I'm so tired. All I want to do right now is sleep."

Dollar opens his closet door and grabs hold of a black North Face book bag, and out the door he runs.

Three hours have passed and Dollar is just returning. Unique is dressed and waiting. She's sitting on the sofa. Her eyes are glued to the television watching Jerry Springer. Dollar walks right past her with his book bag in his right hand and a Pepsi in his left.

"Damn, you could have bought me something cold to drink. Where's my food I asked for?"

"Hold up one second. We're going to eat!" he shouts as he walks toward the kitchen. The sound of four locks opening echoes throughout the corridor. Then the sound of a door creaking, followed by the sound of him walking down the stairs to the basement, sounds off.

Ten minutes later, he returns with an empty book bag, turned inside out. "You ready?" he asks.

"Been ready," she replies.

He tosses the bag onto the bed and they exit the apartment. Fifteen minutes later, they're parking in front of a restaurant, which has a sign that reads "Shaky Hut" across the canopy.

Unique notices the word "Halal" posted everywhere in the restaurant. She's no stranger to the word halal. Muslims populate Philly in abundance.

The restaurant is packed. As soon as they walk through the door everyone's attention is drawn to Dollar's escort. They can't believe their eyes. They try and look away in respect of Dollar, but seconds later their eyes end up right back in her direction. Dollar absolutely loves all the attention. He shakes hands throughout the entire restaurant. She now realizes he must be well known.

"Dollar, what's good, my nigga?" they ask him.

"Not too much," he replies.

"Yeah right. If I had your hands, I'd turn mines in."

"Go ahead, knock it off," he says while blushing.

After eating, they make their way to Short Hills once again. She has a feeling that this is about to be her favorite mall.

They top their action-packed day off at the nail salon, where they sit side-by-side enjoying manicures and pedicures from two beautiful Asian women. This is something that Sha-Rock would never do. He's too masculine to get this done. He swears that any man who gets his nails done is a homo. Unique begs to differ. She thinks the whole metro sexual thing is very sexy. Damn, a sister could really get used to this, she thinks to herself. Dollar sure knows how to take care of a woman. She's been thinking that the entire day.

—————————◆◆◆—————————

Two Days Later

As Jimmy hops into the van, he closes his gigantic umbrella. It's pouring outside. It's only six o'clock but judging by the darkness it appears to be eleven o'clock. The bright Exxon sign is the only source of light. The giant raindrops bang against the windshield.

"What up, Chulo!"

"You, Pa," he replies.

"This spot was a bad decision, Homey. The train (Task Force) runs through here all night."

"No, me get gas, Pa. That's it." After the attendant finishes pumping the gas, Chulo speaks again. "Which way, Pa?"

"Bear to your right at the corner," Jimmy instructs, while pointing towards West Market. Chulo's driver follows the instructions perfectly. "I got half of the dough right here. My cousin has the other half. You know, just in case we get pulled over, all the money won't be in one car. I ain't got no $100,000 to pay them boys if shit get fucked up," he explains.

"Okay, okay, that's smart."

"Make the right here and a quick left. My cousin should be there," he says as he stares up the block. "Oh, there he is on that porch, in the middle of the block."

"Pa, I ran into a little problem," Chulo says as his driver gasses up. "I couldn't get all ten."

"You couldn't get all ten?" he asks in a high-pitched tone. "Come on, man! Why the fuck you didn't tell me that? I got them boys' money. They gone think, I'm bullshitting them. Yo, you playing fucking games!" Jimmy shouts at the top of his lungs. He's pissed to no end.

"Me play no games, Pa. Me peoples no have ten for me."

"Well, how many did you get?"

"Five," he mumbles.

"Five? What the fuck am I gone do with five? I need ten!" he shouts. "So, you can't get five more from nowhere?" he asks desperately.

"Not today. Maybe tomorrow."

"Listen, I got the money. When can you get five more?" Jimmy gets the feeling that Chulo doesn't trust him. "Why didn't you tell me this on the phone?"

"Me no talk on the phone, Pa. That's no good."

"You could have told me something. Pull over and let my cousin in."

Sha-Rock snatches the door open and hops in directly behind Chulo. He's holding a small black duffle bag in his right hand. "What up, what up!" he greets.

"Bullshit, man!" says Jimmy.

"What happened?" Sha-Rock asks.

"He ain't got all the work. He couldn't get it."

"Nah, don't tell me that shit! How many he got then?"

"Five!" Jimmy shouts.

"Five? Come on, man! That's some bullshit. Them boys waiting for seven. At least get two more, so we can take care of them. We were banking on this move."

"Word up," Jimmy agrees. "We can wait for ours."

"This is it," Chulo says. "Me try, me can't get them."

"Alright, fuck it!" Jimmy shouts. "What price are you going to give us for five?"

"Eighteen."

"Alright, give him … how much is that? $Ninety thousand. Give him that out of your bag," Jimmy demands.

Sha-Rock unzips his bag and digs both hands deep inside. He then looks Jimmy directly in the eyes. Jimmy gives him the head nod. Sha-Rock snatches his hands from the bag quickly. His hands tightly grip two twin Smith & Wesson .357 Magnums. "Don't nobody fucking move," he says calmly as he rests the pistols onto the back of their heads.

Chulo doesn't have a clue of what's going on. "Pa?" he says desperately as he attempts to look at Sha-Rock.

Sha-Rock clunks him with the butt of the gun. "I said don't move. Now listen, move slowly so I can see everything," he advises. "Driver, touch the roof, slowly."

The driver places his hand on the roof as instructed.

"Chulo, you pass the work over to my man slowly."

Chulo slowly passes the bag behind him.

"Okay, now slowly empty your pockets," he says calmly.

Chulo hands over a neat stack of twenties.

"Driver, you got money on you?" Sha-Rock asks.

"No Papi`," he replies nervously.

"Check him. I'm telling you now, if I find something it's going to get real ugly in here, early!" he shouts. "Y'all got guns on y'all?" No one replies. "Y'all better tell me, 'cause if I find it!"

"Yeah, yeah," Chulo interrupts.

"Ok, where is it?" Sha-Rock asks.

"Me waist," Chulo answers quickly.

"Jimmy, reach up there and get it. Listen, don't nobody move."

Jimmy leans up to the front seat and pats Chulo's waist until he locates the bulge. He lifts Chulo's shirt and snatches the chrome .45 from his waist.

"Got damn, you wasn't playing, huh Chulo? What were you going to do with that, huh?" He clunks him again. Chulo grabs his head tightly. The pain from the blow is excruciating. "Was that for us, you dumb motherfucker? Check the driver."

Jimmy frisks him carefully. "Nothing, he ain't got nothing."

"See what greed got you? You so fucking stupid!" says Sha-Rock. "You don't know us from a can of paint. All you saw was a come-up, right? Now turn around slowly and look me in my face."

Chulo turns his head around. Fear is in his eyes. Sha-Rock places his pistol on Chulo's forehead, while his other gun rests on the back of the driver's head.

Jimmy is peeking around nervously, watching out for police.

"Chulo, repeat after me," Sha-Rock advises. "Say ... You."

"You," he mumbles.

"Louder, I can't hear you. Say. . . You."

"You," Chulo repeats.

"Caught," says Sha-Rock. "Say it ... Caught."

"Caught," Chulo repeats.

"Me," says Sha-Rock.

"Me," Chulo mumbles innocently.

"Slippin'!"

Chulo hesitates.

Sha-Rock bites down on his bottom lip enraged. "Say it ... Say Slippin'."

"Slippin." As soon as the words exit Chulo's mouth, the sound of the two cannons goes off simultaneously. With very little time in between, five other shots follow.

The driver's head crashes into the steering wheel, while Chulo's twisted body slides underneath the dashboard. Sha-Rock raises up and bangs the driver in the head two more times before shooting Chulo three more times.

"Let's go," Sha-Rock shouts before pushing the doors open and exiting the van, leaving both victims lying there motionless.

Unique exits the bathroom and walks into the bedroom, where Dollar is waiting patiently. Finally, the day he has been waiting for. Her monthly is finally over. Before going into the shower, she grabbed a box of Massengil, and the most revealing teddy of all from the Vickie Secret bag.

He's so anxious. His curiosity is killing him. He hopes and prays that his performance is up to par. He wants everything to be perfect. As soon as she's done in the shower, he's going in. He has his favorite cologne stashed in his pocket. She told him that she loves the fragrance. That's all he needed to hear. Now every time he's expecting her, he drenches himself in the cologne.

As the water stops running, Dollar can hear Unique singing loudly. He's shocked at her beautiful voice. He never knew a woman as perfect as Unique existed. Every time he's around her, he examines her to find a shortcoming, but she seems to have none. To the naked eye, she's flawless; her tiny feet, her perfectly shaped head, pearly white teeth, long beautiful hair and smooth skin all make up one hell of a package. She's a dream come true. God broke the mold with this one. Dollar is sure that deep down inside, underneath all her beauty something has to be wrong with her. They say know no one is perfect. He doesn't know what it is now, but he's sure one day the truth will come out.

Unique steps out of the bathroom elegantly. Her pink teddy fits her perfectly. It's pink satin trimmed in lace. The way her nipples peek through the lace turns him on instantly. He zooms past her and grabs her from behind. As he leans forward to kiss her neck, the sweet smell of watermelon greets his nostrils. He grabs a handful of her wet hair and swoops it over her left shoulder before biting down passionately on her shoulder. She leans her head backwards so he can get a better grip of her flesh. She lifts her hands over her head and grasps the back of his neck as he nibbles her shoulder blades. Suddenly she begins grinding on him. The stiffening of his mankind excites her. She stops grinding, and backpedals a few steps until he bumps into the wall. She then turns around to face him. She plants soft kisses all over his face before jamming her tongue deep inside his mouth. She places her index finger on his chin to lift his head, before pecking him all over his neck. From his neck to his chest, she licks him like a lollipop. She leaves a tongue trail from the middle of his chest down to his belly button. While she's tracing little circles inside his belly button with her tongue, she slides her hands down his pants in search of her prize. She strokes him vigorously. A warm sensation shoots through his body. He snatches her hand out of his pants and gently pushes her away.

"Hold up, let me shower first," he insists.

"Come on," she begs. "I'm hot now," she says in a low whisper.

"Stay hot, Ma. Give me ten minutes. I'll be right out," he says as he exits the room.

The entire time he's in the shower, he's talking to God. Please God, let my performance be impressive, he pleads. Dollar has a premature ejaculation problem. A lot of times it's over for him before it even starts. Please God, don't do this to me tonight. Please let me last all the way through, he begs, as he scrubs away. He looks down at his third leg and speaks. Come on champ. It's all or nothing, he whispers.

Finally, he dries himself off and sprays damn near half a bottle of his cologne. He's drenched in it. "Aghh," he sniffs himself. If he doesn't knock her dead with the sex, he's sure to knock her dead with all the cologne he just used.

He steps into his black silk boxers and exits the bathroom. As he steps into the bedroom, darkness greets him.

"Unique?" he calls as he steps into the room. He focuses on the bed, hoping to find her there.

"Yes?" she whispers. Her voice comes from the direction of his left.

"Where you at?" he asks while quickly turning his head to the left. Suddenly an unsuspecting head twisting blow crashes into the back of his skull, knocking him off balance. He stumbles forward clumsily. Just as he's about to catch his balance, another blow lands directly on the top of his head. This blow can be compared to a center block being dropped from a building. He falls face first onto the floor. That's when the stomping begins. He can't see how many people there are but he can feel at least two different boots kicking him. This catches him totally off-guard. He curls up to protect himself, but how can he stop blows that he can't see coming? The pressure of someone standing on the back of his neck makes it hard for him to move. Everything is happening so fast that he can't gather his thoughts. He doesn't know what's going on.

"Tie this dumb ass nigga up!" shouts the voice.

Dollar squirms, trying to work his way up from the floor, but another blow to the head sets him straight. He lays there submissively, as his hands are being tied behind his back. As soon as his hands are tied, he feels the rope being tied around his ankles. The rope is tied so tight that it's actually cutting through his skin.

He hears the sound of duct tape being unwound. Seconds later they extend the tape from his mouth to the back of his neck. After five rounds, the taping process comes to a halt. He takes short gasps through his nose, because he can't breathe through his mouth on the count of the tape being airtight. They grab him by the shoulder and turn him over. He lays there face up, staring into the darkness.

"Turn the lights on!" shouts a voice. Light appears instantly. Dollar lays there staring at a huge black, bald-headed man with a chrome .45 in his hand. He tries to identify the man, but the gun is distracting him. Suddenly his mind replays this character behind the wheel of a red Porsche. It's Unique's boyfriend. What the fuck, he thinks to himself. He replays the entire incident slowly. He comes to the conclusion that this is a set-up. Unique was in on it all the while. He feels like an asshole right now. How the hell could he fall for this bullshit, he asks himself.

"Remember me, player?" the boyfriend asks. "You thought you got that off, huh? About to fuck my broad and brag to your little homeys about it, huh?" He strikes him once again, causing blood to leak from the corner of his eye.

Who the fuck are they? Why me? These are the questions that are running through Dollar's head. He's scared to death. His heart is racing. He's sure that he's about to get murdered. Did he find out about her cheating and make her come here so he can kill him, he wonders. She did say he was crazy jealous over her. While he's in thought, Unique appears in the doorway, fully clothed. She looks him dead in the eyes with no remorse.

Sha-Rock drags him to his feet and shoves him into the rocking chair. He immediately pulls out the rope and ties him to the chair. "Jimmy, come here."

Jimmy, Dollar thinks to himself. Not my man Jimmy? A frail young man appears in the doorway, answering Dollar's questions. Yep, Jimmy, my man. Now he's really confused. Maybe they won't kill me,

45

he thinks. Jimmy won't let him kill me. They'll just take the money and leave. Nah, Jimmy knows I saw him. He'll make sure he kills me. He knows my young boys won't have this shit. They'll be on him as soon as they untie me. Why, he asks himself. Jimmy was his connect. Dollar used to cop at least four bricks a week from Jimmy. He spent $100,000 a week faithfully with Jimmy until Jimmy started falling off board, where he could no longer cover the order. How can he flip on me like this?

For once they lock eyes. Jimmy's eyes show a slight bit of pity, while Dollar's show pure confusion.

"Yo man, I'm fucked up. I have to get right," he mumbles, trying to justify his reason for his criss-cross. Deep down inside he feels terrible. He thinks back on the day he told Dollar he couldn't cover the order. Jimmy was shocked when Dollar gave him the money up-front so Jimmy could purchase the bricks. Dollar even allowed Jimmy to take his normal profit off the top. They worked it that way for a few flips before the connect fronted Jimmy a half a joint, and he never paid the connect back. Jimmy's intentions were not to beat the connect, but as soon as he got the work, things went haywire. A few of his soldiers got bumped, with product and money. He took his last $5,000 to the gambling hall in search of a come-up. He was hoping to double his money, so he could at least pay the connect back. He used to gamble for fun, that time he was gambling for survival. His luck was going so bad that he lost the five grand in less than one hour. Last year, everything he touched turned to shit.

"Where's the bread?" Sha-Rock asks Miranda.

"I'm not sure, but there is something in that closet."

"Go look inside," he advises. Miranda races to the closet. After fumbling around, she steps out of the closet holding an empty duffle bag. It's the exact same bag Dollar carried back and forth. "Oh, the basement. I'm sure something is in the basement," she shouts.

"Hit the basement then," Sha-Rock replies.

Miranda and Jimmy take off toward the kitchen, leaving Dollar and Sha-Rock all alone.

"Damn, Dollar, out of all the bitches in the world, why my bitch?" he asks. "That's fucked up, man. When I went in the store, you should have left her alone. You couldn't though, right?" he asks. "Too pretty, right? Or did you just want to play me out? Fuck my broad, clown me and talk real bad about me? I must admit, you have a good heart though.

You was about to take her away from all that bullshit, right? You thought you was about to take the only girl I ever loved. Damn, I would have went crazy."

Dollar is getting more and more nervous by the second. He can see the rage in Sha-Rock's bloodshot red eyes. The anxiety is killing Dollar. It feels as if he's waiting to die. He almost wishes he would hurry up and pull the trigger, just to get it over with.

"You was about to move her up in the hills and give her a better life? Miranda loves her life."

Miranda, Dollar utters to himself. The whole Unique thing was a lie, too. Stinking ass bitch!

"You a fool. You really thought you was about to fuck that pretty little motherfucker, right? Got your little dick all hard. I should at least let you fuck her before I murder you, right?"

Dollar is sure that he's crazy now. Why did he fuck with that bitch, he asks himself. His intentions were only to fuck her at first, but after listening to her fake ass story, he started feeling sorry for her. Look at what I get for trying to help her out. He can't believe the mess he has gotten himself into.

Miranda and Jimmy walk into the room. Jimmy is holding a clear plastic bag full of powdered cocaine and one un-opened brick. Miranda is holding three shoeboxes full of money.

"Where was it at?" Sha-Rock asks.

"In the basement," Jimmy replies. "He had it stashed in an old ass rusted boiler."

"I must admit, you are smart," Sha-Rock says. "Is that everything y'all?"

"Yep," Jimmy replies.

"Y'all sure?"

"We looked everywhere. This is it."

"Alright then ... show over."

Dollar's heartbeat speeds up drastically. His bowels loosen. The moistness in the seat of his drawers tells him that he's just shitted on himself. He just gave new meaning to the phrase "scared shitless."

Miranda leaves the room. She can't stand the sight of it. She's done this a few times, but she still hasn't gotten used to it. She doesn't have the heart to stand there and watch Sha-Rock execute anyone.

Dollar closes his eyes, preparing for death. Sha-Rock snatches the tape from Dollar's mouth. Dollar stretches his eyes wide open and begins to scream desperately. "Oww, oww!"

Sha-Rock clunks him twice with the butt of the gun. "Shut the fuck up!" After the two stunning blows, he comes back to his senses and shuts his mouth.

"Repeat after me," Sha-Rock whispers. "Say ...You."

Dollar doesn't reply. He can't understand what's going on.

"I said repeat after me! Say ...You!" Sha-Rock instructs.

Instead of repeating after him, Dollar screams at the top of his lungs. "Mrs. Jones! Mrs. Jones!"

"Shut up," Sha-Rock whispers while pointing the gun at Dollar's forehead.

Fear is in Dollar's eyes. He's screaming his head off.

"Don't worry," Miranda says, from the other room. "The lady upstairs, Mrs. Jones, is deaf. There's no way she can hear him."

Sha-Rock grabs an oversized pillow from Dollar's bed, and sets it directly on top of Dollar's head.

Dollar shakes his head and screams even louder.

Sha-Rock buries the nose of the gun deep into the pillow. He then squeezes the trigger four times back to back.

"Lights out!"

The Next Day

Jimmy and Sha-Rock sit in the living room of Jimmy's apartment while Miranda is in the bathroom showering. In total, they retrieved 1500 grams of cocaine and $37,000 in cash from Dollar. Between Dollar and Chulo they've managed to score 6500 grams and $38,500 in cash.

"You should be alright now, right baby boy?" Sha-Rock asks. "Now you'll be able to get right."

"Yeah, this will definitely do it," Jimmy replies. "How are we going to divide it up?"

"Listen, you take the four keys. I'll take everything else. Fair enough?" That'll leave Sha-Rock with 2,500 grams and $37,500 in cash.

"No doubt," Jimmy shouts, with a look of joy in his eyes. He was almost sure Sha-Rock would want the majority of the score being that he did the dirty work. Jimmy doesn't have the least bit of remorse of what he did to Dollar or Chulo. His main concern is getting back on top.

"Listen," says Sha-Rock. "Now we had a deal. Shit don't stop here. Don't forget, you promised me. Your exact words were, 'if you help me get back on board, I will turn you on to a few dudes.' Please don't renee on me. Round a couple more of them dumb ass niggas up, and I'll handle the rest."

That was the deal they made. Up until now, Jimmy has always done fair business. Neither of them has ever played by these rules. Jimmy and Sha-Rock both have always been hustlers. Jimmy has always been about making money. He's never been a killer or a tough guy, just a money getter. Sha-Rock on the other hand has always made money, but he also lived for the drama. He always kept a gun on him and couldn't wait for the time to use it. He just loved to put in work. In Philly, he has a reputation for playing the murder game. Everyone in town knows he's a coldhearted murderer.

While Sha-Rock and Jimmy were down Northern State, they became so fly. They attracted like magnets. They both had big plans. They promised each other that they would get rich together. They planned to take everything over from Newark on down to Baltimore. Sha-Rock had heard so many stories about Jimmy and how smart he was. They said he was one of the strongest cocaine dealers in Newark. Sha-Rock truly respected his hustle and his mind. He had planned to take the backseat and let Jimmy drive. He was going to let Jimmy run everything. His role was going to be the muscle. Sha-Rock told Jimmy that he lost the drive for the hustle thing. He had been hustling ever since he was fifteen years old. He was tired.

Sha-Rock knew it would take more than just his muscle to lock down all those states. That's where his crew would come in. He would have to bring in his two main men. Skip and Calvin the Albino, a.k.a. Killer Cal. Skip is currently doing a bid in Trenton State Prison. Killer Cal, well that's a whole different story. Skip and Cal were like Sha-Rock's bodyguards. Sha-Rock kept them around for security purposes. They both are highly dangerous. He didn't really need them to protect him because he could put in his own work. He mainly kept them around to keep them out of trouble. Without him keeping them on point, dudes would have it hard. Their game was really robbery, murder and extortion.

Killer Cal taught Sha-Rock and Skip to play that game at an early age. Cal is almost fifteen years their senior. Sha-Rock's parents knew that was a problem in the beginning. They would not accept the fact that their fifteen-year-old son was hanging out with a thirty-year-old man. They always knew Cal was bad news. They always told him that they didn't raise a flunky or a follower. How true were they? They didn't raise a flunky. They raised a boss.

Sha-Rock has always been the black sheep of his family. His father is a reverend and his mother is an evangelist. Once again the myth is correct. "The Reverend's kids are always the worst kids."

At first Sha-Rock made a few moves with Skip and Cal, but he never really liked that game. He felt like he was too smart for that. He wanted to make his own money, and that he did. He got his first package and took off like a rocket. He blew up pratically overnight. He promised his boys that they wouldn't have to rob ever again because he was going to hold them down. Their run lasted for years until Sha-Rock caught the drug beef and had to go away to prison. Skip and Cal had to go back to what they knew. Skip ended up catching a robbery beef that landed him in Trenton State.

Jimmy was released before Sha-Rock. Jimmy took care of Sha-Rock once he hit the streets. He made sure everything was alright, from money orders for Sha-Rock to mortgage payments for Sha-Rock's mother and father. He even paid a few months' tuition for Sha-Rock's sister's kids. He was an all-around good dude.

Sha-Rock came home with the plan of blowing up again. When he finally made it home, his first stop was Newark to meet with Jimmy. He was shocked when Jimmy admitted to him that he was broke. Jimmy never told Sha-Rock how bad he was doing because he didn't want Sha-Rock to lose hope. He knows how important hope is when you're incarcerated. Anyhow, he figured he would get it right by the time Sha-Rock came home, but he ended up doing worse. That's when Sha-Rock's other side jumped out. He came up with the bright idea of getting money the "ski mask" way" as he calls it. Jimmy didn't like the idea, but he didn't have much of a choice. They have a common fear, and that is being broke.

Sha-Rock hears Miranda coming out of the bathroom. He quickly dumps the cocaine and the money into his duffle bag. He doesn't want her to know exactly how much they made. The more she sees, the more she'll want.

She steps into the room fully dressed.

"Are you ready, Ma?"

"Yep, whenever you are."

Two hours later, Miranda and Sha-Rock arrive in Philly. It feels so good to be home safe and sound, they both think to themselves. As soon as they drop off their bags at home, they head right back out the door. They're on their way to their jeweler. Sha-Rock has a big surprise for her. Today is the day he'll pick up her custom-made, diamond fluttered Wonder Woman bracelet.

She almost faints when the jeweler places it on her wrist. Sha-Rock spent over half of the earnings on the bracelet. He paid a total of $24,000 for it. The things Sha-Rock would do to please his lady!

———————■◆◄————————

12

One Day Later

"Little Sis, your husband home?" Sha-Rock asks.

"Yeah, he's in the backroom playing that damn game as usual."

"Tell him, don't leave. I'll be right over."

Twenty minutes later, Sha-Rock is standing on the porch ringing the bell. His younger niece answers the door. "Hey Uncle Sha," she shouts as she jumps into his arms.

"What's good, little Mama? Where your little chump ass brother at?" he asks in a playful tone.

"Right here, Uncle Turkey," his nephew shouts.

"I got your turkey. Come here," he shouts as he chases the little boy around the table. After catching him, Sha-Rock tickles him until he starts crying. "Now who the turkey? Stop crying like a little punk," he teases. He finally lets the little boy loose. "Here Shonda, get some sneakers for you and the little crybaby right here," he says, while handing her two, $100 bills.

"Thanks!" she shouts.

"Thank you, Uncle Turkey," his nephew shouts as he dashes up the stairs at top speed.

He loves those kids more than anything in the world. He doesn't have any kids, so he treats them as if they're his own.

Lisa, his little sister, is his pride and joy. He's so proud of her. She looks, thinks and acts just like his mother. His mother did a good job of raising her to be a woman. The only thing Sha-Rock hates about Lisa is her punk ass husband. He can't stand him but he never admitted that to her because he knows how much she truly loves the guy. He would hate to do anything to alter the good relationship him and Lisa have. Sha-Rock hates to believe it, but he thinks if he put his sister in a position of choosing between him and her husband, she might choose her husband. That's why he refuses to admit his true feelings. He just lets her do whatever it is that makes her happy.

Sha-Rock thinks Lisa's husband is the corniest dude alive. Sure he gets a little money, but that doesn't change the fact that he's squarer than SpongeBob SquarePants.

"Lisa, what up?" he greets her with a big hug. "How have you been?"

"Alright," she replies. "It's not like you care. I haven't heard from you in weeks."

"I'm sorry, baby. I been on my grind."

"Here you go! You back on that bullshit again. I thought you were done?"

"I am done. What are you talking about? The grind don't have to be negative."

"Well, I know you. So I know what the grind is for you."

"See, that's where you're wrong. I'm on some other shit. Ah ah," he laughs in her face. "See what you get for thinking. I'm up in Jersey promoting parties and shit. My man brought me in." he lies.

"Whatever boy, tell me whatever. All I know is if you get into trouble you're on your own this time."

"I ain't getting into no trouble. Damn, you sound just like Mommy."

"Yeah, speaking of Mommy, she's pissed at you. She said you have not called her in over a month. She says she hopes you're alright. She's praying for you. You need to call her."

"Alright, alright, I'll call her," he replies. She's right, he hasn't called her in over a month. He loves his mother dearly. She's been putting so much pressure on him since he first went to jail. He hasn't called her because he knows the moment she hears his voice, she's going to ask him what he's been doing. He hates to lie to her. When he lies to her he gets this creepy feeling that she knows he's lying. Ever since he was a kid, his mother has had this strange power. It actually scares him. She makes predictions that almost always come true. Everyone in the church goes to Mother Ford when they have a problem. As a kid, Sha-Rock watched people melt at her fingertips. They would start catching the Holy Ghost and crying and carrying on. It was so bad that Sha-Rock was scared to go to church. He thought his mother was a witch or something. Sha-Rock still to this day believes that his mother's prediction sent him to prison. The day he caught the case, she told him she had a dream of him standing behind bars. He's scared to call her because he thinks she may already know what he's been up to. "You looked stress, you alright?" he asks, trying to change the subject. "What up? You need something?"

"I'm good. I don't need anything, but if you throwing out. I'm not going to refuse it."

"Nah, if you don't need it, don't worry about it. I'm only giving to the needy," he laughs. "Here," he says while handing her a stack of twenties.

"Thanks," she replies.

"Don't worry about it. I have to take care of Little Sis. You the only one I got. Oh, I almost forgot about the other one. What's up with his homo ass, anyway?" Sha-Rock is referring to his twin brother, who happens to be gay. Sha-Rock hates him more than his worst enemy. They're identical twins. He has always felt cursed behind that. His brother has always been effeminate since they were kids. Sha-Rock played all sports while his brother played the role of his cheerleader. He would embarrass him so much. He hated to bring him along, but his mother made him. It got so bad that Sha-Rock and his boys would beat his brother violently. Sha-Rock called it "beating the fag out of him." Eventually his brother got tired of the ass beatings and he stopped tagging along with him. While Sha-Rock was in prison, he would think back on how bad they used to beat him and he would feel terrible. He didn't feel bad for beating him, he just felt bad that he allowed someone else to put their hands on him. One Sunday, he came to visit Sha-Rock. He was with Miranda and Lisa. That was the worst visit ever. He wanted to kill his brother. The way he pranced around there, snapping his fingers really pissed Sha-Rock off. Sha-Rock thinks he done it to pay him back for how bad they treated him as a kid. After that visit, Sha-Rock was the talk of Northern State. A couple of his associates made jokes about it until they saw how touchy he was about the situation. Months later, his brother tried to visit again. Sha-Rock walked into the visiting hall, saw him and left right back out. They have not spoken since.

"He's alright. You know he's getting married next month, right?"

"Married?"

"Yeah married. He's marrying some white man."

"Lisa, I don't want to hear that bullshit."

"Seriously. Your invitation is over there on top of the microwave."

"Yeah, whatever. You going?"

"Yeah. That's my brother. When you get married wouldn't you

want me there?"

"Hell yeah, but I ain't no fucking faggot, marrying no white man!"

"Love is love," she replies.

"Lisa, I know you ain't taking them kids are you?"

"That's their uncle," she replies.

"Girl, you done lost your mind. You gone fuck around and ruin them kids."

"They'll be alright. They know better."

"I don't know. Little Rahiem does cry a lot. I'm telling you now, if he ever come out the closet, I'm killing him."

"Stop playing boy, Rahiem is not going to be gay!"

"I'm just telling you. We already got one in the family. Ain't gone be no more. Anymore born, I'm killing them myself. Mail that invitation back to him. Tell him I said fuck him and his faggot ass lover. I wish I would go to man on man wedding!" Sha-Rock is getting furious at the thought of it. Just to be at the wedding watching a mirror image of him standing there kissing another man. He would rather die than go to that wedding. A verse from his favorite underground rap group Mob Style comes to his mind. "Man on top of man. I can't understand. Throw them all in the garbage can because they trash. Who would like it in the ass?" he sings aloud. He quickly erases the terrible thought out of his mind. "Here goes $500. Get a money order and send that to your mother. She ain't gone take it from me. She thinks all my money is blood money," he says sarcastically. "Where Fam at?" Fam is what he calls Lisa's husband. He and Lisa have been together for fourteen years and he has never said his name. That's how much he despises him.

"Rahiem is in the back."

Sha-Rock walks into the room. Rahiem is laid across the bed playing the video game. He continues to focus on the game without even acknowledging Sha-Rock. He's so self centered and arrogant, that he thinks the world revolves around him. Sha-Rock becomes slightly agitated. The fact that he's ignoring him is really killing him inside. One of these days Sha-Rock is going to give him what he has been asking for. He really thinks it can't happen to him. If it weren't for Lisa, he would have done him dirty a long time ago.

"Fam, what up?" Sha-Rock forces himself to ask.

"What up," he replies nonchalantly.

Sha-Rock closes the door behind him. "Yo, I came by to let you know that I got something you might could use."

"Something like what?" he asks.

"Some girl. My man up the way owed me some scrilla, so he just dropped some powder on me," Sha-Rock lies.

"Oh yeah," he asks without even taking his eyes off of the screen.

Sha-Rock expected a different reaction from him.

"I'm good," he mumbles.

"Huh?" Sha-Rock asks.

"I'm good," he repeats.

"I'm telling you, it's flavor," says Sha-Rock.

"I'm alright. I just flipped."

"I got an offer you can't refuse," Sha-Rock claims.

"And what is that?"

"Twenty-one a gram," Sha-Rock replies.

"Twenty-one a gram?" he laughs.

Sha-Rock doesn't have the slightest idea what he's laughing at. He thinks he's giving him a damn good price. He's been gone a while, and the closest thing he's been to the game is the meeting with Chulo, who was charging nineteen a gram, and that's up north. He figures twenty-one down here should be a good price.

"I pay seventeen and a half for the whole thing, and I sell it to my peoples for less than you're trying to charge me. You're trying to hit me over the head."

"Damn, Sha-Rock thinks to himself. It's kind of hard to top that. He was expecting to make at least $50,000 total off of the work. "Alright, you drive a hard bargain. I'll give it to you for seventeen even," he offers. That totally cuts his profit, but he just wants to get rid of it. Anyhow he didn't pay a dime for it so it's all profit for him.

"Man, I just flipped. I'm loaded. I got a couple of dollars laying around though, if it's the right food."

"Trust me, it's the right shit. I got it in the car if you want to take a look at it. If not, I already got a sale for it. This kid gone give me twenty-one for it," Sha-Rock lies.

"Get your money then, nigga. I can't do nothing with twenty-one."

"Nah, I'd rather you get it. You take care of my sister and the kids. I'd rather keep the money in the family."

"Let me check it out?"

Sha-Rock races out of the room. In less than three minutes he's back. As he unzips the bag, the strong aroma of cocaine fills the air. Rahiem doesn't even have to look at it. He can tell it's official, just by smelling it. He looks at it, just to play it all the way out. After examining it, he tosses it to the side as if he's not impressed.

"It's alright, but nothing to write home about."

"Alright? This that New York flavor. I know blow."

"It's alright. It can't fuck with the shit I got though," he claims.

Sha-Rock is once again getting pissed. "Look, you want it or not?"

"How much you got?"

"I got two and a half bricks."

He begins calculating. "I got $41,000 for you."

"$41,000? Come on, nigga. How much that come out to?" Sha-Rock asks.

"Like $16,500 a joint, give or take a dollar."

"Knock it off man!"

"Hey, that's what I got. Take it or leave it?" he propositions.

Right now Sha-Rock wants to stick his gun so far down Rahiem's throat and take everything he's got, but his love for Lisa overpowers his hate for Rahiem.

After finalizing the deal, Rahiem goes to the closet and opens his safe. He pulls out approximately $200,000. Sha-Rock feels so stupid watching him peel the $41K from his stash. "I thought you said, that's all you had?" Sha-Rock asks.

"Did I say that?" he asks sarcastically. "I meant, that's all I'm willing to give you," he laughs.

Sha-Rock is heated. I should rip him for everything, he thinks to himself. Nah, Little Sis loves this clown, he rationalizes with himself.

"Pleasure doing business with you. If you come across some more holler at me," Rahiem shouts. Rahiem isn't buying Sha-Rock's story at all. He believes Sha-Rock is hustling again and not admitting it. Maybe he thinks Rahiem will tell his sister. Little does Rahiem know, a man died over those kilos.

Sha-Rock doesn't reply. I'm going to holler at you alright, he thinks to himself. He walks out feeling like a rape victim. He doesn't have a clue how badly he just played himself. Rahiem told him he pays seventeen and a half; in all reality, he pays twenty-one and a half. He just made a hell of a come-up. He just saved himself five points. He'll make an extra $12,500 profit. He buys them for $21,500 and sells them for $25,000. That gives him a total profit of $21,250 off of two and a half birds. It gets no sweeter than that. Normally he would have to break it down on the street to profit like that. His normal profit off of 2 and a half bricks would be $8,750. If Sha-Rock knew this he probably would rob him for everything.

As Sha-Rock is leaving the house, he utters to himself the words, "Laugh now, cry later. Sometimes the things that make you laugh, will make you cry too."

━━━━━◆◆◆◆━━━━━

13

One Week Later

Miranda floats in the king-sized waterbed. She's in the apartment of her best friend, Tamara. She and Tamara have been friends for only a little over three years, but it seems like forever. They met a few months after Sha-Rock went away. Miranda told Sha-Rock so many stories about her while he was in prison. When he came home and finally found out whom Tamara was he almost fainted. His face went white like he had just seen a ghost. One year before he went away, he had met a fine little chick at a party his homeboy gave. She knew all about his girlfriend and everything. But she never knew her name. He refused to tell her that. Although they did date once or twice, they never had sex. They didn't end their little rendezvous on bad terms, they just sort of fell out of touch. That little fine chick was Tamara.

Miranda and Tamara have become so close that Sha-Rock can't find the heart to tell her. At first he begged Miranda to stay away from Tamara because he feared that she would probably tell about the dates they went on. Sha-Rock was shocked the day that Miranda formally introduced him to Tamara. She acted as if she never saw him a day in her life. Sha-Rock still wonders if she really didn't recognize him or if she was faking.

During the little time Miranda and Tamara have known each other, they've been through so much together. When it comes to men, Tamara must be cursed. She has always had difficulty finding good men. She always gets stuck with the losers. She's been through it all from the jealous, insecure man who thinks he doesn't deserve you so he beats you to keep you, on down to the lovable, pretty boy kind that thinks women are supposed to take care of him because he's a cutie.

Tamara and Miranda tell everyone that they're sisters, which is easy to believe because they look a lot alike, except that Tamara's hair is dyed blond and it only falls a little past her shoulders. Tamara is also two times thicker than Miranda. She's stacked in all the right places, especially her extra wide hips. She makes Miranda look like just another pretty face.

Those two beautiful women walking the street have caused a many of accidents. Men can't keep their eyes off of them.

Right now Miranda is doing a favor for Tamara while she's at work. She asked Miranda to wait in her apartment for the furniture man to arrive.

Some guy Tamara met a few months ago is fully furnishing the entire apartment. This doesn't shock Miranda. All Tamara's newfound relationships start out like this, but sooner or later his true colors will show. He'll end up doing something crazy or admit that he has a wife, or he's bisexual. Something will steer them apart. She told Miranda she's only living for the moment. When it's over, it's over. She refuses to put her feelings into another guy. She's been hurt too many times.

Miranda has been waiting for hours already, but she has no problem doing her the favor. She'll do anything for Tamara and vice versa. They're tighter than sisters. They even have keys to each other's apartments. That's how close they've grown. The only secret Miranda keeps from Tamara is Sha-Rock's occupation. Tamara would be distraught if she knew the things Sha-Rock and Miranda have been doing for money. Miranda told her that Sha-Rock gets his money up north. That isn't too hard for Tamara to believe because she knew how Sha-Rock was rolling back when she met him.

Deep down inside, Miranda hates her new lifestyle, but she'll do anything for her man. He promised her that this is only temporary. He told her after he gets right, he's done with his new hustle. She had no clue that it would last this long. They have been working it like this ever since he first came home. He's been doing little dirt from town to town, only calling her in when he really needs her. There's nothing she won't do for Sha-Rock. He's always been there for her, and she plans to always be there for him.

Miranda would love to live a regular life. Tamara lives Miranda's dream life. Tamara really is a model. She does pretty well with it too. She has appeared in several music videos, magazines and television commercials. There's no doubt in Miranda's mind. She knows she could be right there with Tamara if not further.

Miranda modeled while Sha-Rock was away. Just when it was all about to come together, Sha-Rock was released from prison and he made her stop modeling. She never told Tamara why; she just said she wasn't feeling it. That was a boldfaced lie. There's nothing that makes her happier than modeling. Since Miranda stopped, Tamara has stolen pictures of Miranda and taken them to agents who have fallen in love with her beauty. Miranda would love to take the offer from the agents. Some of them have come at her with big deals, but she knows Sha-Rock is totally against it. He's so jealous that he's afraid she'll run off with some rich Hollywood guy and he'll never see her again.

While Miranda is waiting, she dazes off and starts reminiscing about her childhood. She stands in front of her kindergarten classroom of about thirty students. Her teacher just asked her the famous question. "Miranda Benderas, what are you going to be when you grow up?"

Miranda stands up joyfully, wearing her favorite pastel colored, flowered sundress. Her straight, black hair is parted down the middle with two pigtails hanging to her hips. She strikes a pose and smiles the cheesiest snagged tooth smile. "I'm going to be a thupermodel," she slurs.

Miranda is the product of a biracial marriage. Her mother was African American and her father is of Cuban descent.

Every since birth her beauty has made her an outcast. She had gotten accustomed to praise at an early age. Her mother would always tell her that her looks would make her rich. Her mother was a model at one time as well.

Miranda's father hated the attention that Miranda received. He always knew that her looks were a curse just as much as it was a gift. He knew if he didn't raise her right, her looks would lead her to destruction. He spent a great deal of his time trying to raise her to be the perfect woman. The last thing he wanted was for her to get pregnant by some loser like so many other young girls have done. He hoped and prayed that she would grow up to be an independent successful woman.

At age thirteen, Miranda won first place in her school's Miss Teen Beauty Pageant. That was by far the happiest day of her life. The only disappointment was the fact that her father couldn't share the special day with her. Two months prior, he was sentenced to life in prison. Edwin Benderas was convicted of leading a drug ring that operated across the entire East Coast. This was a traumatic experience for both of them. They were so close. She was daddy's little princess. He left her young and yet so ripe. He never got the chance to instill all the values in her that he wanted to. He feared what she would become.

Hours pass and the furniture guys still haven't arrived. At 3:04 P.M. exactly, Tamara struts into the apartment and finds Miranda knocked out cold. "Wake up, girl!" Miranda awakes instantly. "They didn't get here, yet?" Tamara asks.

"Nope."

At 4:30 in the afternoon, the deliveryman finally arrives. After the delivery, Miranda and Tamara head over to the Gallery Mall on Market Street where they shop the evening away.

They top their evening off with dinner on South Street at their favorite restaurant.

They're eating at a small table two feet away from the curb. Just as they're finishing the remains of the meal, a teal green Mercedes SL500 with butterscotch colored interior pulls alongside of them. Tamara jumps up instantly and rushes toward the driver. He quickly climbs out of his car, as if he's just as happy to see her. This must be Tamara's new friend, Najee. Najee is the friend who furnished Tamara's apartment. This is Miranda's first time ever seeing him. He's everything Tamara said he was. He stands about six feet even. He's slender with a golden complexion. His hair is cut in a low Caesar, and his beard has the five o' clock shadow effect. It's mainly stubble but it's shaped up neatly. Tamara met him at a photo shoot in New York. He's also a model. He's from Harlem. Miranda can tell that by his pretty-boy style. He's wearing a pink three button Lacoste shirt and dark blue denim jeans. He's wearing white and pink Air Force Ones to match his outfit. His diamonds are excessive. Miranda never knew you could ever use the words "too much" when referring to diamonds, but now she knows. He has way too much ice. She can't believe her eyes.

They hug tightly before Tamara snatches away and pulls him toward Miranda. "Come here. I want you to meet my big sister."

He walks toward her. He doesn't believe his eyes. It's like he's seeing double. "We finally meet," he says while extending his hand for a handshake. "Pardon my staring, but I can't believe it. Y'all look just alike. "Excuse me, I gotta call my twin brother. He ain't gone believe this. It's two of y'all, and two of us. We'll shock the world. You have to meet my twin," he shouts.

Damn, another twin, she thinks to herself. She wonders, does he look as good as he does? Maybe he's a homo like Sha-Rock's twin? "Do you really have a twin?" she asks.

"Yeah, I'm about to get him on the phone, right now!" he shouts as he dials. "Looks just like me, same eyes, same hair, weight, height. The only thing, he's as black as tar."

Black as tar, she utters to herself. Uh oh, that's Miranda's weakness. She's always been attracted to dark handsome men.

"Yo, Najim, you ain't gone believe this. Tammy got a twin! You gotta see her. No bullshit. I'm getting this one for you! No doubt! One!" he shouts before hanging up the phone.

"Oh no you ain't," Tamara denies. "Ah ah, she got a man. Fall back!"

Miranda sits quietly just smiling away.

"Here take his number anyway, just in case you change your mind." He grabs a pen from the table and scribbles a number with a 917 area code onto a small piece of paper. "Here," he says as he shoves the paper to Miranda, who tucks it into her purse. "Tammy, I got something for you!" he shouts as he trots to his car and opens the trunk. He returns holding a plastic Chanel bag. "Here, this is just a little something-something," he claims. "I'll be back in three days. I have to meet the agent in D.C. I'll holler at you as soon as I get there!" he claims before giving her a wet passionate kiss.

He then hops into his Benz. While he's sitting there, his top drops automatically. In a matter of seconds his entire roof disappears. "You make sure you call my brother. He's waiting for you!" he shouts before peeling off. The sound of his tires screeching distracts everyone.

As soon as his car is out of sight, Tamara digs into the plastic bag. She's anxious to find out what he's bought her. She's happy to find the Chanel pocketbook that she's been saving her money for months to get. She mentioned to him how bad she wanted it, and now he has surprised her with it. It's a $2,000 pocketbook. She picks it up by the straps. She notices the bag has a peculiar amount of weight to it. In no way does this bag feel empty. She unzips it only to find three stacks of money wrapped in rubber bands, with a small note attached. The note reads, "they say it's bad luck to give someone a purse with no money in it." The note makes her crack a smile. She quickly fumbles through the stacks of twenties. She estimates the amount at about $3,000. "That boy is crazy. He gives gift after gift. I'm not complaining though. I do deserve it, all the drama I been through with these tired ass niggas."

"I know that's right," Miranda agrees. "Get it while it's there."

"It's like, he's too good to be true. I know he's going to do something wrong. I just know he is."

"How do you know?" Miranda asks. "Maybe this is the one. Maybe God sent you this one to make up for all the other losers. Maybe God sent you all the other ones first, so you'd be able to appreciate a good man. Don't think so negative. Give him a chance."

"I am. All I know is, I have never been this happy in my entire life. Najee makes me feel so complete. I just hope I can find perfect love. The kind of love you and Sha-Rock share. That's all I want."

Careful what you wish for, Miranda thinks to herself. She doesn't have a clue how "Dangerously in Love" they are.

One Week Later/ August 22, 2004

Two days ago Lisa called Sha-Rock and told him he had mail at her house. He was shocked to receive a letter from his man, Skip. Skip is doing his time in Trenton State. He's been there for almost two years now. The letter states that he wants Sha-Rock to come visit him. Skip is locked up for robbery. Right now, they're into the same line of work, but Sha-Rock has taken it to the next level. Skip is locked up for petty street corner robbery, but Sha-Rock doesn't fault him. He knows Skip had to do what he knew how to, just to survive. When Sha-Rock got sentenced he wasn't worried about himself. He was more worried about Miranda, Cal and Skip. He knew how much they all depended on him. In the letter, Skip also asked Sha-Rock to check on Cal. Killer Cal is the eldest of the bunch. He practically raised Sha-Rock and Skip.

Killer Cal, a.k.a. Calvin the Albino, is extremely dangerous. Sha-Rock kept Cal close to him up until a couple of months ago when Cal lost his mind. He had a nervous breakdown. The cause was too much pressure. Cal had it rough from birth. He's always been an outcast because he was born an albino. Out of his parents' seven children, he was the only one out of the bunch who was born with the disorder. His pinkish colored skin, and red pupils have always caused people to fear him. He's always had it rough. At six years old, he lost his entire family in a fire. He was the only survivor out of his six siblings, his mother and his father. That alone made him a walking time bomb.

From six years old to fourteen years old, a foster family raised him. The man of the house was sexually abusing Cal. One night, Cal couldn't take it anymore. He killed the man while he was asleep. Cal waited for him to get drunk, then he struck him in the head with a hammer.

From then on, the streets raised him. At age nineteen, he fell in love with a girl, whom he eventually married. She managed to persuade him to change his life around. He enlisted in the United States Marines.

Months later, he was shipped to the war. He lasted only a few short months before they realized that his past had a traumatic experience on him. They labeled him as mentally ill and released him. He then found himself a job painting the lines on the highway late at night. He was straight. It was a union job paying $25 an hour. One particular night he left the job early because he was feeling sick. To his surprise he walked in his house and found a strange man in his bed on top of his wife, wailing on her as she screamed for more. Cal hasn't been the same since.

Before Sha-Rock went away, Cal's mind would fade in and out. He would be okay, as long as he took the medication the doctor prescribed. His mental condition isn't the reason Sha-Rock cut him off. He's been half crazy for years, and that never put a damper on their relationship. When Sha-Rock came home he found out that Cal had started getting high and drinking heavily. The intoxicants and his mental condition didn't mix. He would always talk off-the-wall stuff that Sha-Rock had no clue of what he was talking about. Sha-Rock hung around him for a few weeks. He continuously tried to talk him into getting help, but Cal kept refusing until Sha-Rock eventually faded away from him. Sha-Rock hasn't seen or heard from him in months.

Sha-Rock is cruising slowly through the block, trying to see the addresses on the houses. Skip gave him Cal's address. He's looking for eighty-seven. As he approaches ninety-three, he slows down. Sha-Rock is shocked at the house which appears to be eighty-seven. It's a shabby little two-story house. The aluminum siding is stripped off of the entire house.

Sha-Rock parks and gets out. He has to walk up the steps carefully because every other step is missing. The steps that are there are very loose. He finally reaches the front door. He presses the doorbell, only to find out that it doesn't work. He then walks over to the window and peeks inside. Through an opening in the curtain he sees junk scattered around the front room. It looks as if someone just moved out. He then walks down the stairs and backpedals toward the curb, looking upward. He notices that all the windows are stripped. The attic also looks abandoned. He pulls Skip's letter from his pocket, just to make sure he has the right address. After confirming it, he walks to the alleyway. The small door is slightly opened. An extension cord stretches from the second floor through the doorway. He peeks further and sees a light, which tells him there is some sign of life.

Sha-Rock peeks his head through the doorway. A pungent odor

makes him step backward. He regroups and peeks his head inside again. This time he holds his breath. "Yo!" he shouts. No one replies. "Yo!" he repeats.

"Yo, what?" someone replies aggressively. "Who are you looking for?"

"I'm looking for Cal!"

Silence fills the air.

"Who wants him?" the voice asks from a distance.

"Is that you, Cal?"

"It depends on, if you are who I think you are," Cal replies.

"Who do you think, I am?"

Cal finally peeks his head through a doorway in the back. "What's happening, Baby Boy?" he shouts with a great big smile on his face.

"Nothing much," Sha-Rock replies while still trying to hold his breath. The smell is overwhelming. He can't understand how Cal is living down here with that smell.

Cal runs over to Sha-Rock and hugs him. As they separate Sha-Rock catches another bad odor. Cal smells like he hasn't showered in years. Sha-Rock gives him a complete overlook. Cal looks terrible. It looks as if he just crawled out from underneath a rock. His clothes smell of funk and mildew. His thick golden dreadlocks are matted onto his head like an old rug. His nappy beard is well overgrown, and his mustache has curled over his lip into his mouth. Green mucous fills the corners of both of his eyes. His breath smells like horse shit.

"What's good with you, big homey?" Sha-Rock feels bad looking at his man suffer like this. "Yo man, what the fuck is up with you? Ain't this house abandoned? And what the fuck is that smell?"

"One question at a time, Baby Boy. The sewer backed up. That's what you smell. And yes, this house is abandoned," he shamefully admits. "What else can I do? I'm fucked up."

"Come on, Bro. You can't be that fucked up."

"Shit! I'm fucked up, fucked up."

"Come on Killer Cal, this ain't you. How you living? What are you doing for yourself?"

"I'm trying to put it all together, but shit been rough for me."

"Are you still fucking with that shit?"

"Hell no!" he snaps. "I been clean for two months. That's a

closed chapter of my life."

"Well what's the problem then?"

"I have been having a hard time getting on my feet," he claims. "You know I hit rock bottom fucking with that shit? For a while I was pissed at you. I felt like you left me when I needed you the most. We are a team. You were supposed to be my crutch."

"Cal listen, you were running one hundred miles an hour. It's cool to ride in the fast lane, but every once in a while you have to pump your brakes just to make sure they're still working. I tried a lot of times to get you to register in a program, but you refused. I had to bounce before you got me into a fucked up position, feel me?"

"Yeah, I feel you now, after sitting back and analyzing the whole picture. The main thing about that shit is you have to be ready to stop. I wasn't ready. I loved that shit," he admits.

"What was it that made you want to stop, then?"

"I never wanted to stop. I started fucking up big time. To be honest, the only thing I remember is waking up in a straight jacket with a bunch of looney tune ass doctors around me. I was bugging out, watching all them crazy motherfuckers eating their own shit and drinking their piss. I asked myself what the fuck am I doing here?"

Sha-Rock is shocked. "You were in the crazy house?"

"Yeah. They had my ass up in Greystone, in New Jersey. My doctor wouldn't tell me what happened. He just kept telling me I had a nervous breakdown from too much stress. You know, my family, the war and that shit with my ex-wife. Everything!"

"Yeah, I got you." Sha-Rock begins to feel a great deal of pity for Cal. Especially being that he wasn't there for him during that time. "Enough of the past. What are you going to do now? You can't live like this. You look like a caveman. Look at this shit, it's abandoned."

"Yeah, but it's home. To be honest, Baby Boy, I don't know what I'm going to do. Everyday I pray that something will come through. I look at all my suffering. I know I done a lot of dirt, but damn! How much payback do I deserve? I just hope something comes through, real soon."

"Say no more. Shit going alright for me again. And you know if I'm alright, you alright. I got some major things brewing. Don't worry no more. It's over."

"Yeah? It's like that?" Cal asks.

"Like that!" Sha-Rock replies. "In two days I scored almost seven kilos and close to forty grand in cash."

Cal's eyes damn near pop out of his head. "Oh yeah?"

"Hell yeah!"

"How?"

"Nigga, I stepped my game up. That's how. I'm fucking around up in Newark."

"Newark, Delaware?" Cal asks.

"Nah nigga, Newark, New Jersey. Them cats getting a lot of bread! They ain't got no loyalty though. They'll set one of their homeys up in a heartbeat. Everybody all over the world knows that. Even in the prisons, Newark niggas don't even fuck with Newark niggas, cause they're all so grimey. They can't even trust one another. In the pen, any Newark nigga who is about something clicks up with out-of-towners. I can't understand it. I don't care how much I don't like a motherfucker, I ain't gone let no out-of-towner come down here and cross the home team, feel me? That's the bottom line. Fuck that!"

"For sure," Cal agrees. "I heard them niggas up there is wild as hell, though."

"Yeah, they live. I ain't gone deny that. They put in work. See, I'm dealing with the element of surprise. We gotta catch 'em slippin'. I got some major shit on the way. I'm bringing you in."

"Baby Boy, fill me in with all the details, and it's a wrap!"

————————◆————————

Days Later

Sha-Rock sits in the crowded visiting hall waiting for Skip to enter. Sha-Rock never visits anyone in jail but he really needs to speak with Skip. They haven't seen each other in over three years.

Here comes Skip, finally. He's so wide that he damn near has to squeeze through the doorway. He only stands five feet six inches tall, but he's as wide as a superhero. He stated in his letter that he's the strongest man in the prison. His bench-press is recorded at 525 pounds.

Skip sits down. Both of them try hard to remain emotionless but their eyes tell it all.

"What's good, my nigga?" Skip asks.

"Hey man, barely breathing, that's it."

They kick it for minutes. Skip tells Sha-Rock that he hasn't seen or heard from his lady and his kids in months. Sha-Rock can see the bitterness in his eyes as he's speaking. He doesn't know what to tell him, so he decides to change the subject.

"Yo, I saw Cal the other day."

"Oh yeah? What's really good with him?" Skip asks.

"He doing fucked up, but I got him. I'm about to bring him in with me. He's homeless and the whole shit."

"You should have been brought him in," Skip snaps. "If I was home I would have never let him slip like that."

Sha-Rock is shocked at the tone Skip is using with him. "What? So you saying it's my fault?"

"Nah, I ain't saying it's your fault, but we are a team. You don't turn your back on the team like that."

"First of all, obviously you don't what you're talking about. Cal was already fiened out before I came home. When I first checked in, he was already at an all-time low. I tried to step in, but he was too far gone. I had to get myself right first. At that time, he would have just been dead weight. What the fuck was I supposed to do?"

"Hold him down," Skip replies. "You left him for dead!"

"Left him for dead? You stupid! He's a grown ass man. If he

wants to get high, ain't shit I could do about it."

"Whatever man! I had to rip a nigga up in here. Nigga was clowning my dude, telling me my man cookoo for cocoa puffs, all up in Greystone and shit. I didn't have nobody to be mad at but you. I felt like it was all your fault," he admits. "I felt like if anybody could have saved him, it would be you."

"Yo Skip, it ain't on me. I tried to help him but he was in love with that shit. He just admitted it to me. He told me during the time I was trying to register him in the program, he wasn't tired yet. Come on Skip, you hurt me, Big Bro. I would never turn my back on the family. You know that more than anyone else in the world. Now that he's clean, I'm about to bring him back to life. On the real!"

"I hear you," Skip mumbles. "What's good with you though?"

"Right now, I got some surefire plans up in Newark. When I first came home shit wasn't right, so I had to make it right, feel me?" he asks, while Skip looks him straight in the eyes trying to figure out exactly what he's talking about. "I had to do some shit that I really didn't want to do, but it's all turning out for the better. I'm making more money this way, than I ever made the other way."

"What way is that?" Skip asks.

"The ski mask way," Sha-Rock whispers.

"Street corner shit?" he asks. Skip can't believe his ears. He never thought he would see the day when Sha-Rock would be glorifying robbery. That totally goes against his code. Back in the day, he hated when Cal and Skip talked about stings. Now this? "What you mean, the ski mask way? What's up with you? You changed baby. You going against the code. You know the rules, never go outside your element. You know what happens when you go against the grain."

"Street corner shit?" Sha-Rock repeats. "Hell no! Bigger than that. I'm catching them niggas with everything, pants down."

Skip shakes his head in dispute. 'That's a dangerous game you're playing."

"I'm a dangerous nigga," Sha-Rock replies.

"I know that but who you rolling with? I know you can handle yourself, but who got your back?"

"Up until now, I've been dolo, but from here on out I'm bringing Cal in."

"Alright, that's what's up. I'm still worried about y'all."

"We gone be alright. I just can't wait until you check in."

"That's why I wanted you to come down here. I should be home in a few weeks. I have to play the halfway house for a few months though."

"Oh yeah? Alright, bet."

"I got some other shit on my mind though. Bigger shit, way bigger. I have been using my time wisely, just planning moves for us. Just do what you're doing until I get there, then it's over."

"Moves like what? Give me an idea. Are they major?"

"From here on out, everything I do will be major. One thing, I need you to holler at one of my young boys. He's from Newark, somewhere. He was my junior down here. I told him once I came home we would connect the dots. He's a good dude with a lot of heart. He'll hold you down. Get with him. He knows the do's and the don'ts of that town. He already knows you. I told him all about you. His name is Bree. When you go back up there see if you can locate him."

Normally, Sha-Rock wouldn't even consider the idea, but if Skip says someone is cool, it must be official. He's still not sure though. Sha-Rock doesn't trust anyone.

"Are you going to look for him?"

"I don't know. You know I ain't with that meeting new friends shit. I'll probably just wait until you check in."

"Nah, he's good. This is an OG call. Take my word for it. Have I ever steered you wrong?"

Instead of answering the question, Sha-Rock debates with himself. He really does need some help, but he's not sure. For so many years their crew only consisted of the three. Skip asking him to add an addition to the family is surprising. This must be one hell of a guy if Skip is willing to bring him in?

———◆◆◆———

Sha-Rock is really considering what Skip asked him to do the other day. He asked Jimmy if he ever heard of the kid, Bree. Coincidentally, Jimmy knows some of the same people he knows. A few phone calls here and there lands Sha-Rock and Bree on the phone.

Jimmy's phone rings. "Hello," he answers.

"Yo, can I speak to Sha-Rock?"

"Who is this?" Jimmy questions.

"Bree."

"Hold on."

"Yo," Sha-Rock answers.

"What's shaking, daddy?"

"Nothing much. I heard a lot about you. My dude said it's imperative that I get with you."

"For sure," Bree replies. "I've been waiting for your call ever since I got home. When can we meet? Homeboy told me so much about you, it feels like I already know you."

"What are you doing right now?" Sha-Rock asks.

"Shit. I'm up in Orange Projects. Do you know how to get here?"

"He in Orange Projects," Sha-Rock whispers to Jimmy. "How far is that?"

"Ten minutes away," Jimmy replies.

"Yeah, I can find it," Sha-Rock tells Bree. "Give me fifteen minutes, I'll be there."

"Bet, when you get here, call this number back," says Bree.

Ten minutes later, they arrive on Parrow Street. Jimmy pulls to the very end of the block while Sha-Rock calls the number. Sha-Rock gets out at the corner and stands in front of the little bodega, on Oakwood Avenue.

"What's good," Bree answers. "You here?"

"True," Sha-Rock replies.

"Where you at?"

"I'm on the corner, walk down."

"What are you riding in?"

"I'm standing outside," Sha-Rock replies.

Minutes later Sha-Rock spots a tall slender kid walking toward him. He's extra cool, and his swagger strikes Sha-Rock as being way too much. He looks like he's over doing it. He's wearing a blue fitted Yankees cap well over his eyes. His white tank top exposes his bony frame, and his baggy jeans sag well over his crisp suede Timberland construction boots. They say never judge a book by its cover but Sha-Rock looks at this kid as harmless.

"Sha-Rock?" he questions, as he approaches.

"Yeah, that be me. What's the deal?"

They greet each other with a handshake and a quick gangster hug. As they part, Bree's hand drops to Sha-Rock's waist, at the exact area where his gun is. This was not accidental. It was purely intentional. An ordinary guy wouldn't pay attention to it, but Sha-Rock is well aware of his tactic. In fact he uses the same tactic regularly.

After feeling the bulge of the gun, Bree backs away slightly and presses his back against the wall. It's not that Bree doesn't trust Sha-Rock but just for his own sanity, he needs to know if Sha-Rock is holding or not.

As they're talking, Sha-Rock pays close attention to Bree's eyes, which constantly scan the area. He's very alert. This let's Sha-Rock know that he's definitely on point.

Sha-Rock is a good judge of character. Judging by the tactic he used, his wandering eyes, and his slick body movement, Sha-Rock can tell he's definitely one of them. He shows the characteristics of a nigga with massive game. Now his heart and his loyalty is something totally different. That could take a lifetime to figure out.

"What's good with you, homey?" Sha-Rock asks.

"Not too much. Just trying to keep my head above the water, that's it. I ain't doing nothing major. I ain't with the hustling shit, but I gotta do something. I was trying to wait for Big Bro to check in. He said he got a lot of shit planned. I'm ready to eat!"

"I feel you," Sha-Rock replies, before shutting his mouth. He figures, the less he talks, the more Bree will talk. He finds that tactic to always be successful. Something about silence makes a guy nervous.

Usually one will overtalk in order to make the next man open up.

The tactic works. Bree starts speaking again. "I just been scoping shit out, waiting for Big Bro, so we can do us."

The words "scoping out" strikes a light bulb in Sha-Rock's head. "Oh yeah?" he asks.

Bree realizes that he has Sha-Rock's undivided attention. "Yeah! I got a few moves I wanna make. I just need a team. I can't go in by myself, feel me?"

"Go in?" Sha-Rock asks, as if he doesn't have a clue of what Bree is talking about.

"Yeah in. I told you I ain't really with that hustling shit. On the real fam, I rather wait for a nigga to make the trap, and I take it from him. I tried that hustling shit, but I really ain't got the patience for it, feel me?"

"Yeah, I feel you, somewhat," Sha-Rock claims. "That ain't my thing, but right now, I'll try anything. A nigga's ribs are touching."

"I'm telling you Fam, I been doing my homework."

"Big shit?" Sha-Rock asks.

"Big, big shit," Bree replies.

"Yo, if you need me, I'm here. Anytime, just holler."

"Alright, let me put a few things together and I'll get with you."

"I haven't made any money in a while," Sha-Rock lies. "I been sitting around, letting my old lady take care of me. I ain't with that shit! That ain't my style. It's time to do something. I'm starving."

"Starving? Hustlers don't starve. You need something? I ain't got a lot but I do have a few dollars."

"Hey man, that would be a blessing," Sha-Rock replies. Sha-Rock in no way needs a handout. He's only trying to see where the kid's heart is.

Bree pulls his phone out and starts dialing. "Yo little nigga, come to the front!" he shouts into the mouthpiece. "I need to holler at you." He hangs the phone up. "My little man is on his way, hold up. I got a little something-something for you."

Sha-Rock is overwhelmed. He can't believe this kid is about to hit him off. The question is, how much does this kid think he's worth?

Minutes later a fat sloppy teenager walks toward them. "Huh?" he asks.

"How much you got on you, fat ass?"

"I'm finished. I got everything on me. I was just about to put it up."

"How much is it altogether?" Bree asks.

"Like $2,100."

"Give me a G."

The fat kid walks lazily to the alleyway and counts the money out. He returns with a hefty knot and passes it over to Bree.

"Alright, I'll be there in a minute. Go tell shorty to give you that last brick."

The fat boy drags away slowly.

"Here you go, Bro. This ain't much, but it's something to keep the lint out your pocket, feel me? Things will get greater later!"

"Good looking out, baby" Sha-Rock shouts gratefully. He sounds like he really needed the money. Bree just won Sha-Rock's heart. He's truly impressed. Giving $1,000 to a total stranger? Bree doesn't have a clue of how much money this small investment will make him.

"Just let me put shit together," says Bree. "As soon as I finalize everything, I'll get with you. Just hold tight, shit gone be alright. If you need me, hit me. You don't have to budget that. Do what you need to do. I should be calling you in about a week or so, alright?"

"Alright," Sha-Rock confirms, before they part. Sha-Rock waits for him to disappear into the back of the projects before he steps toward Jimmy's car.

As they're riding, he can't help but think of Bree. He likes his style. He can't believe he second-guessed Skip's judgment. This can be the beginning of a beautiful relationship.

Two Weeks Later/ September 9,2004

It's 9 PM. Sha-Rock waits for Miranda in front of Tamara's house. They're on their way to Jersey for business.

As Miranda is walking down the stairs, Sha-Rock notices a Mercedes SL500 parking in the space in front of him. Just as Miranda is grabbing hold of the door handle of Sha-Rock's car, the driver of the Benz hops out. It's Tamara's friend, Najee. Sha-Rock has never seen him before.

"Miranda, what's up lady?"

"Nothing much," she replies before seating herself.

"Sha-Rock looks him up and down from head to toe very attentively. Once he goes inside the house, Sha-Rock switches his attention to the kid's ride. The foreign plates strike his curiosity. "Who is that?" he asks.

"That's Tamara's boyfriend."

"Do you know him like that?"

"Like what?"

"Like Miranda," he mocks in a feminine voice. "He acts like y'all knew each other for years."

"I just met him the other day," she admits.

"Yeah, alright! What's good with him?" he asks.

"I don't know," she replies defensively.

"You don't know?" he asks sarcastically. "That's your best friend and she didn't tell you nothing about him?" he asks in an aggressive tone, as if he doesn't believe her. "I ain't going with that. As much as y'all females run y'all mouth?"

"All I know is he's a model."

"Just a model?"

"No. Not just an ordinary model. He's supposed to be like the next poster boy of the models. Even Ralph Lauren wants him."

"Oh, say that then. Don't just say he's a model, like he's just a plain old model. Ralph Lauren, huh? That explains the Benz. He's from New York?"

"Yes."

"What part?"

Miranda sees exactly where Sha-Rock is headed with this. "Harlem, somewhere."

"Somewhere? You don't know the street?"

"Nope."

"You slippin', Ma. That ain't like you!" he shouts.

"I ain't slipping. I just wasn't trying to cut into her like that."

"Well, cut into her!" he shouts. "Listen Miranda, all money is green. Whether it's drug money or model money, I don't discriminate. It all spends the same!" he shouts as he blasts the radio and prepares for the ride to Jersey.

Two hours later they arrive in front of Jimmy's house where they park Sha-Rock's black Nissan Quest van that he just bought two days ago. He bought it just to work in. He and Miranda hop out of the van and get into Jimmy's Ford Taurus.

Minutes later, they turn onto Evergreen in East Orange. They pull into the parking lot of Club Brokers. Sha-Rock passes his gun to Jimmy. Jimmy takes his gun along with Sha-Rock's and places both of them into his stash box.

Sha-Rock and Miranda stand at the gate, waiting for Jimmy. They reunite and the three of them step toward the entrance. Within fifteen feet of the club, Sha-Rock halts and he looks Miranda dead in the eyes. "Here we go, Ma. Go get that money," he whispers.

"I'll do my best," she replies."

"Give me a kiss," Sha-Rock suggests.

After a long passionate kiss, Miranda walks off and steps into the club. Two minutes later, Sha-Rock and Jimmy follow.

Once they get inside, Sha-Rock immediately finds a corner to melt into. Jimmy walks to the bar area to order a drink, while Sha-Rock scans the floor trying to locate Miranda. That won't be hard to do. All he has to do is find the VIP section, and he knows she'll be somewhere close.

Jimmy returns holding a glass in each hand. "Here," he says while handing Sha-Rock a drink.

"What's that?"

"Hennessy and cranberry."

"I'm good. You know I don't drink. I need to be focused. This is work."

"I know. Just hold it and make it look good. Not only are you an out-of-towner, and you're not going to drink? People are already staring at you. You stick out like a sore thumb. Everyone knows you're not from here. If you stand here without drinking, you'll make niggas nervous."

Sha-Rock reaches for the drink, while still looking for Miranda. He looks to his left. At the far end of the room, he sees heavy activity. The ropes and the huge bar bouncers tell him that's the VIP section. Not to mention the multiple bottles of champagne that is being passed around.

One particular booth is getting the most attention. A short stocky kid is standing on a table with a bottle of champagne in both hands. You can see the reflection of his diamond watch bouncing all over the place. Women line up behind the rope, with their mouths stretched wide open as he pours champagne down their throats.

Sha-Rock looks deeper into the crowd, where he finally locates Miranda. She's busy at work. She hasn't been in the club ten minutes yet, and she already has a victim. They're talking and drinking away. Sha-Rock looks him over. He looks like an average dude. Hopefully she won't waste too much time with him. He knows Miranda well. She's probably just using him to warm up.

Sean Paul's "I'm Still in Love" comes on. The crowd goes wild. The dance floor fills up instantly. Miranda goes to work. She starts off conservatively, just bopping her head and sipping her drink. All of a sudden, she goes buck wild. She sexily seduces her no-rhythm-having dance partner. He doesn't know what to do. She's too much for him. She's winding like a ghetto belly dancer. Just as she heats up, Nelly's "Drop Down and Get Your Eagle On" jumps through the speakers, and she does exactly what Nelly instructs her to do. The crowd opens up for her. Everyone backs away and forms a tight circle around her and old square pants. The crowd cheers and applauds as she gives them the show of a lifetime.

The kid on top of the table stops pouring the champagne. He's busy watching Miranda. He jumps off of the table like a wrestler. He lands directly in the center of the dance floor. He pushes the kid away from Miranda aggressively. He then grabs Miranda by the hand and drags her with him. She doesn't put up a fight. She's just rolling with the flow. Her performance just got her a front row seat in the VIP section. He grabs an unopened bottle of Cristal and hands it to her. The females who are lined up at the rope watch with jealousy. They have been getting teased with the champagne all night, while trying to get into the VIP section and she walks right in the club and gets a formal invitation inside the booth.

Sha-Rock watches her discreetly as the kid sits close to her, feeding her lobster, and whispering in her ear. He lifts the bottle of champagne to her lips, while she sips away. Afterwards he even has the nerve to pat her mouth dry with a napkin. What a playboy, Sha-Rock thinks to himself.

"Bingo," Jimmy mumbles. "She's got a winner."

"Oh yeah? Do you know him?" Sha-Rock asks.

"We alright. Just hi and bye, nothing personal. His name is Hollyhood. He definitely lives up to his name. He's the biggest show-off in this town. The nigga brags all the time that he's a millionaire."

"Do you believe him?"

"Nah, I don't think he's a millionaire but I think he has some dough. He's one of the only niggas in this town who has had a ten-year run without going to jail. So he should have something. Did you see that white 745 Beamer in the parking lot?"

"Yeah, I saw it."

"That's his. He's the first one to have one in this town. That's all he brags about. He cashed it out for like $80,000. The bitches in this town love him."

"Well he got the right bitch now. She'll bring him right to daddy."

"Oh shit, that's my broad over there. I ain't seen her in months. Yo kid, that mouth is crazy. I gotta get some of that tonight. Damn! Her ass got fat as hell, too. I have to go put my bid in. Hold up, let me go holler at her for a second."

One second turns into thirty minutes. Sha-Rock doesn't notice the time since he's so busy watching Miranda being treated like the queen of England. Even though they've done this many times, he still hasn't gotten used to it. Jealousy still fills his heart as he watches her at work. He feels like killing the kid, just for hugging and touching on her. His temperature is boiling. He's so angry right now. Sha-Rock has to admit to himself, the kid isn't half bad-looking. It's evident why the ladies may love him. He can actually picture Miranda falling for a guy like him. He wonders if she has looked at him like that?

"Yo," Jimmy shouts, interrupting Sha-Rock's insecure thoughts. Sha-Rock turns his head quickly. "Damn, what were you thinking about?

I called you four times already. The Hennessy must have you off point," he clowns.

"I didn't drink that shit!"

"Look straight ahead at the bar," Jimmy instructs. "Do you see the girl with the lime green blouse on with the low rider jeans?"

"With the fat ass?" Sha-Rock asks.

"Yeah, her."

"What about here?"

"That's that bitch right there. They call her the First Lady. She's like Hillary Clinton of the hood. She get a lot of money, boy."

"What kind of money," Sha-Rock asks.

"That dirty money, nigga. That bitch loaded. She got a nice piece of the town on lock."

"Word?"

"Word. Her brothers were major, but all of them either dead or knocked off. She's *made,* but she still wants to be a hood rat."

It's easy to believe Jimmy because her jewelry game is crazy. "Is her dude in here somewhere?"

"I don't think she got a main dude. She just like a nigga. She comes to the club to find something to fuck, and then she puts his ass out in the morning. I heard she take care of her niggas though. She buys them cars and the whole shit. But if they step out of line, she ain't got no problem embarrassing the hell out of them. I have seen her pimp smack niggas and the whole shit. I couldn't believe it."

"What the nigga do?" Sha-Rock asks.

"Shit, just stand there and look stupid. Don't get it fucked up. She got some dudes that'll put that work in for her if she needs it. She busts her gun, too. She then popped a few bitches over her little dudes. She mainly fuck with them young ass broke niggas, so she can control them. She took one chick's husband. The girl came to her house, disrespecting the First Lady. One late night I was leaving Bogies parking lot, all I heard was boc, boc, boc! I couldn't believe it when I saw that little shorty stretched out in the parking lot. Seconds later, I heard two more shots. The girl's husband tried to break for the car, and she caught his ass and lit him up too. Bitch crazy, son."

"What she sell?" Sha-Rock asks.

"That heroin. Trust me, she's heavy in it."

Sha-Rock has never moved out on a chick before, but he has no problem doing it. "Do you know where she rests?"

"Nah, she on the low. She ain't no dummy," Jimmy replies.

Sha-Rock bounces his attention back and forth from Miranda to the First Lady. He knows Miranda can handle herself; so most of his attention is going to the First Lady, whom he has witnessed down four shots of whatever it is she's drinking.

Three shots later, the First Lady looks as if she's about to leave. Sha-Rock looks over at Miranda who happens to be looking right at him. He gives her the head nod, gesturing her to wrap it up. He then looks over at the First Lady. She's kissing, hugging and preparing to leave. The First Lady looks to her left, where some weird-looking dude is standing about ten feet away. She snaps her fingers and he runs over to her. Sha-Rock has never seen anything like this. The dude grabs hold of her pocketbook, and she grabs his hand as he leads her away from the bar. Sha-Rock can't let her out of his sight. He hopes Miranda doesn't take too long. He glances back and forth. The First Lady stops to talk to one of the bouncers, who appears to be trying to get some play.

Miranda extends her hand for the phone number. Afterwards they depart giving each other the biggest hug in the world, which makes Sha-Rock so jealous. He sure hates to see her working. His trust for her is enormous, but sometimes he can't help but get jealous. After all, he's only human.

Miranda passes Sha-Rock and Jimmy as if she doesn't know them. She carefully walks down the rounded staircase. Sha-Rock and Jimmy follow within feet of her. Once they get to the bottom of the staircase, they see the First Lady making her way down the stairs. It's evident that she's drunk by the way she's staggering. If it wasn't for her little flunky she would have fallen a long time ago.

They all walk out the door. Miranda leads them to the parking lot. As she approaches the car, Jimmy hits the remote to open the car doors. Miranda peeks around to make sure no one is watching before getting into the car. Sha-Rock and Jimmy get in seconds later.

"Do you know what she drives," Sha-Rock asks.

"She has a few cars. Ain't no telling what she could be driving," says Jimmy as he looks throughout the parking lot. "This is the only parking lot, so she has to be parked in here."

No soon as the words part Jimmy's lips, the First Lady enters the parking lot, walking with a slight stagger. She hits her remote. The lights of a dark colored Mercedes G500 truck shines brightly.

"I told you. She doing the G5 thing tonight. I told you the bitch got trap."

Jimmy starts his car up as the kid is opening her door for her to get in. He helps her step up into the vehicle. That was a fairly big task, being that she only stands about five feet tall with heels on. After the kid finally jumps in the driver's seat, they pull off immediately.

"Jump on her," says Sha-Rock. Jimmy lets them get a small lead before tailing them.

"Don't play her too close. You never know, she might have been schooled."

Jimmy fades back as the G5 nears a red light.

"Miranda, what's up with homeboy?" Sha-Rock asks.

"Easy as pie," she replies. I probably could have brought him in tonight if I really wanted to," she boasts. "He's such a show-off. His arrogance will be his downfall. He's the type that has something to prove, and I'm the type to make him prove it. All I have to do is second-guess his position and he'll show me everything just to make me a believer."

"Well, that's what it is then," Sha-Rock replies.

"Did you see that watch?" Miranda asks.

"Yeah, I saw it from the other side of the room."

"I know he paid a lot for that," says Miranda.

"We will soon find out," says Sha-Rock.

The driver of the G-500 makes the left onto Central Avenue. Seconds later, Jimmy makes the same turn.

He's heavy on the gas. He zooms down the avenue at a reckless speed. Jimmy has to mash the gas pedal just to keep within eye's distance. His swerving lets them know that he's as drunk as the First Lady.

The driver bears to his left as he nears the parkway entrance. Jimmy steps on the gas in order not to lose him. He makes the quick left. Jimmy catches the light in the nick of time. Once they get onto the parkway, Jimmy mixes in with the rest of the traffic. All of a sudden, the driver opens up full speed. The awkward-looking truck bounces up the highway doing at least 120 miles an hour. Jimmy is having hell trying to keep up with the truck.

"Who is he?" Miranda asks.

"It's not him that we're on," Sha-Rock replies. "It's her. That bitch is the heroin queen."

Uhmm, Miranda thinks to herself. This is a first.

The driver slows down as he approaches the Bloomfield exit. A quarter of a mile later, he tapers off. Jimmy follows him at a moderate speed until he finally pulls into the garage of a beautiful little house.

She staggers out of the car. She's even drunker now than when she first got into the truck. The last drink must have just kicked in. Not once has she peeped her surroundings. The driver is so busy trying to keep her from falling that she has his full attention. How unpolished are they? The First Lady doesn't even realize that she has formally invited danger to her home.

Miranda sits back. She's not in favor of this vick. Her sensitivity gets involved. She hates to cross the men up the way she does, but a woman is a different story. She thinks about the reality of it. This is somebody's daughter, somebody's mother, sister, or aunt. Damn, she thinks to herself. She would love to call it off, but she and Sha-Rock will have the argument of a lifetime. The best thing for her to do is just sit back and mind her business.

Days Later

Miranda and Tamara are in the middle of their traditional Saturday morning shopping spree. Right now they're zipping through the Gallery Mall, spending money in abundance.

Spending money is something they both enjoy doing. Miranda is so glad to see Tamara as happy as she's been these past couple of months. She was dirt broke up until she met Najee. All her bills were backed up, and her car just got repossessed. Miranda was tired of watching her struggle. They still shopped the weekend away but Miranda paid for everything. Whatever she bought herself, she bought Tamara, only in a different color.

Tamara makes good money modeling but she was just in a terrible relationship last year that she's paying for dearly. Her last boyfriend left her stuck not only with her bills, but he also left a bunch of his as well. He was a fake ass baller who claimed to be getting out-of-town money, but come to find out the only hustle he had was hustling women. He used women for everything he needed; room and board, clothes, and food. He didn't have to pay for anything anywhere he went. Once a woman started complaining, or asking for help, he would leave her. He wouldn't even help out with the cable bill. He didn't believe he should help with the rent because he didn't stay at any of his girls' houses enough nights back to back, to consider himself living there. Tamara finally cut him off, and she's been trying to get back on her feet ever since.

Today, Tamara paid for everything. She wouldn't take no for an answer. She literally forced the gifts on Miranda. She must have spent $2,500 easily, all compliments of her boyfriend. He's taking good care of her.

After the shopping spree, they make their way to their favorite restaurant, where they finish off all of their Saturdays.

Miranda is enjoying her Caesar salad and a Diet coke, while Tamara devours a tray full of marinated mussels with tomato sauce. She washes them down with a glass of white zinfandel.

"Tamara, I look in your face and I see a beautiful glow. It makes me feel so good to see you happy like this. In fact I think I'm happier than you."

"Thank you baby," says Tamara. "You have been by my side all the way through all of my struggles. I couldn't have overcome that shit without you. You've been more than a friend. You've been more like a mother. I don't know what I would have done without you."

"The same thing you done with me," Miranda replies.

"Nah girl, I'm serious. It's been so rough."

"But now it's over," Miranda claims.

"For the moment," Tamara challenges.

"It's over."

"You know the saying, 'don't count your chickens before they hatch?' I'm just taking it one day at a time. I'm living for the moment."

"Makes sense don't it!" Miranda shouts, quoting the words of her favorite rapper, Jay-Z. They clap hands in harmony, while giggling away. "Nah, serious girl, just enjoy it. Don't ruin your happiness by worrying about when or how it's going to end," Miranda advises.

"I try not to, but it's hard. Najee is too good to be true. Sometimes I look at him and ask, do I really deserve him? I examined him thoroughly. I can't find any flaws. He's tall and handsome. He's caring and sharing. He has a beautiful body, nice car, a good sense of humor, and his dick game is to the heavens!" she laughs.

"Uhmm, uhhm," Miranda sighs. "Don't tell me the dick got you sprung?"

"I ain't sprung, but girl let me tell you. He's hung like horse. Have you ever heard of too much dick?"

Miranda laughs to herself. Yes, she has. She thinks the same thing about Sha-Rock, but she'll never tell another woman that secret. Her mother told her that several years ago. She said never discuss bedroom secrets with your girlfriends. Before you know it, they'll be trying to find out for themselves if what you're saying is true.

"Like that?" Miranda questions.

"Like that, girl," Tamara replies. "I mean too, too much dick. Fill my whole body up. I can't even exhale while he's in me. It took me months before I got the heart up to give him some. He thinks I made him wait because I'm a good girl, and didn't want to give the coochie up too fast. He don't know I been wanted to give him some, but one day I saw him get out of the shower. I almost fainted. I swear to God, hitting him at the kneecaps. Do you hear me? At the kneecaps," she repeats. "I was like, is this nigga human? Is he a man or a beast?"

"Girl, you're crazy!" Miranda laughs.

"I'm serious. How many niggas have you met that have the full package? Good looks, money, and holding? You're lucky if you get one out of three. To get two out of three is unbelievable." Tamara's phone rings. She lifts it up to view the display. "This is horse dick, right here," she laughs. "Hold on."

Miranda just smiles. It's funny to hear Tamara say that. That's exactly how she feels about Sha-Rock. The only difference is she's finally used to his breathtaking size. Losing her virginity to him was a total nightmare. There was so much blood in the hotel room that the room smelled like a slaughterhouse. That was hell for her. At that time Sha-Rock was a full-grown man. It took her years to fully enjoy sex with him. In the beginning sex with him was for his pleasure only, but now that she's a grown woman, she's learned to appreciate his third leg. Now she takes him in its entirety and bounces up and down on him, like he's only half the size. Sha-Rock isn't used to being handled like that, so every now and then he feels belittled and he will punish her. He doesn't know that Miranda loves that as well. Punish me, she screams to herself as he pounds away at her.

After finishing the last of their meals, they go to the post office. Miranda has to mail a money order off to her father. She sends him a money order of $250 every month, faithfully. Miranda is the only help on the outside that her father receives. She refuses to turn her back on him.

After the post office visit, they make their way over to Tamara's house. Miranda hasn't been here in weeks. She's truly impressed with the apartment. It looks brand new. Najee has bought her so many new items for the house, like plasma TV screens throughout the whole apartment, and thick, plush carpets. He even bought her a nice little Jacuzzi for her bathroom. Miranda falls in love with it at first sight.

The Jacuzzi is beautiful!" Miranda shouts. It's pink marble with solid gold fixtures on it.

Miranda runs the water. As the Jacuzzi fills up, Tamara adds the bubbles to the water. She then lights some candles and dims the lights. The aroma of fresh peaches fills the air. The sound of the Jacuzzi purrs. Just as the bubbles float to the top, Tamara speaks. "Get in," she offers.

Tamara quickly exits the bathroom, just as Miranda anxiously peels off her clothes. Seconds later, she drops herself into the Jacuzzi. The hot steaming water feels lovely on her soft nude flesh.

Tamara returns holding a bottle of Remy Red and two wine glasses in one hand. In the other hand she holds a large ceramic bowl full of big red cherries. Tamara is not wearing a stitch of clothing. Miranda gets a full view of Tamara, up close and personal. Any man should consider himself lucky to see this picture, let alone to have her intimately. Her bodacious body glows of youth. Miranda thinks to herself, how beautiful Tamara really is. She's flattered that everyone thinks that they look like twins. Just to think that when they see her, they see a Tamara look-a-like makes her appreciate her own beauty.

Tamara fills the glasses with Remy and seats herself into the Jacuzzi. Soapsuds cover Tamara's entire body, except for the peeking of her dark nipples.

After sipping two glasses of Remy apiece, they both become totally relaxed. Tamara reaches over and grabs a long handled scrub brush from the side f the Jacuzzi. She then scoots around Miranda until she's sitting behind her. They sit flesh to flesh. She gently scrubs Miranda's back. Afterwards, Miranda returns the favor. Once that's over, they both extend their right legs high in the air as the other one scrubs away.

Girls pampering each other? This is something that men will never understand.

━━━━━━━━━━◆◆◆━━━━━━━━━

Later That Evening

Jimmy pulls in front of West Side High School on South Orange Avenue. His client spots the car and immediately jumps out of his black Suburban.

He hops into the passenger's seat of Jimmy's car holding a black shopping bag in his right hand.

"What's the deal, J?" he asks.

"Chilling, chilling," Jimmy replies.

"Yo, that last shit was off the rocker!" he shouts. "Motherfuckers clucking. My phone been going crazy. You see how fast I shook them last two? What it take like, a day and a half?" he asks.

"Yeah, something like that," Jimmy agrees, as he circles the block. As he cruises down Eleventh Street, he hands the client a bag containing three kilos.

"Yo, my nigga, we gone have to do something about that price. I know you can do a little better? My man told me his peoples went down for him. I heard that prices are down everywhere. I'm like the only nigga still paying twenty-six. My man be buying like 100 grams at a time, and he pays $26 a gram. You know that ain't right. He said I could probably get the whole thing from his man for like twenty-two. I know if I come for three, he'll bring that number all the way down," he assumes.

"It ain't all about the number. It's about the quality. I sell it just the way I get it. I could hit it and sell it to you for twenty if you want, but the quality won't be the same. I bet you it'll still be better than what your man getting. My shit come back line for line. Take your man to the lab with you, and see who shit come back bigger. If you put ten lines of my shit in the shaker, you gone get ten lines back. Your man will be lucky if he gets six lines back. Stop talking to 100-gram niggas about kilos; they'll never understand you. I could sell bullshit, but I ain't with it. I ain't got time for niggas calling me back complaining. But if you chasing a number, I'll sell you the cheapy-chop. It's on you."

"Nah, nah, I feel you. Just keep it like you got it."

"I have seen that shit done so many times before. Nigga sell the garbage and get rich in three months. By the fourth month, he can't give a nigga that shit. Now whatever he made in them three months, he has to live off all year. Now his street credibility is gone, while a nigga like me still doing me, feel me?"

"Yeah, I feel you," he replies while looking inside the plastic bag. He's so busy examining the work that he doesn't even see Sha-Rock who has popped up from the floor like a jack-in- a-box. He's sitting quietly, right behind the kid.

Jimmy makes a left turn onto Thirteenth Avenue, followed by another left onto Twelfth Street. Jimmy pulls behind a small Toyota that is parked alongside of the graveyard. The block is pitch-black with no sign of light on the entire block.

The client looks over at Jimmy trying to figure out why he has stopped. "Nah, take me to my car, son." Jimmy looks straight ahead as if he doesn't hear him speaking. "Jimmy!" he shouts.

The feeling of cold hard steel bangs against the back of his skull. "No need to look back, kid. Caught you slippin'. No need to try and reach for your gun. I already got the drop on you," he whispers aggressively. "Pat him down, and get his banger."

Jimmy reaches under the seat and fumbles until he locates his black leather gloves. After putting them on, he reaches over and pats his waist. He snatches his chrome .40 caliber from his waist.

"What's up? What's this about?" he asks Jimmy. Jimmy is doing a good job of ignoring him.

"Get out!" Sha-Rock shouts.

"Huh?"

"Get the fuck out, I said!"

"Come on, son. You ain't gotta do it like this."

"Nigga, get the fuck out!" Sha-Rock shouts before striking him across the head with the nose of the .357.

"Unghh," he grunts.

Sha-Rock opens the back door and climbs out while still holding the gun to the kid's head with his left hand. He stands on the curb and snatches the door open with his right hand.

"Please don't let him kill me," he begs. "Y'all got the bread already. It's over, please."

Sha-Rock snatches him out the car by his collar. The boy struggles to stay inside. He's doing a hell of a job of fighting Sha-Rock off. He's fighting for his life. He knows once he gets him outside of the car it's over for him. "Please, please," he begs. "You got the money. What do you want?"

Sha-Rock finally gets a grip of his ankle, and he drags him to the ground where he falls face first onto the cement. A loud thump sounds off when his face bangs onto the ground. "Don't kill me! Please, don't kill me. Help! Please, somebody help me!" Sha-Rock releases three shots to the back of his dome, killing him instantly.

"Give me his gun," says Sha-Rock. Sha-Rock then lays the kid's gun right next to him. He jumps into the car and Jimmy pulls off nonchalantly.

That was the fastest and the easiest $72,000 Sha-Rock or Jimmy ever made. They'll split the profit at $36,000 apiece.

Sha-Rock has to be the most cold-hearted individual in the world. He shows no remorse. Jimmy can't understand him. This is only the third murder Jimmy witnessed Sha-Rock do, but he has been observing him closely. Sha-Rock's look never changes. His eyes don't even cringe and afterwards he never even brings the incident up again. He just carries on as if nothing has happened.

What Jimmy doesn't realize is, Sha-Rock is no stranger to murder. He's fairly new at the stick-up game. He only made petty street corner robberies with Killer Cal and Skip back in the day. He has put a few guys under though. He never killed anyone for robbery purposes, but he has partaken in murder for security purposes. Back in the day, if he even got the word that someone was plotting on robbing him, he would finish them off before they got a chance to execute their plan. He's a seasoned veteran. All this is only work for him. There's nothing to discuss. Only a new jack would brag about murder or continue to talk about it. Killer Cal taught him that. Jimmy has to get accustomed to it. Some people never get used to it.

"Can I ask you a question?" Jimmy questions.

"Go ahead, fire away. And I don't mean literally," Sha-Rock jokes.

"How did you get so raw like that?"

""What do you mean?" Sha-Rock asks.

"How you just put a nigga under like that, then go on with your regular life afterwards?"

"Hey man, I was raised by the best," he claims. "I have been doing this for a while. I really can't explain it. I'm not gone tell you it's nothing. I'll tell you my secret. I never told nobody this. You better not ever tell nobody this in life. Back in the day, me, my twin brother and my sister were in the playground during the lunch period. I was on the basketball court and my brother and sister was jumping rope."

"Your brother was jumping rope?" Jimmy asks, thinking that Sha-Rock made a mistake.

"Yeah, jumping rope," he repeats. "That's another story right there," he explains. "Well anyway, I'm on the court doing my thing, and I hear my sister and brother screaming their heads off. I stop dribbling the ball and look over to the fence. I see the school bullies tossing my brother and sister around like rag dolls. I run over to rescue them. By the time I get there both of them are on the ground. By this time the entire playground has formed a circle around us. As soon as I try to swing, one of the bigger boys grabs me and slams me to the ground too. Now all three of us are on the ground squirming to get up but they're holding us down. It was about ten of them on us three. All of them were older and bigger than us. Like two of them was holding each of us down while the other ones took our sneakers off of our feet. After they had them off, they lifted them in the air and showed the whole playground our raggedy sneakers. All I could hear was laughing. I closed my eyes because I was so embarrassed. I peeked up and all I could see was big gigantic potato holes in the bottoms of all our sneakers. My sister had cardboard in the insole of her sneakers so her stockings wouldn't peek through the hole. They reached inside and pulled the cardboard out and flung it like a Frisbee. That broke my heart. It wasn't about me. It was about my little sister. I felt like I let her down. I couldn't protect her because it was too many of them and they were much bigger than me. I looked into my sister's eyes and I saw embarrassment. She looked over at me. She didn't say a word to me, but her eyes spoke a million words. Her eyes said, get up from there. How could you let them do this to me? They finally let us up. There we were standing with just socks on. Mines were the filthiest because I had been running up and down the court for an hour, and I had to keep tucking my sock under my foot so it wouldn't peek through the hole. The biggest kid grabs all the sneakers and takes off. I chase behind him but he's too fast. One kid grabs me from behind as the big kid tosses our sneakers over the telephone wires in the middle of the street, one by one. We had to walk home with our socks on. When we walked in the house without our sneakers my mother gave me the beating of a lifetime. My sister didn't get whipped because she was a girl, and my brother got spared because he wanted to be a girl. Every day that I went into that playground, I would take a sneak peek at those telephone wires and see our sneakers up there. That was a constant reminder of that embarrassing day. I promised myself that one day, I would murder every one of those dudes one by one. I was about eight at the time. In 1993, I finally ran into the biggest kid of the bunch. I asked him did he know who I was. He didn't have a clue until I told him the story. He laughed like it was a joke, until I pulled that 9-millimeter out. Then he screamed and begged for me to stop, the same way my little sister and my brother was screaming. I put three holes in his head to represent the three holes that were in our sneakers. I never talk to my sister about street shit, but this was different. The next morning I cut the article out of the paper, and I gave it my sister. I asked her did she know that dude. She said no. Then I explained to her who he was. Tears filled her eyes. Not because she was sad, but because it reminded her of that terrible day. I had to show her that I was still her protector, even though they got that off, feel me? I didn't get the rest of them yet, but I know all of their faces, trust me. So anytime I stand over a dude with that gun in my hand, I make believe that I'm standing over one of those cowards that did that to us."

Jimmy looks into Sha-Rock's tear filled eyes and he sees revenge. He had no clue that Sha-Rock's anger ran that deep. That answers his question, but that doesn't soothe his pain. He feels bad. He realizes that in the game, it's stick-up kids against the hustlers. His motto has always been, never mix the two because shit can get ugly. He feels guilty because he's setting up other hustlers. He realizes that he's breaking the code. "Yo, shit alright now," Jimmy says. "We both got a few dollars now. We can just go ahead and do us, feel me?"

"What do you mean, do us?" Sha-Rock asks. "You doing you and I'm doing me. You sell coke, that's what you do. I get that money. I'm a hustler. Do you know what a hustler is? A hustler never limits himself to just one hustle. I did the math on it. I been selling coke over half of my life and I still ain't rich. Nine times out of ten, I ain't never gone be rich. Man, I'm thirty-four years old. I ain't really with that hustling shit no more. When I first came home, I was willing to do it, only because I had to. I was broke. I didn't have no other choice. I ain't got time for that shit. You can do what you have to do, but don't go getting soft on me. We had a deal. Now that you're back in position, you're alright, it may be easy to forget. A couple of months ago you was all with the program. Don't forget the pact we made. All a man got is his word, feel me? My word was, I'm going to help you get right. Your word was, you would give me the dudes, I need to do what we had to do. I held my end of the bargain. I made you four kilos and $36,000 richer already, and we just getting started. Lord knows how much profit you made off it already. That doesn't matter to me. That's your business. Just hold your end of the bargain, feel me?"

"Oh, I'm going to do that regardless. I know what I said. You don't have to remind me. I'm just saying, how long do you think this will last, killing motherfuckers at will? If the cops don't get us, you're going to kill all the hustlers in the town. It ain't gone be nobody left to sell shit too," he says sarcastically.

"How long do you think you gone last, selling kilos to motherfuckers at will?" he questions with an agitated tone. "All good things come to an end, one day. Nothing lasts forever. I know the consequences to what I'm doing, and I'm prepared for it. Whether it be niggas coming at me or one hundred years in the box. It is what it is. If it's selling kilos or killing niggas over kilos, you get the same time. Are you prepared?"

The Next Day

Sha-Rock sits in front of Tamara's house once again waiting for Miranda to come out. She's been staying here for the past couple of days while Sha-Rock has been in Jersey.

Sha-Rock looks at the black-on-black convertible BMW 645 that is parked in front of him. He wonders who it belongs to. Who on this block would have New York plates, he asks himself. It can't be Tamara's boyfriend. He has a Benz.

The sound of women laughing disturbs his thoughts. He looks up to Tamara's porch. Here comes Miranda, Tamara, and her boyfriend.

Sha-Rock studies him carefully. His earrings are the size of quarters. The charm on his necklace reads Harlem World. The letters spread across his whole chest in fancy print. The diamonds gleam flawlessly. His watch changes Sha-Rock's opinion of him. Sha-Rock judges a man by his jewelry. His big dumb chain says he's young, ignorant, and arrogant. Only a show-off would want such a big chain. Now his watch says something completely different. He's wearing a plain leather band, square faced watch. It's very simple, with no diamonds. The average person wouldn't pay attention to it, but not Sha-Rock. Back in the day when he was on top, his hobby was collecting watches. There's no watch that Sha-Rock is ignorant to. That particular watch the Harlem kid is wearing happens to be a Patek Philippe classic. The price exceeds over $60,000 without diamonds. That tells Sha-Rock that the kid does have some class about himself. Back in the day, a Caucasian man schooled Sha-Rock. He told him a well-to-do white man would never put $10,000 rims on a Mercedes, or decorate an expensive watch with a bunch of cloudy diamonds. It's already expensive. Why overdo it, he asked. He told him that will only depreciate the value.

When they get to the bottom of the steps, Tamara and her friend jump in the BMW. That explains the New York plates, Sha-Rock thinks to himself. He peeks around the side to view the rims. They're standard BMW rims. That's another plus for him, in Sha-Rock's eyes. Now Sha-Rock is sure this kid isn't fronting. He must really have some money.

The brokest nigga would put rims on his truck to prove a point that he has money, while a rich nigga wouldn't give two fucks what the next man thinks. He knows he can get rims, and that's all that counts. Sha-Rock gets a kick out of analyzing dudes. That's one of his strong points.

Miranda hops in and greets Sha-Rock with a great big welcome kiss. "What's up, Smook?" Smook is what she calls him when she's in a good mood.

"You," Sha-Rock answers blandly. "What's good with pretty boy? He's a real comedian, huh?"

"Why do you say that?" she questions.

"He keeps you smiling!" he says sarcastically. "All teeth; I counted all thirty-two in your mouth. Oh, by the way, you have a cavity in the back," he teases.

"Psstt," she sucks her teeth out of frustration. "Stop it, please."

"No you stop it. I don't think I want you over here staying the night anymore. Where does he be, when you spend the night?"

"He's not here when I spend the night. I wouldn't play myself like that!"

"I don't know," Sha-Rock says sarcastically. "Is that his car, too?"

"Tammy said it's his brother's."

"Oh, why did she tell you that? Do she want you to get with him? Y'all probably already double-dated," he accuses.

"Please Sha-Rock, don't start," she begs.

"Nah, I'm just saying. That's how it goes. You mean to tell me, as fine as you are, he didn't say nothing about meeting his brother?" Sha-Rock questions.

"No," she lies.

"Please Ma. This is Sha-Rock. I been doing this a long time. Don't play me like a square from nowhere! I ain't going for it. Why didn't you introduce us? You probably told him, I'm like a brother to you, or some shit like that."

"Sha-Rock, I would never do that. He knows who you are."

"How did that come up? Y'all be having personal conversations?"

"No, but he knows you're my man, though."

"He asked you who I was?"

"No, Tammy told him."

"Why he asking about me? I'm the last nigga he need to know!"

"Sha-Rock, what is wrong with you?"

"Ain't nothing wrong with me. I just hate slick shit!"

"Ain't nobody being slick," she pleads.

"I might have to keep you away from him. I don't want you to get weak. Pretty boy look like he got some game with him. Fuck around and ask for a ménage 'a trois!"

Miranda can't believe her ears. "What the fuck did you just say? I know you didn't. You black motherfucker, don't you ever disrespect me like that. I don't believe your ass! That jealousy shit is getting on my nerves. Nigga, I love you. I won't ever cross you. I been had mad opportunities. If I didn't love you, do you think I would be living this crazy ass life? Do you think this is what I want out of life? When I was in school everybody just knew I was going to be a supermodel. And I could have been, but you stopped me. Look at me; I'm a fucking Murder Mommy! You're my man. You say jump, I ask how high. You say go get him, I reel him in, no questions asked. I never fucked any of them. I only fuck one nigga at a time. Right now, that's you and it has been for years now," she claims. "You might have to keep me away from him," she repeats sarcastically. "How could you say that? You can't trust me with him, but you can trust me sleeping overnight with strangers. How that sound? ménage 'a trois? Psst, boy please!"

Sha-Rock sits there looking and feeling stupid. He has a loss of words. She has made some great points. "I'm sorry, Ma. I'm just scared to lose you." He comforts her with a kiss and a hug before driving off.

While looking straight ahead, he asks, "So what did you find out about him?"

"Nothing, I didn't ask nothing," she replies.

"I know you have to know something. She had to tell you something."

Yeah, he got a horse dick, she thinks to herself. She laughs hysterically inside. Sha-Rock would kill her if she told him what Tamara really told her about him. They always say "never ask questions that you don't want to know the answers to." You can't handle the truth, she teases in her mind.

"Well, what did she tell you?" Sha-Rock continues to ask.

Miranda has a good mind to say it, but she knows he'll probably smack her head off.

"He's riding hard. His jewelry game is crazy. He smells like money to me. What do you think?" Sha-Rock pesters.

Miranda realizes that he's not going to leave her alone unless she tells him something. "All I know is he's a model."

"Model? Come on now, Miranda. You're not that stupid!"

"Nah, for real. He just got a few big contracts," Miranda repeats what Tamara told her. "Tammy says he's on billboards all over New York. Some designer supposedly is about to back him with his clothing line."

"Clothing line? Come on, you have to get that info ASAP. Stop bullshitting, alright?"

They make their way home. Sha-Rock only had plans of hanging out with Miranda for a few hours and working off a little steam with some hard-core sex before bouncing back to Jersey, but his jealousy wouldn't allow him to leave her alone. Even after Miranda's long, touching speech, he still doesn't want her staying at Tammy's house. Eventually he'll get over it, but not right now.

Sha-Rock ended up taking Miranda back to Jersey with him. He has a big meeting, bright and early tomorrow morning.

At ten o' clock, they arrive at the Soho Grand on West Broadway in New York. Sha-Rock reserves a room for two nights. Miranda is shocked at the price. He paid $4,400 for a two-night stay in a luxurious penthouse suite. He never ceases to amaze her.

The Next Day

The shabby looking crack-head opens the chain lock before pulling the door open. A chrome 9 millimeter aimed at his face greets him.

"Freeze! Police! Back up in the hallway, nice and quiet." The other officer closes the door behind them. The cop snatches the crack-head by the collar and pulls him to the door of the first floor apartment. He then turns the hallway light off. He pushes the crack-head close to the door, while pressing the gun against his side. "Knock on the door," he whispers.

"Who?" the voice on the other side of the door asks.

"Me," the crack-head whispers.

"Speak up, motherfucker," the officer whispers.

"It's me, Gene."

The clicking of the peephole sounds off. One second later, the door opens. The officer pushes the door open and shoves the crack-head inside first. Both cops follow with their guns waving in the air.

"Freeze! Police! Nobody move!" all the cops shout simultaneously. Everyone is surprised. The room has four occupants besides the crack-head. Three of the occupants are young females. The other one is a man who appears to be in his early twenties. "Everybody, lay the fuck down!" the officer shouts. The three young women begin screaming at the top of their lungs. "Y'all too. Everybody to the center of the room. Lay down, everyone."

The second officer dashes to the back of the apartment. By now all the occupants are laying in the center of the room, just like the officer instructed them to do.

The sound of someone attempting to open a door catches the officer's attention. "Get the fuck over here!" shouts the officer from afar. "Don't move!"

"Partner, you alright?" the officer asks.

"Yeah, everything is good. I caught one trying to slip away," the officer yells from the back room.

"Bring 'em here!"

"Hold up, I have to let Ron in," he shouts.

The two officers come into the living room along with another male. The escapee, is about five feet ten inches and stocky. His chiseled-looking face looks like the face of a monster. His pitch-black skin is dry and ashy. His dreadlocks extend down the middle of his back. 'Look at what we got, Sarge," says the first officer. "He thought he was about to get away."

"You should have shot him," the officer says aggressively. "Justifiable homicide!" he adds.

The females are going crazy. They're yelling and screaming.

"Listen, y'all better shut up!" says the officer.

"Where were you going?" the sergeant asks the escapee. "The party is just getting started, and you trying to leave already?"

The escapee doesn't respond. He just looks at the sergeant with a cold stern face.

"Some boss you are. About to leave all your employees," the sarge says sarcastically.

That statement alerts the escapee. His eyes stretch wide open. "Boss? What are you talking about, boss?" he asks with a look of confusion on his face.

"That's right, boss. You know exactly what I'm talking about," he says aggressively. "Did y'all frisk him?" the sergeant questions his officers. "He's labeled as armed and dangerous."

"Yeah, I checked him. He's clean."

"Whoa, that's surprising," says the sergeant.

"Yo, y'all must have me mixed up with somebody else," says the escapee.

"Oh yeah? Just sit down and put your hands on top of your head!"

He sits down slowly. "What the fuck?" he shouts.

"Oh, you don't know what the fuck?" the sergeant asks him. "Don't act stupid. We have been watching your stupid ass for months."

"Me?"

"Yeah, you motherfucker!"

"Y'all really got me mixed up!" he claims.

The sergeant laughs in his face. "Oh yeah, Rasta Rab?"

His face looks startled.

"So you're not Rasta Rab?"

"No, my name is Raymond," he corrects the officer.

"Yeah, Raymond Anthony Bell, but the streets call you Rasta Rab!" The sarge kicks the crack-head up the ass. "Hey you, Stinky, get up slowly."

The crack-head does as he's instructed.

"What are you doing in here?" sarge asks the crack-head.

"I, I, I," he stutters.

"I, I, I, my ass," the sarge repeats. "Strip!"

"Huh?"

"If you can, huh, you can hear! You heard me, I said strip!"

"Man," he sighs. "They're ladies in here."

"Strip, I'm pretty sure they've seen dick before."

The crack-head is moving hesitantly.

"Listen, strip before I strip you!" the sarge threatens.

The crack-head slowly pulls his jacket off first. He pulls off his shirt and stands there with a dumbfounded look on his face. "What?" he asks.

"Take everything off!"

"Come on, officer, please," he begs.

"Strip!"

The crack-head finally pulls his soggy jeans off, revealing his extra large shorts, which have bulges lined up along the waistline.

"Take the shorts off too," says the sergeant.

Fear is written all over the crack-head's face. He slowly slides his shorts down to his ankles. The stench of foul body odor fills the room instantly. Ziplock bags filled with tiny bags off marijuana fall to the floor.

"What's that?" the sergeant asks. "I, I, I," he clowns. "Sit your sour smelling ass, down! Damn, Rasta Rab, I mean Raymond Bell, we even got your transporter. Smart, but not that smart. He'll tell everything before he hits the holding cell. He has a dope habit, stupid! Do you think he's ready to kick for three days? He'll do anything to stay on the outside. He can't live without that dope. You would have been better off, letting them little girls transport it. You have to use your head, Raymond. Boys, y'all go and search the apartment. I got them covered."

The sergeant backs up against the wall, as the other two officers disappear. Sarge pays close attention to Rasta Rab, who is trying to give head signs to the other male. "Rasta, shut up. Don't move again," he says calmly. "The next time you move, I'll splatter your brains on the sofa. I can see the article in the paper now. Known felon, Raymond "Rasta Rab", Bell, wrestles with police sergeant Darryl Jenkins, attempting to take the sergeant's weapon. Sergeant manages to fire one deadly shot," he says in a news reporter's voice. "You know they'll believe me. You have a history of resisting arrest and cop abuse. I wish like hell you would run up on me. I ain't like them other cops you ran into. I can fight. I'll beat you to a pulp, and then I'll bust yo motherfucking head open. Please, get up and fight me like you do all the other cops. Please," he begs. "When they told me about you, I knew you weren't a fool. You pick and choose who you do that dumb shit with. I ain't them other cops. I pray for the day you step to me!"

Rasta Rab looks the sergeant directly in his eyes. His bloodshot red eyes show fury. Had this been any other cop, he would've already made his move on him. Rab is the most feared drug dealer in all of Elizabeth. Even the cops fear him. It usually takes the entire force just to restrain him. He has knocked out a total of eight officers in two years. As of right now, he has no drug convictions. His jacket consists only of resisting arrest and aggravated assault.

The officers return. One of them is holding a shoebox filled with money in one hand and a big black garbage bag in the other hand. The other is lugging a total of three huge garbage bags. "We got 'em good," says the officer with the three bags. "Just in time."

"We got two nines, too."

"Yeah, this will definitely hold y'all. This is your first drug charge, huh Raymond? Cuff 'em boys!"

All the girls look up with shocked faces. The two officers walk toward the center of the room with three sets of handcuffs dangling.

"Y'all cuff them. Let me get old tough ass over there. Hopefully, he'll make my day," says Sergeant Jenkins.

"Psst," Rasta sucks his teeth. 'What about the ladies, Sarge?"

'What about them? Cuff them too. Everybody's going to jail today," he replies.

The word jail strikes a soft spot. The girls begin crying hysterically.

"Don't cry ladies. No need to cry now. Your tears mean nothing to me. Y'all should have thought about the consequences while y'all was sitting around here. Y'all know exactly what was going on here."

The officers handcuff the crack-head and the other male together. He hasn't said a word throughout this whole ordeal.

The sergeant walks toward Rasta. "Turn your punk ass around!" he shouts as he drags him onto his feet by the collar. He cuffs him and pushes him to the floor where he falls face first.

"Can I please say something?" the older looking girl asks.

"Be my guest," Sergeant Jenkins replies.

"What do we have to do with this?" she asks innocently.

"You're in here. For all I know, y'all three can be his connects. Maybe Rasta works for y'all. If not, y'all can still get conspiracy charges. Y'all can face twenty-five years for that."

They begin crying even louder now.

Sergeant Jenkins calls a huddle. All three cops walk to the far end of the room and indulge in deep conversation. Minutes later they return to the center of the room. "Ok, we came to a conclusion. If Rasta admits everything is his, and he signs the form stating so, we'll cut the women loose."

"You crazy as hell!" Rasta shouts. "That ain't mine. I didn't know that was in here. This ain't my apartment."

"Alright smart ass. See y'all, I tried. Now everybody gotta go!"

"Please don't take us," the younger, and by far the prettier looking, girl begs. "Please," she cries.

"Look at these pretty young girls. I know they're innocent, and you know they're innocent. Are you really going to let them go to jail for life?" Sergeant Jenkins asks Rasta.

All the girls look at Rasta desperately.

"What are you going to do? Are you going to cut them loose or what?"

"I ain't taking the weight. It's not mine," he claims.

"It ain't his," the quiet kid shouts.

"What?" Sarge asks.

"It's mine," he mumbles.

"This ain't yours. This is Rasta Rab's operation. Son, don't be stupid. You can go to jail for life."

"It's mine," he repeats.

The sarge looks at him sternly without speaking for a matter of seconds. "Uncuff him," Sarge finally says. After the cuffs are off, Sarge instructs him to come over to him. Sarge leads him into the kitchen. Everyone else lies on the floor, nervously awaiting the verdict.

Minutes later, the sergeant walks back into the room flagging a sheet of paper in his hand. "Uncuff all of them, and cuff this one! He claims everything is his. He signed the form. Rasta, today is your lucky day. Ladies, y'all need to hug this man before he goes away. He saved your pretty little lives."

"Damn!" the officer shouts. "Sarge, that ain't his. His dumb ass is just taking the weight!"

"He signed the form," Sarge replies.

Rasta shows a look of relief, but he also shows a look of confusion. He can't believe his little man is actually taking the weight, just like a true soldier is supposed to do.

The officers release the cuffs off of everyone. The sarge drags the kid by his cuffs. "Let's go!" he shouts.

The other officers grab hold of all the evidence.

"Have a nice day, everybody! Ladies, please don't let me catch y'all in here again. The next time, I'll make sure everything is yours. Oh, and Rasta, you haven't seen the last of us. You got saved today, but we'll be back. Make sure your shit is tight, cause I'm going to take you down!" Sergeant Jenkins shouts.

They walk outside, jump in their minivan and pull off. "I told you it would be simple!" the officer shouts. The only thing is, he's not a real officer. This is actually Bree. The sergeant is Sha-Rock, and the other officer is Sha-Rock's man, Killer Cal. Their first vick together is a success.

This whole scam was Bree's idea. He's been planning it for months. He just needed a thorough team to go in with him.

The would-be prisoner is really Bree's little cousin. He's been working for Rasta for a few years. At one time he was a true soldier, up until four months ago when he caught a major drug charge and Rasta left him in jail with no bail money. Bree and some other family members had to scrape the money up to bail him out.

"Got his dumb ass," the kid shouts.

"How much bread was in there?" Sha-Rock asks.

"I'm counting it now," says Bree. "So far, I counted over $14,000."

"Damn," Sha-Rock shouts. "Does he keep everything in here?"

"Yeah, that's the stash house. He doesn't work outta there. The fiend nigga comes and gets what he needs for the block. There's been times, that he has had like thirty pounds of weed, and like $200,000 in cash laying around in there."

"Damn, we caught him at the wrong time," Sha-Rock says greedily.

Hours Later

The scandal was a success. Everyone parted happy and satisfied. Altogether they scored $22,000 in cash and at least ten pounds of goodness. Sha-Rock really had no use for the smoke. He kept only a tiny amount of it, along with $20,000 in cash. Bree and his little cousin took the weed and the $2,000. Sha-Rock really played himself. He thought he was getting over on them. He didn't know the value of the smoke until Bree's cousin informed him about what they really have. Sha-Rock thought it was just plain old backyard boogie, but he taught him differently. He said the smoke is exotic. He said he could sell each pound for $6,500, if he wholesales it. That's a grand total of $65,000. Who knows how much they'll make if they sell it bag for bag on the block.

Sha-Rock felt like a total asshole once they explained that to him, but it was already too late. The deal was already final. Anyway, he doesn't know the first thing about selling weed. He probably would get stuck with it. He doesn't know one person he would be able to sell it to.

Bree's cousin will never be able to go back to Elizabeth again. Bree has given him a spot in Orange projects. As of right now, no one sells smoke up there, so they should be able to get rich overnight.

Sha-Rock gave Cal $5,000 out of his $20,000. Even though Cal received less than anyone else, he was still grateful. He's just so happy to be eating again. He hasn't made a dime in months. If that were Sha-Rock's vick, he would have seen to it that Cal had made a bigger percentage. He had to talk Bree into bringing Cal along. He really didn't want to split up the earnings with a third party. Sha-Rock didn't feel comfortable rolling with Bree alone. Cal and Skip are the only dudes Sha-Rock is confident in moving out with. He's sure they have his back. With them it's not only about the money. They also have loyalty amongst each other. Bree was dead set against Cal coming along until Sha-Rock told him he didn't feel comfortable moving with anyone except Cal, and if Cal wasn't going, he would rather fall back.

After dividing the trap, they all went their separate ways. Bree and his cousin headed back to Orange. Cal jumped on the next train to Philly, and Sha-Rock went back to New York to get with Miranda.

Sha-Rock and Miranda decide to spend the rest of the day in the Village. This is actually Miranda's favorite place in the entire world. As they soar the Soho section, Miranda is as happy as a kid in a toy store. She skips not a store. She has to at least peek her head inside each and every one of them. Something about this part of New York makes her feel like she's made it. It makes her feel like she doesn't have a care in the world. She shops away like there is no tomorrow. Normally, Sha-Rock would be complaining, but today he's just sitting back and letting her do her. Although doing her is getting quite expensive. She's already spent $3,000 of his earnings.

By the way, Tamara was absolutely right. Miranda has counted at least ten billboards with Najee's face on it. His billboards are on damn near every corner. Sha-Rock actually brought the billboards to Miranda's attention. As soon as he saw them, his brain started working overtime. Since then, every question that has come out of his mouth has been about

Najee and Tamara. That's probably why Sha-Rock is allowing Miranda to shop without complaining, like he usually does. He's probably trying to butter her up, so she'll give him the information that he needs. Miranda sure wishes that he didn't see the billboards. Now he'll never forget about Najee.

They end up in BBQ's on Eighth Street. All the shopping has both of them starving. Miranda is living on the edge today. She orders the barbequed half chicken with macaroni and cheese and cornbread, instead of her normal Caesar salad, which she normally orders from anywhere she goes. Sha-Rock is having barbequed half chicken and barbequed ribs, two sides of macaroni and cheese and a hefty order of crab cakes. They both wash their food down with big pitchers of Pina Coladas.

The ringing of Miranda's phone interrupts their meal. "Hello?" she answers. It's Hollyhood, the kid she met at Brokers the other night. They have been staying in contact on a regular. She's tried to hook up with him a few times already, but he always complains about being so busy. Sha-Rock bugs her about pushing the issue of setting up a date, but she doesn't want to seem so anxious. She gets the feeling Hollyhood is a lot sharper than the average baller. She doesn't want to scare him away with her persistence.

"What's good, sugar?" he asks.

"You," she replies.

"Yeah, sounds good."

"It is good," she counters.

"I hope so."

"Hope? No need to hope. It's only one way to find out, but you're always so busy."

"I know, I know. I'm about to make some time for you. I promise. It's crazy for me. I've been back and forth out of town, feel me? And this Atlanta thing ain't helping. You know I have to go out there at least once a week?"

Miranda senses that he wants her to ask what he's doing in Atlanta, but she refuses to ask him.

"Yeah, ATL is what's up! Have you ever been there?"

"No," she lies. Sha-Rock has taken her there a million times. There are not too many places he hasn't taken her. That's another thing she loves about Sha-Rock, she has been places that most girls only dream of going. She did the Barbados, Cancun, and the Bahamas thing when she was seventeen years old. He did a good job of spoiling her. His motive was to show her everything so the next man couldn't step in and tempt her with trips and material. She must admit, his plan worked.

"No? Do you mean to tell me you have never been to ATL? Damn, what kind of nigga you got? You have to get out more. That don't make no type of sense. Don't worry about it though. I'm getting a house built from the ground up. You'll spend plenty of time down there, once they finish building it."

Miranda was right. He was dying to tell her that. It was eating him up inside. Sha-Rock had the right idea. If Miranda were a naïve young girl, Hollyhood would have started a beef between her and Sha-Rock, the way he just downplayed the fact that she's never been anywhere. That would have been all the fuel he needed to swoop her away from her man.

"Oh yeah?" she asks.

"Yeah, it's a little something-something. It's not what I really wanted but it'll do," he downplays.

"Oh," Miranda replies, hoping he'll change the subject.

"I only paid a half a million for it. The one I really wanted cost 2.5 mill, but I ain't ready for that, yet."

"You'll get it. Just keep working at it," says Miranda.

"Oh, for sure. I can get it now. I just don't want the pressure, feel me? You know how these haters are? If they find out how I'm really living, they'll put the man on me, feel me? Plus, I ain't in the position that I want to be in, yet. What's the purpose of having a $3,000,000 home, with no wife and kids to share it with?"

Oh boy, please shut up, Miranda thinks to herself. This is why she hates to talk to this clown. All his conversations start and finish with him. He never gives her any time to talk about her. In all the conversations they have had, he has never asked her real name, her age, or even if she has a man. As soon as he's done bragging about himself, he finds a way to end the conversation.

"Who is that?" Sha-Rock whispers.

Miranda raises one finger in the air, gesturing to hold up for a minute.

"So, when will I finally get a chance to see you?" she manages to slide in, before the next topic about himself. "I have forgotten what you look like, it's been so long. That's messed up how you tease a sister like you did. Told me all that good shit that night, and then you stay away. Is that how you do all your women? Oh, I know what it is, you're playing hard to get. You want to make me sweat, right? You want to see how long I'll chase you?"

"Nah, it ain't like that. I'm definitely going to make some time for you."

"Ok, I'm going to hold you to that."

"I tell you what," he blurts out. "What are you doing Friday night?'

"I'm not sure, why what's up?"

"I got tickets to the American League Championships. Do you watch baseball?"

"No, not really, but if that's what I have to do to finally spend some time with you, then I'll force myself to watch it," she laughs.

"Ok, that's what's up, then. Don't forget me alright?"

"Like you forgot me?" she asks sarcastically.

"Knock it off. Friday it is!" he shouts.

"Ok, we'll see. I'll give you a call tomorrow, alright?"

"Ok, that's what it is, then. Later!"

"Ok, bye!" she shouts before hanging the phone up.

"Who was that?" Sha-Rock asks.

"That was the kid Hollyhood."

"What is he talking about?"

"He wants to get together Friday. He says he has some tickets to some baseball game."

"Alright, now we gambling!" Sha-Rock cheers. "It's about time!" Sha-Rock is so anxious to get this one over with. He's sure Hollyhood will be a big payday. He's confident that it will be well worth the wait. Jimmy told him that Hollyhood claims he's worth a couple of million, which may be hyped up. Jimmy says at the worst case scenario, he should at least have a couple of hundred lying around. Sha-Rock can't wait to find out. The anxiety is killing him.

The Next Day

Bree lays in the king-sized bed. He sparks a Newport and takes a big pull. Smoking after sex is a habit for him. What he just had was more than sex. He just had one of the most fulfilling fuck sessions he has ever had in his life.

His sex partner, Kia, waddles into the bedroom belly first. She's six months pregnant. Even with her stomach protruding the way it does, she's still has massive sex appeal. She wears her pregnancy well. Her hair has grown full and long. Her skin has the pregnant glow, and her breasts have filled out tremendously.

She resembles an angel, but she's far from one. In fact, she is maybe the skuzziest chick on the planet. No, she's not Bree's baby's mother. She's pregnant by some heavy hitter. Well at least she's putting the baby on him. She probably doesn't even know whose baby it really is.

Judging by the stories she tells Bree, he believes she just got pregnant by the dude just to keep him. She claims they've been together for five years. Bree has been dealing with her for a few months and he only hears of the guy coming and going. He never spends an entire week there. She claims he's always out of town.

Whether she's his main girl or not, it really doesn't matter. He takes good care of her. She told Bree that she hasn't worked since she met the kid. Her beautiful apartment, lavish wardrobe and her new Lexus are all funded by him.

Kia stands next to the bed. She leans over and plants a kiss on Bree's shriveled up manhood. Her soft kisses turn into tongue lashes. Before he knows it, she has devoured him entirely.

She stops and snatches away from him. She looks at him with a frustrated look on her face. "Damn, what's up? I'm sucking the little soldier and he ain't even responding. And I do mean, little soldier," she emphasizes.

"Little?" Bree asks with a defensive tone. "My shit dead. What do you expect? You wasn't saying that a few minutes ago, when I had you running up the wall. Talking about my baby, my baby," he teases.

"Naw, you was trying to be funny," she replies. "Trying to go too deep."

"Damn, right. Bang the little motherfucker right on his head. Come out with my dick print on his forehead. Father be like, I know you been fucking somebody else," he jokes.

She laughs while stroking him gently, attempting to get a response. "Come on, Bree, break a sister off," she begs. "Let me get some more."

"Damn, I can't fuck no more. I'm tired. You busted about four nuts already."

"And?"

"And? How many more do you want?" he asks.

"Four more," she replies.

"Shit, not from me. That's it! I ain't fucking no more. You ain't killing me in this motherfucker. I see I have to bring two extra dicks with me when I come over this motherfucker. Now, I see why homeboy barely comes by here. You ran the mothefucker away."

"Hey it ain't my fault you niggas can't fuck. My pussy stay wet. Not cause I'm pregnant either," she denies.

"You got white liver. That's what you got!"

"No, I got wet pussy!"

"Yeah, right?"

"Seriously, my pussy is wet twenty-four hours a day, seven days a week. I wake up horny," she claims.

Bree is denying it to her, but he knows she isn't lying. He always tells his boys how wet she is. Every time he checks, no matter what time of the day, or what mood she's in, she's always soaking wet.

The thought of her juicy coochie excites him, giving him an instant erection. He reaches over and pets her love box. His finger accidentally slides inside of her. Her creamy interior swallows his finger. She grabs his hand and snatches it out of her.

"Fuck that finger shit. Give me some dick!" she shouts before hopping on top of him and bouncing crazily with no regard of the baby inside of her.

Just as she gets into the groove, the phone starts to ring. She's so caught up in the moment, that she's not even considering answering it. She eases off of him and crawls to the foot of the bed. She reaches back for his hand and leads him toward her. He crawls behind her on all fours until he reaches her. He slowly grinds on her from a doggy style position. "Faster, faster!" she shouts. He speeds up the grinding as he applies a little more force with each thrust. He heightens her pleasure by slowly fingering her cave. This drives her wild. She throws it back at him hard and rough. He's so caught up in the moment that he's ignoring the fact that she's pregnant. The louder she screams, the harder he pounds. The sound of her cries is exciting him. He wails on her with long deep strokes. "Ah ah, my baby," she cries. He totally ignores her. He continues to wail on her until she crawls away. "My ass," she whispers. "Please, take my ass," she begs. Bree doesn't hesitate. He does as she says before she can change her mind.

He's covered with her juices, which makes it easier for him to enter her back door. From the very second of his entrance, he rams himself into her.

She has mixed emotions. Her cave pulsates from excruciating pain, while her sweet opening feels neglected. Her mind is so far from here. Bree has her on cloud nine. She quivers uncontrollably as her muscles tighten. The sudden grip causes an unexpected reaction for Bree. He grunts as he releases. Seconds later, he falls backwards onto the bed. He sneakily cracks one eye open and finds Kia sitting there waiting for more.

Damn, he thinks to himself. She still hasn't had enough. Bree closes his eyes trying to fake her out. He's hoping she'll catch the hint, and go to sleep as well.

The ringing of the phone starts again.

Saved by the bell, he thinks to himself. Please, answer it, please. "Hello," she answers. Yes, he cheers in his head. "What the fuck, you calling for, now? I called yo ass two days ago. You ain't shit, nigga. Some father you are! You don't give a fuck about your baby. I almost had a miscarriage, and you wasn't nowhere to be found. Don't worry, I'm alright now. You a fucked up ass nigga." She pauses for a second. "You a got damn lie! You wasn't out of town, shit. Motherfuckers told me they saw you riding down South Orange Avenue, stop lying!" She pauses again. "Whatever! Nah, don't come here now. I bet you I don't open the door. I'm telling you, don't come." She sits there pouting like a baby. "Ok, don't believe me. Don't get mad, now. Your baby was mad two days ago, when he almost died and you wasn't even there for him," she

111

claims. "Bye motherfucker!"

Bree cracks both eyes open. "Is he on his way?" he asks hoping she'll say yes, so he can leave the apartment still holding onto his pride and dignity. He knows there's no way in the world he'll be able to get it up again.

"No, not right now. He won't be here until late tonight."

Damn, Bree thinks to himself. Please somebody save me. "I didn't know you almost had a miscarriage," he says trying to take her mind off of fucking.

"I didn't. I just said that," she shamelessly admits.

"That's a fucked up lie to tell." He can't believe she would tell him a lie like that. That really makes Bree believe that she purposely got pregnant just to hold onto the guy.

"Whatever. You stay out of it. Just worry about how you gone get that shriveled ass dick of yours back up. I'm ready to fuck again!"

As much as he hates to admit this, he has to. "Kia, I'm done," he whispers. "Anyway, your dude is on his way here."

"We got time. He's coming all the way from Durham, North Carolina. He's not even in Maryland yet."

"What's in Durham?"

"You know what's down there," she replies.

"So, he spends the majority of his time down there?"

"Yep, him and his cousin take turns going there. They both stay there three days at a time," she informs.

"How do you know all of that?"

"How I know?" she asks with a goofy look on her face. "I been with him for years. That ain't nothing. You would be surprised at all the shit I know!"

Is that so, he thinks to himself. Thoughts race through his mind two hundred miles per hour.

Killer Cal arrived back to Philly a few hours ago. He's really appreciative that Sha-Rock brought him along. He hasn't had money in so long that he almost forgot how it felt to have it.

He lies across his tiny twin-sized bed. He has an uncontrollable headache. His head pounds like a drummer. Tears creep down his face. The pain is unbearable. He has to deal with this pain almost everyday.

Suddenly, the vision of him walking in on his wife having sex with another man replays in his head. Her moans and gasps sound off clearly. He closes his eyes and shakes his head, hoping to shake away the vision. As he's shaking his head, the smell of his family's burning flesh blows past his nose. He can actually hear them screaming. The fire trucks, the police sirens, and everything is so clear to him. He remembers the very first time his adoptive father sexually abused him. His feeling of violation rekindles. He shakes his head even harder, but he can't seem to shake it away. He stands over his adoptive father. He looks so innocent as he lays there snoring loudly. The smell of cheap liquor blows through his nostrils each time he exhales. He raises the hammer in the air and with all his might he digs into the forehead of the sleeping victim. Blood gushes excessively. Fear takes over his young body. He races out to the backyard. He climbs over the fence into the yard of the house, which sits behind theirs. He runs over to a tree in the far corner of the yard. Using a broken mop stick, he begins to dig a hole. Minutes later, he plants the hammer into the dugout and fills the hole with dirt. Now they're dragging him out of the house in handcuffs. The social workers drill him over and over everyday. He finally admits that he's been tampered with sexually. After running tests, they finally believe him. The manslaughter charge is downgraded. They admit him to a boys' home. He wakes up in a straightjacket, inside Greystone Mental Hospital. "Mommy!" he screams aloud. "Help me, Mommy!"

His headache worsens. The memories of his childhood cause several emotions. He feels helpless, scared, and furious all at the same time.

He reaches over to his nightstand where his medicine is sitting in clear view. He grabs hold of it. As much as he hates to take it, he knows he has to. This is his only hope of attaining piece of mind. His mouth becomes as dry as cotton. He bangs his head against the wall violently, with no regard of pain.

He opens the bottle of pills and quickly dumps three of the horse pill-sized tablets into the palm of his hand. He hesitantly dumps them with no water. He gulps hard as the pills lodge into his throat. He finally manages to swallow them. He's breathing hard and his heart is racing.

The pain of his headache lessens. The pace of his heartbeat slows down tremendously. His visions disappear. He starts to feel drowsy. His body feels like it's floating. He falls face first onto his bed where he falls asleep instantly.

Sweet dreams?

-23-

Tamara and Miranda are zipping up I-95 North in Najee's convertible SL500. Dark shades cover their eyes. They're looking like two movie stars. It's a beautiful autumn day. Although it's only sixty degrees, they still have the top peeled back with the heat blasting. The wind blows fiercely through their hair.

They're on their way to a fashion show. It's not just any fashion show. It's Najee's fashion show. Tonight is also the night of his premier party. This is the first time anyone will ever see his clothing line. He will have models showing off all types of clothing from jeans to dress clothes.

Tamara is so proud of him. He's been working so hard on the clothing line. He has barely time for her. She understands the situation he's in. She hasn't put the least bit of pressure on him.

Hours Later

Tamara and Miranda finally arrive. The show is almost over. They interrupt everyone's attention as they enter the auditorium. Everyone focuses on them as they elegantly step down the aisle.

"Got damn!" shouts a rude male from across the auditorium.

Today, they're dressed alike, only wearing different colors. They both have on extremely short leather skirts, with leather jackets to match. Their long leather riding boots add much pizzazz to the outfit. Tamara's suit is brown, while Miranda's is tan. They're wearing their hair in the wet and wavy style. Miranda's leather suit fits her beautifully, but Tamara looks awesome. Her bodacious body is enough to make any man drool all over himself. The leather skirt grips her curves perfectly. Her thick, juicy thighs are the focal point of every onlooker.

They finally take their seats, allowing everyone to focus back to the show. Right now, two models strut down the runway, wearing denim jeans and leather motorcycle jackets all designed by Najee's brother Najim. Najim is the designer and Najee is the model. Together they make a perfect combination.

The models walk to the rear of the stage. The lights dim as they disappear behind the curtains. The auditorium is pitch-black. R. Kelly's "Bump and Grind" faintly sounds off through the speakers. "Ladies, what you all have been waiting for!" the male announcer shouts in a womanly tone. "This, my dears, is too much for TV. If you have the kids with you, I suggest you make them close their eyes!" The lights begin to brighten slowly. The volume of the music increases. The women scream at the top of their lungs as Najee confidently steps down the stage. He's shirtless and barefoot, wearing only extended briefs. His rounded chest bounces with each step. His abdominal muscles are rippling. His slender but muscular body sparkles with baby oil. He stops at the center of the stage and strikes a pose. The women go crazy.

Miranda can't help but notice the big bulge in the front of his briefs. She laughs to herself silently as she thinks back to the day when Tamara called him "horse dick." Miranda unconsciously compares Najee to her Mandingo, Sha-Rock. She tries to size him up, to see if he can compare. She can't tell this way, but she has to admit, he is holding. Any woman with eyes can see that. Miranda and every other woman in the building have their eyes glued to his bulge. He spins around slowly, giving them a clear view of his firm rear, which he flexes as he steps away. They beg for more as he fades into the back of the stage. The women scream, while the men boo him.

The lights go dim. Najee leaves an auditorium full of wet panties behind. Miranda looks over at Tamara. She's wearing the cheesiest look on her face. Her head hangs low close to her lap. Her cheeks are blushed. Her embarrassment is evident.

"Uhhmm, uhhmm girl," Miranda sighs. "They're going crazy over your boo," she whispers.

"I see," Tamara replies goofily.

The announcer speaks again. "Everyone, thanks for coming out. We truly appreciate your support. You've made this show a success. Najee and Najim, come out. Everyone please give them a nice big round of applause."

They walk out side by side. Najee is still barefoot. He's wearing a black satin robe. Najim is wearing, baggy dark blue denim jeans, suede Timberlands, with a tight fitted T-shirt which exposes his huge biceps. Their company design sets in the center of his shirt and his black baseball hat. His hat turned backwards gives him a thugged out look.

Miranda can't believe her eyes. Him and Najee are identical except their complexion. His skin is as black as tar, just the way Miranda likes them. For a second, she loses focus until the reality of Sha-Rock sets in. He'll surely kill her and Najim if he knew she even entertained the thought. She wonders if they're identical in all ways? She tries to size him up through his jeans but his pants are way too saggy.

Her mind just wonders. She would never go as far as to find out. Her thoughts are innocent.

Two Hours Later

Tamara and Miranda have just entered Fort Lee, New Jersey. Tamara pulls into the driveway of a beautiful one-family house. The house is breathtaking. It's all white. Beautiful life-sized statues spread over the lawn. Miranda is overwhelmed. "This house is beautiful," she admits.

"Wait until you see the backyard," Tamara replies.

As they walk up the alleyway, Miranda spots a huge swimming pool in the yard. A built-in deck with a countertop and bar stools sit directly across from the pool. There's even a lifeguard chair setting in the corner. A volleyball net stretches across the yard. To the left of the yard there sits a gazebo. "Oh my God, they even have a gazebo back here!" Miranda shouts, losing her cool. Having a gazebo in her backyard has always been her dream. "That is so beautiful." Miranda's mind runs wild. There has to be something more to Najee than what Tamara is telling. There's no way a rookie model can afford to live like this. If there's one thing Sha-Rock taught her it would be how to recognize game. He always tells her that game recognizes game.

They enter the house through the back door. To Miranda's surprise it looks nothing like the outside. It's the typical, messy, bachelor's pad. The sink is full of dirty dishes. Old pizza boxes and Chinese food cartons cover the table. The garbage can is overloaded from soda bottles and beer cans. The ashtrays are filled with cigarette butts and blunt remains.

"Look at this mess," says Tamara.

"Girl, it's alright," Miranda denies. "It just needs a woman's touch. And from the looks of it, you're the woman that will be touching it."

"Girl, please."

"For real, Tammy. This is all you. That nigga is crazy over you."

"You think so?" Tamara asks.

"Think? I don't think, I know. You don't see the big picture. It's all about you. You got your own key and all. Just think of everything he's done for you. Ain't no nigga gone do all of that for a chick he's just playing around with."

"I don't know, girl," she replies as she leads Miranda through the house. They walk up the circular staircase. "This is the bathroom," she says as she points to her left.

The bathroom has Polo everything, from the shower curtains on down to the floor mats. Pictures of little teddy bears and Ralph Lauren signatures are everywhere. How ghetto, Miranda thinks to herself. Although, she is impressed by the dual toilets that set against the wall. "Damn, he even got you your own toilet. His and hers, huh?"

Tamara blushes. "This Najee's room," she says as they exit the bathroom. Najee's room is terrible. Mounds and mounds of clothes are piled up on his king-sized waterbed. Sneaker boxes cover the entire floor leaving no space to walk. "Ain't this room a mess?" she asks.

"A woman's touch, girl. Remember what I told you."

They step further down the hall. "This is Najim's room," she says as she points to a closed door. As they're passing, Miranda is so eager to peek inside. She knows that she's violating his privacy, but she can't help herself. She turns the knob and cracks the door. She peeks inside. She's shocked. Najee and Najim may have identical looks, but don't live the same. His room is the complete opposite of Najee's room. It's so neat. He has a custom-made shoe tree against the wall, which has at least one hundred pairs of shoes on it. He has all kinds of shoes from Ostrich, to pony-haired shoes. He has them separated according to color and skins. Versatility is one thing she admires. She loves it when a man can mix it up. She loves to see Sha-Rock in jeans and sneakers, but he drives her crazy when he wears a suit and tie. She looks over to his closet. He has about forty suits lined up with a wall full of assorted ties. His bed is neatly made and his walls are sparkling clean.

"He's neat, huh?" Miranda asks.

"Very," Tamara replies. "He's never here though. That's why the room looks like no one sleeps here. Girl, that boy got so many bitches, he ain't never gotta sleep here."

That figures, Miranda says to herself.

"Fine, chocolate nigga like him? You know bitches are falling at his feet. I heard he got 'em all over the world, too. He's slinging dick from state to state. He got about twenty kids."

"Get out?"

"Damn near, shit! He got a baby momma in Atlanta, two in Harlem, one in Brooklyn, two in Baltimore, one in Virginia, one in Chicago, and one in Miami. He even got one in Puerto Rico. He got some more, I just can't remember where. And them just the ones he claiming."

"Shit! He leaves a baby everywhere he travels too, huh?"

"Yeah, that's another reason why I can't trust Najee. I wonder how many kids he got over the world? Now what the fuck do you think he's doing while his brother is trying to fuck everything that's moving? I know he ain't just passing up all that pussy. He's fucking too!"

"Not necessarily, Tammy."

"Please!"

"How many kids does he have?"

"None, so he says."

"None? Girl, I know you a fool now. You better bust a hole in that condom or something," Miranda teases.

Tamara laughs.

"I'm serious girl. You got a good thing. You better not let it slip away," Miranda says as she closes the door behind her. They walk down the staircase that leads to the front of the house. The living room is at the landing of the staircase. The living room is so average that it disgusts Miranda. They have the typical big screen television with the same old leather sectional, just like any other ordinary bachelor's pad.

Tamara turns the TV on from the remote. Miranda is not surprised by what's on the screen. Hard-core porno, how typical, she tells herself. Tamara flicks the stations until she finally locates HBO, where her favorite show "The Wire" is being aired. She left Najee's party early just so she could catch it. She won't miss that show for anything in the world.

"This is my shit!" Tamara shouts.

"Ain't no way in the world I would have left my man alone at that party with all of them dick hungry bitches," says Miranda. "Did you hear how they were cheering for him?"

"Girl, he ain't going nowhere. Besides, he definitely got enough dick to go around. Trust me, I won't get cheated. In fact, help a sister out. Save me a little pain. Let him shift their insides around. Let my poor little pussy rest. I'm tired of walking around with swollen coochie

119

lips and stomach aches," she jokes.

They both laugh as they sit across from each other. They sink into the butter-soft leather. Miranda recognizes that this isn't that cheap leather from the local furniture spot. This is fine Italian leather. She does give them a plus for that.

Ten minutes into the show, Tamara races to the kitchen. She returns with a bottle of merlot and two glasses.

Three glasses later, Miranda digs into her purse and fumbles inside. She snatches her hand out, holding a paper towel in her palm. She lays the paper towel onto the coffee table carefully trying hard not to spill the contents. She opens it carefully. The aroma of goodness fills the air.

"That's what I'm talking about!" Tamara shouts as the fragrance entices her nostrils. "That's goodness, right there!"

"It sure is!" Miranda confirms.

"Where did you get that?"

"Ain't important, I got it," Miranda says in a joking manner. She stole it from the little stash Sha-Rock had. She doesn't know where he got it from. Truthfully, she knows he must have gotten it from a robbery, but she doesn't know all the details. He never discusses other *vicks* with her. He tells her only the details that she needs to know to do what she has to do for the ones that she's involved in.

Miranda pulls a blunt from the box as she's watching television. She stuffs the blunt with so much goodness that she can barely roll it. She seals it and sparks it up. She anxiously takes a few pulls before passing it to Tamara. If Sha-Rock could see her now. He has no clue that she smokes. She picked the bad habit up while he was away. Tamara is busy smoking like a chimney. Just as they begin to buzz, the sound of the door lock opening startles them. Tamara looks for an ashtray to dud the blunt out. She's so nervous that she doesn't even notice the one that's sitting on the table. She duds it out in the palm of her hand. "Aghh," she sighs.

Miranda's eyes are stretched wide open. She's so busy watching Tamara make a fool of herself, that she has totally forgotten about the paper towel full of smoke that's laying in the center of the table. Tammy passes the remainder of the blunt to Miranda. She tosses it into her purse, just in the nick of time. Their smoking is their little secret. They would never reveal that to any man. They would never smoke openly in front of any man and risk him losing respect for them and start treating them like hood rats.

Najee walks into the living room, along with Najim, another male, and the homosexual announcer.

Najee sniffs the air. "Aghh! No wonder y'all left our corny little party. Y'all having a party of y'all own. Damn! It smells good in here. Can I smoke?" he asks sarcastically.

"Smoke?" Tammy asks defensively. "Ain't nobody smoking," she lies.

"Oh, y'all wasn't smoking?"

"No."

"Ok then, I guess y'all won't be needing this over here," he says while pointing to the paper towel with the weed spread across it.

Their faces blush from embarrassment.

Najee reaches for the box and starts rolling away. He rolls three blunts that triple the size of the one Miranda rolled. He sparks his, after passing the other two off to Najim. Najim takes a big puff of his. He exhales with his mouth wide open. "Unghh, unghh, this some good shit," he teases. "Purple Haze," he adds.

The girls try and watch TV as if they don't hear him. Miranda sneakily peeks at the other dudes. She's trying to see who they are.

"Miranda," Najee calls out. "What's good, lady?"

"Nothing," she replies, giving him much attitude.

"Let me introduce you to everybody. This right here is my evil twin brother, who happens to be crazy over you."

She blushes.

"Stop it, Najee. I already told you!" Tammy shouts.

"Yeah, you told me. She didn't. Stop talking for her."

Najim extends his hand to her for a handshake. "How are you doing beautiful?"

"Fine, and you?" she replies. Miranda finds his deep voice rather sexy.

"This right here is my announcer. He doesn't find you beautiful at all," he jokes. "He's strictly dickly," Najee says sarcastically.

"Damn right!" the announcer shouts. "I don't want nobody's fish! Just kidding, doll. How are you?"

"I'm good," she says.

"And this motherfucker came here just to meet you. He's been bugging me ever since he saw you and Tammy walk into the auditorium tonight. This is my agent, Todd. He wants to holler at both of y'all."

"Hello, gorgeous. Tammy already knows me but she insists on playing games. If she had hooked up with me, I would have had her face all over the world by now. The agent she has is a rookie. He's using her to build up his resume. My resume is already extensive," he says with a sharp tone. "Miranda, have you ever thought about modeling?"

"Nah," she replies instantly. She knows where he's probably headed with this. She thinks Tamara has something to do with this.

"Why not?" he asks.

"Ah, ah," she replies. Ever think of modeling, she asks herself. All day, everyday, she answers herself.

"You really need to consider it. You have exactly what it takes. You are cover girl material. You're just right. Not too hippy, either," he says sarcastically as he looks over at Tammy, insinuating that her hips are too big. "Please think about it. I would love to represent you. We could work wonders together. Will you think about it?" he asks.

"Nah, I'm keeping it real. That isn't for me."

"Why? What are you doing now?"

She laughs to herself. You don't want to know, she thinks to herself. She's stumbled. She has to think of something quick. She can't tell him she's not working. She'll look like an airhead. "I have my own business. I don't have the time," she says quickly.

"What kind of business?" he asks nosily.

"If I tell you that, I'll have to kill you," she jokes. I mean that literally, she laughs to herself.

"Please, take my card," he insists, as he hands her the card.

She constantly catches herself peeking at Najim. She pulls her phone out just to interrupt her bad thoughts. She dials Sha-Rock and whispers into the phone. "Hello? What's up, babe?"

"Nothing much," he replies. "Where are you?"

"On my way home."

"Who you with?"

"Tammy, we're leaving New York right now. I have something to ask you later, alright?" she asks.

"What is it? Ask me now. Is it bad?"

"No. As a matter of fact, it may be good." She knows he's going to flip when she asks him about modeling. They have been through this same argument so many times already. "I'll call you when I get home. Are you still in Jersey?"

"Yeah, I'm working as we speak," he replies, giving her the hint for her to leave him alone while he's doing whatever it is that he's doing.

"Oh, ok, I'm sorry. Be careful, alright? Hold up, before you hang up, make sure you keep an open mind when I ask you what it is I have to ask you, alright?"

"No doubt," he replies. "Hit me when you touch down."

"Will do. I love you," she whispers.

"You better," he jokes, before hanging up the phone.

"Are you ready?" Tamara asks.

"Yeah, I have to get up early tomorrow."

"Damn, y'all out so early? The night is just beginning," says Najee.

"Don't even think about it!" Tamara shouts. "Najim won't get his hands on this one."

Najim stands there with a guilty-looking smile on his face.

Najee escorts them to the front door. Him and Tamara kiss passionately while Miranda waits patiently.

"I'll come over there if you feel left out!" Najim shouts to Miranda.

"No, I'm alright," Miranda replies.

"At least take my number," he suggests.

"Your brother gave it to me already."

"Yeah, and you haven't used it yet. Why?"

"I have a man," Miranda replies. Damn, she could kick herself up the ass. Those words sort of slipped out. That must have been her conscious speaking. She truly believes two individuals live inside her. Her bad twin is doing the thinking, but the good one is doing the talking.

"Think about it, alright?" Najim asks.

"Nothing to think about," she quickly replies. Damn, she spoke again. "I'm faithful, and I'm madly in love with my man."

"Oh, much respect. But don't forget, I'm here if you need me."

"Bye, y'all," Tamara shouts, purposely interrupting Najim.

Miranda and Tamara jump into Najee's car and peel off. They're Philly bound.

Meanwhile

A few miles away, Sha-Rock sits parked in his van along with Jimmy. It's extremely dark inside the tinted van. They have been parked out there for two hours already. They're sitting approximately ten houses down from the First Lady's house. Her house sits right next to a vacant lot, where it looks like they may be in the process of building another house. This angle is perfect because Sha-Rock can watch the house from front to back from this very spot.

Sha-Rock and Jimmy aren't speaking much. Sha-Rock is busy observing, while Jimmy sits there with a huge attitude. There are so many other things he would rather be doing than sitting out there. He has missed so much money while sitting out there.

Jimmy's phone rings again for the hundredth time. "Yo," he answers. "Not yet, bee," he replies with an agitated voice. "I'll hit you when I get back around, alright?" He hangs the phone up and jams it into his pocket angrily.

"Damn, your joint blowing up," Sha-Rock teases, adding insult to injury. ""Shit looking real good for you, huh?"

"Yeah, it picked up a little," he replies modestly.

"A little? All them calls, I know you could have sold least two joints by now? Hold up, here go some lights," Sha-Rock whispers before allowing Jimmy to reply.

A small car slows down as it nears her house. Finally it comes to a complete stop before turning into the two-car garage. The car is a red convertible SLK compressor, Mercedes Benz.

"That's her other car," Jimmy says.

Damn, two Mercedes, Sha-Rock thinks to himself. What a big payday this is going to be.

It's her car, but she's not driving. A tall, slim male crawls out of the tiny car. He's so tall you would never believe that he could fit into the little car.

"That's her flunky, from the other night," says Jimmy.

"Oh, alright. His face looks familiar, but he didn't look that tall the other night," Sha-Rock admits. "He's always with her, huh?"

"Yeah, that's her flunky. He's always glued to her hip."

"Who is he?" Sha-Rock asks.

"Nobody, a nondescript. He's a straight duck. He used to be with her brothers before they got pinched. He was the only one who didn't get caught up in the Fed beef. They say him and her used to fuck around, but after she blew, she cut his lame ass off."

"What's up with him? Does he put in work?"

"Not at all. He's a straight coward. She's tougher than him. I told you he's her servant. He washes her clothes, washes her car, and probably fucks her when she needs to be fucked."

"So, he's just her servant?" Sha-Rock asks.

"No doubt. Fag ass nigga probably scared of his own shadow. Me and him went to school together."

The dude walks to the trunk lazily. He grabs an arm full of groceries and runs up the stairs, goofily, without looking in either direction. He pulls out his key and sticks it into the door without even watching his back. "He's a dumb ass nigga," says Sha-Rock, as he pulls out his pen and pad. He glances at the clock, while jotting down the time of his arrival.

Two hours pass and neither one of them have said a word to each other. The only noise has been the sound of Jimmy's aggravating phone, which has been ringing every twenty minutes faithfully. The more his phone rings the angrier he gets. He hates to miss money. He wants so badly to tell Sha-Rock to drop him off, but that will start the argument of a lifetime. He'll give Jimmy the long speech about how he has to be a man of his word, and how he kept up to his end of the bargain. Jimmy is oh-so-tired of hearing that. If he knew Sha-Rock would bring that up so much, he probably would have reconsidered the deal.

Sha-Rock notices lights approaching from behind him. The way the lights are reflecting against the sun visors in the van, Sha-Rock can tell they're not the lights of a car because the lights are up too high. He realizes that the lights have to belong to an SUV. He sure hopes it's the First Lady. He looks back, and the first thing he notices is the Mercedes Benz emblem that sits in the center of the truck. "This is her!" Sha-Rock shouts.

She slows down as she approaches her house. You can see the silhouette of her head through her back window. She's looking around observantly, paying close attention to her surroundings. She passes right by her house.

"That is her, right?" Sha-Rock asks.

"Yeah, that's her truck," Jimmy replies.

"Where the fuck is she going?" She makes a left at the corner. "Do you think she saw us?" Sha-Rock asks.

Two minutes later, she approaches again. Sha-Rock is impressed. Someone must have schooled her, and taught her better than to jump right out her car without circling the block first.

She pulls into her garage slowly. She walks out of the garage while glancing around. Her head is moving consistently. Either she's a nervous wreck or she's on point like a *Sniper,* Sha-Rock thinks to himself.

Sha-Rock pays close attention to her right hand. She hasn't taken it out of her jacket pocket one time, not even to open the gate up. "I think that broad got a banger on her," says Sha-Rock.

"She probably do," Jimmy replies. "I told you, she get down like that. She ain't your average broad," he adds.

"It don't matter. I don't give a fuck! She could have ten bangers on her and she still ain't no match for me. You could dress a bitch up in whatever outfit you choose, but she still gone be a bitch. You don't create gangsters; they're born that way. She ain't built like that. When it's all said and done she's still a girl. She ain't no killer. She ain't ready for the game she playing. She thinks she is, but time will tell. When I put this cannon down her throat, watch the bitch jump out of her. Mark my words," he says arrogantly.

Before stepping outside of the gate, she turns around completely and takes one last look before backpedaling up the stairs. Once she reaches the top of the landing, she digs into her pocket with her left hand. She continuously peeks around as she sticks her key into the door.

Sha-Rock has to admit, he does admire her awareness, even though it's going to make his job a lot harder. It's obvious that she's no new jack. Her brothers must have taught her well.

A few minutes after she closes the door, Sha-Rock sees the light at the back of the house come on. He assumes that must be her room back there. He finally busts a U-turn and pulls off nonchalantly.

Four Hours Later

It's 4 A.M. and Sha-Rock is back, sitting in the exact same spot as he was sitting four hours ago. This time he's by himself. After he dropped Jimmy off, he came right back. He's on a real mission. It may take him some time to put everything together, but he's sure it will be well worth his time and energy.

No one has left the house, and there hasn't been a light on since 1 A.M. Jimmy knows very little about the First Lady. All he knows is she's heavy in the heroin game. He doesn't know anything about her internal moves. Her game is airtight. Sha-Rock knows his work is cut out for him. He may have to follow her around for weeks just to put things into their proper perspective. He needs to know everything about her before he makes a move on her. He can't afford to miss anything. He wants to know where every one of her stash houses is. He needs to know what beauty parlor and nail salon she goes to. He has to find out where all her family members reside. He'll also need to know the last ten niggas she has dealt with, just in case she's still linked to any of them. Who knows where she may have the dope stashed? Judging by the way she moves, he seriously doubts that she's keeping anything in her house. She appears to be way too smart for that. Whatever she has and wherever she has it, Sha-Rock is sure he'll find out. He has one advantage working in his favor, and that's the fact that he used to be a drug dealer. He's up on any game that hustlers play. There is no way any hustler can pull wool over his eyes. He was smart as a hustler, so that will make him extremely dangerous on the other side.

At 6 A.M. a light finally comes on. Sha-Rock assumes it must be the bathroom light by the patterns that are on the curtains. He jots the time down in his notepad.

Ten minutes later another light appears from the back of the house. A few bottles and jars are lined up at the window. This tells Sha-Rock that this has to be the kitchen. Five minutes thereafter, the front door opens. Sha-Rock's heartbeat speeds up.

The First Lady peeks her head through the cracked doorway. After a few seconds of peeking, she steps onto the porch and walks to the entrance of the gate. She's wearing a pink and gray jogging suit.

She grabs hold of her gate and starts stretching, while looking around her surrounding area with a paranoid look on her face. After a ten-minute stretching/observing session, she busts through the gate entrance like a horse in a horse race. She runs up the block in the opposite direction of where Sha-Rock is parked.

Sha-Rock gives her a two-block head start before he tails her. He ends up following her to a small park about ten minutes away from her house. He parks several blocks away and watches her workout. He thinks that maybe someone will meet her there and he can witness a transaction; unfortunately, it doesn't happen. All he did witness was the jiggling of her loose, shapely spread as she bent over doing pushups. Sha-Rock couldn't really see her the other nights because it was dark. Today he really saw her clearly. He didn't realize how beautiful she is. Her *doobie* falls about an inch below her shoulder line. Her auburn colored hair matches her red-boned complexion. She has sexy eyes and seductive looking, very full, pinkish colored lips. She stands about five five inches, with an ass as big as Texas. Her beauty almost made him back away from her. He had to remind himself that it's business and not pleasure. He watches her up until she completes her workout and exits the park, which happens to be approximately one hour later. He lets her take a big lead before following her back to her house.

At 10 A.M. the First Lady comes out again. This time she jumps into her SLK Compressor and takes off at top speed. Twenty minutes later, she makes her first stop at a Catholic school, where she stays for approximately two hours. From there she rides for another twenty minutes to pick up another girl. Their next stop is Friday's on Route 22, where Sha is in the parking lot, waiting patiently.

His phone interrupts his boredom. He looks at the display. Normally, he doesn't answer the phone while he's working, but it's Miranda. He has to focus. He doesn't need any distractions. He does realize how smart the First Lady is. He has to keep all eyes on her. He doesn't want to miss a beat. "Yo?"

"Baby?" she whines.

"What up?"

"I'm on my way to Jersey."

"Alright, what time does the game start?" Sha asks.

"I'm not sure, I think he said like 4:30."

"Alright, just hit me once you get up this way."

"Ok, love ya."

"I love you, too," Sha replies. He sits there for another thirty minutes before the First Lady and her friend finally exit the restaurant. As he pulls out of the parking lot, he lets at least ten cars get in front of him before he decides to proceed onto the highway. He wonders where they'll lead him to next?

When Miranda steps out of Newark Penn Station, the first car she sees is Hollyhood's white BMW with the spinning rims. How could anyone miss it, as loud as he has the music playing? He has Snoop Dog's "Drop It Like It's Hot" blasted to the max. He stands at the passenger's seat of the car. Everyone watches him as he puts on a concert for the onlookers. He's imitating the Crip walk. He has his New York Yankees cap pulled down real low over his eyes, and he's just dancing away, using heavy hand gestures to emphasize certain verses.

Miranda's stomach gets queasy just looking at him. She hates a show-off. She knows its only business, but the bad part is the fact that people probably think he's her man. She can only imagine what they're saying about her. She has had several men approach her on the train, and off. She shot them all down, telling them she has a husband. Then for her to come out and have a buster like him out here waiting for her is a disgrace. They're totally mix-matched. She's way too classy for a guy like him.

He honks the horn to catch her attention, when in all reality he knows she already saw him. He just wants everyone to see her walking over to his car. Miranda walks over to him gracefully even though she feels like a clown just being in his presence.

He walks over and meets her halfway. Hollyhood has to be a true Yankees fan because he's representing them to the fullest. He has on so much Yankees attire that he could be mistaken for one of the players. He has on an oversized blue satin Yankees jacket. Underneath the jacket he's wearing a Yankees jersey, which has the numbers and the letters trimmed in rhinestone. His hat is encrusted with rhinestones as well. He's wearing big baggy Yankees sweatpants, that appear to be triple his size.

Throughout the entire ride to Yankee Stadium, all Hollyhood did was brag, brag, brag. Everything that came out of his mouth was "me" and "I". He told her everything about his life, starting with his first day of kindergarten, when he told his teacher he would be rich by the time he turned twelve. He claims he was off by only one year. According to him he has been rich ever since he was thirteen. He told her how he first got started in the game and how he eventually took over his projects. He told her he's the richest dude in Newark, and everyone either picks up off of him or works for him. She knows his dreams, his goals and his fears.

She was so happy to finally make it to the stadium so he could focus on something other than himself, but unfortunately the game couldn't even shut his mouth. He babbled on and on for nine innings.

Miranda hates his cocky attitude. The entire game he attempted to place bets with Boston fans. He stood there for hours, talking really loud, holding a handful of $100 bills. Miranda was so embarrassed that she wanted to crawl up underneath the bleachers. His arrogance is nerve-racking, but it will work to her advantage. He'll fall right into her trap. He'll be so busy showing off that he won't be paying attention to anything else.

Right now they're walking to the car. Hollyhood hits the alarm to open the doors and automatically start the car. Instead of walking to the driver's side, he steps toward the passenger's side. "Drive," he insists, while hopping in. As soon as he sits down, he leans his seat way back and sits real low. He's wearing a cocky look on his face like he's sure he just impressed her. He kicks both feet onto the dashboard as she pulls out of the lot. She can feel him watching her. He turns up his volume to ten pumping the same Jay-Z song that he replayed over and over ever since she first got into the car. He sings the song loudly. It's obvious that the song has an effect on him because he's acting cockier now than he has been acting all night. There's something about Jay-Z's music that Miranda can't understand. His songs make the poorest nigga in the world feel like he's a big time baller.

Miranda looks at him. She's sick to her to stomach, but she can't let him know it. He's bouncing around in his seat and screaming at the top of his lungs. Everyone stares into the car as they pass by them. She sure wishes his windows were tinted. A show-off like Hollyhood would never tint his windows. It would kill him if no one knew it was him inside. That would defeat his whole purpose of buying the car in the first place.

"Damn, you love you some Jay-Z, huh?" Miranda asks.

"Hell yeah! This is my dude. I swear this nigga is rapping about my life!"

Oh boy, not another one of these motherfuckers, Miranda thinks to herself.

"I told you, I used to fuck with them dudes, right?" he asks.

Please, she mumbles under her breath. "No, you didn't tell me that. You did?" she asks, flattering him.

"Well, not really Jay, but Dame Dash. That's my dude! Harlem is my second home. I'm in Harlem more than I'm in Jersey. I was the first nigga pumping Jay in Jersey. Them Mob Style niggas, them my dudes too, Az, Whip Wop, Gangster Lou, all of them. Have you ever heard of them?" he asks.

"No," she replies quickly, hoping he'll shut up with all his lies. She has heard this same story so many times before, just from different dudes.

"Oh, listen to all their songs, they all shout me out. Ma, I'm somebody in the world!" he shouts. He pulls a stack of money from his pocket and counts it. After the song plays out, he switches the CD to another one, which happens to be another Jay-Z joint.

He's been counting this same stack of money all day, Miranda thinks to herself. He's counted the money so many times that she's sure he knows the serial numbers on each bill by heart.

After counting the money four more times, he spreads it across his lap, as he sings over the words of Jay-Z and Jermaine Dupree's "Money Ain't a Thing."

Right now, Miranda is all Jay-Z'd out. "Is that all you have in here?" she asks.

"Just about," he admits, as he flicks through his CD album. He finally plays R. Kelly's "12 Play" CD. He simmers down, just bopping to the music. Miranda can't believe he has finally shut his mouth.

Before the thought could even vanish, he starts up again. "Damn! I bought all this money with me for nothing! I thought I would at least catch a few motherfuckers to bet against me. They knew better than to bet against my Yankees. I brought $10,000 with me, for nothing," he claims, as he tucks the money into his jacket pocket.

Please, Miranda thinks to herself. He has counted the money so many times that she even knows how much is there. It's nowhere near $10,000. At the most, it's only $3,500.

He sneakily reaches over and strokes her hair. "Your hair is beautiful," he compliments. "Is it yours?"

"You feel it," she replies with bitterness in her voice. "You tell me," she says arrogantly.

He tugs at it gently. "Yeah, it's yours. Are you mixed?" he asks.

"Yeah, my mother was black and my father is Cuban."

"Was black?" he asks.

"Yeah, was. She passed away years ago."

"I'm sorry to hear that. How?" he asks.

"I rather not talk about that, if you don't mind?"

"Oh, no problem. I'm sorry," he replies as he strokes her hair. Suddenly, his fingers fall to her neckline, where he traces little circles.

She rolls with the flow. She leans her head back seductively. She closes her eyes for a quick second. She's faking him out, trying to make him believe that his touch is making her weak. "Stop," she shouts. "You're going to make me have an accident."

He laughs, as his tiny circle tracing turns into a massage. "Okay, when I crash, don't get mad," she laughs.

"Get mad?" he asks. "I'll never get mad over that. This is only material. Crash this one, and we'll be at the BMW dealer tomorrow. I want that convertible 645 anyway. That will just give me a reason to cop it!" he brags.

"Stop," she begs.

"Why?"

"Just stop."

"Why should I?" he asks in a sexy whisper.

"That's my spot, that's why."

He ignores her wishes, as he continues to massage her neck. Every now and then, he peeks over at her just to make sure he's having an effect on her.

He decides to make his move for second base. He traces a few circles around her belly button, just to se if she'll tell him to stop. To his surprise she doesn't say a word. She wants to stop him, but she also wants him to feel comfortable.

Hollyhood spots a police car up ahead about a mile away. "Slow down, the pigs are up there to your right."

Thank God, she thinks as she snatches his hand away from her stomach. He was so close to his goal. He already had two fingers underneath the elastic of her panties. She doesn't have a clue of how she was going to make him stop. She needs him to feel comfortable, and the only way she knows how to do that is to make him think he's about to fuck. He'll be so busy concentrating on getting some ass, and that will make her job so much easier.

132

They approach the area where the police car is sitting at a moderate speed. Just as they pass, the cruiser swerves recklessly behind them. He follows for a few minutes before finally turning his sirens on.

"Damn, this motherfucker," he sighs.

Miranda's nerves begin to work. "Your papers are good, right?" she asks.

"Hell yeah! I'm legit."

"Pull over," the cop says over the loud speaker. Miranda bears over to the shoulder and comes to a complete halt before the officers jump out. Both of them have their hands on their guns as they approach the car. One officer steps toward Miranda's side while the other one steps to Hollyhood's side. "Good evening," says the cop at Miranda's window. "You do know why I pulled you over, right?"

"No," Miranda replies innocently.

"No?" he repeats. "Neither of you are wearing seat belts. License, registration and insurance, please?'

Miranda digs her hand into her purse to retrieve her license. After locating it, she hands it over to the officer.

"Where's the registration and insurance?"

"Right here," says Hollyhood, as he digs into his glove compartment. It takes him a matter of seconds to find it due to the mess he has piled up inside. As soon as he passes it over, the officer begins reading.

"Whose car is this?"

"My mother," Hollyhood replies.

"Helen Francis?"

"Yes, sir."

"This is your mother's car, with $15,000 spinners on it?" he asks sarcastically. "Mom's doing it big, huh?"

Hollyhood cracks a cheesy smile.

"Where do you live? With your mom?"

"Yes, sir," he replies.

"How old are you?"

"Twenty-seven."

"Twenty-seven and still living with mom? You got a license?"

"Nah." He shamefully admits.

"Nah? So why do you have the car, if you don't have license?"

"I'm not driving."

"Oh, so mom let you hold the car?" the officer asks Miranda. She doesn't know what to say. She sits there with a baffled look on her face. "Don't lie for him, beautiful. I know this is his car. He's not fooling me. I'm about to run the paperwork and make sure everything is okay. I'll be right back." The officer asks for the keys and both of them walk back to their cruiser.

"Dick-riding as Pig. I hate police!" Hollyhood shouts.

Miranda's heart is pounding. She hopes all his paperwork is in order. The last thing she needs is to get locked up, messing around with this buster. If she even gets a ticket, the mission is over because they'll have all her information. Sha-Rock will be so upset with her. He's really looking forward to this sting. If she blows it by driving this car, she'll never hear the end of it.

The cops finally return. "Everything is good. Tell hip-hop mom she better stop giving you her car until you get a license," he says sarcastically.

"Eat a dick," Hollyhood mumbles only loud enough for Miranda to hear.

One hour later, Miranda exits Route 280 at the West Orange exit. Hollyhood coaches her to the parking lot of a suburban housing complex. He instructs her to park while he runs inside for a second.

While Miranda is waiting, she looks around for a street sign so she'll know exactly where she is. After locating it, she jots it down along with the address of the house he ran into.

Minutes later, he slowly drags himself to the car. After sitting down, he kicks his feet up on the dashboard and instructs her on which way to go next. His instructions lead them to a secluded block about fifteen minutes away.

A teenage boy is standing on the porch of a little shabby-looking shack. When he spots Hollyhood's car coming, he races off the porch and jumps in the backseat as the car is still rolling.

"What up?" he shouts.

"You," Hollyhood replies.

The young kid hands a sloppy knot of money over to Hollyhood, who in return hands him a small brown bag.

"Hit me when you finish, lil nigga," Hollyhood says in a loud arrogant tone. He peeks over at Miranda as he says it, to see if she's

134

watching. She looks straight ahead as if she's not paying him any attention at all. "I got the new shipment coming in, and I'm going to need your help moving it."

"Alright, bet!" the kid shouts in an excited tone.

"I got a lot of shit coming," Hollyhood emphasizes. "No bullshit. We about to really take over, feel me?"

"I feel you," he confirms.

"Make sure you hit me."

"No doubt," the kid replies, while opening the car door to get out.

"Pull off," Hollyhood instructs. Miranda pulls off without saying a word. That was the fakest shit she has ever seen in all her life, she thinks to herself. Talking about corny! She looks over at him. He doesn't have a clue of what position he just put himself into. His stupidity is about to cost him dearly. She humors him by saying, "I know you didn't just do what I think you did?"

"It depends on what you think I did," he says.

"Was that a drug deal?" she asks in her most naïve voice.

He snickers. "Go ahead girl."

"Go ahead, my ass!" she shouts, as she acts like she's furious. "Don't be putting me in the middle of that shit!"

"Calm down, calm down," he whispers. "My bad, the little cat couldn't wait, and I wasn't ready to drop you off just yet. I apologize."

She goes on and on. "Shit, don't be using me as no fucking get-away girl!"

He laughs arrogantly, paying her no attention at all.

Meanwhile back at the First Lady's house, Sha-Rock is parked in his normal spot. He's so tired that he can barely keep his eyes open. The First Lady has taken him on a little crusade. She hasn't made the slightest business move all day, but he did learn a few things about her. He jotted down all her movements. After lunch, she went back to her house to change cars. After getting into her truck, her and her friend went back to pick up the two little girls from the Catholic school. Next they ended up at the mall before going to Red Lobster. Finally she pulled up to a beautiful house in a quiet suburban area. Some corny-looking, suit and tie type dude pulls up in a white Mercedes S500. Him and the little girls go inside the house. Sha-Rock figures the dude must be her brother, and the girls are probably her nieces. After that, the First Lady and her friend go back to the First Lady's house, where they have been ever since.

Sha-Rock is about ready to pull off, but he's scared he may miss something. This job may take longer than he expected it to, but that doesn't discourage him. He has nothing but time on his hands.

He decides to go ahead and punch out. He's extremely tired. Tomorrow, he'll have to pick up from where he left off. He has to get some rest if he expects to keep up with her. Her day starts at 6 A.M. and ends at 1 A.M. She sleeps only five hours, so that means he has to sleep less than that in order to keep an eye on her. Maybe, he's bit off more than he can chew.

-25-

Two Weeks Later

Two weeks have passed and everything is going as planned. Miranda and Hollyhood have been speaking on a regular basis. He's wide open for the taking. Sha-Rock had intentions on finalizing the deal days ago, but his concentration has been on the First Lady. She's driving him crazy. He's been following her around day and night for weeks and he still hasn't seen her make one move. He has found out a great deal of information, though. Her brother, the dude with the S500, works for the City of Newark. He's a building inspector. She picks the girls up from school everyday and drops them off to him in the evenings. Sha-Rock has it narrowed down. The dope is either stashed in her best friend's house or her brother's house. Those are the only people that she sees everyday. Sha-Rock has followed her brother, the best friend, and her flunky and none of them has given him any leads. The suspense is killing him. This vick is more than just business. It has turned personal. He's determined to find out where she's working her operation from and how it works.

As for Bree, he just walked onto Kia's doorstep. He rings her doorbell twice. Normally, she answers after the first ring. He's sure she's in there because he just spoke to her about five minutes ago.

He rings the doorbell again, this time leaning on it. Seconds later, she finally opens the door. She waddles in front of him, with her cordless phone glued to her ear. She's ranting and raving. "You a motherfucking lie! Motherfucker, I been trying to contact you for over two weeks. I'm sick and tired of this shit! You have been treating me like shit ever since I got pregnant! I knew I should have got a motherfucking abortion! You doing me dirty as hell," she cries.

Bree has never seen her act this emotional. She's usually so gangster. Maybe the pregnancy is making her sensitive?

"I swear to God, I hate you! Oh, it's funny? Are you laughing at me?" she asks with a surprised look on her face. "I wish you were dead!" she screams before hanging up on him. She sits on the edge of the bed, and plants her face into the palms of her hands. She's crying loud and hard.

Bree sits right next to her. He wraps his arms around her and pats her back to comfort her. "Don't cry," he says in a sympathetic voice.

"I'm tired of this shit. This motherfucker waits until I get pregnant to start shitting on me. He barely answers my calls. My bills are backing up. My rent is late, and my car note was due a week ago."

This is shocking news to Bree. This is her first time admitting this to him. Normally, she brags about how good everything is and how he treats her like a queen.

"Kia, stop crying. It'll be alright."

She continues to cry as if she doesn't hear him.

He kneels down, on the floor in between her legs. They're face to face. "Listen, stop crying. It's gone be alright. Later for him. I'll help you," he offers.

"No! This is his baby, not yours. You don't understand how much I hate him. How could he shit on me like this?" she asks. "He's cheating on me; bitches calling my house disrespecting me, asking for him. Bitches coming to my house, scratching my car up and busting my windows. Before this baby, he was crazy over me. Now that I'm pregnant, he's making my life a living hell. If I knew he was going to flip the script on me like this, I would have got an abortion. He ruined my life!" she cries. "I really wish he was dead!"

Thoughts race through Bree's head. He suddenly gets a bright idea. "I got a proposition for you that can be beneficial for the both of us. Just hear me out," he insists, as he fills her in on all the details.

Meanwhile down in Philly

Killer Cal is running around his apartment ass naked with a green army helmet on his head. He's carrying an eight-inch army dagger in his hand. He hasn't taken his medicine in days, and it's affecting him terribly. Besides the visions of his traumatizing past, his paranoia is at an all-time high.

He has both doors barricaded with sofas and coffee tables. He has nailed the windows shut and tacked blankets against them so no one can see inside.

He stands at the back window, peeking through a small slit in the blanket. He grips his dagger tightly in the palm of his hand. His heart is racing and his mind is replaying scenes of the war.

The sound of his doorbell ringing startles him. He kneels down to the floor, trying to make as little noise as possible. He lies onto his stomach, and inches forward by slowly crawling. He still grips his dagger in his right hand. The sound of bombs bursting and loud explosions sound off in his head. His mind tells him he's fighting a war. The only war that he's fighting is the war against his sanity.

The doorbell rings again, just as he makes his way to the door. He pulls himself up by scaling the wall. He presses his nose against the crack in the door and takes a number of sniffs like a frisky puppy. After his sniffing session, he leans his head over with his ear close to the door, listening closely.

The bell rings once again. He squints his eye through the peephole. He feels safe to see it's not a member of the other army invading. The visitor is his female acquaintance. Something tells him to hold up. Maybe they have captured her, and now they're using her to get inside. He debates back and forth before deciding to open the door for her.

He grabs hold of the sofa and snatches it aggressively. He starts unlocking the doors, starting with the slide lock on the very top of the door. In total, he has seven locks on the door. After unlocking the middle lock, he grabs hold of the two-by-four that extends across the door. Two silver posts hold in it place. The last lock is slide-bolted into the floor. He lifts it up using his bare foot. Finally, he snatches the door open. "Hurry up," he whispers. "They're on their way," he adds.

"Listen, if you gone start that crazy shit, I'm out of here!" she shouts.

"Shhh," he says.

"Shhh, my ass! That's why I don't like fucking with you," she says while climbing over the arm of the chair.

Cal slams the door behind her and locks all of his many locks.

The woman looks terrible. It's amazing how her skeletal frame can carry her enormous head. Her Aunt Jemima scarf covers her entire head except for the row of naps that are on the back of her neck. Her eyes are blood-shot and her lips are extremely chapped. You can barely see her high yellow complexion due to the many dark scabs that blanket her face.

She kicks off her filthy sneakers. She then removes her raggedy, oversized flannel jacket and her fuzzy cotton sweatpants, revealing her nudeness. Her worn out body is an awful sight.

She holds ten vials of crack in her hand. Cal grabs his pipe from the nightstand. He places the pebble into the top of the pipe, lights it, and takes a huge blast. The woman sits to the right of him. Her eyes show greed as she stares at the glass. Cal takes pull after pull without even thinking of offering her a hit.

If Sha-Rock could see him now? Cal told him he stopped getting high. It was all a lie.

The woman fears that Cal will smoke it all by himself. She realizes that she has to do something to persuade her to give him a hit. She desperately falls to her knees. She leans her head over his leg. She buries her face into his lap, and goes to work. She sucks away as Cal kisses the glass. He's so busy blasting that he's paying no attention to her. She sucks harder and harder until she finally gets his attention. He snatches her head away and tilts her head back. He takes a huge pull without exhaling. He leans over as if he's about to kiss her. She eagerly waits with her mouth stretched wide open. He slowly exhales, blowing the smoke in her face. She absorbs all the smoke as she inhales anxiously.

He finally passes the pipe over to her. He crawls behind her as she's smoking. In a doggy style position, he rams himself into her violently. The crack and his lack of medicine changes him into a madman.

He hunches over and grabs her tightly, like a dog in heat. He's damn near squeezing the life out of her and she doesn't even realize it. The only thing on her mind is smoking all the crack she can before he decides to take the pipe from her. He pounds on her furiously.

Finally, the pipe is empty. She slyly reaches over and attempts to get another vial without him knowing. Cal realizes what she's trying to do. He reaches over and snatches the vials off of the bed. He digs deeper inside her. She screams loudly. Her scream is not a scream of pleasure. It sounds more like fear and agony. "Please stop," she begs. The louder she screams the harder he pounds. His deranged mind tells him she loves the pain. She screams louder. He covers her mouth with his huge hands. She tries to squirm away from him but he has her in a tight hold.

Talk about rough sex.

Days Later/October 18, 2004

It's 5 A.M. Sha-Rock, Bree and Killer Cal wait patiently in Bree's little raggedy hooptie Chevrolet. They've been posted up for about twenty minutes already.

They're sitting in front of Kia's house, waiting for Kia's boyfriend to come out. Bree talked her into helping them out. He explained to her how it could benefit the both of them. She was so mad at the guy that she didn't hesitate to tell Bree everything he needed to know.

He came up from North Carolina at about 11 P.M. last night. He came straight to Kia's house before he could get a chance to stash his earnings. Kia called Bree and told him that her dude would be leaving by 6 A.M. because he had business to handle. She also stated that he makes all his transactions before the sun comes up.

They all sit quietly as they impatiently wait for the door to open. All of them are entertaining their own private thoughts.

Bree can't believe that Kia would be down for something as grimey as this. How could she set someone up who has taken care of her for so many years? Temporary love is what it's called. She doesn't really love him. She loves what he does for her. Dealing with females like Kia helps him stay on point. In his life, he has seen some of the best dudes get jammed up behind a girl. They cheat with a dude, not knowing who he is or what he's about. They're so busy being sneaky that they end up telling all the dude's business without even knowing it. The man with the biggest dick wins, he laughs to himself. He beats the coochie up crazy, and she tells him whatever he needs to know. With females like Kia around, it's hard for him to trust a woman. Whatever happens to this guy is his own fault. This foolish mistake is about to cost him a lot of change. The biggest mistake he ever made was letting Kia know his every move.

Sha-Rock is here in the physical form, but his mind is on the First Lady. She's literally driving him crazy. He hasn't found out anything solid about her yet. He's been on her a few weeks already and he has learned very little about her personal life and nothing at all about her hustle. It's really beginning to frustrate him. He knows he has to control his temper. He can't let his frustration make him do something stupid and blow the whole operation. He has to find out where she stashes the dope. He's sure patience is the key, but he's already used what little patience he had.

Approximately one hundred thoughts per minute are racing through Killer Cal's head. Will the church say amen, a voice says inside his head. We are gathered here today to pay our respects to the Collins family, says the preacher. "Mommy!" Cal blurts out unexpected.

Bree and Sha-Rock look at Cal simultaneously, while Cal sits there as if he doesn't have a clue of why they're looking at him.

"What did you just say?" Sha-Rock asks.

"Huh?" Cal replies.

"What did you say?" he repeats.

"I didn't say anything," he claims.

"Cal, you said something. I heard you," says Sha-Rock.

"Baby Boy, I didn't say anything. You must be going crazy."

"Well, we both must be going crazy 'cause I heard you, too," Bree adds.

Cal gives at Bree with the dirtiest look without replying. Bree's smile turns into a cheesy smirk. He gets the feeling that Cal is not too fond of him anyway. It's nothing personal though, that's just how Cal is. He's very antisocial. He doesn't speak around people until he feels comfortable around them.

"Yo, that's him," says Bree, successfully breaking the tension. The tall stocky kid walks down the stairs. His lazy walk shows sign of fatigue. He's wearing a black leather Pelle Pelle jacket, with a New York Yankees fitted cap on his head. He holds a shopping bag with a sneaker box in his hand. He may have others fooled, but Bree knows exactly what's in the box.

The guy continuously rubs the sleep from his eyes as he makes his way to his car. Little does he know, they're parked directly behind his bright red Dodge Magnum. He has it hooked up beautifully with dark tinted windows, chrome rims and chrome pipes.

"Y'all ready?" Sha-Rock asks.

"Yep," Bree replies. Cal doesn't say a word. He responds by flicking the lever of the safety and loading one bullet into the chamber.

"As soon as the dude grabs hold of his door, we're on him," says Sha-Rock.

142

The dude is now two cars away from his car. He glances around as he approaches his car. His eyes pass over their car. He sees someone's reflection. His neck snaps back as he double takes. He stops dead in his tracks and squints to see who's in the car.

"I think he sees us," says Sha-Rock. "Don't move," he whispers.

It's obvious that he does see them. He slowly backpedals away from his car. After about four steps, he turns around and goes into flight.

"Get him!" Sha-Rock shouts. Bree and Cal rush out of the car with their guns aimed to the sky. The dude has a huge lead on them. He's trying to make it back to the house. He's about two houses away from Kia's house. There's no way they'll be able to catch him.

Bree aims at his back and squeezes the trigger of his .40 caliber twice. He's unsuccessful. The shots make him run even faster. Now he's one house away. Bree squeezes five more times recklessly. Once again he hits nothing.

Cal stops running. The dude is halfway up the steps of the house. Cal inhales and holds his breath before aiming his 9 millimeter at the porch. A red dot appears on the side of the dude's face. Cal squeezes. Bingo. The dude tumbles down the stairs backwards. Once he hits the bottom step, he falls flat onto his back. He's lying slightly upside down. His feet are on the steps, but his head rests on the concrete.

The red dot reappears. This time it shines on his bald head. Cal fires two more times. His head jolts as his skull absorbs the shots.

Totally in shock, Bree runs over to him. Blood is everywhere. He grabs hold of the sneaker box, which is lying next to the lifeless body.

Sha-Rock pulls up, and Cal jumps in the car. Bree follows seconds later. They peel off recklessly, leaving the corpse twisted on the pavement.

Bree snaps back into reality and realizes they've just made a big mistake. "Damn!" he shouts. "You killed the motherfucker! Man, we're going to jail!"

"Yo Baby Boy, the nigga was getting away with that scrilla!" Sha-Rock says defending Cal.

"Man, I could have caught him. Anyway, he could have hit him in the body. You saw the beam. He aimed at the head from the rip! Damn! I hope that bitch don't tell!"

Cal sits in the backseat nonchalantly. He has no remorse for what he's just done. His mind is somewhere else. He smiles to himself as he stands over his sexual abuser. The hammer drops and blood gushes everywhere.

Bree's phone rings. He looks at the display. It's Kia. What the hell am I going to tell her, he asks himself. He lets the phone ring with no intention of answering it. Murder was not a part of Bree's plan. He thought they could get the money and bounce without anyone getting hurt. What he didn't know is every robbery Cal was ever a part of resulted in a homicide.

One Hour Later

Sha-Rock and Bree ride in Bree's hooptie, while Cal follows closely in Sha-Rock's van. They pull into Checker's parking lot on Central Avenue in East Orange. They've already counted the money. In total, they counted $50,000.

"Yo kid, I hope that broad don't flip," says Bree. "I didn't really plan on mirking the nigga. If that was the case, I wouldn't have gotten her involved. I gotta go over there and prep her to make sure she knows what to say when the cops start questioning her like crazy."

"I hope she's a trooper," Sha-Rock says.

Bree takes several stacks of money out of the sneaker box and hands the box over to Sha-Rock. "How much is this?" Sha-Rock questions.

"Twenty cent," Bree replies confidently.

"Twenty cent? What about my man?"

"Five of that is his," Bree replies.

"Ho, ho, ho," says Sha-Rock with an agitated look on his face. "Hold up. Let me get this straight. A $50,000 sting, you keep thirty and break me off twenty, and five of that is for my man? My man just murdered this dude and all you gone give him is five punk ass thousand?" Sha-Rock raises his voice. "Fam, I ain't even trying to hear that shit! That's my dude. I can't let nobody play him like that. Hell no!" he shouts. His voice is filled with anger.

"Listen kid, I have to break Shorty off with at least fifteen," Bree claims. "That's the only way I'll be able to get her to keep her mouth shut," he explains.

"Yo, give that bitch $10,000 and send her on her way!" Sha-Rock shouts. "Give the extra five to my man. You can't keep shitting on him like that. He's an asset. He put in work. You saw him. If it wasn't for him, we wouldn't have scored shit. In all due respect, he should be getting more than us, but if you break him off ten cent, I'm sure he'll be happy with that."

Bree shakes his head in disgust. He really hates to have to give Cal more money. Especially being that he didn't want Cal to come along anyway. "Alright, that's what it is then! I hope ten is enough for shorty. If not, I'll just have to give her $5,000 out of my money," he claims.

Well that's what you'll have to do then, Sha-Rock thinks to himself. Silence fills the air.

"Alright, later Fam!" Sha- Rock shouts. "I'll hit you later. Make sure you get shorty to keep her mouth shut, no matter what. This can get real ugly."

"I know," Bree agrees, as Sha-Rock exits the car.

Sha-Rock jumps in his van and proceeds onto Route 280. He's headed home. He promised Miranda that he would be home early. Tomorrow marks their six year anniversary. Even though he would love to finalize the deal with the First Lady, he knows how much tomorrow means to Miranda. He has a very special surprise for her.

The Next Day

Bree just arrived at Shop Rite on Route 22 in Hillside about ten minutes ago. Now Kia is cruising through the entrance in her pearl white Lexus SC430. It was all Bree's idea for them to meet here. Kia begged him to come to her house. She claims that she's so distraught that she can't drive. Bree refused to go to her house on the count of him not being sure if she's trying to set him up or not.

She parks parallel to his car and gestures for him to get into her car. He quickly denies the offer and gestures for her to get in with him. He has to be prepared just in case the police try and box him in. He made sure that no cars were parked in front of him. He has a clear path straight to Route 22. He promises that he'll take them on the chase of a lifetime. He hasn't put the gear into park. He's sitting there with the car still in drive, with his foot on the brake.

Kia struggles to climb out of the low-seated vehicle. She finally gets out, stomach first. She looks a mess. Bree has never seen her look this bad. She's wearing a baseball fitted cap on top of her wild hair. Her eyes are swollen shut from crying, and dried-up tears stain her face. She's wearing a denim jacket over top of her silk maternity dress. She drags her slippers lazily while rubbing her stomach all the way to Bree's car.

He reaches over to open the door for her. She slowly drops herself into the seat. Bree is clueless as to what he should say to her. He just looks straight ahead as he bounces to imaginary music. He slowly pulls off and exits the parking lot, paying close attention to his rearview mirror. He's trying to see if she brought the police to him.

"Why?" she blurts out. "Why? Bree, I thought you were only going to rob him. I didn't know you were going to kill him," she whispers. "Why?" she repeats.

"Kia, it wasn't supposed to go like that. I swear that was not my intentions. He reached for his gun," Bree lies. "What was I supposed to do?" he questions. "We were just going to rob him, like I told you."

"But now he's dead," she cries. "What the fuck am I going to do?" she asks. "You killed my baby's father. She'll never know her father, all because of you!"

"Because of me? You the one who said you wish he was dead! He was shitting on you, anyway. Fuck him," Bree says, trying to get her back on his side. He's hoping his little mind trick works on her.

"I didn't really want him dead," she admits. "I was just mad at him at the time," she explains. "He treated me good. I was just being greedy. How could I do this to him?" she cries.

Bree doesn't like the sound of this. "Kia listen, the man is dead, and we can't bring him back. I'm sorry. I told you it wasn't supposed to go down like that but it did. Me or you can't change that. Now we have to worry about our next step. Dig this, the police are going to take you down for questioning."

"They already did," she shouts while crying.

Bree's heart races. Uh oh, he thinks to himself. "Oh yeah? What happened?"

"They questioned me for almost three hours."

"What did you tell them?"

"I told them, I don't know nothing. I was sleep when he left."

"Then what," Bree asks with a nervous look on his face.

"They kept asking me the same questions over and over."

"Kia listen, you have to stick to that story. If you don't, me and you are going to jail," he threatens. He realizes he has to reassure her that she's in this situation along with him. Then she'll think twice about telling.

"Aghh!" she screams. "I didn't kill him, you did!"

He ignores her outburst. "Kia, we're in this together. Our destiny is in your hands. If you break under pressure we're going to jail forever. If you stick to your story, we're good. You hear me?"

She nods her head up and down. "I don't know what to do," she cries. "His family is threatening me. His sisters came to my house trying to fight me."

"Fight you for what?"

"They think I set him up. They never liked me anyway 'cause me and the oldest sister used to mess with the same boy back in the day," she explains.

"Kia, don't worry about it. I got you," he reassures her. "I just need a little information on dude. Does he have any brothers?"

"No, but he has a lot of cousins."

"Do you know where they're from?" Bree has to know who he needs to be on the lookout for.

"They're from all over. It's a lot of them. They have a big family. I'm scared they're going to do something to me," she cries.

"Kia, I swear, you don't have nothing to worry about. Just remember, you have to stick to the script. I'll handle the rest, alright?"

"Alright," she whispers.

"Here goes $10,000 for you. Do you have anywhere you can stay besides your house? A sister, your mother, anybody?" he asks.

"No," she replies. "My family ain't from up here. Only me and my brother are here, and he's locked up."

"Damn. Don't worry, though. I'll make sure that you're alright," Bree claims.

"Can I stay with you?" she asks desperately. "I'm scared."

He hesitates before speaking. What can I tell her, he asks himself. "Ain't no room at my spot. You know I live with my sister and her kids," he lies. Bree doesn't even have a sister. He lives with his girlfriend. "Just calm down. It will be alright." Hopefully, he thinks to himself. "I promise," he says to comfort her.

Meanwhile in Philadelphia

Miranda and Sha-Rock walk into their apartment. Sha-Rock leads her inside. He has her blindfolded. The aroma of food and freshly baked pastry greets her at the door. The heat from the oven is blazing.

"Here, sit right here," he insists, as he guides her to the chair of the kitchen table.

"It smells so good in here," says Miranda. "Where are we?" she asks without the slightest clue. "Can I take the blindfold off, yet?"

"No, not yet. Wait a minute. I'll be right back." Sha-Rock runs into the living room and turns on the DVD player. The Dolby surround system plays so clear. The sound of "Anniversary" by Toni, Tony, Tone rips through the speakers as Sha-Rock races back into the kitchen. "Let me take that off for you," he says as he slowly unties the blindfold.

Miranda is in total shock. She had no clue that she was in her own home. The lights are dim. The table is decorated beautifully. She has to gasp for air. She thinks her eyes are deceiving her when she sees an obese white man standing in the doorway wearing a chef's hat as a waiter dressed in a tuxedo walks toward her holding a bottle of red wine and two glasses.

Sha-Rock hugs Miranda tightly. "Baby, I love you," he whispers in her ear, as he fumbles inside his pocket. In his hand he holds a tiny velvet box. He hands it to Miranda. Tears fill her eyes at the very thought of it. This can't be happening, she thinks to herself. "Open it," he demands. The anxiety is killing her. Her hands are trembling so much that she can't get the box open. Finally she gets it open, and there sits the most beautiful engagement ring she has ever seen. The huge stone has to be at least seven karats. It sits on a beautiful platinum baguette-filled setting. Tears blur her vision. This is the happiest day of her life. "Do you like it?" he asks.

"Like it? I love it!" she cries. She can barely look him in the eyes on account of her blushing. He places the ring on her finger. He drops down to one knee. She can no longer fight the tears. Huge droplets fall from her eyes. She looks away from him bashfully. "Miranda Benderas, will you marry me?" he asks.

She can't find the words to answer him. She just nods her head.

"I take that as a yes," he replies.

The waiter and the chef applaud loudly in the background. Sha-Rock leads her to the middle of the floor. He pulls her close to him, and they slow dance to the music. Miranda lays her head on his chest, just savoring the moment.

After twenty minutes of dancing, the waiter pours the wine. "Congratulations, you two. You make a perfect couple," he adds.

While they're drinking the wine, the food is being served. The food looks delicious. Miranda loves Italian food. The waiter brings out all types of Italian dishes including chicken parmesan, baked ziti, spaghetti, lasagna, fettuccini and shrimp alfredo. She doesn't know where to start. She gets a tummy ache just looking at all the food.

After serving their meal, the chef and the waiter stand off to the side. "Anything else, Sir?" the chef asks.

"You can just line the deserts on the counter, and that's about it," Sha-Rock instructs.

The chef and the waiter do as they're told, and Sha-Rock escorts them to the door. Sha-Rock passes the chef an envelope before sending him away. He found the chef in the yellow pages. The chef charged him $1,200, but he tipped them another $300 for the lovely service. The look on Miranda's face is well worth it. She'll never forget this anniversary.

After finishing up the last of her meal, Miranda prepares for desert. Feeling slightly groovy from the several glasses of wine she consumed, she wiggles out of her skirt and panties while still in a seated position. She then reaches over and snatches his pants down to his ankles. She staggers over to him and straddles herself over his lap. Her naked kitty presses against his firm cannon. The smooth silk from his boxers separates their flesh and teases the both of them. She begins grinding, in a slow winding motion. During all the movement, Sha-Rock's eleven-inch Louisville Slugger manages to peek through the slit in his boxers. She positions herself and inhales as she prepares for his entrance. He rips through her tight opening. She continues to hold her breath as he fills her insides. He pinches her nipples to increase her excitement. She moans loud and hard as he grabs her by her waist and slides her up and down on him. She sighs after each landing. She can't get used to the pain. It gets more and more painful as they go along, but she loves it. While she bounces up and down, he reaches over the table and grabs the bottle of wine. He holds it up to her mouth as she gulps away. The wine drips down her chin. Before the drop can drip onto her blouse, he catches them with his tongue. He then pulls her blouse over her head. He's greeted by her stiffened nipples. He slowly pours little drops of wine over her shoulder blades. As it leaks down her chest, he begins to lick her like a lollipop. She's so excited now. She starts to buck like a wild horse, losing all respect for his massive penis, which is banging against her walls painfully. He stands up on his feet while still inside of her. She wraps her legs around him tighter, making sure she keeps all of him inside without losing one inch. Her head is laying on his shoulder as she squeezes his neck, damn near choking him. He walks over to the counter, where he sits her on the edge. He teases her by pumping slowly with long deep strokes. The more he teases, the more she wants. Goosebumps cover her beautiful body. She tightens her legs around his waist and throws it back at him. She trembles as if she's about to come. He suddenly snatches himself out of her. "Aghh," she sighs.

He just fucked up her flow. With one sweeping motion of his left hand, he reaches up to the refrigerator and knocks down all the items that occupy the top of the refrigerator. He grabs her by the armpits and places her on top of the refrigerator. He grabs her by her tiny waist and positions her so she's sitting on the edge. Her mid-section is exactly at his eye level. He grabs hold of her tiny size five foot, lifts it to his mouth, and plants soft kisses from her insole up her thigh. He then places her left leg over his right shoulder and her right leg over his left shoulder. He spreads her legs as wide as he can, and enjoys the view of her love tunnel. Her swollen clit pulsates. He reaches over to his right and digs his hand into the scrumptious looking freshly baked chocolate cake. He scoops a huge sloppy handful and slaps it in between her legs. Dripping hot chocolate covers her kitty. He goes in for the attack. He uses his tongue to find his way to her sweet opening. After a few tongue lashes, he locates the man in the boat. He tugs at it gently with his teeth, before jamming his tongue deep inside her. She props her head against the cupboard. Her body is lifeless. He's taken her to ecstasy. An uncontrollable trembling takes over her body. She tightens her legs around his neck as she force-feeds him, damn near suffocating him. Suddenly, the trembling stops, and she slowly unlocks her legs from around his neck, allowing him to breathe again. She leans forward and licks the cake from his face, before giving him the sloppiest, wettest kiss they have ever shared. The chocolate cake and the sweet taste of her love juice drives her insane. He grabs her by the armpits once again and pulls her down from the refrigerator. While her legs dangle in the air, he zooms in for seconds. She can't control herself. All the blood in her entire body rushes to her legs. She wants to lean back to allow easier access, but she fears falling out of his arms. He slowly stands her to her feet. As soon as she lands, she drops to her knees in a submissive position and returns the favor. She starts off by planting soft kisses all over his shaft, before wrapping her tulip shaped lips around it. The warmth of her wet mouth feels so good to him that he can't take it. The pleasure is just too much. He tries to back away from her, but she has a super grip on his shaft. The faster he backs away from her, the faster she crawls toward him. He backpedals through the hallway, as her lips remain glued to him. He fumbles for the banister and sits on the bottom step. He climbs up the stairs one by one in a seated position. When he finally reaches the landing at the top, he stands up and continues to backpedal away from her. While on all fours, she continues to please him with her mouth. He finally approaches their bedroom. His sac tingles as the tension quickly builds up. As he bumps into the bedpost, he grabs hold of her hair. He tugs away as he unloads. "Aghh!" he sighs as he collapses on the bed. As soon as his head touches the pillow, he falls sound asleep.

　　Miranda makes her way into the bathroom. Minutes later, she re-enters the bedroom with a bucket of hot water and a washcloth, and a bar of Irish Spring soap. She wets him down before gently sliding the bar of soap across his body. Soapsuds cover his body entirely. She then washes him like a newborn baby as he snores away.

Kia sits in her living room holding her only portrait of her baby's father. She's holding it against her chest while crying hysterically. She's been calling Bree all day, but he barely answers her calls. When he does answer, he constantly instills in her the importance of sticking to her story. He makes sure that she's aware that they're in it together. He hopes that will make her less likely to tell.

Her phone rings. She sure hopes it's Bree. "Hello?" she answers desperately.

"Yeah, bitch," the caller whispers.

"Who is this?" Kia asks.

"This is Samirah, Jay's sister, bitch!" the caller shouts. "Don't think it's over, bitch. I know your trifling ass had something to do with my brother's death! I hope you know you're going to get yours? I'm telling you, don't bring your trifling ass to the funeral, either! If you do, they gone be burying your ass next!"

"Listen Samirah, I didn't have nothing to do with that," she lies. "I wouldn't do no shit like that. I love him. I'm pregnant with his baby," she cries.

"Not for long, bitch. I'll see to that. Even if I have to cut the little motherfucker out of your stomach, my damn self. You gone get yours! Mark my words. Somebody is coming for you, and your baby!" she shouts before Kia slams the phone down.

"Why?" Kia screams. How could she let Bree talk her into that? She lays on her bed and cries herself to sleep.

Two hours later, her doorbell awakens her. She's scared to death. She thinks it's Jay's sisters coming for her. She's not going to answer it. She's afraid to move, on the count of someone might see her shadow moving around and decide to kick her door in or come through her window. She has to answer it. Maybe it's Bree. She really needs his comfort right now.

She reaches underneath her bed, and grasps hold of her steak knife. She walks to the window and peeks out. She's surprised to see three white detectives standing on her porch. They spot her peeking through the curtain.

The first detective taps on the window. "Kia, please open the door," he begs. "We need to speak with you, again."

She's not happy to see them at all. She's not sure who is worse as a visitor, the detectives or Jay's sisters? She hesitantly walks to the door, without even realizing, she's still carrying her knife.

"Ma'am, we need you to come with us? You won't need that knife either. Please hand it to me?"

She hands it over without hesitation. "Where are we going?" she asks in a frightened tone.

"To the precinct. We need to talk."

"We already talked," Kia replies. "Why can't we talk right here?"

"Ma'am, please lock your doors so we can leave. We'll explain everything when we get to the station."

Kia is full of fear. A bunch of questions formulate in her head. Is she going to jail? Do they know that she set Jay up? Why can't they discuss whatever it is that needs to be discussed, right here?

-29-

━━━━━◆◆◆━━━━━

Two Days Later

Hollyhood lays stretched out in the middle of his living room floor. His ankles are tied together, and so are his wrists. Thick, gray duct tape seals his mouth shut.

Killer Cal sits approximately ten feet away from him, while Sha-Rock and Miranda literally tear the apartment up, looking for money and drugs. So far they've found $9,000 and twenty-five bricks of heroin in his safe. They've been inside for over an hour already. All of them are getting frustrated with him.

Sha-Rock runs over to Hollyhood and stomps him out for the tenth time. Hollyhood is in so much fear that he doesn't feel the pain. Something told him to hook up with his man. Him and his man were to supposed to hook up with two girls from D.C., but after Miranda called and told him she was dying to see him, he cancelled his plans. As he walked out of his apartment to go meet her at the parkway exit, he was shocked to find out that she was already at the door, along with Sha-Rock and Killer Cal. They caught him slipping dead to the rear. Not in a million years did he suspect this.

Sha-Rock kneels down and snatches the tape from his mouth. "Listen you dumb fuck, where is the rest of the fucking money? This is my last time asking you. Next time, I'll blast you!"

"I swear to God, that's it," he cries. "I swear, that's all I got!"

"What the fuck do you mean, that's all you got?" Sha-Rock questions.

"I swear. You have to believe me. If I had more, I would have been gave it to you. I swear. Please don't kill me," he begs. "You already got everything!"

"This can't be everything. You got more somewhere," Sha-Rock insists. "Yo Cal, niggas say this nigga is a millionaire."

"Man, that's just talk, man. People always talking. I swear you got everything."

"That's it, Cal. I tried, and he ain't cooperating, do you."

"Now?" Cal asks.

"Yeah, now."

"No, please, no! I swear on my mother's life, that's it. Ain't no money nowhere else! That's it," he cries.

"So, you're trying to tell me that's all you're working with?" Sha-Rock asks.

"That's it man."

"I ain't going with that. You running around here like you a Don, and you telling me, that's it?" Sha-Rock questions.

"Man, I swear! My man just fronted me fifty bricks two days ago. I sold thirty of them, and I have twenty left. I ain't lying to you."

"Your man fronted you fifty bricks?" Sha-Rock is heated. "So basically, your fronting ass wasted our time for fifty punk ass bricks?" Sha-Rock strikes him with the pistol across his face. Hollyhood screams like a baby. "You fronting ass niggar. You wasted my fucking time," he shouts as he beats blood out of Hollyhood's face. "You running around here like you rich! You broke motherfucker." Sha-Rock is furious. He's so angry that he doesn't realize that Hollyhood is knocked out cold. The last blow just woke him. "Yo, I think this nigga lying. My man told me he's holding."

"Hold up. I can make him talk," says Cal.

Sha-Rock stands up and kicks him in the head one final time. "Fucking fronting as nigga!" he shouts as he backs away, turning him over to Cal.

Cal bends over and wraps his hands around Hollyhood's neck. Cal's appearance alone is enough to scare the life out of someone. Hollyhood can barely look at Cal, with his pale white skin and dirty gold dreads. His heart pounds as he looks into Cal's wicked looking eyes. He's never seen anyone more demonic looking than Cal.

Cal tightens his grip as he snatches Hollyhood to his feet. He's gasping for air. Cal's grip is stopping his oxygen. Hollyhood's temples are throbbing. A huge pulsating vein protrudes through the center of his forehead. Cal is as strong as an ox. He has Hollyhood in the air, about two feet away from the floor. He's fading in and out. "Listen bitch, this is your final chance. Where's the fucking money?" Cal snarls.

Hollyhood is no longer gasping. He's run out of oxygen. He continuously fades in and out.

"Hold up," says Miranda as she enters the room. "Y'all doing all that for nothing. Look what I found in his drawer," she says while holding a small booklet in the air.

Cal loosens his grip, allowing Hollyhood to intake a little air.

"What the fuck is that?" Sha-Rock asks.

"His payment book for his car," she replies. "It's leased!" she shouts.

"Leased?" Sha-Rock repeats. "He got motherfuckers thinking his shit paid for! I don't believe this shit. A fucking waste of time, fucking with this fake ass baller nigga!"

Hollyhood stands there with a blank look on his face. He never knew his lying and exaggerating would ever get him into a situation like this. "Please," he manages to beg. "Please?"

"Miranda, go start the van up," Sha-Rock instructs. "Back up right in front of the door."

Miranda knows this is her cue to leave. She would hate to witness this bloody mess. She hurries out of the apartment.

Sha-Rock dumps Hollyhood's Rolex and jewelry in the shopping bag with the money and dope. "Cal, game over! Put the lights out," Sha-Rock whispers.

"No!" Hollyhood screams.

While his mouth is stretched wide open, Cal jams his gun deep inside. Hollyhood pukes a little vomit as the nose of the gun presses against his tonsils. Boom! The shot roars. Hollyhood slides down the wall. Red and black matter stains the wall in the exact same spot where his head was. It's evident that Killer Cal blew his brains out of his head. Cal uses the tip of the gun to scrape the matter from the wall. Residue sticks to the gun. He raises the gun close to his face and examines it. "I wonder what the fuck was on his mind?" Cal asks sarcastically.

They run out of the apartment, leaving Hollyhood dead, lying in a pool of blood.

-30-

The Next Morning

Sha-Rock and Cal are waiting patiently in front of the house where the First Lady's brother lives. Last night after their unsuccessful robbery, Sha-Rock drove Miranda back to Philly, and him and Cal came back up north. They have a lot of work to do.

Today Sha-Rock is determined to find something out. They've been parked out here for one hour already. Sha-Rock sits behind the wheel. He can't believe how much of a waste of time Hollyhood was. He had the entire town believing he was a millionaire, and he wasn't even holding onto five figures. It was all an illusion. Sha-Rock gave the dope to Jimmy to sell for him. Jimmy let a few junkies test it and found out that the dope is garbage. To make matters worse? Jimmy couldn't believe it when Sha-Rock gave him all the details. He's been bragging to the women in this town for years now. They would be so upset to find out that they've taken all his abuse and slick remarks for nothing. In all reality, he was just as broke as they were. Sha-Rock feels like an asshole. He should have known better. Sha-Rock has come across some real millionaires in his lifetime, and none of them ever broadcast it. You would never know it. It never fails. The one who runs around bragging about everything he's doing is usually doing nothing but talking. Sha-Rock is sure the First Lady isn't a hoax. This sting should make up for the loss of time and effort they put into Hollyhood.

Sha-Rock has it narrowed down. This is the only house that the First Lady visits everyday faithfully. He assumes that there has to be something in there. Right now he's good and frustrated. Hopefully today he'll get some kind of clarity on the matter.

Killer Cal sits there with his eyes closed. He laughs to himself as he envisions himself in heaven. Him, his mother, father, and all of his siblings are flying around like one big happy family. His mother stops to talk to Hollyhood. Hollyhood's head is huge. His brains hang from the hole in the back of his head. Cal flies extra fast to catch up with his mother. It's a trick, he yells to his mother. Hollyhood is trying to get even with him by killing his mother. Her and Hollyhood fly away from him quickly. Cal is flying as fast as he possibly can, but he can't seem to catch up with them. They're flying away into the soft white clouds. Hollyhood falls behind slightly. He looks back at Cal and sports a devilish smile. He then pulls a bazooka from underneath his long white gown. "No!" Cal shouts aloud.

Sha-Rock looks over at him, with a shocked look on his face. "Now tell me I didn't hear that either?" he asks sarcastically. "What the fuck is wrong with you?" He knows exactly what's wrong with him, but he doesn't have a clue to what degree it has gone. "Have you been taking your medicine?"

"Yeah," he lies.

Sha-Rock looks at him with a look of disbelief on his face. He doesn't know that Killer Cal is an official nut case.

"Why do you ask that?" Cal asks innocently.

"Never mind," Sha-Rock brushes him off. For once Cal is starting to make him nervous. As much as he hates to believe it, his man is sick.

The two little girls come running down the alleyway playfully. "Here we go," says Sha-Rock. The man steps out looking sharp as a tack. He's wearing a beige pinstriped suit with a bright yellow tie. He dumps his briefcase into the trunk of his white four door Mercedes as the girls jump in the backseat and strap their seatbelts.

He backs out of the alleyway and drives into the sunset. Sha-Rock has him clocked. He should be pulling in front of their school in about twenty minutes. It then takes him another twenty minutes to make it to his job from there.

Sha-Rock lets ten minutes pass just in case he may have forgotten something and decides to come back to the house for it.

Sha-Rock busts a K-turn in the middle of the street. He parks the van directly in front of the house. He and Cal jump out and walk to the back of the van where they put on hard hats and strap their work belts around their waists. To the naked eye, they appear to be some type of repair and installation men.

They step quickly up the alleyway. Cal picks the locks open as Sha-Rock watches his back. It takes Cal only a matter of seconds to get in.

After shutting the door, they immediately start their hunt. The first room they enter is the kitchen. It's spotless. It hardly looks like a kitchen that belongs to a bachelor. "Make it quick, Cal. You hit the kitchen. I got the living room!" They begin tearing everything apart, being very observant so that they won't miss any small details. They're flipping appliances over and emptying cupboards. They're even going through the garbage.

It takes them about twenty minutes to search almost every room. They even searched the kids' room. They saved the best for last. They attack the master bedroom together.

Cal starts his search in the closet as Sha-Rock flips the mattress over. He then pulls every drawer from the dresser, dumping all the contents on the floor. One particular drawer catches his attention. The drawer contains several photos of the dude, the First Lady, and the girls in family portraits. Other photos are of them vacationing in amusement parks, like Disney World. Another photo is of the dude and First Lady kissing. This can't be her brother, Sha-Rock thinks to himself. He's confused. How can this be her boyfriend? They don't even live together, and she never stays here overnight. Sha-Rock thumbs through the photos. One particular one absolutely takes his breath away. The First Lady is lying across the bed of this room, stark naked with her fingers jammed into her pussy. The next picture is a close-up view of her bent over from the back. Both of her holes nearly jump out of the picture, like they're in 3D. What a freak, he thinks to himself. A third picture has her standing straight up, with her back facing the camera. Sha-Rock has to admit, her body is beautiful. Her wide ass stretches across the picture from border to border. His eyes are glued to the photo. She's very photogenic. She looks into the camera seductively. Her eyes say, "Fuck Me." He stuffs the photos into his pocket.

Next he comes across the deeds to two houses. One is the one they're in and the other is the house the First Lady lives in. He also finds the bill of sales to all three Mercedes. The First Lady is not fronting. The proof is right here. Her houses are paid for and so are the cars. Hollyhood could have taken a few lessons from her. He also finds the spare keys to all three cars and another key ring that holds several other keys. Bingo, he thinks to himself.

Ten minutes later, it's over. They've found neither drugs nor money. Not even an emergency stack.

Sha-Rock stares at the keys that he holds in the palm of his hand.

Hopefully these are the keys to paradise, he thinks to himself.

Sha-Rock and Cal grab hold of a few small appliances on their way out, just to make it look like an official break-in.

Two Weeks Later/ November 6

Things have been very quiet. Miranda has been in Philly with Tamara for the past few days. A couple of days ago, she took Hollyhood's watch and jewelry to a little pawn shop not too far away from their home. She was surprised to find out that even his jewelry was a fraud. His Rolex turned out to be nothing but a good replica, and his jewelry was made up of cubic zirconium. Hollyhood really had everyone fooled. Talk about perpetrating.

Killer Cal has been almost sane for the past couple of days. Sha-Rock was so worried about him that he decided to keep him with him for a few days, just to keep a close eye on him. He's been making sure that Cal takes his medicine as prescribed by the doctor. He hasn't been talking to himself or making any sudden outbursts.

Sha-Rock has switched his attention from the First Lady to her good friend. He thinks that maybe her friend makes all the moves for her. He's been following her closely.

Bree has his work cut out for him. Kia has been driving him crazy. He can sense that she's getting weak. He fears that she may crack and flip on him. She's under so much stress.

The funeral services were held last week. The kid's sister has been at Kia's house damn near every night harassing her. She has vandalized Kia's car and busted out her house windows. Even worse than that, the police come to her house every other day questioning her. She tells Bree that she's sticking to her story, but it's hard for him to believe her. She's not built for this type of pressure. This is their job. They're trained to force the truth out of professional criminals. They're putting her under too much pressure. He doesn't know how long she'll be able to withstand it. Just the other day, Bree had to rush her to the hospital. She almost had a miscarriage. The doctor kept her in the hospital for three days before releasing her. The time away from home probably did her some good. At least she could rest without worrying about Jay's family coming in there to kill her. Bree is on his way over to pay her a visit, to make sure she's alright.

Kia answers the doorbell after the second ring. She cracks the door open with just barely enough space for Bree to slide in. She walks as fast as she can to her apartment door, while Bree follows way behind. As she walks through the narrow hallway that leads to her apartment, she speaks while looking straight ahead. "My baby has been kicking her ass off, today."

Bree doesn't reply.

"Did you hear me?" she asks as she turns around slowly.

Boom, boom! Two shots to the dome leaves her splattered across the hallway. Killer Cal strikes again. She invited Bree. He took it upon himself to bring a friend.

She's squirming around fighting for her life. She holds her stomach, as the blood leaks out of her mouth. Killer Cal stands over her and aims at her forehead. He squeezes. Boom! "You are the weakest link!" he shouts, imitating the famous game show. Watching too much television is not good for Cal's mental condition.

Bree hated to have that done, but he knew it was mandatory. He got the vibe that her breaking point was near. He had to cover his own ass.

He stares at her until she finally stops moving. Better safe than sorry, he thinks to himself, as they exit the apartment. Sha-Rock is parked out front waiting for them.

Jimmy just left his apartment. He has a ton of business to handle. Things are going lovely for him. Slowly but surely his financial situation is starting to come back together, thanks to Sha-Rock, whom he hasn't heard from in weeks. He doesn't mind though. It's better for him that they haven't seen each other. He does worry about Sha-Rock though. Jimmy knows on the overall, he's a good guy. It's just his greed that makes him so cold. Jimmy often wonders how he's making out. He won't go as far as to call him because he's afraid Sha will want him to bring someone else in. At times his conscience beats him down terribly. He knows how wrong it was to set those guys up, but being on the bottom was driving him crazy.

Jimmy can finally breathe again. Just the other day he met a new connect. The work is quality and the prices are beautiful. Jimmy won the connect's heart when he copped six kilos for $114,000 cash, then two days later he copped eight more. This could be the start of a beautiful relationship. Jimmy hopes the connect shows love with no limits.

As Jimmy reaches for the door handle of his car, his attention is drawn to a small white paper that lies underneath his windshield wiper.

He smirks as he's opening the folded paper, thinking that one of his female neighbors has left another phone number for him. This is the normal for him. He snatches it from the window and reads it carefully.

His smirk turns to a frown in a matter of seconds. The note leaves a bad taste in his mouth. It reads: "Jimmy, a man was murdered some time ago. He was on his way to meet you, and he never returned. It's imperative that we meet ASAP. We need clarity. Get at me before I let my hounds loose. It's not a threat. It's a promise. You are not hard to find. That's obvious, right?"

The note is signed by "Trauma."

Jimmy looks around nervously. Trauma is a loose cannon. He's from the projects. He gets major money. He's known for taking over blocks. If your block is getting money, he'll move you out and slide right in. He's the brain but he has a team of young boys who murder at his command. Everyone knows them as the Trauma Unit. It's evident that Trauma is referring to the kid that Sha-Rock murdered at the graveyard.

Jimmy wonders how the hell he knew where to find him. Up until now Jimmy was under the impression that no one knew where he lived. He has never brought anyone to his house. So there's no way anyone could have told him. Maybe they followed him, he thinks to himself. No way, he thinks. He has definitely been on point when it comes to watching his mirrors. That's one good thing about dealing with Sha-Rock. He made Jimmy sharpen his game up. Watching Sha-Rock at work taught Jimmy so much.

Jimmy hops into his car and pulls off quickly. He feels so uneasy right now. The Trauma Unit doesn't play. They murder for fun. He didn't have a clue that the kid was linked to them. If he had known that, he would have found an easier vick.

Jimmy snatches his gun from his waist and tucks it under his right leg. As he's driving he studies his mirrors carefully. He pulls out his cellular phone and dials Sha-Rock.

"Yoooo," Sha-Rock drags in a playful voice.

"Sha!"

"Yo, what's good?"

"Sha, where you at? I need to holler at you!" he shouts sounding like a nervous wreck.

"Yo, stop yelling in my joint. I'm on my way upstate with my fiancée." The word fiancée sounds strange coming out of his mouth. He's so used to saying "my girl." It will take time for him to get used to saying it. Miranda has to get used to it as well. She blushes every time he says it. "Why, what's good?" he asks.

"Ain't nothing good. I walk out my house and I got a letter on my windshield. Somebody peeped my spot!"

"What the hell, you talking bout?"

"I can't talk on the phone. Hit me when you get finished, whatever you're doing."

"No doubt!" Sha-Rock shouts as he hangs the phone up. He's completely lost. Jimmy has confused him terribly. He can't wait to find out what has him acting so crazy.

Hours Later

The long trip was tiring. Miranda drove the first half of the ride until she could no longer keep her eyes open. That's when Sha-Rock had to take over. He tore the highway up in her little 350Z. It's nowhere nears as fast as his Porsche, but it gets the job done. Miranda wasn't aware that her car could move that fast.

As they pull into the parking lot, Sha-Rock gets butterflies in his stomach. His stomach does flip flops, just thinking about prison.

This will be Miranda's first time seeing her father since he was arrested almost nine years ago. They have always communicated through letters because he was always so far away from home. In the nine years that he's been locked up, he's been shipped all over the world. This prison is the closest he's been to Philadelphia.

As they line up, Miranda becomes nervous all of a sudden. Her underarms are sweating embarrassingly. She hopes no one can see the sweat rings that are forming on her sweater. Sha-Rock isn't much help. He's just as nervous as she is.

They finally make it through the frisking procedure and walk into the visiting hall. The inmates begin filling the room. Miranda looks around anxiously, waiting for her father to arrive.

Sha-Rock pays close attention to her eyes. He wants to see the initial expression on her face when she spots her father. Sha-Rock is well aware of how special this day is for Miranda. He's just happy that he could partake in this event with her. She loves her father so much. Not one day passes that she doesn't tell him at least one thing that her father used to say to her or do with her. Her father has a great impact on her life. Sha-Rock has never met him, but if he's the man who produced her and instilled in her the values that Miranda has, Sha-Rock is sure that he must be one hell of a man.

Sha-Rock is feeling a bit nervous about meeting Miranda's father. He fears he may question him. During the entire ride he's been rehearsing what he's going to say to him. Hopefully, he'll ask the questions that Sha-Rock rehearsed.

Miranda squints her eyes tightly as if she's trying to zoom in on something. Sha-Rock turns his attention to the direction of where Miranda is looking. A chunky, Cuban man about five feet eight inches tall walks into the room glancing around with a lost look on his face. Miranda gets the feeling that this is her father. She gets a strong vibe from him, but he looks so different compared to how he looked almost a decade ago. He has picked up at least sixty extra pounds. All of it appears to have gone to his potbelly and his rounded butt. His complexion has lightened about two shades. The shiny jet- black hair that he used to have has been replaced with a head full of silver hair with the exception of the small patches of black that remain around his ears. His thick bushy mustache is still jet-black. Crows feet extend from the corner of his eyes. His puffy jaws sag like they're filled with air. Old age and stress has taken over but she still finds him to be the most handsome man she has ever laid her eyes on.

He finally spots her. His eyes light up as he picks up his pace. Miranda meets him halfway. Sha-Rock stands up attentively. Miranda and her father embrace each other gratefully. He picks her up off of her feet and spins her around. Everyone in the hall has their attention focused on Miranda and her papi.

After about a minute of hugging, he finally drops her onto her feet. They clasp hands and walk to the table. Tears of joy drip down both of their faces. This was a touching moment for Sha-Rock as well. He managed to wipe his eyes with his sleeve before they got back to the table. Miranda is wearing the biggest, prettiest smile Sha-Rock has ever seen. He feels slightly jealous. Sha-Rock hasn't seen her cheese like this since the day he first came home from prison, and that smile comes nowhere near the one she's rocking now. Her father's smile transforms to a look of stone as he stands before Sha-Rock.

"Papi, this is Sherod, my fiancé," she says hesitantly.

Miranda's father replies with a slight head nod.

"How are you doing, Sir?" Sha-Rock asks, while extending his right hand for a handshake. He immediately realizes how stupid that question is. The man has less than ten years in on a lifetime sentence. How good can he possibly be doing?

He reaches over and returns the handshake with an extremely firm grip, almost crushing every bone in Sha-Rock's hand. Sha-Rock tries hard to keep a straight face because he knows what his motive is. He's trying to intimidate Sha-Rock through his grip.

They all sit. Sha-Rock feels very uneasy. The tension is visible. Miranda's father doesn't feel comfortable talking around Sha-Rock. Sha-Rock catches the heat. He excuses himself and fades away from the table.

"How have you been, Princess?" he asks as soon as Sha-Rock steps far enough away from the table that he won't be able to hear him.

"I'm good, Papi. It feels so good to finally see you again. I miss you so much."

"Princess, I miss you even more," he claims. "How is life treating you? What are you doing with yourself? Are you still modeling?"

"Yes," she lies.

"That's beautiful. Follow your dreams."

That breaks her heart to hear him say that. If he only knew she stopped modeling. He would really hate Sha-Rock if he knew she stopped for him.

"So, is that your boyfriend you have been telling me about?" he asks with a look of disgust on his face.

"My fiancé," she blurts out confidently, hoping that will make matters a little better.

"Fiancé?" he repeats, with his nose turned up.

"Yeah, he just proposed to me on my birthday!" she shouts joyfully.

"Umm?" he sighs. "Princess, marriage is a big move. Are you sure you're ready for that? Why don't you wait until your career is stable first? First you get married. Then you get pregnant with one baby and have to stop modeling. Then you have another baby. You sit around the house for about five years, and put on a ton of weight. And boom, your modeling career is over. Next thing you know you're divorced with two kids and no stability."

"Oh Papi, I'm not even married yet, and you already have me fat and divorced with two kids," she laughs.

"That's how it usually goes. I don't want to see you fall to the wayside like so many have fallen before you. You have to move wisely. Papi, is not on the outside. I can't pick you up and kiss the boo-boo when you fall. You'll have to kiss the boo-boo yourself and keep on trucking."

Miranda thinks back to the times that she would fall off of her bike and her father would run to her rescue and pick her up. She could be in the worst pain, and all he would have to do is kiss the boo-boo, and her screaming would turn into a whine. After he kissed her wound, she would be good to go. She'd jump right back on her bike just like nothing ever happened.

"What's his name, Shark?"

"No Papi," she laughs. "His nickname is Sha-Rock, but his real name is Sherod."

He gazes deep into her eyes. "Princess, you've grown to be so beautiful. You're the spitting image of your mother," he says.

"Thank you, Papi, and you're just as handsome as I remember

you. You've managed to fight old age," she lies. "Except for that big pot-belly," she jokes. Miranda remembers her father being much taller and slender, but at the time she was only four feet tall, everyone was a giant to her.

Miranda looks at her father closely. He fits the description of a Cuban who has just come off the boat, as the saying goes, but he speaks better English than many people who were born in this country. Her mother made sure of that. One thing she didn't play was him speaking in broken English. She would correct him like an English professor. He would get so frustrated with her. Eventually he got tired of her correcting him and he started thinking before he spoke. She didn't correct him to belittle him. She just didn't want Miranda to grow up talking like that.

"So, is Shark treating you good?" he asks, purposely mispronouncing Sha-Rock's name. "What line of work is he in, again?"

Miranda has to think back for a second. She has told so many lies that she has to remember what exactly she told him. "Construction, construction," she lies.

"Construction? Oh yeah? The same kind of construction I had you telling your teachers I did?" he asks sarcastically. He looks down at her ring.

She looks away from him. She always had a problem lying to him. He could always see right through her.

"Miranda, I'm going to ask you again. Please don't lie to me, Princess. What kind of work does he do?" he asks sternly.

She fixes her eyes on the table. "He doesn't work, Papi," she replies, sounding like a four-year-old.

"So, he's a street kid, huh?"

"Yes," she shamefully admits.

"I already knew. Princess, you can't game a gamer. I've been around for a long time. And anyway, there's no way a construction worker can afford a ring that size, unless of course it's fake?" he asks with a smirk on his face. "And I know my little princess won't dare allow that. I raised you better than that," he laughs.

I know that's right, Miranda thinks to herself. "No Papi, it's real."

"But back on a serious note, your mother told me about him long ago. It broke my heart, but eventually I got over it. That was my biggest nightmare. The last kind of person that I wanted you to get involved with was a street person. I prayed to God for years and years for him to keep you away from those kinds of men. Before I met your mother, I was hard on women. I dogged so many of them. Then the doctor told us you were a girl, I felt like I had been cursed for all the dirt I had done to women. Those women were someone's daughters. I said to myself, this is God's way of paying me back. Please don't pay for my mistakes," he begs. "Plus, you deserve better. You're too smart to settle for that. You can have so much better. There are so many single doctors and lawyers out there. They would love to have a wife like you. You have beauty, brains and charisma. Please don't sell yourself short. You deserve more than a jive ass slick talking street man."

"But Papi, you were a street man. How can you downplay him when you were the same kind of man?"

"Princess, that was different. At that time the circumstances were much different. I came to this country with nothing, no education, no money, nothing. I came here with the intention to make money, and that I did. All the risks I took, I took for my family; you and your mother. My intentions were to take the risk so you wouldn't have to. And now look, I'm sure you have to take more risks now than if I were out there with you."

"Papi, please. You could have been stopped taking risks. You were rich. You continued to take those risks because of your greed. Don't say you did it for me because I didn't need all the riches. I didn't need the big houses, the fur coats and expensive cars. I just needed a father to be present at the P.T.A. meetings. I just needed you to spend a little time with me, Papi. Even when you were home, you weren't there. You spent the majority of your time on the phone or pressing the keys of your calculator. Papi, I had a best friend in school. She was so poor. Her mother worked at a bakery and her father worked at McDonald's. I used to laugh at her when her father came to pick her up from school in his McDonald's uniform. I would tease her by calling her father Ronald McDonald. She would cry from embarrassment. But guess what? He never missed a parent-teacher meeting or class play. After you went away, I realized that the joke was on me, because her father still was around. Last year, I saw all of them at McDonald's. They now own three McDonald's back in Philly."

Tears fill her father eyes. Pain is written all over his face.

"Papi, I love you dearly, but sometimes I feel cheated," she cries. "Do you know, I never told any of my childhood friends what happened to you? I lied to them all. I told them the United States Army shipped you to a war overseas. What else could I tell them?" she asks. "One day you were here, and the next day you were gone. Papi, I realize my life could have been so much easier if you were active in it. Sometimes I just needed that extra push or some words of encouragement to make me know that I could do it."

"Princess," he interrupts. "Guess what? You are doing it, and you didn't need me to tell you. Do you know why?" he asks.

"Why?"

"Because you always knew you could. Miranda, you're a female soldier. You have always been. I'm sorry. It is all my fault," he admits as his eyes leak years of sorrow and regrets. "I take full responsibility. The first couple of years into my bid I eased my pain by saying, 'Hey, chalk it up. I did this for my family' but then I realized my family wasn't caught up in the hype of the Hollywood lifestyle. I was. I had to have lobster and filet mignon. You and your mother's favorite restaurant was White Castle. Any expensive habits that y'all may have, you got them from me. I can't begin to apologize to you. I wish I could have been there, but shit happens. I cried for years. I still cry to this day. I just want the best for you. Please don't sell yourself short," he begs. "This is it for me. I may as well be dead. The only living I can do is through you. I want you to be more than some Kingpin's old lady. You deserve much more. Your mother deserved more. She begged me to stop. She knew we had more than enough money to stop, but like you said, my greed kept telling me I didn't have enough to stop. When the Feds caught me, they put a freeze on all of my bank accounts. At that time I was worth $10,000,000. Now I'm worth nothing behind this wall. Your mother, I miss her so much. Not being able to attend her funeral took a big chunk out of me. I never stopped loving her. Even after I found out that her and Kiko were having an affair."

Miranda is shocked. She never knew her father was aware of that. Kiko is supposed to be Miranda's godfather. He was her father's best friend and his business partner. After Miranda's father went to jail, he was supposed to take care of Miranda and her mom. That he did. He moved right in and took Miranda's father's place. As Miranda grew older she started to look at her mother differently because of that situation. Miranda could never understand how she could do such a thing. A part of her hated her mother for committing such a scandalous act. "Papi, I didn't know you knew about that?"

"Of course, I knew. I heard the story so many times. I was the joke of the century. I hated to believe it. That crushed me. At first I hated your mother, but again, I take the blame. I left her out there vulnerable. I left another man in charge of my wife. I expected him to play the role of me. Wanted him to feed her, and clothe her, but I how could I expect him not to want to fuck her? Please excuse my language, Princess," he pardons. "That was very stupid of me. She was human. I did everything for her. She lived like a queen, and then I got sentenced to life in prison. One monkey don't stop no show," he quotes. "The game doesn't stop because the point guard breaks his ankle. Nah, the coach has to pull someone off of the bench. He may not be better than the original guard, but he's there when you need him," he explains. "That's what your mother did. She found the next best thing to me. Kiko has always been suave and debonair. The ladies always moved at his command. I never dreamed that he would use his powers on my wife. We had a pact. There are billions and billions of beautiful women in the world. Did he have to fuck mine? Excuse my language," he begs. "I think back at all the times the Feds begged me to tell. That went on for years. I never even considered the thought. Just to think, if I had told this would have never happened because it would have been the other way around. I would have been on the outside attending P.T.A. meetings with my wife and daughter, and he would have been behind this wall. The phone conversations they had on tape? That wasn't me! I never talked on the phone recklessly. The informants never said it was me. Everyone knew it wasn't me including the judge, but I was the only one who knew who the voice belonged to and where he was. I could have came home a long time ago. All I had to do was rollover. Sometimes I ask myself, was it worth it? I saved a dirty, piece-of-shit of a man. I saved him and it came back to haunt me. He's in my house, in my bed, fucking my wife, and tucking my daughter to sleep after reading her a bedtime story. How do you think I feel?" he asks. "Like shit," he answers himself. "But guess what? If I had a chance to do it differently, I wouldn't," he admits. "I'm sorry you got caught up in my pride issues, but I still have my dignity. I don't know how much that means to you, but it means a hell of a lot to me. I'm still a man. Over half of these guys in this prison can't say that. The majority of them have rolled over on somebody. Not me. I never did and I never will. I walked into prison a man and I will die as a man. Just because a slime ball back-doored me, I still won't change who I am. I could have easily done that. The Feds even knew he took my wife. They informed me, hoping I would tell on him, but I didn't. If I would have folded, I wouldn't have been able to live with myself. The worse part of it all wasn't him fucking my wife, it was him giving my daughter orders and instilling bad values in you. I just imagined you hugging him and kissing him, and calling him Papi," he cries.

"I only have one Papi," she reassures. "I never kissed him, hugged him, or called him Papi. I was a child, but I knew what they were doing wasn't right. The values and morals that you instilled in me made me know better than that. As much as I wish you were there for me, I can truthfully say, I respect your decision. It may sound crazy, but I'm glad you didn't rollover. If you would have, I would have been forced to look at you differently. I would have considered you a fraud. All the times you told me to stand up for what I believe? All the times you told me never to tattle-tale? You always told me, a man that doesn't stand for something will fall for anything. Papi, you're still standing, and guess what?" she asks. "You're not standing by yourself. I'm standing with you. When your legs get weak, you can lean on me. Papi, I never tattled on anyone and that's because of you. I walked in here with a little bitterness in my heart, but I'll walk out with understanding. Your belief and your pride was on the line. You did what you had to do and that means everything in the world to me. You took responsibility for your actions. That was another one of your golden rules. It affected me drastically, but I'll get over it. I'm a big girl," she says in a little girl's voice.

He smiles bashfully. "You were so young when I told you those things. How do you still remember that?"

"Papi, I never forgot anything you told me. I pull it out of my memory bank when I need a reminder to keep me going. I just want you to hear this, right here, right now. I love you. I respect you, and I will always be here for you when you need me."

Her father is crying without shame. "Princess, I know that. You're all I got."

"Listen Papi, on the outside, that man standing over there is all I got. He's the man I chose. You made your decision and I respect it. Now I'm asking you to do the same for me. He drove me all the way up here to see you, at least make him think you're grateful."

His stone face melts into wet cement. "Sha-Rock, come here!"

he shouts. He winks his eye at Miranda. "Anything for you, Princess. You're all I got."

Miranda smiles on the outside but she's crying a river on the inside. Hearing her father's pain about the Kiko situation really ripped her apart. He may not be mad at her mom, but a part of her will never be able to forgive her mom. There are just some things you don't do, and replacing your husband with his best friend, is one of them.

-33-

Two Days Later

Miranda and Tamara are at Najee's house in Fort Lee, New Jersey. They have just arrived. Tamara is hysterical. She's so distraught that she couldn't even drive here. Two hours ago Miranda and Tamara were in Tamara's house celebrating Miranda's engagement, when Najee called with an alarming collect call. He, his brother, and a few friends got caught up in a raid. He claims he's innocent, and he was just at the wrong place at the wrong time.

Up until now, Tamara wasn't completely sure about her feelings toward Najee. She now realizes how much she loves him. She can't even think straight. If it weren't for Miranda, she couldn't have made it here. For the entire ride she sat in the passenger's seat of Najee's car while Miranda drove. She just dazed into space, without saying a word. Najee gave her a series of instructions. Tamara didn't tell Miranda what they are. Hopefully, she'll remember what to do.

Miranda doesn't know all the details but the little that she does know sounds suspect to her. She's starting to agree with Sha-Rock. Najee has to be involved in something else besides modeling. It's just not adding up.

Tamara walks through the house in a daze. She still hasn't said a word to Miranda, whom is following close behind. Her nosiness will not allow her to miss a beat. Tamara leads her to the attic.

Tamara walks directly to the closet, just like Najee instructed her to do. Near the back of the closet, there sits a pile of Gucci luggage. Tamara pulls the luggage from the closet piece by piece. At the bottom of the pile, there's an old black trunk lying there. The trunk is trimmed in solid brass. It's so worn out that it looks like it's been passed down from century to century.

Tamara struggles to drag the heavy trunk to the middle of the floor. She digs into her purse and pulls out a small piece of paper. She reads from the paper as she turns the dial of the combination lock. She's unsuccessful at the first try. Her nervousness is getting the best of her. She tries again, but still no luck in getting it open. She slams the paper down with frustration.

"Calm down, girl. Give it here," Miranda says eagerly. Her anxiety is killing her. She's so curious to find out what's in the trunk, that she gets it open with her first try. The lock pops open, and Miranda backs away. "There you go," Miranda boasts.

Tamara opens itslowly. Miranda's knees get so weak. She feels as if she's going to faint. She's overwhelmed. She has never seen so much money in her life. Her heart thumps loudly. Suddenly, she feels so out of place, here witnessing this. She's sure Najee would be furious if he knew Tamara brought her along. Miranda gulps as her eyes comb through the stacks. Ben Franklin stares into Miranda's eyes from each stack. Miranda never paid attention to how sexy Ben Franklin is, until now. She's truly in love with him. She finds his huge bald head and his silver-gray shag so attractive.

Each stack is held in place with two rubber bands. Tamara grabs five stacks and sits in the middle of the room. She slowly fumbles through the first stack as she counts it carefully. She's counting so slow that Miranda is five to ten bills ahead of her.

In total, Miranda counts one hundred Ben Franklins. Math has always been Miranda's favorite subject. She calculates in her head; $100 X 100 = $10,000. The tiny stack holds $10,000. Miranda looks at the trunk. If all these stacks hold $10,000, someone is filthy rich, she thinks to herself. She seriously doubts that all the stacks are the same.

Tamara fumbles through the other four stacks at the same speed. To Miranda's surprise, they are all equal. Miranda counts fifty grand on the floor, and a trunk-full still remains. She can't believe this.

Tamara pulls fifteen more stacks out and quickly fumbles through them. Miranda looks at the trunk and discovers that only a corner is missing. She quickly counts through the stacks. She can only estimate about how much money is in there. The way she sees it, there must be at least 100 more stacks in, which equals approximately $1,000,000 still in the trunk. Her panties are wet from just looking at all the currency.

Tamara cuts her lifeline by slamming the trunk shut. Tamara locks the combination and spins it around several times. She then dumps the stacks into her Chanel backpack. "Help me take this to the car," Tamara asks as she grabs hold of the trunk.

My pleasure, Miranda says to herself. They each grab a handle. Together they struggle out of the apartment. After dumping the trunk into the back of Miranda's car, Tamara hits the house alarm. Miranda cruises off. Her mind runs wild. What would the police say if they were to pull them over with all that money? What would Sha-Rock say? She can't help but think about Sha-Rock. He would put Tamara to sleep right now if he knew how much money they're chauffeuring around.

Now not only is Tamara riding in silence, but Miranda is just as quiet. She can't believe what she just saw. No one would ever believe her. Something about that picture isn't right. An unknown model, with a brand-new Mercedes, a half-a-million-dollar home and a trunk-full of Ben Franklins? Miranda is no rocket scientist, but she can put one and one together. The answer is, somebody is bullshitting. Either Najee is lying to Tamara or Tamara is lying to her. Tamara is a little gullible at times. Maybe she does believe he earns his money by modeling? Nah, she can't be that gullible, Miranda hopes.

Twenty minutes later, Tamara is pulling into a parking lot on Sixth Avenue in Manhattan. They walk across street into a huge office building. Tamara uses her finger to scroll down the directory. Her finger stops at the slot that reads Davidson and Fickleberg.

The lawyer meets them in the reception room. Miranda takes a seat as Tamara walks into his office and closes the door. Miranda stares at the Tamara's backpack. No one would ever suspect her to have $200,000 stuffed into that little bag.

Two hours later, they're back in Philly, and Tamara and Miranda are lugging the trunk into Tamara's house.

Miranda has been eagerly awaiting some kind of information. Tamara hasn't told her anything. She so badly wants to ask her what the lawyer said, but she knows she'll be totally out of place. She already knows more than she should.

Miranda sits with Tamara for approximately one hour before she decides to go home. "Girl, I have to get home. I have a lot of cleaning to do. Are you sure you're alright?"

"I will be," she replies sadly. "This is just too much. I don't know if I'm ready for all of this?"

Ready for all of this, Miranda asks herself. Miranda gets the feeling that Tamara wants to tell her what's going on. "All what?"

Tamara shakes her head negatively. "Nothing, nothing."

Miranda is sure she can get some answers with a little prying but she doesn't want to pressure Tamara.

"Miranda, I love you."

"I love you, too."

"I hate to disrespect you like this, but," she hesitates before finishing her statement.

"But what?" Miranda asks defensively.

"But, I need you to promise me, you won't tell anyone what you saw today. I mean no one. If Najee knew I took you with me, he'd kill me. He doesn't trust anyone. I would hate for him to feel like he can no longer trust me. He specifically told me to go alone."

"Girl, I promise!" Miranda shouts as she crosses her fingers behind her back.

Jimmy got in touch with Trauma and they set up a meeting. Sha-Rock's initial words were "Fuck Trauma!" Jimmy begged to differ. Sha-Rock isn't from this town, so he doesn't really know the rules of this town. Jimmy knows without this meeting, things can get rough for him. He knows he won't be able to make money, ducking a dodging Trauma. This incident with Trauma made Jimmy realize how stupid he was for bringing in an out-of-towner to set up his own people, but it's too late now. If Trauma or anyone else from this town ever finds out, he knows he's a dead man. There's a certain code you play by in this town, if you expect to be allowed to play in the game.

Trauma wanted Jimmy to meet him in the projects, but Jimmy denied. He feared that they would have left him for dead down there. He wants to meet on neutral grounds.

Sha-Rock and Jimmy slowly pull into the entrance of Weequahic Park. They're riding in Jimmy's car. Sha-Rock is disguised today. He's wearing a dreadlock wig, with a baseball hat glued onto the top of it. Pitch-black shades cover his eyes. He looks like a real Rastafarian.

Sha-Rock spots the black Ford Excursion parked across from the pull-up bar.

"That's him," says Jimmy in a high-pitched squeaky voice. He takes a deep breath. Sha-Rock can see the fear in Jimmy's face. Sha-Rock doesn't know anything about Trauma and he doesn't care to know anything about him.

When Trauma spots them pulling in, he slowly climbs out of the truck. All the doors open simultaneously. Six young boys get out of the truck after him. They all disperse into the green pastures. They all spread out, going their separate ways. Trauma stands about ten feet away from the truck. One kid accompanies him. He stands by the hood. They are spaced out so far that it's hard for Jimmy and Sha-Rock to watch all of them at the same time.

Trauma thinks they have them greatly outnumbered, but what he doesn't know is Sha-Rock is no fool. Sha-Rock's van sets parked about ten parking spaces away. Bree sits in there ready for war. He's dressed in black with his ski mask on. He grips the handle of the AK47 assault rifle, waiting for action. He didn't hesitate when Sha-Rock mentioned the name Trauma. It's all his pleasure. Bree has a long time vendetta against the Trauma Unit. They killed one of his good friends two years ago, while Bree was locked up. He's been anticipating getting even, but he didn't have the manpower he needed to go against them. Now that he has a team, he can finally handle his business. He didn't tell Sha-Rock about them killing his friend. Jimmy and Sha-Rock think he's rolling just because.

"Hand me your gun," Sha-Rock demands. Jimmy passes it off quickly. Sha-Rock sticks the rubber gripped 9 millimeter Ruger into his left jacket pocket. In his right pocket, he has a chrome .40 caliber. Altogether, he's holding a total of thirty-four rounds.

Jimmy pulls parallel to the Excursion. Five spaces separate them. Sha-Rock has one more trick up his sleeve. Approximately fifty feet behind them, right next to the pull-up bar, there sits a huge tree. A construction worker sits against the tree, eating his lunch and reading the newspaper, which is spread out across his lap. The man is no construction worker. He's Killer Cal. Underneath the newspaper lies an Uzi with an extended clip, which holds sixty rounds. That should even everything out.

Jimmy and Sha-Rock get out of the car simultaneously. Trauma slowly lifts up his black hooded sweater and spins around slowly, letting Jimmy know that he doesn't have a gun on him. Jimmy spins around and does the same. They meet each other halfway.

Sha-Rock looks Trauma over. He doesn't look like the killer Jimmy makes him out to be. He actually looks like a sucker to Sha-Rock. He stands about five feet six inches tall. He's smooth complexioned, but you can hardly see his face because his huge bifocals swallow his little face.

Trauma points at Sha-Rock as he follows Jimmy toward him. "You back up! You don't have nothing to do with this. This meeting doesn't concern you," he says calmly but sternly. "This is between me and Jimmy. I don't know you, and obviously you don't know me. Let's keep it like that. Ask around. I'm really not the kind of you guy you want to get to know," he says arrogantly.

Sha-Rock is burning inside. Who does this little punk think that he's talking to like that? He must have lost his mind. "Listen, it's obvious that you don't know me either. I don't care to know you. I'm here on the strength of my man. This ain't about you," he says in a calm manner.

"Listen homeboy, you starting off on the wrong track. You're already on my bad side, and that's bad. I'm trying to give Jimmy the benefit of the doubt, but you're about to fuck that up for him," he threatens.

Jimmy looks at Sha-Rock with fear in his face. His eyes are begging Sha-Rock to stop.

"Yo, all that intimidating, big mafia talk, don't do nothing for me. I'm not fucking it up for Jimmy. This thing can go either way!" Sha-Rock shouts.

Sha-Rock's voice alerts the Unit. They tighten up their circle, but Trauma waves them off, gesturing that it's nothing. "Do you really believe that?" Trauma asks sarcastically while snickering. "Please do me a favor? He pauses for a second while looking Sha-Rock directly in the eyes. "Whatever you do, don't ever raise your voice at me in your life. My boys hate that. The next time I won't be able to stop them," he claims.

Sha-Rock has both hands inside his pockets, gripped tightly around both guns, ready for all-out warfare.

"Now, let's start this over. He extends his right hand, gesturing for a handshake. Sha-Rock denies the gesture. He leaves Trauma's hands dangling in the air. He draws his hand back embarrassingly.

"My name is Trauma," he introduces himself. "I never saw you before, so I'm assuming you must be an out-of-towner? Which is another negative for Jimmy over there. I'm sure he knows the rules when it comes to taking sides with out-of-towners. That can get ugly. Know what I mean, Jimmy?" he asks with a demonic look on his face. "Like I said, I'm Trauma, let me brief you on who I am. I'm one of the most dangerous cats in this town. I play for keeps," he says as he pats both hands against his chest. "My resume is extensive. I put in work. That's not meant to intimidate you. I'm sorry that you find my persona to be intimidating. I'm just forewarning you. Those kids you see out there," he says while pointing around the park. "Those are my young boys. Stay out of our way, and we'll stay out of yours. We actually hate beef because beef results in murder, and murder gets costly. You know, bail money for my young boys and lawyer fees? I'm tired of spending unnecessary money, feel me? Hopefully we can resolve this matter with words?

"A short time ago, the brother of one of my young boys was murdered. This is him to my left," says Trauma as he points to the kid who stands at the hood of the truck. Rumor has it that you, Jimmy, was the last person he saw. He was supposed to link up with you to cop some powder. His body was found a few blocks away from his truck. We need to know when you saw him. Did he: A, get murdered before you saw him? B, get murdered after you saw him? Or did you, C, get him murdered?"

"Me," Jimmy asks defensively while pointing to himself. "Trauma, you know me. I'm a hustler not a murderer. I don't rob."

"Rob? Who said something about rob? You're jumping the gun, and I do mean that literally," Trauma threatens. "To keep it real with you, my young boy really didn't want to talk with you. He just wanted to do him. This meeting thing was all my idea. Please just tell my young boy something to make him change his mind about this?" he begs. "We just need clarity. Sure, I know you're a money getter, but this is the hood. Shit happens, feel me?"

"Nah, I ain't feeling you at all, right now," Jimmy admits.

Their attention is drawn to the entrance where a sheriff's car is slowly pulling in. He halts when he sees the crowd. They all become nervous. They try and act nonchalantly, but it's evident that they're ready to break out any minute.

The sheriff is on the radio. Apparently he's calling for back-up. Seconds later, three other vehicles appear at the entrance with their sirens on.

"Go!" says Sha-Rock, as he dashes off. Sha-Rock runs so fast that the wind snatches his wig and shades off, giving Trauma a clear look of his face.

Jimmy and Sha-Rock hop in the vehicle and peel off, while Trauma jumps into his truck along with the murder victim's brother. They pull off immediately.

The other members of the Trauma Unit disperse throughout the park. The sheriffs disregard them. They're so busy concentrating on the Taurus and the Excursion. They both are speeding recklessly through the park.

Jimmy is driving like a professional race car driver. He refuses to get caught. He promised himself that he'd never do another bid. Two guns will definitely land him another one.

Sha-Rock is just as shook. His life is in Jimmy's hands. "Go!" he shouts as he looks back at the many sheriff cars that trail them. Jimmy exits the park, finally. He has a huge lead on them. He takes an even greater lead on them as he crosses over the Hillside borderline.

Jimmy's car is so far ahead of them that they switch the chase to the Excursion. They must have realized that it will be a lot easier to catch the huge awkward truck.

Jimmy and Sha-Rock exhale a sigh a relief. Luckily they got away. Sha-Rock is worried about Bree and Cal. He hopes they didn't get caught up.

Jimmy is busy worrying about the Trauma Unit. He's left in suspense. They didn't have a chance to come to some kind of conclusion. He wonders if they believe his plea of innocence?

Killer Cal is fine. Well, as fine as he can be despite his mental condition. The sheriffs didn't pay any attention to Cal or Bree. Although, they did catch three of the Trauma Unit members on foot. Word has it that they also caught Trauma and the other guy, after Trauma crashed into a tree.

Killer Cal is on another one of his crazy missions. He lies under his bed, ass naked as usual, wearing only his army helmet. His lips wrap tightly around the glass pipe. The foggy room smells of burning crack and the stomach-turning foul odor that always lurks in the apartment.

As he's blasting away, his mind goes on another adventure. He envisions Hollyhood walking toward him with his brains dripping from his head. Hollyhood is not alone. He walks side by side, hand in hand with Kia. She has a giant bullet hole which takes up the majority of her face. Blood covers her silk pajamas. She lifts the bloody blanket from the baby's face to show Cal the baby. Cal is so surprised to see his brother that he lost in the fire. His face is burned to a crisp.

Cal's head starts pounding. The harder it thumps the more crack he inhales. The heat from the glass pipe burns his palms, but even that doesn't stop him from puffing. His brother jumps out of the blanket, and crawls away at an incredible speed. Cal chases him, but his brother is so far away, he's sure he'll never catch him. Hollyhood laughs satanically as Kia cries. "My baby, my baby! You killed my baby!"

-36-

One Week Later/ November 15

Miranda and Tamara sit in Tamara's house, when Najee enters the house through the kitchen door. Him and his boys were released about two days ago. Miranda can't believe that Tamara still hasn't mentioned anything else to her about their case.

Najee has been staying here for the past couple of nights. Tamara said he's staying because he missed her so much, but Miranda thinks he's afraid to go home for whatever reason. She assumes that he feels safe here, because no one knows his exact whereabouts. He may have Tamara fooled but he'll need a little more game to pull one over on Miranda.

He hasn't been the same since he's been home. He's usually a happy-go-lucky comedian. He always has a funny remark, or he's usually clowning Miranda or Tamara. They know better than to do or say anything foolish while he's around. He'll ride them to the end. Both of them stay on their toes when in his presence.

Today his face looks much longer than usual. Stress is evident. Big bags from lack of sleep are under his eyes. "Hey," he greets in a very bland manner.

"Hey?" Tamara asks sarcastically. "Is that all we get?"

"My bad, y'all. Hello. My head is somewhere else."

"That's obvious," Tamara replies. "Anything I can help you with," she offers.

"Nah," he replies. "I have to fight this battle by myself."

"Are you hungry?" Tamara asks.

"Yeah, I'm starving, but I ain't got time to eat. I have to get right back to New York for a business meeting," he claims.

I wonder what kind of business, Miranda says to herself.

Najee walks to the bedroom leaving Miranda and Tamara alone. Minutes pass before Tamara decides to accompany him.

When she enters the room, he's at the closet pulling a few stacks of Ben Franklins from his treasure trunk. He dumps about twelve $10,000 stacks into a black garbage bag.

"Honey, are you alright?" she asks while standing face to face with him.

He hesitates before replying. "Not at all, Tammy. I'm stressed the fuck out," he whispers. Tamara feels sorry for him. She doesn't like to see him looking like this. "I just need to clear my mind," he sighs.

"Let me see if I can help you clear it," she whispers in a seductive voice as she grabs hold of his hand and jams the tip of his index finger into her mouth. She drops to her knees slowly while looking deeply into his eyes as she descends. She anxiously unbuckles his pants and lets them fall to his ankles.

It's no shock to her to see that he's not wearing a stitch of underwear. He claims he hasn't worn underwear in any of his adult years. At times Tamara gets extremely wet just watching him walk, knowing that his bat and balls are bouncing around freely. The thought alone makes her cum.

With only three gentle tugs his withered snake stretches to a full-grown anaconda. She teases him by slowly licking around his rim. That drives him wild. She knows that's his weak spot. Just as he's getting into it, leaning his head back from pleasure, she stops all of a sudden. He looks down to see why she has stopped. Now she knows she has his full attention. She grabs him by his tip and lifts him high before dropping his sac into her mouth. One by one, she juggles his balls with her tongue before dragging the tip of her tongue up his rod until she reaches the head. She wraps her mouth around him and makes a slow jerking movement. The buckling of his knees excites her, giving her a feeling of control. She reaches inside of her own jeans to pet her cat. She's soaking wet. It's so slippery that her finger accidentally slides inside of her. She fingers herself as she sucks away. She gets so excited that she forgets how huge he is. She attempts to deep throat him. Reality sets in when his tip bangs across her tonsils and only half of him is inside her mouth, which makes her gag. He grabs the back of her head using both of his hands as he slowly grinds her mouth. He grinds faster as he enjoys the heat of her mouth. Right now, she's just as excited as him. She pulls away suddenly, causing a loud, embarrassing, sucking noise. She sure hopes Miranda didn't hear that.

She jumps up from the floor and immediately snatches her skintight jeans off of her. Tamara is without panties as well. She picked up that habit from Najee.

Najee can't help but stare at her picture perfect, clean-shaven twat. He licks his lips sexily. He always tells her that she has the perfect porno pussy.

Her pink lips pulsate as her love juices drip down her thighs. Najee drops to his knees and buries his face into her pelvic section. He catches each drop before it evaporates into her skin. He then drags his tongue across her opening, before stuffing his tongue inside. She grabs his shoulders and gently forces him backwards as she falls onto his face, in a 69 position. As soon as his back hits the carpet, she gobbles him up. She grinds on his face as he sexes her mouth.

They're both very close to reaching their peak. Neither one of them is happy about that. They want to savor the moment. They wish it could last forever, but all good things must come to an end. She grinds faster as he pumps harder.

Suddenly Tamara stops while Najee is still jack hammering her mouth. She tightens her thighs around his neck. Her grip makes it impossible for him to move. Her body quivers tremendously as she leaks a puddle of love onto his face. "Aghh," she sighs, as she jumps up leaving him at full attention.

"Come on," he insists.

She laughs out loud. "Come on, what?" she asks playfully as she picks her jeans up from the floor.

"Tammy, stop playing," he says, while she steps one leg into her pants.

"What? I already got mine," she laughs. "You didn't cum?"

"Stop playing, Tammy. Don't leave me like this?" he begs. His hopes shatter. He realizes that she's not playing once she zips her jeans up.

She smiles. "That will give you a reason to come back here tonight," she teases. She stares at the cannon. She would love for him to fill up her insides, but she can't give in. She has to prove to him that she has *coochie control*. She walks over to him, bends over and pulls his pants up, while he's still lying there desperately.

"Please Tammy," he begs as she tucks his rod in between his legs to prevent him from getting caught in the zipper. "Please don't do this? You gone give me blue-balls."

She buttons up his pants. "So what time will you be coming back?" she asks in a joking manner.

"About ten," he replies.

"Ok, I'll be waiting. Ta, ta," she whispers as she walks out of the room.

Miranda sits in front of the television, watching attentively. "Oh, no he didn't?" Tamara shouts referring to the show she was watching before Najee came in. Tamara's suck-fest has worked up a huge thirst. Her mouth is as dry as the desert. She plops onto the sofa with her eyes glued to the television. She reaches for her glass. As she lifts it, she realizes that her glass is empty. She then slides her hand over about an inch away, and locates Miranda's glass. She turns it up to her mouth and wets her whistle.

Najee walks out. He's still as hard as a brick. As he approaches Miranda he places the plastic bag full of money over his bulge. Little does he know, Miranda isn't watching the bulge. Her eyes are on the plastic bag. The plastic is stretched so much, due to the weight of the money, that the bag has become transparent. She can see the stacks clearly. That informs her that the trunk of money is still here. Where can he be taking that money to, Miranda tries to figure out. She has to get to the bottom of this. She will not be able to rest until she finds out exactly what he's into.

Miranda slowly reaches for her glass. She turns it up and gulps away. If only Miranda knew where Tamara's mouth just was.

-37-

Days Later

Sha-Rock just got back into Philly late last night. Miranda has been complaining so much about his lack of quality time that he decided to spend the night at home, instead of working. He thinks the ring has brought about the change in her attitude but it's really the talk her father had with her about selling herself short and settling for less. Deep down inside, she always knew that she could do whatever she chose to do, but hearing her father break it down to her simple and plain, made it all clearer for her.

She also plans to follow her dream of modeling. Coincidentally, Tamara told Miranda that Najee has a big show coming up, and he really needs her to model for him. She debated for a while, and she plans on doing it. Not for Najee, but for herself. She can no longer let Sha-Rock put her goals on hold. She has yet to tell him her plan because she doesn't know how to break it down to him. She can only imagine the argument that will stem from her telling him that.

It's 8 A.M. and Sha-Rock is already fully dressed and ready to go. Miranda is highly upset with him. He came in late last night and he's already leaving. She planned on breaking the news to him, but he didn't give her enough time to get the courage up.

Sha-Rock comes into the bedroom. Miranda is sitting up in the bed with her head propped up against the headboard. She's so pissed off that she just wants to scream. The tension in the room is very thick.

Sha-Rock eases his way toward her nervously. "I'm out, Ma," he whispers. "I'll be back in two days for sure," he claims.

She ignores him.

"You hear me?"

"You come in late last night, fuck me, then I roll over first thing in the morning and you're not even in the bed? I'm tired of this shit, Sha. I never complain to you but the loneliness is killing me. I don't hold you down. I let you do you. I don't argue with you or ask you where you're going, but this is starting to be too much. I lived without you for three years. You promised me, you'd never leave my side ever again. Now

189

look. You've been home for months, and I can count the nights that we've spent together."

Sha-Rock knows this must really be bothering her because she hardly ever complains. Normally, she just rolls with the flow. "Hold up, first of all, I don't fuck you," he says humbly. "Let's get that straight, first. You're my fiancée. We don't fuck. I'm sorry that you feel like we're only fucking," he says hoping that will change the subject. "Secondly, I know I have been running wild but in a minute it will all be over. Trust me, I'm tired of running, too. I just gotta get right. I just need one big hit so I can fall back. Hopefully it's on the way. I'm closer than ever."

"Sha, you're putting too much time into that. If you really wanted to get right, you could have been done that. You know, I look at you and I'm starting to think you love what you're doing. I hate it. I only do it because you asked me to. I won't sit here and preach to you like I'm a goody-two-shoes. I'm not gone front, I like the fast life too. I just don't like what we do to live that life. I never told you this because I didn't want you to think I was weak, but that shit bothers me so. I know selling drugs is wrong but I rather you do that than to do this other shit. Sha, this is ain't you. You're not a thief. And this damn sure ain't me. Sometimes I wake up hearing gunshots. My heart is pounding and I'm so wet from sweat that my clothes stick to me."

"I didn't know that," he interrupts.

"How would you? You're never here with me."

"Promise me, the next one, you'll do what you have to do to get on your feet?" she begs.

He hesitates. He can see the hurt in her eyes. He hates to put her through this. He loves her so. It's his selfishness that allows him to involve her in his drama. It started out as a gesture, when she told him she loved him and she would do anything to help him get back on. He didn't really think she would do it. She surprised him when she agreed to it. He realizes either a real down ass chick or a fool would go to those limits for her man. He believes she's a down ass chick because she's never been a fool. "I promise," he whispers as he looks into her beautiful eyes. He hugs her and gives her several kisses before he walks away. "Miranda, I love you!" he shouts as he turns toward her while grabbing the doorknob.

I can't let him leave, she thinks to herself. I didn't get a chance to tell him about the show. "Sha!" she yells. It's now or never, she prepares herself. How am I going to tell him? What will he say? I have to tell him. This is my life.

Sha-Rock pops his head back in. "Huh?"

Miranda is at a loss of words. Her mouth is open but nothing is coming out. The cat has her tongue.

"Huh?" he repeats.

"I, I love you," she stutters.

"I love you too," he says while walking out of the room.

After the door closes behind him, Miranda starts to cry like a baby. She couldn't find the courage to tell him.

Twenty Minutes Later

Sha-Rock is parking in front of Cal's raggedy shack. He hits the horn several times with no response from Cal.

Sha-Rock gets out of the car and walks through the alleyway. The foul smell smacks him in the face as he approaches the door. His stomach turns as he inhales the odor. He has to hold his breath while knocking on the door. He can't understand how Cal can live in there with that smell. Inhaling those vapors all day has to be dangerous.

Cal peeks through the curtain, trying to be careful so whoever is on the outside won't be able to see him, but Sha-Rock sees him anyway.

"It's me, motherfucker! Open the door."

"Hold up, here I come!" he shouts from behind the window.

"No, open the door!" Sha-Rock insists. He really doesn't want to go inside. He just wants to see if Cal will let him in. He wants to make sure Cal isn't hiding anything from him. He has to keep him on point, just so he won't slip again.

Cal takes a matter of minutes before slowly opening the door. Sha-Rock steps toward the door, just to see how Cal is going to react. Cal's tense reaction makes Sha-Rock decide to go in. The smell rips through his nostrils.

"Baby Boy, I got company," says Cal as he points toward his bed. The filthy blanket covers her from the waist down, slightly showing the crack of her behind. The woman with the high-yellowed complexion lays face down. Her bare back assures Sha-Rock that she's naked. Her auburn colored, kinky textured hair spreads over the entire pillowcase. Ever since Sha-Rock has known Cal, he has always been a sucker for a yellow

191

woman with long hair. Up until the situation with his wife. After that, Sha never saw him look at light skinned-women. He always went for the fattest, blackest chick in sight. Sha assumes that Cal must have gotten over his hate for yellow women.

"Look at you," Sha-Rock teases. "Mack Daddy," he whispers. "Who is that?" he asks as he walks toward the bed to get a better view of her.

"A friend of mine," Cal replies quickly. "Cool out, man. Don't wake her," he whispers as he grabs hold of Sha-Rock's arm and escorts him out of the apartment.

Sha-Rock waits in the car as Cal gets dressed. Ten minutes later, Cal walks out of the alleyway alone. He left his female acquaintance in the bed.

Cal hops into the car.

"Damn, you got in-house pussy, huh? Shorty must be special?"

"Something like that. She's one of my main joints. She stops by about four times a week," he brags.

Sha-Rock is glad to find out that Cal is back in the swing of things. His wife had hurt him so bad that he vowed never to fall in love again.

Cal falls asleep as soon as they jump onto the turnpike.

Later That Evening

Tonight is the night. Sha-Rock can't take it anymore. He's been tailing the First Lady for months and he has not found a clue. He's sick and tired of playing cat and mouse with her. Besides, Miranda is starting to get on his nerves, too. He has to get this over with.

Right now, it's 10 p.m. The First Lady and her best friend went in over two hours ago and haven't come out yet. He's waiting for the First Lady to drop the girl off, then when she returns he'll catch her going inside. Who knows how long that may take?

Being that he was unsuccessful in following her and finding out where she keeps everything, he'll have to do the next best thing, and that's put the pressure on her and make her take them to the money. He's sure that shouldn't be a problem. Grown men bitch up when they're put into that position, so he can only imagine how fast she'll cooperate. He's expecting it to be as easy as taking candy from a baby. He already told Cal to mask up, so she won't be able to identify them. He feels that there's no need to kill a girl. She's harmless, despite the image she portrays for the rest of the town.

It's 11 P.M. and they're still inside. Sha-Rock is good and frustrated now.

At 1 A.M. the First Lady's Mercedes truck creeps up the street. Her flunky is driving. He must be on his way in from a go-go bar or something. They witnessed him leave hours ago. They were about to follow him but Sha-Rock decided not to. He's fed up with him, too. Sha-Rock followed him for two weeks straight, and he led him to nothing but go-go bars and errands. All Sha-Rock found out about him is the fact that he's a flunky and a pervert.

"Change of plans," Sha-Rock blurts out. "If we wait for the First Lady, we might sit out here forever. I say we grab the flunky and make him take us in. What you think? Think quickly!"

"I don't think. I just react!" Cal shouts, while sliding a bullet into the chamber of his Heckler & Koch .40 caliber.

"Listen Cal, no murder, alright? Remember this is a bitch.

Smack her up a little, but we ain't gone kill the hoe. Ya dig?"

"Yeah," Cal replies angrily. He truly looks forward to murder. That's his specialty. To him, a robbery without murder is as dry as peanut butter without jelly.

The kid pulls into the garage slowly. Killer Cal and Sha-Rock jump out of the van and close the doors quietly. They tiptoe across the street. It's pitch-black outside, and both of them are dressed in all black. They can hardly be seen.

After successfully making it across the street without him walking out of the garage they walk alongside the houses until they finally make it to the First Lady's house.

The dude's voice echoes throughout the garage, as he yells into his cell phone. Sha-Rock gestures with a head nod for Cal to wait on the porch. Cal walks to the alleyway and quietly climbs aboard the porch. He stands in the darkness with his back against the wall.

Sha-Rock peeks into the garage. The kid has his back facing the entrance as he yaps away. He lifts the hatch of the truck and fumbles through a few laundry bags. "Alright, I'll hit you later!" he shouts as he hangs up and grabs the two larger duffle bags from the truck. He slams the trunk closed and turns around.

"Don't make a noise," Sha-Rock whispers while aiming the gun right at his mouth. "Shh," he whispers.

His eyes stretch wide open as he looks at the masked gunman. He wants to scream, but nothing is coming out of his mouth. Paralysis has taken over his body. His feet feel like they're glued to the ground.

Sha-Rock snatches him by the collar and pulls him closer. He pats him down to make sure he doesn't have a gun on him. "We gone make this real simple," he whispers into the kid's ear. "It will only get as ugly as you let it. Do as I say, and I'll do my job and leave without hurting anyone. Go against my wishes, and you'll make the newspaper, feel me?" Sha-Rock asks. "Don't talk, just nod your head if you feel me?"

The dude nods his head up and down.

"Listen, we're going in the house with you. You open the door, and I'm right with you. Remember, no funny business, and you'll live to learn from your mistake, but if shit doesn't go right, you'll have to pay for your mistake, tonight. Also, anything goes wrong, you're the first to die, don't forget that," Sha-Rock threatens. "Now, we're going out here.

You close the garage as usual and walk up the steps. Don't even think of running. I got a serious aim, plus I have this," he whispers as he aims at the kid's face and slightly squeezes the trigger, showing off the infrared beam. "And I have a silencer, so no one will hear my bark," he informs. "Ok, let's remember, everything nice and smooth," he says as he pushes the kid toward the entrance. They walk out side by side. Sha-Rock has the gun pressed up against the boy's side.

The boy is so frightened that he's pissed on himself without even knowing it. He closes the garage door, just as he was instructed to do.

Sha-Rock forcefully leads him to the gate. They enter and walk up the small flight of steps. Sha-Rock can't believe he's so close. It's like a dream come true to finally be walking up these steps. He glances around to see where Cal is. He can't see him until he lifts his head up. His red pupils glow in the dark like the eyes of a cat. He's laying on the porch flat on his stomach. "Get yo ass up," Sha-Rock whispers.

The boy gets even more nervous once he sees another masked man. He can't believe this is happening. Never in a million years did he expect this. Home invasions are popular in this town, but he never expected it to happen to them.

"Now open the door," Sha-Rock mumbles. The boy pulls his keys out and inserts it in the lock. Cal slowly pushes the door open. Nice and easy, Sha-Rock says to himself.

They peek around very observantly. The house is dark except for the room in the back, which Sha-Rock thinks is the First Lady's room. Sha-Rock guides the boy to the back of the house, while Cal spins around nonstop, aiming his gun high and low. He's prepared to bust at any second.

They finally make it to the door. Sha-Rock gestures for Cal to open it. Cal grasps the doorknob cautiously. He slowly turns it. After a complete turn, he suddenly pushes the door inward, and aims his gun at the center of the room.

What they witness is a beautiful sight. The First Lady is standing ass naked. She has one leg up on the edge of the mattress. Her good friend is on the floor on her knees with her hands holding the First lady's voluptuous hips while she feasts away. The distraction makes them turn toward the door.

"Oww!" the girl screams.

Sha-Rock can't believe his eyes. He's in a state of shock. The

girl is not her best friend. She's her lover. No wonder they spend
so much time together. Maybe that's why she's no longer with her
daughters' father, Sha-Rock thinks. He's wasted a matter of seconds, just
enjoying the view.

He finally snaps back into reality, and remembers what he's here
for. He pushes the boy inside the room aggressively. "Don't stop on the
count of us. We'll just watch," says Sha-Rock.

Killer Cal is also enjoying the view. He gets an instant erection
watching the two nude bodies in the center of the room. Sweat plasters
their smooth skin, giving their high yellow tone a glossy effect. The
room smells of women's sweaty sex mixed with sweet perfume. The
combination of the mild funky aroma drives Sha-Rock and Cal wild.

Both women display looks of innocence. "What the fuck?" the
First Lady manages to blurt out.

Sha-Rock aims the gun at her while approaching her. "You know
what the fuck!" he shouts. "Cuff 'em," he instructs Cal. "Everybody to
the center of the room. Get up, beautiful," he says to the girl who is on
the floor. She stands up slowly. Her frame is awesome. Sha-Rock can't
help but stare at her huge tits. They're perfectly rounded without the least
sag. Her perky nipples excite him. This is business, he reminds himself
as he looks over at the First Lady. Her tits are only half the size of her
friend's but her firm rear makes up for her disadvantage. Both of them
are definitely *Playboy* material. "On the floor," he shouts. "You too,
dummy," he says to the dude. He quickly runs to the center of the room
as he remembers what Sha-Rock told him about going against the plan.

The First Lady has a series of thoughts running through her mind.
Who are they? Who would have the heart to do this? How did they know
where to find her? She's sure it has to be somebody from somewhere
else. No one from this county would have enough heart to do this to her.
Everyone is aware of the repercussions of this. Maybe her flunky set
her up? Maybe this is all a hoax? She's sure she'll find out, and when
she does she'll have all of them killed. Maybe it's her little girlfriend?
Her ex-boyfriend did follow her here before. The First Lady is more
concerned about who they are than the actual robbery.

Cal pulls three sets of handcuffs from his pocket. He pulls the
girlfriend by her long hair until she's shoulder to shoulder with the First
Lady. He cuffs them together, squeezing the cuffs extremely tight.

"Aghh," they both cry as the cuffs cut into their little wrists. He grabs the other set of cuffs and uses them to cuff the dude to the First Lady. He uses the last set to cuff the First Lady's left ankle to the dude's right ankle.

The First Lady leans against the bed with her legs spread wide open without shame. Cal backs against the wall and enjoys the view. All kinds of sick thoughts occupy his perverted mind.

"Listen bitch, let's make this snappy," says Sha-Rock. "I ain't got time for the bullshit. Where's the dope and the money?" Sha-Rock inquires while looking into her eyes blankly.

"You talking to me?" she asks innocently with her little squeaky voice. Her voice and her size match perfectly.

"No bitch! I'm talking to myself. Don't act stupid. Stupidity will get your dumb ass blasted in here tonight. Now, I'm going to ask you again. Where's the smack and the money?

"Smack? What is smack, and what money are you looking for?" she asks.

"Still acting stupid, right?" Sha-Rock asks in a frustrated tone. "Killer, search the house! The bitch got some money in here somewhere. If she don't cooperate, I'm about to start doing me," he threatens.

Her little girlfriend bites on her bottom lip and cries silently. Sha-Rock feels sympathy for her as he looks into her cute little baby doll eyes, but he knows he can't show them a sign of weakness. He quickly looks away from her. "Homeboy, I see they gone make it real hard for you. The more she bullshits me, the more you'll suffer. I don't hit bitches, so you gone have to take the weight."

"Come on man," he cries. "I ain't got shit to do with it."

"Nah? You just live here, right? Don't play me like I'm stupid!" he shouts. "Where's the shit?"

"I don't know nothing," he claims.

"Oh, you don't know nothing, huh? You've been hanging yo flunky ass around her for years, and you don't know shit? Nigga, shut up before I bust yo fucking head open!" he shouts as he aims at the boy's head. The girl lets out a loud cry. "Bitch, shut up. I don't want to hear your mouth again," Sha-Rock threatens.

The First Lady isn't going for this. She's sure this is a set up. They sound like they're reading off of a script. Something tells her that her dude is behind this. "What is this all about?" she asks. "Ain't shit here. I ain't got shit," she says.

"Bitch, don't play stupid!" Sha-Rock shouts.

"That's enough bitches," she says sternly. "I ain't gone be too many more of them."

"Bitch, you gone be how many bitches I call you, bitch! Bitch, bitch, bitch!" he shouts sounding like an angry child.

She smirks at him. "I don't believe this shit," she mumbles under her breath.

"Please believe it, bitch."

She snickers even harder as she looks at him fearlessly. She knows that she's getting under his skin.

Sha-Rock realizes that this is going to be a little harder than he expected. "Let me tell you something, bitch. Don't think I won't kill your stupid ass. I came here to get what I want and leave. Go against the plan and you're a dead bitch!"

She smirks again. "Let me tell you something, *gangster*. I'm the First Lady. Obviously you don't know the repercussions of fucking with a *bitch* like me? If you did, you would rather kill your mama than to fuck with me. From any city in this country, I'll have your wack ass touched, bottom line. I don't know who souped you up to do this but they must hate you. I got $5,000 in the bottom of that closet over there," she says as she points toward her left. "The best thing for you to do is, get the five grand and get the fuck out of my house," she says in a calm manner. "No hard feelings, no repercussions. I promise. I'll just charge it to the game. You caught me slippin'."

"First of all, I didn't catch you slippin'. I must admit, yo shit is airtight. I caught yo fool ass flunky slippin'. Secondly, I'm not a fiend. Five thousand ain't gone do it for me. Either you tell me where the mother load is, or I'll have to finish yo ass in here. That's the bottom line."

"You're not smelling me," she says. "I'm telling you to take the five and bounce. Do you. I'll chalk it up as a loss."

"Obviously, you're not smelling me. Keep the five. I want the mother load or none of y'all are going to make it out of here." Sha-Rock truly respects her *gangster*, but now she's starting to make him angry. He does not intimidate her at all. He knows that a man can never win in a debate with a woman. It's just their nature to challenge men. He's come to the conclusion that the only thing she's going to respect is pressure. "I ain't even gone ask you no more. When my man comes back from his search, if I don't get what I want, it's going down," he says as he leans against the wall nonchalantly.

Ten minutes later, Cal walks in the bedroom empty-handed. "Nothing, Baby Boy," he says sadly.

"Fuck it then. This is my last time asking you. Where's the shit?" The First Lady looks straight ahead without replying.

"Bitch you heard me?" Sha-Rock asks. He's getting more frustrated with her.

"I already told you where it's at."

"Oh, you think I won't kill a bitch, right?" Sha-Rock asks hoping his voice will intimidate her. "You right, but I don't give a fuck about killing a nigga!" he shouts as he walks toward the dude that sits at the end of the chain gang. "Playboy, I told you, if shit don't go right, you the first to go, right?"

The girl cries louder.

"Playboy, you got two seconds to tell me where the shit at," says Sha-Rock.

"I swear I don't know," he cries.

Sha-Rock slaps him across the face with the nose of the gun. "I'm about to ask you again. Where's the shit?"

"Please?" he begs. "I don't know."

Sha-Rock slaps him again. This time his eye swells immediately. "Where's the shit?"

"Please tell him," the man begs as he looks toward the First Lady. "Please," he begs. The First Lady ignores him.

Sha-Rock slaps him again. This time the gun lands directly on the bridge of his nose. His nose bone shifts to the left and the blood pours rapidly. "Aghh," he cries. "My nose is broken."

"Shut up, you bitch ass nigga! Where's the dope?" Sha-Rock asks.

"I don't know," he cries.

Sha-Rock looks at the First Lady. "That's the wrong answer. Do you want to help him?" Sha-Rock asks as he rests the nose of the gun on the top of the kid's head, making the gesture that he's about to shoot him in the head. His face looks hideous. Both eyes are swollen. His nose is also swollen and crooked. The blood hasn't stopped pouring yet. Sha-Rock is not getting the reaction that he expected from her. He thought she would have given in by now. "Is there anything that you would like to ask the First Lady before I put yo bitch ass out of your misery?"

The boy looks her in the eyes. "Please don't let him kill me," he pleads. His begging does hit a soft spot in the First Lady's heart, but a part of her still is in disbelief. In her heart, she really believes this might be a set up. She doesn't think they'll kill him. She thinks that they're using him to reel her in. He better hope they kill him because if they don't she'll have him murdered for pulling this stunt.

"Please tell them," her girlfriend pleads. "Don't let them kill him."

"Please," he begs once again.

First Lady looks into his eyes. He looks scared. Actually he looks real scared. He's putting on a hell of an act, she thinks.

"Only you can save him," Sha-Rock claims.

Shockingly, the First Lady says, "Kill the bitch ass nigga."

No one can believe their ears. He starts to cry like a newborn.

"You think this is a game, huh?" Sha-Rock asks. "Killer, show this bitch this ain't a game."

Killer Cal pulls the handcuff key out of his pocket and opens the cuffs. He then snatches the boy to his feet. He looks the First Lady in her eyes. This is actually the first time she has stared into his eyes. The looks of his eyes alone are frightening. "Bitch, this ain't a movie," he shouts as he pushes the kid out of the room. "Bring them, too," says Cal as he tosses Sha-Rock the key.

Sha-Rock takes the cuffs from her ankles and cuffs her hands behind her back. He does the same to her girlfriend. He then pushes the both of them out of the room. He doesn't have a clue of what Cal is about to do. Actually, he's probably more scared of the outcome than they are.

Cal leads the boy into the bathroom. "Sit them bitches down! I'm about to perform a baptism," he says as he smiles peevishly.

"No," the boy cries. "Please tell him."

Cal runs the water at full blast. The steam from the hot water makes the room extremely foggy.

The First Lady still believes all of this is staged. She sits there nonchalantly, wondering just how far they're going to take this.

"One more time," says Sha-Rock hoping she'll give in. "Where's the shit?"

She's still not responding.

By now about a quarter of the tub is filled. Steam rises from the hot water. Sha-Rock sure hopes she gives in before Cal goes through with it. Sha-Rock knows Cal is not bluffing. There's no doubt in his mind about that.

The water just about reaches the halfway mark. Cal pushes the boy to his knees as the boy screams at the top of his lungs. He tries to put up a fight but Cal is way too strong for him. Cal grabs him by the back of his neck and mashes the boy's face into the tub of water.

The boy tries to squirm his head from Cal's grip. He tries to reach back and snatch Cal's hands off of his neck.

The First Lady is starting to feel a little nervous. This is a bit much, she thinks to herself. Maybe this isn't a set up.

Cal snatches his head out of the water.

"Unghh," he gasps. He pants loud as he tries to catch his breath. "Please tell them," he begs. The blood has completely been washed from his face. His eyes are swollen shut. He can barely see out of them. Patches of his skin is peeling from his face from the scalding hot water.

The girl screams at the sight of his face.

"Shut the bitch up," says Cal.

Sha-Rock pulls a roll of duct tape from his pocket. He then snatches a purple satin thong from the shower rod. He stuffs the girl's mouth with the thong and tapes her mouth shut. The tears drip rapidly down her face. She's scared for her life. She's living a nightmare, right now.

"Ask her again," Cal instructs.

"Where's the shit?" Sha-Rock asks.

"I told you I don't have shit."

"Dear people!" Cal shouts. "We are gathered here today to witness this holy ceremony!" he says mimicking a preacher. He mashes the boy's head under water. In the name of Jesus, he thinks to himself as he brutally baptizes him against his will. The boy continues to fight for his life. Cal snatches him up again. Burns are all over his face. "Ask her again!" he shouts. "Time's up," he shouts not even giving her time to reply, let alone giving Sha-Rock time to even ask the question. "In the name of the Father, the Son, and the Holy Ghost!" he shouts before dumping his head underwater again. This time he holds his head underwater for double the time of the last two times.

He finally snatches him up. "Ask her again," he says in a demonic voice.

The First Lady still refuses to answer. She's starting to believe that this isn't a scam, but her stubbornness won't allow her to tell them anything.

Using all of his strength, he once again mashes the boy's face into the hot, bloody water. This time his face is so much deeper in the water. Bubbles flow from his mouth. Cal's mind takes him back to the day when he got baptized. He was so scared that he ran around the entire church trying to get away from Reverend Walls. It took the whole congregation to corner him off. He struggled so hard to keep his head from going underwater. He always had a fear of drowning. He almost choked as his head was immerged into the water. He could hear everyone laughing at him as he struggled for his life.

He remembers his mother's words: "Baby, after this you won't have any problems. You'll be protected by the blood of Jesus. You will be well taken care of."

He was sure taken care of all right. The very next week, his entire family was killed in the fire. Cal was the only survivor. "Thank you Jesus," he says aloud as he continues to hold the boy's head underwater.

Let that boy up, says a voice. It's not the voice of someone in the room. Cal recognizes the voice but he can't recollect it because he hasn't heard it in so long. Let that boy up, the voice repeats.

Dad, is that you, Cal asks in his mind.

Yeah, this me, boy. What the hell are you doing? Let him up!

Cal snatches his head from the water. He's barely conscious. His head hangs low, and he's not crying anymore.

Sha-Rock's heart pounds in his chest.

The First Lady turns away. She can't stand the sight of it but her stubbornness still won't allow her to tell them anything. Her brothers taught her to hold it down. They told her if they were to ever get in a situation like this and someone called her with a ransome call, not to give up anything, no matter what. Their orders were, let them die before giving the money away. She's now crying, but not on the outside. Tears drip down her soul as she watches her best friend in the whole world dying because of her stubbornness. Maybe she should tell them where the money is, she thinks. Hell no, I refuse to let them get rich off of my brothers' blood, sweat, and tears. Fuck that, she thinks to herself. The only reason they're doing this is because I'm a girl. My brothers never had a problem like this. I have to hold it down. I'm about to set the record straight right now. Shit is not sweet, just because I'm a female.

Cal's father's vision fades from his mind. "Last and final chance!" Cal shouts.

Sha-Rock's heart pounds harder as he looks at the boy's hideous face. He sure hopes the First Lady tells because right now, he even wishes Cal would stop. He knows if he stops him, the First Lady will never give in. He has to play it all the way out. "Where's the shit?" he asks desperately.

The First Lady rolls her eyes as she turns away.

"In the name of the Father, the Son, and the Holy Ghost." Cal dumps the boy's head into the water. The kid is no longer putting up a fight. He's dead, but Cal is still holding his head underneath the water. "We are gathered here today to say our farewells!" he shouts. Cal's mind takes him back to the first time his adoptive father made him kiss his private part. The feeling of violation rekindles in his heart. Calvin, let that boy loose, his mother says. "Okay, Mommy," Cal says in a little boy's voice.

He snatches the kid's head out of the water. His head dangles loosely. Cal turns the man's head toward the girls so they can get a clear view of him. Mucus fills his eyes and his nostrils. Blood covers his lips. His blackened eyes are completely closed.

The First Lady can't stand the sight of him. She turns away. Vomit fills the other girl's mouth but she can't spit it up because the tape has her mouth sealed.

Sha-Rock tries to act like he's not bothered by the sight, but it's eating him away inside. He's never witnessed a drowning before.

"Look at what you've done to him," Cal says as he stands up, while still holding the dead man by his neck. After he stands completely to his feet, he lets the dead man's neck loose. His head descends rapidly. The water splashes loudly as his head smacks into the tub of water. "I don't think he meant much to her," says Cal. "Give me her little girlfriend."

Sha-Rock hesitantly grabs the girl's wrist, hoping the First Lady will give in. She still isn't replying though. Cal drags the girl by her hair. She tries to squirm to the best of her ability. Cal picks her up into his arms. Her soft nude body gives him perverted thoughts, but he quickly erases them. Sha-Rock prays that she tells where the money is. There's no telling what Cal is about to do next.

Cal holds her body over the tub of water. Her head is near the bottom, where the dead man is leaning over into the water. She's kicking and squirming; yet she feels so helpless with her arms cuffed behind her. Cal drops her body into the water. She falls hard into the pool, causing a big splash. Cal laughs at her landing. She can't manage to get up. She lands directly on the man's head. This freaks her out. She can't believe this is happening in real life. She feels like she's starring in a horror movie. "Listen bitch. I ran out of patience," says Cal. "I'm going to ask you one time and one time only. Save your little pretty girlfriend," he says as he aims the gun at her head. "Where's the goods?" he asks. "I'm counting to five! Three!" he shouts, skipping over one and two. "Four!"

"Hold up," Sha-Rock interrupts. "He's only asking you once, and I'm asking you once. Listen, you see he's not bullshitting. He already killed your homey. You know he'll kill your little girlfriend. Just give us the money, so we can leave," he compromises.

The First Lady looks at her girlfriend. Helplessness and desperateness fill her big beautiful eyes. She begs the First Lady to tell She's not begging with words. Her eyes are doing the begging. As much as she would love to cut her loose, she can't. She refuses to go against the code. She's about ready to break. She's feeling weak. The money means nothing to her, but if she tells where it is, she'll get more innocent people involved. She's sure they'll kill them as well. She knows she has to ride this one all the way out. She leans her head back against the wall and closes her eyes. Boom, boom! The shots ring. The girl lies there motionless. Blood fills the entire tub as it leaks from her head. The First Lady cries silently.

"Now are you ready to cooperate?" Cal asks. "I gave your boy several chances. I gave your bitch two chances. You have only one." He grabs her to her feet and pushes her to the bedroom. She's not putting up the least bit of a fight.

He slams her onto her bed. Her naked body looks oh so delicious to him. How he would love to have his way with her. He envisions himself lying on his back while she's riding him. He closes his eyes for a second. When he opens them, he gets the scare of a lifetime. Hollyhood's head and Kia's head are stuck together like Siamese twins. Both heads are attached to the First Lady's body. He tries to force them off of him, but he can't. As they're riding him, the double heads lean closer to him. He closes his eyes to shake the vision away. Instead, the vision of the

First Lady's girlfriend's face appears in the place of the other two. She's on top of him, but she's not moving. She's just staring into his eyes. She's trying to talk to him, but she can't because the tape is covering her mouth. Cal finally shakes the vision away.

"Call somebody, right now," says Sha-Rock. "We need that scrilla. I know you smell me now!" he shouts. He just witnessed her first tear drip down her face, finally. She's broke. All that tough shit is over. She's ready to cooperate. He can see it in her eyes. He has to admit, she is a lot tougher than he expected her to be. The average man breaks down as soon as you aim the gun at him. "Are you ready to cooperate?"

She nods her head slowly in agreement.

Sha-Rock grabs her cell phone. "What's the number?"

She calls it out quickly as he dials. Someone answers, and he places the phone against her ear. "Hello," she cries. "Listen, the wolves finally got hold to Little Red Robin Hood," she says as she's about to give in and tell them she needs money to get free. She pauses for a second. She can't go out like this. She'll be a disgrace not only to her brothers but the game as well.

Sha-Rock nudges the phone, gesturing for her to finish her statement.

"You know the rules. Don't give them shit!" she shouts.

Sha-Rock and Cal are shocked to hear those words come out of her mouth. They were sure that she was ready to cooperate.

"Tell my daughters I love them!" she shouts as Sha-Rock snatches the phone away and hangs up the phone immediately. "That's it. Kill this bitch!"

Cal doesn't hesitate to walk over to her.

"Kill me," she cries. She has no fear. In fact she would rather die, than to live with the memories of this horrifying night. She wouldn't be able to live with herself, knowing that her lover and her best friend lost their lives behind her. "Go ahead and kill me. You don't have a choice now. You could have taken the $5,000 and split, no strings attached, but now you'll die, too," she threatens. "Kill me!"

Boom, boom, boom! Cal squeezes three times at close range. She dies instantly.

Sha-Rock runs to the closet and locates the five grand, before running out of the door.

What a disappointment.

November 21, 2004

Miranda is so nervous that she can barely stand on her on two feet. She can't believe that she allowed Tamara to talk her into doing this. She debated for days but she finally gave in. She never built the courage up to tell Sha-Rock what she was planning to do. She feels deceitful about going behind his back, but at this period in her life, she doesn't care how he feels about it. For so many years, she's been so busy worrying about everyone else that she has totally forgotten about what she wants out of life. She's been thinking hard about what her father said to her that day at the visit, and he's so right. She does deserve more. Not that she'll leave Sha-Rock for her modeling career, but he has to know that she's willing to lose him if he's not supportive of what she wants to do. She has been supportive of any and everything that he wanted to do, whether it is legal or illegal, moral or immoral. She just wants the same from him.

Miranda stands close to the curtain. She hasn't modeled in so long that she forgot about the queasy feeling that runs through her stomach before each show. Normally she has to move her bowels right before every show. The hardest part of it all is the fact that Tamara isn't here to support her. She's doing a show about twenty minutes away. Actually, Miranda is doing this show as a favor for Tamara. She already had a previous booking before Najee put this show together. She didn't want to let Najee down, so she bugged Miranda to fill in for her.

Miranda peeks through the curtain. The size of the audience frightens her. She glances around and notices that each seat is occupied. There's not a single empty chair in sight. People are even lined up against the wall. This by far is the biggest show Miranda has ever done. Never in a million years could someone have told her that she would be doing a show in the Apollo Theatre. As a kid she watched all the stars on television performing here and just to be standing in this very building is blowing her mind. She hopes and prays that she does well. Her biggest fear is tripping, or even worse, falling in front of all those people.

"Whoa," says the model, which just left the runway. "I didn't know there were so many people out there," she says, instilling more fear into Miranda. She's doing it purposely because Miranda told her earlier how scared she was.

Suddenly, thoughts of sneaking out of the back door run across Miranda's mind. She looks over to her right where the exit is. It would be so simple, she thinks to herself. She could walk right out the door without anyone seeing her. She can't, she debates with herself. That would be a cowardly act, but she's more concerned with disappointing Tamara.

"Go girl," the announcer shouts. That's Miranda's cue. When she hears those words that means the model before her is walking up the runway. She looks at the door once again. She has taken five steps toward the door without even realizing it. She can't go through with the show. She peeks to her left and then her right to make sure no one is watching her. The coast is clear. She pushes the door open quietly. Just as Miranda steps one foot out of the door she hears, "And now we have sportswear." Miranda stops in her tracks. She's not sure of what she should do. Tamara will be so upset with her.

"Ay girl, where are you going?" a model asks.

Her voice startles Miranda. "Huh?"

"Where are you going?"

"Nowhere. I was just trying to get some air," she lies as she steps back inside. Damn, too late, she utters to herself.

"Girl, you better go ahead. You already missed your cue."

"And now we have sportswear by our beautiful model, Miranda," says the announcer.

"Here we go. It's all or nothing," Miranda says aloud to prepare herself. She rips through the curtains. She looks straight ahead, trying not to focus on the audience. Her eyes are glued to the wall in front of her. If only the audience knew how scared she really is.

She looks awesome in her all leather outfit. Her leather motorcycle jacket matches her tight leather pants. The suit fits her beautifully. She's wearing tall black leather riding boots that extend over her knee. A black leather bandanna is tied around her head, and her long silky hair falls down her back. Her dark shades give her a bad girl look. In her right hand, she holds a black German motorcycle helmet.

Everyone watches quietly as she steps thuggishly down the runway. Her bowlegs add so much sex appeal to her. After the first ten steps, the butterflies are no longer in her stomach. She walks the runway like a seasoned veteran. Once she gets to the end of the runway, she halts, and then she strikes a pose. She then turns her head to the left then the right. Finally, she looks to the center of the audience, where she spots Tamara sitting in the crowd. Miranda gets a sudden boost of confidence, just seeing her face. Miranda snatches her shades off and winks at Tamara before spinning around and stepping away. Ten steps later, she makes her way over to the Harley Davidson that sits on the edge of the stage. She jumps on and starts it up. The crowd is surprised. They thought the bike was only a stage prop. Miranda puts the helmet on and straps it up.

She revs the motorcycle up a few times before cruising away. The crowd is going wild. Their cheering and applauding echoes throughout the auditorium.

Two Hours Later

Miranda and Tamara are sitting in Tamara's living room. Miranda is so proud of herself. She can't believe that she really pulled it off. She just wishes Sha-Rock could have seen her. She truly believes that he would support her if he knew how good she is at modeling.

Tamara took so many pictures of Miranda walking the runway, and most importantly, riding that motorcycle. Miranda can't wait to send the photographs to her father. She knows he'll appreciate them.

Miranda had no clue that there were so many agents in the audience. When the show ended they attacked her like vultures. She collected over a dozen business cards. All of the attention flattered her. A modeling career is right at her fingertips. The hard part is getting Sha-Rock to see things her way.

"Girl, I tore that runway up!" Miranda brags. "Child, did you see me?"

"Yeah, you know I saw you," she laughs. "I knew you could do it. You sound shocked."

"No, I'm not shocked. I was just nervous. I had to work the butterflies out."

"I know," Tamara says as she looks away. She pauses before speaking again. "Miranda, I have something to tell you."

Miranda doesn't like the sound of her voice. "What?" she asks anxiously. Tamara can't look her in the face. "What?" she asks again.

The anxiety is killing her. "What?" she repeats.

"Don't get mad, alright?"

"Girl, what? Be mad at what?"

Tamara finally looks her in the eyes. "I lied."

"Lied about what?"

She hesitates. "About the show. I didn't have a show to do. I just told you that to get you to do that show. I was in the audience all the while," she admits.

"What?" Miranda asks. She's heated. "How could you lie to me?"

"It was for your own good."

"My own good?"

"Yeah, I can tell you really want to model. You just need a boost. I swear, you looked so beautiful on that stage. I was so proud of you. You should have seen yourself. You're a natural. You really need to stop playing and take it serious. You can go so far." Miranda looks at her blankly. "Please don't be mad at me?" she begs. Miranda's eyes show no emotion. "Are you mad?"

"Hell yeah, bitch!" Miranda shouts. Her words shock Tamara. Miranda has never spoken to her with that word or tone. She looks at Miranda with a surprised look on her face.

Miranda cracks a big smile. "Girl, I'm playing! I could never be mad at you."

Tamara jumps up from the chair and gives Miranda a big hug. The ringing of the phone interrupts their bonding. Tamara runs through the house in search of her cordless phone. While Tamara is in the kitchen on the phone, Miranda steps toward the wall unit to retrieve the remote that's sitting on top of the speaker. Right next to the remote, there sits a large newspaper clipping. The headline catches Miranda's attention. It reads: "*Double Jeopardy for Harlem's Own Twin Kingpins.*" Miranda automatically knows what it's about. She sneakily peeks into the kitchen to make sure Tamara is not on her way into the room. She reads the article and all her questions are answered. Sha-Rock's assumptions are absolutely right. Modeling is nothing but a front. Najee and his brother are allegedly, the biggest heroin distributors in New York. The arrest is the result of a two-year investigation. In total there were over two dozen arrests. They operated in New York, but all their clientele came from other states, like Massachusetts, New Jersey and Virginia. The

Feds retrieved a total of ten thousand bags of heroin, ten handguns and over $300,000 in cash. What shocks Miranda the most is the last couple of paragraphs, in which the article gives a complete run down of Najee. They know everything about his modeling and his clothing line. There's no doubt in her mind now. This is no mistake. He may have Tamara fooled, but Miranda is on to him. She's astonished. She loves juicy gossip. She can't wait to tell Sha Rock that he was one hundred percent correct.

-40-

Two Days Later

"Listen, you know how much time I put into that. I thought that was the one. It ain't my fault," Sha-Rock claims.

Miranda sits at the kitchen table extremely agitated with him. She's staring at the wall with her lips twisted. She's not even trying to hear what he's saying. His presence is making her sick.

The look on her face is pissing him off as well. "What the fuck is wrong with you? Why have you been acting like this lately?" he asks. "I know what it is. I've been checking you out lately. I haven't been talking, I been watching. I can tell something isn't right. Somebody must be whispering in your ear, souping you up. He's probably telling you how much easier your life will be if you fuck with him? Somebody gassing the fuck up 'cause lately your whole attitude has changed. You go ahead and be a fool for that nigga. When it's all said and done, and you find out that all he wanted to do is fuck you, don't come back running to me!"

He strikes an emotion. She finally speaks. "There you go accusing me again." Miranda hates it when he accuses her, but she has to admit, he does have a point. She does hear all those slick remarks everyday. She's accustomed to it, so she's positive that her attitude toward him didn't change because of that. Her attitude has changed, though; reason being, she's getting so frustrated with their lifestyle. She just wants to carry on with her modeling career. She's also frustrated with herself because she still can't manage to build up the courage to tell him what she plans to do. "Sha, this isn't about a nigga. This is about us. I told you before, I'm not feeling this." She decides that this is the perfect time to ease it in. "Sha, you're being selfish."

"Selfish? Selfish?" he repeats, as he looks at her in awe. "Ain't this a motherfucker? I'm selfish, but you walking around here with $25,000 bracelets and $40,000 diamond rings. I ain't got one diamond, but I'm selfish. I ain't selfish, you're just ungrateful!"

"Ungrateful? Sha, I didn't ask you for none of that shit."

"You didn't have to ask because I know my role. Matter of fact, you should be more appreciative, being that you didn't have to ask for it. I didn't ask you for that," he repeats sarcastically. "I don't believe this shit. Yeah somebody got you gassed up. You better slow down before it's too late. I'm telling you," he threatens.

"Sha, this ain't about no nigga. And I'm grateful for everything you have ever done for me. It's just ..."

"Just what?" She pauses for a second. She's hesitant, but she realizes that it's now or never. "Just what?" he repeats.

"Sha, there are things that I want to do with my life. I have supported you in everything you've ever done, but you refuse to do the same for me."

"I see where this is going. You might as well stop right now. We've been through this shit a thousand times already. Fuck that modeling shit!"

"See what I'm talking about? You're selfish."

"Now I got you. I know what this is about. I knew I was right. You hanging around Tamara and them faggot ass Harlem niggas. That's the problem. Niggas promising you a better life. Persuading you to model now. Fuck what I'm talking about, and how I feel about it, huh? Pretty boy want you to do it," he says sarcastically.

"They don't have anything to do with me wanting to model. You know that has been my dream ever since I was a little girl."

"Whatever! Tamara got her dude. Don't let them fuck up what we got!"

"You're going to fuck up what we got," she says in a calm manner.

"Well, it's like this, if you want to model, you gone have to do it without me. I ain't with it! You make the decision 'cause I don't want to fuck up what we got." Miranda looks at him and shakes her head in frustration. She realizes that she's fighting a losing battle when it comes to this. "Yo, if you ain't gone do what I asked you, I'm about to head up to Newark. I gotta get some money from somewhere," he mumbles. Miranda stares at the ceiling. She's steaming right now. Sha-Rock wants her to go up north with him so they can put something in motion. He really didn't want to ask her on the count of how she's been acting lately, but he really needs her right now. His money is getting low and he doesn't have anything brewing right now. He was really banking on Hollyhood and the First Lady. "Well?" he asks.

"Well, what?"

"Are you rolling, or do I have to go by myself?" he asks. She rudely ignores him. "Miranda, you know if I didn't need you, I wouldn't ask," he says. "Please, just this last time," he promises.

"Sha, please?"

"Please what, Miranda? I need you. I tell you what ... Either roll with me or promise me you'll get all the info on them Harlem dudes like I been asking you to do for the longest?"

Oh boy, Miranda thinks to herself. There he goes with that again. Not one day passes without him asking about Najee. Miranda is quite sure that he'll never let that rest.

"Something tells me that you're holding out on valuable information about them," he says.

Miranda swallows the lump that formed in her throat. Is he a fucking mind reader, she asks herself? Sometimes he makes her so nervous with his accusations because nine out of ten times he's usually on point.

"Miranda, why haven't you turned me onto them? I feel like you're not telling me something," he says as he awaits her answer. He doesn't want to accuse her again, but deep inside he feels like Miranda is fooling around with a member of that clique. That's the only reason that he can come up with on why she won't bring him in. "Miranda, I need you to keep it real with me. I'm not accusing you, I'm asking you. Keep it real, alright?"

"I always do," she replies.

"What is it? Why won't you bring him in?"

"I don't know shit about him," she lies.

"Miranda, knock it off. Bitches talk. As close as y'all are, I'm sure she told you something. And don't talk that he's a model shit to me. You and I both know that's some bullshit!"

Damn, there he goes again, she says to herself. He's batting a hundred today, Miranda laughs to herself. He was right all the while.

"Why are you protecting him?"

"I'm not protecting him. I don't know shit," she lies.

"Miranda, are you fucking with one of his boys?"

"What?" she asks. He must think I'm a fool, she says to herself. Like, if I were I would admit it to him. I might as well put the gun to my head and pull the trigger myself. "Sha, no, I am not fucking with any of his boys," she says in her most convincing voice.

"How about his brother?"

"I don't even know his brother. I only seen him once."

"And you mean to tell me, he didn't try and push up on you?"

"Sha, niggas push up all day everyday."

"I ain't talking about niggas. I'm talking about Pretty Boy's brother. Did he ever try to push up on you?"

Miranda's left eye jumps. That always happens when she gets nervous. Sha-Rock peeps the movement of her eye. "Miranda, please don't lie to me," he begs. "All I ask is that you keep it real," he says with sincerity.

She can't lie. "Yes, he did," she admits.

"And?"

"And I told him I have a man."

"And?" he asks again trying to put pressure on her, hoping she'll crack.

"And nothing. That was it. Sha, you don't have anything to worry about. I'm not fucking around on you. I love you too much to do that. Yeah, I've been acting funny lately, but I told you what that's about."

"Miranda, I need that for something. Something tells me that he's a heavy hitter."

Heavy hitter is an understatement, she thinks to herself. The phone rings and Miranda excuses herself to answer it. Saved by the bell, she laughs. "Hello?"

"Miranda, what's up, girl?" Tamara screams on the other end.

"Nothing much, just in here talking to Sha."

"Oh well, I ain't gone keep you long." Keep me as long as you like, Miranda says to herself. "I just want to invite you and Sha to Thanksgiving dinner. I'm cooking a real big dinner over at Najee's house. His brother and a few of their boys will be there. Y'all are invited. Please come, alright?"

"Thanks. I'll let you know," Miranda replies quickly.

"Okay, call me later," says Tammy before hanging up.

Damn the devil is working full time. How coincidental is this? Miranda refuses to tell Sha about the invitation. He would love to go and see what's up with them. It's not that she's protecting Najee. She doesn't give two shits about him. It's Tamara that she's protecting. Through all of her bad relationships, she's finally found peace and happiness. Just to think, usually Tamara spent her Thanksgivings and every other holiday at home weeping. Miranda would hate to do something to interrupt her happiness. The last thing she wants is to see Tamara in pain again. And that's exactly what will happen. Miranda knows Sha will kill Najee. There's no doubt in her mind about that. She wouldn't be able to live with herself knowing that she was behind it. Even worse than that, the trunk of money is hidden in Tamara's house. If Sha finds that out he may kill Tamara. If there was some way that she could put Sha onto the money without it linking back to her or without anyone getting hurt, she would be more than willing to do it. Someone will have to get hurt because no one else knows that the money is there, so Miranda knows she'll be the first one they'll point the finger at. Sha-Rock would definitely have to kill them. Although there is enough money in the trunk for Sha to do what he has to do, she just doesn't want her friend to get caught up in the mix. Who knows, Najee and his boys may kill Tamara if they think she staged the robbery. It's just too much of a risk, Miranda utters to herself.

"Who was that?" Sha-Rock asks.

"Tammy."

"What is she talking about?" he pries.

"Shopping, what else," she lies.

"Go with her," he suggests. "Get that info. Miranda, please bring him in?" he begs. "Stop protecting him. You're making me feel like something is going on. Who knows, this could be the sting that we're looking for. This whole mission could be over with. Think about it," he suggests. "The ball is in your court!" he shouts as Miranda sits there debating with herself.

Cal sits on the closed lid of the toilet seat. The room is pitch-dark. The only form of light in the tiny bathroom is the flame that's covering the tip of the glass pipe Cal is puffing on.

He finally smokes the remains of the crack. He places his stem underneath the sink before walking out. As he walks toward his bed, he enjoys the view of the nude woman, lying ass up in his bed. The blankets are gathered up in a bunch at the bottom of the bed. Her shapely behind takes up half of the full-sized bed.

This is actually the same woman that was laying here the day Sha-Rock came in. She's been staying here ever since. Cal told Sha-Rock she was a good friend of his. What he didn't tell Sha was the woman is actually his ex-wife. He couldn't tell Sha-Rock that, being that Sha is totally aware of the drama she put him through. He was afraid of how Sha-Rock would perceive him if he knew he took her back.

Cal stands over her naked body. Despite the trifling act she committed, he still loves her dearly. He missed her so much. Cal strokes her soft course wooly hair, as he climbs into the bed and straddles himself across her tiny waist. He leans closer to her and plants soft wet kisses on her neck. He massages her gently as he continues to kiss her up and down her spine. He then switches positions, wherein he is now facing her feet. He plants his fingers into her fleshy buttocks, giving her a sensual rubdown. He leans over and plants one kiss on each cheek. He stares at her thick juicy thighs, which has always been his favorite part of her body. He massages them on down to her calves. He then grabs hold of her perfect sandal wearing foot. There's not a corn or callous anywhere. He sucks each toe, one by one.

Words can't describe how happy he is to finally have her where she belongs. Too bad she didn't want to be here. Maybe if she had cooperated, she would still be alive.

Cal climbs off of her and crawls up to the head of the bed. He turns her over by her shoulders. Her eyes are still wide open, as if she's staring directly into his eyes. Dried up blood stains the corner of her lip. Cal leans closer and plants a soft kiss on her chapped lips.

The passion excites him, giving him a full erection. He quickly climbs aboard and proceeds to make love to her corpse.

Thanksgiving Night

It's Thanksgiving night and instead of eating dinner like normal couples, Sha-Rock and Miranda have just walked into Club Envy in Manhattan, New York. She hates the fact that she's here, but Sha insisted. It was either do this or listen to him beg her about setting Najee up. She thought about it over and over. After weighing her options, she decided to stick to her story about knowing nothing about him.

Tamara is so upset that they couldn't make it to the feast. Miranda knows she'll get over it, eventually. Miranda told Tamara that they had planned on going to Sha-Rock's sister's house for dinner. If she only knew this decision was based on her safety. There would have been no way in the world Miranda could have stopped Sha if he had seen Najee's house. That would have increased his desire for him.

Miranda didn't say a word to Sha-Rock all the way up here. She promised herself that this is her last time involving herself in this madness. She was so mad that she didn't even kiss him before getting out of the car, and she never does that. She makes it a habit of kissing and hugging her loved ones before departing because you never know when it will be the last time you get to kiss or hug them. She learned that valuable lesson many years ago, one day when she left for school without giving her father his morning hug. She was still angry with him from the night before, when he didn't let her have her way. She kissed her mother and walked right past him, storming out of the house. She felt so good knowing that she had hurt his feelings. When she came home that afternoon and her mother told her that he had been incarcerated, she fell to pieces. The memory of his saddened face when she walked past him was the last vision she had of him in her head. She held that same vision in her head for nine years. The cheerful look on his face in the visiting hall erased the other one.

Sha-Rock sits at the bar sipping a cranberry juice as he watches Miranda from across the room. She's busy at work. The crowd goes bananas as DJ Funk Master Flex plays Ja-Rule's "New York."

Miranda is by far the baddest chick in the club, which makes her job so much easier. There are so many ballers in the VIP section. Sha wonders which one Miranda will choose. He hopes she'll get two or three. That shouldn't be hard, the way those characters are fighting over her. They've been tugging on her ever since she first came in.

"Excuse me," says a female voice, interrupting his thoughts. "Excuse me," she repeats. Sha-Rock looks to his left. There stands a short cutie. Her creamy dark chocolate skin glistens under the blue light. She smiles, spreading her thick, full lips, exposing her pretty white smile. Sha-Rock's eyes automatically drop to her trim waistline. He leans back slightly to get a view of her goods. Full trunk, he says to himself as he looks up. They lock eyes. She laughs in his face, due to the fact that he wasn't discreet about checking her out. "Damn, straight for the ass, huh?" she asks. "No shame in your game? I like that," she claims.

Sha-Rock's antennas go up; hood-rat alert.

"What you drinking on?" she asks.

"Cranberry juice."

"Cranberry juice? No you ain't! How square is that? Step your game up, nigga. All this Cristal niggas in here popping and you sipping on cranberry juice? Keep going bus driver, wrong stop!" she shouts like a wise ass.

"Damn all them Benzes in the parking lot and you're still riding the bus?" he says returning the sarcasm.

"Ooh, I like that. You got that off, she giggles. "What's good, nigga? Can a sister get a drink out of you?" she begs shamelessly.

Damn, he says to himself. What an easy smash. If I was looking to score, she wouldn't be anywhere to be found. If this were back in the day, Sha-Rock would play her game with her. All that slick mouth usually ends up in hot sweaty sex. Luckily he's not living like that anymore, thanks to Miranda. He decides to humor himself just to kill time while he's waiting for Miranda to score. "What you drinking?" he asks.

"Well, all I drink is Cristal," she claims.

"Oh yeah?" he asks peeping her game. She really doesn't know how plastic she is. Sha-Rock can see right through her. "But what are you drinking tonight, though?" he asks sarcastically. Cristal please, he says to himself. Quarter water ass bitch talking about Cristal, knowing the closest she's been to tasting Cristal is sucking the corks that are laying around on the bar counter.

"Give me a double shot of Hennessy, if that ain't too steep for you? That's about $18. I would hate to break you," she says trying to belittle him.

"Break me? I doubt that very seriously. A hamburger happy meal and a bottle of Hennessey, how could that break anyone?"

"Oh no, you got the wrong one, dear. I have not eaten a burger since I was a kid. Steak and lobster for breakfast. I'm very high maintenance. You might want to check my pricelist before going any further. Even my conversation is costly."

"You know what they say? If you have to ask the price, it's obvious that you can't afford it," he shouts back.

"Don't get in over your head. I like your style, but are you sure you don't want to check my pricelist? You're ego may be bigger than your wallet."

"Nah, I'm sure I can afford it. When there's a price next to an item, that's usually a sign that it's affordable. No price means it's expensive."

"Well, I wouldn't know anything about prices. That's not my field. I'm not in the habit of spending. I get spent on," she snaps.

Sha-Rock laughs in her face. "Lucky you," he says. She gets the impression that he's referring to her last statement, when he's really saying how lucky she is that he's here with Miranda. Boy would he love to give her a run for her money. He loves the overly confident girls. He gets so much pleasure from breaking them down to size. The majority of them are nothing but mouth. They fall in love the easiest.

One hour, six drinks, and one hundred slick remarks later, she finally pops the big question. "What's up, what are you trying to get into tonight?"

"Not too much. I have to get up early in the morning."

"Don't worry, I won't let you *sleep*. I promise to keep you up all night. In more ways than one," she adds while slowly licking her voluptuous lips. The tip of her huge tongue brushes across the holes of her nostrils.

Sha-Rock's mind runs wild. Oh, how he would love to take her up on the offer. He looks over at Miranda to keep his mind right. Not once has he lost focus of Miranda. She's been doing her thing. Sha-Rock witnessed her take at least four numbers. She said only one more vick. He hopes he can talk her into setting them all up.

219

The girl gets frustrated with Sha-Rock. She passes her number to him and staggers away. Sha-Rock aims his full attention toward Miranda, who happens to be leaving the VIP section. She walks down the narrow aisle on the opposite side of the club. Everyone is pulling and tugging on her as she tries to make her way through the crowd. Her face shows signs of aggravation.

Rapper Fat Joe, has the entire club leaning back. Sha-Rock stands up slowly, trying not to make it look so obvious. It takes them a matter of minutes to squeeze through the overly excited crowd.

Finally, they meet at the center. Miranda leads Sha-Rock toward the entrance. She looks back. "I have to go to the bathroom first," she says as she walks inside the restroom area. Sha-Rock leans against the wall, waiting for her. He combs the club with his eyes. He feels tension coming from the far left of him. His senses tell him something isn't right. There are three men standing about fifty feet away from him. Through his peripheral vision he can see them staring and whispering. He waits for the perfect chance to peek over at them.

Flex mixes in Lil Scrappy's "You Don't Want No Problems" and the crowd bops violently to the music. They're going wild, pointing into each other's faces and slam dancing against each other.

Sha-Rock looks at the men. Two of their faces look familiar, but he doesn't know where they're from. In the three years he done down Northern State, he met so many different individuals that it's hard for him to remember everyone. He tries to sneak another peak but him and one of the guys lock eyes. All of a sudden they too start bopping to the beat, pointing in each other's faces but peeking at Sha-Rock as they dance. Sha-Rock slowly turns away from them as he tries to figure out where he knows them from. He then looks again, staring at the shorter man while he's not looking. It all comes together. Oh shit, he thinks to himself. It's Trauma and his Unit. It's obvious that they know exactly who he is. He peeks at them. Now all three of them are staring at him. Sha-Rock turns away nonchalantly, still trying to play it cool. He bops to the music, while peeking at them from the corner of his eyes. He steps away from the wall as if he's about to leave. He stops short in his tracks before making the quick right into the bathroom. He peeks back to see if they're following him. To his surprise they haven't moved. Before walking into the stall he looks around to see if there is a window that he could climb through as an escape. There's not a window in sight. He stands inside the stall and pulls out his cellular phone. His heart is racing tremendously. He's so nervous that he can barely dial the numbers to Miranda's phone. He's totally out of bounds. He would have never expected them to be here in New York. Miranda is his primary concern. He doesn't want her to get caught up in the cross.

Her phone rings ten times before the answering machine picks up. He dials a second time. This time her phone goes directly to the voice mail. He tries again but to no avail. The red "no service" light appears on his phone. Damn, he thinks to himself. He has to hurry up. He doesn't know if they saw him and Miranda talking. If she walks out of the bathroom without seeing him, she'll leave the club and walk to the car alone. They may follow her. He has to go out. "Damn," he mumbles. They have him contemplating on what he should do.

He walks out of the bathroom. As he's walking, the door of the ladies room opens slightly. There's a long line waiting to use the bathroom. Sha-Rock hopes that she hasn't come out yet. He walks to the entrance and peeks his head out. Not only is she nowhere in sight, Trauma and his Unit have disappeared as well. Where are they, he asks himself as he peeks around the club. They're nowhere in sight.

Darkness appears as someone places their hands over Sha-Rock's eyes from over his shoulder. He ducks his head low and backpedals away looking frightened. He shakes the hands off of his eyes and is glad to see that it's only Miranda. "Stop playing so much," he whispers as he pushes her into the corner.

"Sorry," she says.

"Listen, it's going down," he whispers. "Some niggas from Jersey are in here that I had some words with. They spotted me. I went into the bathroom and they disappeared by the time I came out. We have to separate. I don't want them to know that we're together." Sha-Rock can see fear in her eyes. "Don't worry, they don't know you. You stay back, while I go to the car and get the hammer. Then, I'll come back for you."

"No, don't leave me," she whines. "What if they get me in here? Or they may get you before you make it to the car?"

Miranda just made two good points. He debates before speaking. "That's how it gotta go. I'm coming right back for you. Just lay low right here for a few minutes. I'll call your phone when I make it to the car."

Tears well up in her eyes. "I knew we shouldn't have came here," she cries. "I knew it. It's all your fault. Something told me not to come."

Her words rip through his heart. It really is all his fault. If something happens to her he won't be able to live with himself. "Put your phone on vibrate so you can feel it."

He walks through the club, constantly watching his surroundings. As he looks through the mirror he spots a familiar face across the bar. It's the third party. He's standing in the middle of a small huddle. All of their backs are turned. Sha can't see any of their faces. None of them appear to be paying attention to him. Hopefully he can manage to slide by without them noticing him.

He finally makes it to the door. He peeks to the left, the right and then the left again. The coast is clear. He steps out the door quickly. He takes long strides watching his back from every angle.

He's about a hundred feet away from the parking lot entrance, when he hears someone yell from behind him. He looks back and sees two dudes in the middle of the street wrestling around with each other. He speeds up his pace while turning his head in the direction that he's walking. Two cars are in front of him, an interior light shines brightly. The doors of the Excursion fly open. Sha-Rock was so busy watching behind him that he didn't even notice the truck in front of him.

He stops in his tracks. Trauma and the murder victim's brother jump out. The kid holds a chrome handgun the size of a cannon in his right hand. Sha-Rock backpedals three or four steps before making a complete turn. He ducks his head real low and runs around a small Honda that's parked close by him. Boom! The cannon sounds off. The bullet shatters the windshield, and the rear window of the car giving Sha-Rock a warning that they mean business.

They race toward him. Boom! He fires again, hitting the body of the car. The impact of the 44 magnum lifts the car slightly as the bullet rips through the steel. That's Sha-Rock's cue. He takes off at top speed. Boom! One more shot echoes as Sha-Rock runs up the middle of the street. He's running so fast that he's run past the parking lot without even realizing it. He looks back. He has a huge lead on them, but the kid is aiming the cannon at him again. Sha-Rock weaves in and out in a zigzag motion so the kid can't get a clear shot at him. Boom! Sha must have zigged one too many times, because the hot slug rips through his thigh, slowing him down. His leg feels like it's on fire. The pain is excruciating but he can't afford to stop. Fear keeps him in the race, but they're gaining on him. He bends the corner, running to save his life. Boom! Two seconds later, a ball of fire crashes into his back, causing him to flip forward. Boom! This shot pierces his abdomen as he falls on his side.

He tries to get back onto his feet but he tumbles onto his face. He desperately attempts to regain his balance. All he can see is Trauma and the kid coming at him rapidly. It's over, he cries to himself. His entire body is on fire as the bullets shimmy inside his back, thigh and abdomen. He curls his body into a human ball, covering his head with his forearms and closes his eyes so he can't see it coming.

The kid stands directly over Sha-Rock while Trauma speaks. "I told you to mind your business, right? It didn't have nothing to do with you. This was Jimmy's beef. You put yourself into it. Newark niggas discuss Newark business with Newark niggas, not out-of-towners. I did the math on you. You ain't from around here. You should have kept your out-of-town nose out of Newark business," he says as he walks away.

The kid aims at Sha-Rock's head. Click … Click …Click …

Boc, boc! The sound of an automatic weapon sounds off. The kid turns around to the direction where the shots are coming from. Boc, boc! They sound off again.

The kid aims and squeezes. Click … During the heat of the moment, he emptied his gun, wasting shots.

Miranda courageously runs toward the kid. She stops about twenty feet away from him. She aims at his head before closing her eyes tightly. She squeezes, holding her finger on the trigger without giving it a rest. Boc, boc, boc, boc, boc, boc, boc! Cling! The sound of an empty gun sounds off. She just blanked out. She's in a state of shock. She's never shot a gun in her life until now. All she knows is her lover is in danger.

She opens her eyes, only to find Trauma and his boy already halfway down the block. She didn't hit him with a single shot. He dashed away by the third round. She runs over to Sha-Rock. He looks up into her eyes helplessly. He cracks a half a smile, trying to make her think that he's alright, but she can tell he's in major pain. So many tears flood her eyes that she can barely see him. "Come on, baby," she cries. "We have to get out of here."

Sha-Rock fades in and out. One minute he can see her, and the next he can only hear her.

"Come on, baby. Please, you have to get up from there," she says as she attempts to drag him onto his feet.

"Get my arms," he manages to utter. He tries to lift his legs, but he can barely feel them. Miranda lifts his upper body and gets behind him, grabbing him by the armpits. Blood covers his clothes. He's still fading in and out. He can no longer feel the pain. He feels only the burning sensation that fills his body.

With her hands cupping his armpits, she manages to drag him into the car. She reaches over him and pulls the passenger's door inward. She then slides herself into the driver's seat and peels off nervously.

One Hour Later

Miranda is zooming down the turnpike. Sha-Rock lays stretched out in the passenger's seat in pain. He's trying to play it cool, so Miranda won't overreact, but he really wants to cry like a baby. The pain is unbearable, and he's losing blood by the quart. Everything seems to be happening so fast. It all seems so blurry to him. He feels like he's dreaming, but the pain lets him know it's reality.

"Don't worry baby. I got you," she cries. She looks down at the puddle of blood on the floor and she goes hysterical inside. She doesn't want him to see her panic, in fear that he may start to panic as well. The smell of fresh blood fills the air. The aroma almost turns her stomach.

Another hour passes. He's drained. He doesn't have the least bit of energy. Breathing is even a strenuous task. They fly past exit 5, doing 115 miles an hour. "Please baby, hold on," she cries. "I got you," she sighs.

He cracks a half a smile before losing consciousness.

Meanwhile in New Jersey

It's 2 a.m. and Jimmy is on his way to his son's mother's house. He's been staying there ever since his encounter with the Trauma Unit.

He speeds past the vacant parking spot, which is five parking spaces away from her house. He quickly slams the gear into reverse and backs into the parking space.

He jumps out holding a bag of Chinese food. As he's approaching her house, he notices two shadows coming from the alleyway. He stops, while studying the shadows. He sees two masked heads peering over top of the bushes. Without hesitation, he drops the bag and proceeds into flight, running in the opposite direction. Boc, boc, boc! The shots are close. He felt the wind of the bullets zip past his ear. Boc! That one was even closer. He refuses to allow the stick up kids to catch him and take him inside the house. If they get me, they'll have to kill me right here, he thinks to himself. I can't take trouble to my family, he says.

Jimmy crosses the street and dashes through a dark, narrow alleyway. Boc, boc! He hears behind him. He encounters a small gate in the backyard. He hurdles over it like a track star. Boc, boc! The shots make him run even faster. He encounters a second gate, which he hurdles even faster than the first one. He races down the alleyway that leads to the next block over. He finds a bunch of bushes, and he hides behind them. He looks around expecting them to run out of the alleyway, but they're nowhere to be found.

His heart stops temporarily as he hears seven more shots ring off from a distance. The only thing that comes to mind is his girl and his newborn baby. He prays they didn't shoot the house up. He snatches his gun from his waist and leans his head back in suspense. Who the fuck could that have been, he asks himself. He's almost sure that they're stick up kids, coming for his work. He can't believe he just committed such a cowardly act. If Sha-Rock only knew that Jimmy ran with his gun on his waist, he would be very disappointed with him. He violated the code of the street; shoot first and ask questions later. He hopes and prays that his family is alright. If they're hurt, he feels he should die as well. He could have prevented it if he would have just pulled his trigger and blazed back.

⎯⎯⎯⎯⎯◆◆◆⎯⎯⎯⎯⎯

Two Weeks Later/ December 9

Sha-Rock was just released from Temple University Hospital early this morning. Miranda's bravery saved her lover's life. She got him to the hospital in the nick of time. They had to rush him right into surgery. Any longer and he wouldn't have made it. Later she realized how much of a risk she took by bringing him all the way to Philly, but she knew better than to take him to a hospital in New York. She knows they both would have gotten arrested, especially if the other guys would have come to the hospital wounded.

The police questioned Miranda as soon as they came in. She made up a bogus story about someone trying to rob Sha-Rock, and him not giving his wallet up fast enough for the thieves. Sha-Rock told her she's lucky they didn't check her hands for gunpowder residue. He also says he vaguely remembers them checking his.

He's still in a lot of pain, but he's just so happy to be alive that he barely complains about it. The Trauma Unit is a little more treacherous than he gave them credit for. He really underestimated them. He respects the fact that they tried to finish him. The doctor told him that the only thing that saved him was the distance in between them. He says if they had been any closer he would have died instantly. Sha-Rock begs to differ. He believes the only thing that saved him was Miranda. She caught them by surprise. If it wasn't for her, he thinks they probably would have beaten him to death out there.

In total, he had five different surgeries. The shot to the leg went straight through, without tearing any ligaments or nerves. That was truly a blessing. The shot to the back caused a little more damage as the slug lodged into his shoulder. And last but not least, the shot to the abdomen caused the most damage, leaving him with a shit bag attached to his stomach. That bag will last longer than the initial pain. That bag will replace the toilet for as long as he needs it. The doctor couldn't tell him exactly how long he has to wear it. Sha-Rock hates it, but he'd rather deal with that living, than not to be here at all.

Killer Cal just stormed out of the house. He couldn't stand

the sight of Sha-Rock in pain looking like he does. He's about thirty pounds lighter. The dramatic weight loss is quite evident in his face. His cheekbones protrude, and his eyes sink deep into his head.

Cal promises to kill every member of the Trauma Unit, one by one. Sha-Rock believes him. He begged Cal to promise him that he wouldn't go anywhere near Newark until he gets well. Sha-Rock definitely has plans of getting even, but right now, he has to focus on healing.

Jimmy has been trying to contact Sha-Rock ever since that night. Sha-Rock lost his cellular phone during the chase and shooting commotion. Jimmy has been calling everyday. He doesn't know whether to think that Sha-Rock is in jail or dead. Either way is no good for him. All he knows is someone tried to kill him. He was so glad to find out that the gunmen didn't shoot the house up. They only shot all his car windows out.

The next morning bright and early, Jimmy went to the house and grabbed his girl and his little man. He didn't even give them time to pack. He jumped right on the highway heading to Virginia. He figures they'll be a lot safer down there. He plans to stay there until he gets in contact with Sha-Rock and finds out what's going on.

Jimmy has cousins down there who get lots of money and they're always in search of work. Before breaking out, Jimmy met the connect on the side of the parkway. He copped five kilos, packed them up in his rental car and peeled off.

"Ma," Sha-Rock whispers.

"Yes?" Miranda replies, as she applies dressing and gauze to his wounds.

"Thanks for saving my life. You're my hero, like Wonder Woman," he jokes.

"No, we're like Bonnie and Clyde," she replies.

He leans his head back, closes his eyes and puckers his lips tight, gesturing for a kiss. She leans closer without hesitation. Their lips smack loudly as they greet. "I love you," he mumbles.

"You better," she laughs.

227

-44-

————◆◆◆————

December 22

Cal lies in his bed curled up close to his wife's corpse. He has his arm wrapped tightly around her cold, naked body. He holds her hand while singing the theme song of their wedding reception into her ear. Her eyes, still wide open, are fixed at the ceiling. Words can't explain how happy he is to have her back at his side. That's evident with all the trouble he went through to get her back. Her lover hated to see her go. Too bad he couldn't put up much of a fight.

Cal replays the night in his head. His mother's voice told him to go past him and his ex-wife's old house. Cal was so distraught after the incident that he hasn't been anywhere near that house until a few weeks ago. Just seeing the house brought back terrible memories of that heartbreaking night. Deep down inside, he knew he wasn't strong enough to go back there, let alone see his ex-wife. The only reason he went is because his dead mother begged him to.

Cal had been peeking in the window for over an hour or so before deciding to ring the doorbell. He watched her lounge around, doing the normal things she used to do when they were in the house together. The only difference was she wasn't lounging with him. She and her lover looked so happy together. Cal was getting more and more jealous by the second.

Her lover rushed to the door without looking through the peephole. What a terrible mistake that was. He was so shocked to see Cal standing at the doorstep. The last time he saw Cal, Cal was standing over him beating him like a slave. For the rest of his life, he'll never forget the ass whipping Cal gave him.

"Hey, Playboy!" Cal shouts. "You look so different with your clothes on," he says sarcastically as he snatches his dagger from his coat pocket. He grabs the frail man by the neck and pulls him close. He presses the tip of the sharp dagger on the man's neck, pricking him. "Don't talk, just walk," Cal instructs. Cal pushes the man into the living room, where his ex-wife sits with her eyes glued to the television. "Honey, I'm home!" he shouts. "What's for supper?" he laughs.

228

Cal's voice startles her. Her ears must be deceiving her. She knows it can't be true, well at least she hopes. She slowly looks up, hoping it's not true. Yes, it's very true. Cal stands there looking like Satan himself. His red pupils glow demonically. She tries to scream, but nothing comes out. "Don't scream," he suggests. "Screaming will only get him murdered faster. Put your shoes on and let's go," he instructs her.

"Calvin, please," she begs.

"Let's go," he demands.

"Calvin, I'm not leaving with you. Please let him go and leave our house," she reasons.

"Our house, why do I have to leave our house?" he asks as if he doesn't understand what she's saying.

"Calvin, this is no longer your house. You have not lived here in years. Our means, me and him. Now please leave before I'm forced to call the police. I would hate to get you into trouble."

"You're putting me out of our house?" This sounds foreign to him. "You're putting me out of the house that I busted my ass to buy, working day and night, sacrificing just to give my cheating ass wife her dream home. Now I have to leave?" he asks as if he does not comprehend. "Bitch, get dressed. We're leaving!"

"Calvin, I'm not leaving with you."

His mind replays them in his bed when he walked in that night. His temples throb as his head pounds with pain. He jabs the dagger deep into the man's neck once, then twice. "Aghh!" the man screams. His scream snaps Cal back into the present. The man falls to his knees, holding his neck. Cal swings the dagger two more times, both landing in his chest. The man cries as the blood pours excessively. Cal pulls a roll of duct tape from his pocket. He seals the man's mouth shut. He then drags both of them to the bedroom. Using his rope, he ties the man to the rocking chair that's next to the bed.

The chair brings back so many memories. It was his mother's chair. That was the only item that the firemen were able to save. As he stares at the bloody man sitting in the chair, his face vanishes, and Cal's mother's face appears in its place. Calvin smiles as his beautiful mother sings gospel songs and knits. He envisions himself walking over to her to kiss her goodnight. Suddenly, the man's face reappears. "Get out my mama's chair!" he yells aloud before poking him in the arm with the dagger.

"Calvin, please stop," his ex-wife begs.

"Stop? I'm just getting started. Strip!" he shouts.

"Strip?" she repeats, hoping that she heard him wrong. "What are you talking about, Calvin? Don't do this, please?"

"Bitch strip, you heard me. I watched him make love to you, now it's his turn to watch me make love to you," he says with a deranged look in his eyes. "Today is judgment day. Payback is a bitch. Now strip!"

"Calvin, I'm not stripping."

"Okay," says Cal as he swings the knife at the man recklessly. The blade strikes the corner of the man's eye, tearing a thick chunk of meat. His eye looks like it's about to pop out of the socket.

"Strip!" he yells.

She now realizes how serious he is. She has no other alternative. It's either strip, or watch her lover get cut to pieces. She immediately peels her clothes off. Cal slams her to the bed before she gets fully unclothed. She lies there silently begging God to save their lives, as Cal sexes her against her will.

After satisfying himself, he stabbed her lover over forty times, almost shredding his body into pieces. He then dragged her to his apartment where she's been ever since.

For two whole days Cal stayed up nonstop, smoking crack while she watched him in fear of her life. Going into sixty hours with no sleep, Cal began to get tired. His body was beginning to shut down on him. He looked over at his ex-wife. She managed to doze off for a matter of seconds. Cal was tired himself, but he knew if he fell asleep, she would leave him. He refused to live without her. She was finally back in his life, and he would die before he watched her walk out on him again.

He tiptoed over to the bed and grabbed hold of the oversized pillow. In her sleep, she felt him standing over her. She opened her eyes wide. She tried to move, but it was already too late. The pillow swallowed her little head. He applied pressure, not allowing her any air to breathe. She only fought for a matter of seconds before her squirming stopped. He lifted the pillow from her face. There she was with her pretty brown eyes stretched wide open. He kissed her on the forehead before rolling over and falling into a deep sleep.

The ringing of the doorbell brings Cal's mind back to the present day. He's startled. "Cal!" shouts the female voice from the other side of his front door. "Cal, it's me, Miranda!" He jumps up from the bed and puts his robe on quickly. He looks at his beautiful wife lying there peacefully. He kisses her on her lips before covering her face with the nappy cotton blanket. "Honey, don't move. I'll be right back," he whispers. "Here, I come," he shouts. He cracks the door and slides in between the tiny opening. He then slams the door shut. Miranda's Nissan 350Z is parked in the alleyway right in front of the door. Directly behind her car sits Sha-Rock's Porsche. He's sitting in the car waiting for Cal to come over to him. Cal trots over to the driver's side window.

"Cal, we're out. I'm leaving both cars right here in the driveway. Keep an eye out for them."

"No question, Baby Boy," Cal replies. "When are you coming back?"

"In about two weeks, more or less. Here," Sha-Rock says as he hands Cal a stack of fifty $20 bills. "That should hold you until I get back." Sha-Rock is not aware that Cal has acquired a crack habit that could easily cost him $1,000 a night.

"Thanks," says Cal as he folds the money and grips it in the palm of his hand.

Sha-Rock places the remainder of his money into his pocket. In his pocket is his entire life savings of $5,000. That's everything. He would rather stay here and make some money but Miranda's mother's birthday is a few days away and he promised Miranda that they could visit her gravesite. That means they're Miami bound.

Sha-Rock has healed tremendously. His muscles are a little stiffened, but there's no pain. He's gained fifteen pounds back out of the thirty pounds that he lost. He looks somewhat thinner than his usual self, but he no longer looks sickly. The month of rest has done his body good, but it's done his pockets so much destruction. If he could get in touch with Jimmy, he could get a few dollars from him. For the life of him, he can't remember Jimmy's phone number. It was stored in the phone that he lost. He can't seem to recall the last three numbers.

Miranda and Sha-Rock stand at the curb with their luggage, waiting for the cab to come and drop them off at the Philadelphia International Airport.

Miami here they come!

Three Hours Later

Miranda and Sha-Rock stand alongside of the curb of Miami Airport. They feel so out of place due to the fact that they're both overdressed. Miranda, wearing her full-length, hooded wool coat, and Sha-Rock, wearing his gigantic snorkel and skull cap on his head are both burning up. At home the weather was just barely thirty degrees, and Miami is well above seventy degrees in the shade.

After ten minutes of waiting Miranda's impatience sets in. She pulls her cellular phone from her purse. She dials her godfather Kiko's number to see where he is. "Donde esta? Si? Donde? Okay," she shouts as she hangs up the phone.

"What did he say?" Sha-Rock questions.

"He says he's here," she replies as she steps closer to the curb and looks down the ramp.

"Got damn, somebody coming through with the Maybauch," Sha-Rock whispers as the cranberry colored Benz coasts alongside of the ramp. Miranda takes a quick glance at it before directing her attention back to the flow of traffic that's approaching. Sha-Rock admires the Maybauch, which has stopped within feet of them. The tinted window of the rear passenger's side rolls down slowly.

"Miranda, ven aqui!" (Come here!) shouts the passenger of the car. "Miranda!" he repeats.

"Ma," Sha-Rock calls out. "Is that him?"

The chauffeur hops out of the vehicle and walks to the back to open the door for the passenger. The tall, medium-built passenger steps out of the vehicle. He's rather smooth looking. He stands about six feet even. His dark hair is spiked on top and the sides are faded close. His eyes hide behind extremely dark oval shaped shades. He's wearing a bright lime green tank top, and multi-colored Hawaiian type shorts, and he has flip-flops on his feet. His neck, wrist and fingers are all covered with sparkling twenty-four karat yellow gold jewelry.

He stands there as the chauffeur lugs Miranda's Louis Vuitton luggage and lays it carefully into the trunk. Sha-Rock stands there awaiting the driver's return to help him with his luggage but he doesn't return. Instead, he walks to the opposite side and opens the door for Miranda. Miranda and Sha-Rock drag the remainder of the luggage and pack it into the trunk.

"Hola, bonita!" (Hello beautiful) he says as he opens his arms wide for a hug. Miranda returns the gesture by giving him a short brief hug. She peeks over at Sha-Rock. She can sense his jealousy. "Este es mi comprometido, Sherod," (This is my fiancé, Sherod) she introduces.

Kiko responds with a head nod. This bothers Sha-Rock. He looks Kiko up and down with a slight smirk on his face.

They get into the car. Miranda sits in the middle, and Sha-Rock sits behind the chauffeur. The interior of the vehicle is beautiful. The tan leather upholstery is butter soft. Mahogany wood surrounds the interior. The door handles, ashtrays, etc. are trimmed with twenty-four karat gold.

The ride of the luxurious Maybauch is much smoother than the airplane ride they just flew in on.

Sha-Rock feels left out because Miranda and her godfather's conversation is in Spanish. Sha-Rock loves to hear Miranda speak Spanish. He thinks her heavy accent and her deep voice is so sexy.

Sha-Rock can feel a great deal of tension coming from her godfather. It's quite evident that he's not too fond of him. While they're talking, Sha-Rock just enjoys the view of Miami. He loves the scenery. The clear blue skies and the palm trees are a big difference from the hood that he's used to.

Twenty minutes later, the chauffeur pulls into the garage of the most beautiful home both Miranda and Sha-Rock have ever seen. The bright yellow mansion is hidden behind beautiful palm trees. The spacious lawn has several statues spread across it, along with a huge waterfall that sits directly in the center of it. The chauffeur gets out and walks toward the rear of the vehicle. As he drags the luggage from the trunk, Sha-Rock speaks. "Hold up, we're not staying here, are we?" he whispers.

"You don't want to?" Miranda asks.

"Nah, let's stay at a hotel." Sha-Rock will never stay anywhere that he doesn't feel welcomed. His stay will be a disaster if he stays at Kiko's house. So instead of ruining Miranda's trip, he'd rather stay at a hotel.

Miranda turns toward her godfather and says a few words in Spanish. Whatever she said makes him bitter. Sha-Rock can tell by the way he looks at him and rolls his eyes before walking away.

"What did you tell him?"

"I told him you said you would rather find a hotel to stay in."

"Dude hate me," Sha-Rock assumes.

"They're funny like that," she replies. "They forget that I'm Black and Cuban. They think that I'm supposed to be with a Cuban man. It's not my fault that I love *the black mandingo*," she laughs.

"He said that to you?" Sha-Rock asks with an agitated tone.

"Pretty much," she replies. "That's what the entire conversation was about," she admits. "Don't worry, you know I held you down."

"What was he saying?"

"He asked me all kinds of questions about you, like what do you do and so forth. He even had the nerve to ask me about my father, like what does he think of you. I felt funny even hearing my father's name come out of his mouth after all the dirt he's done to him. Like he's really concerned about my father?"

Hearing that just made Sha-Rock really hate him. "How long are we staying, here?"

"We're just going in to freshen up and then he's taking us to get a rental car, that's it. The only reason I called him is so he could show me where my mother's burial site is."

Once they're inside, Kiko gives them a tour of his exquisite home. It's beautiful all the way through, from his antique furniture to his marble floors. Miranda is astonished by his glass roof, which the sun shines directly through. She could just imagine how it looks on the night of a full moon, when the stars are shining bright. Just her and Sha-Rock lying stretched out across the floor snuggled up together, sipping wine, before indulging in some hot and steamy lovemaking. How romantic, she thinks to herself. She then wonders how many times her mother and Kiko layed across that floor enjoying that same vision? Just the thought of it, leaves a sour taste in Miranda's mouth.

While Sha-Rock is in the shower, Kiko takes Miranda to a secluded room. The room gives her the creeps as soon as she walks in. It's full of pictures of her mother. He opens the door that leads to the walk-in closet, and they both step inside. Chills run up her spine as she stares at a room full of shoes and clothes that belong to her mother. It even smells like her mother's favorite perfume. Miranda fumbles through her mother's dresses and suits that are hanging up. The plainest dress of all catches Miranda's eye. She snatches it from the hanger and rubs the fabric across her face. She loves the feeling of pure silk against her soft skin. She pulls the dress over her head, allowing it to fall on top of her clothes. She poses in the mirror. She can't believe how lovely the dress looks on her.

"You look just like your mother," Kiko says with a heavy accent. He's speaking English now because Sha-Rock isn't around. He's right, though. With the dress on she looks just like her mother. Tears drip down her face. She misses her mother so much. Sometimes she feels so alone in the world. Her mother is dead and her father is never coming home, whenever she thinks about it she becomes so scared. Sha-Rock and Tamara are the last loved ones that she really has left. That's why she cherishes them so much. She looks over at Kiko, he's crying also. He gives her a very tight, comforting hug. Despite the fact that she hates him, she still comforts him by patting his back as he sobs quietly.

Suddenly, Miranda gets an uncomfortable feeling. She feels a stiff bulge forming on her thigh. She knows exactly what it is. She backs away and sneakily looks down. The bulge in Kiko's shorts is actually an erection. He stands there with a shameful look on his face. Maybe it was innocent; Miranda tries to rationalize with her self. Maybe it was perverted, she debates. Miranda hears Sha-Rock coming out of the bathroom. Kiko walks away embarrassingly. The thought of what just happened gives her a yucky feeling.

Sha-Rock sits on the porch just relaxing, while Miranda is in the shower. He wonders if he could ever move down here. He knows it would be a drastic change from the polluted air and all the hustle and bustle of the North, but he truly thinks he could get used to it. If his money was right, he would really consider it.

Minutes later, Miranda walks out of the house looking astounding. She's wearing her mother's sundress. She snatches a big red rose from the lawn and sticks it in her hair on the left side of her head. The dress and the flower in her head gives her a sexy Spanish look.

Her and her godfather walk side by side, while Sha-Rock follows close behind. Sha-Rock can't help but appreciate the way the dress fits her. Her booty jiggles loosely with each step, without showing the slightest trace of a panty line. After about six steps, her dress creeps into the crack of her cheeks, which lets Sha-Rock know that she's not wearing underwear. Sha-Rock laughs to himself as she discreetly pinches the wedgie from her crease.

Miranda's godfather hits the remote garage opener. He walks inside the garage as the gate is opening slowly. The sound of an engine racing sounds off. All of a sudden, the most precious, breathtaking automobile appears before their eyes. Sha-Rock's mouth drops open. The Aston Martin blows his mind. It's midnight blue with snow white leather interior. Kiko jumps out with a rather cocky demeanor, leaving the driver's door wide open, gesturing for Miranda to get in. He then speaks in Spanish to her.

"Come on, Sha," says Miranda as she hops into the driver's seat. The chauffeur holds the door of the Maybauch open for Kiko to get in. "Sigue a nosotros,"says Kiko, gesturing for them to follow him.

Miranda is scared of the Aston Martin's power. She's just barely tapping the gas pedal, and the speedometer reads forty-five miles an hour. She switches the gears nervously. The roaring of the engine sounds off several blocks away. Sha-Rock enjoys the ride as they tail the Maybauch to the burial site. He envies Kiko. From the looks of it, he has it all: a beautiful home, a luxury vehicle, and the ultimate sports car. What a life. What else can a man ask for, Sha-Rock utters to himself as he melts into the seat.

Once they reach the graveyard, Kiko directs Miranda to her mother's gravesite. She dusts the dirt from the tombstone still in a kneeling position, she starts to speak to her mother in a low whisper. Sha-Rock stands over her, massaging her shoulders. Kiko walks back to the car, where he waits patiently for her to finish. Just standing over the grave fills the empty space that lies in her heart. For one time in the past couple of years, she feels the bond that her and her mother once shared. Until now she had forgotten the feeling. She stays there for approximately one hour before deciding to leave.

After leaving the graveyard Miranda cruises through the town with no destination. Everyone stares at them as they profile in the eye-catching whip. Miranda changes the radio station dial. Just as the station changes her phone rings. It's Tamara, but she hangs up before Miranda can answer it. She attempts to dial her back but her phone loses service due to poor reception in that area.

"This is WVCG, 1080 AM. You're kicking it with Miami's own, Henry Crespo," the radio show host screams through the speakers. "Miami, I have a special guest for y'all. Today we have urban fiction author of the best selling novels, *No Exit* and *Block Party*."

Those titles ring a bell in Sha-Rock's head. He thinks for a second, trying to remember where he has heard them. "Oh, I read them joints when I was locked up. Turn it up. Let me hear what he's talking about," Sha-Rock says eagerly.

"He's come in all the way from New Jersey," says the host. "Al-Saadiq, introduce yourself to Miami."

"Peace! My name is Al-Saadiq Banks, author and publisher of True 2 Life Productions," he utters calmly.

"And who is this to your right?" the host asks.

"That's my brother, Naim. He doesn't talk much. You'll never get a word out of him."

"Oh, he must be a quite storm?"

"No doubt," Al-Saadiq utters. "He's the other half of the company. It's a family affair," he adds.

"Al-Saadiq, let me start off by saying, I read both of your other books, as well as you allowing me the privilege to review an exclusive copy of *Sincerely Yours*. I must say I enjoyed all of them. I especially like the way you tied all the books together in the last one. You also changed the game a little. I'm not going to give the story away, but it was a good switch. I must say, it was a beautiful conclusion. I had no clue that you would conclude the series in that fashion. What made you change it like that?" the host asks.

"Well, I just wanted to flip the script and show my versatility. People say they're tired of the typical drug stories. Mainly, I did that for the women. I know they get tired of hearing about kilos and murder. So I figured, I'd give them something that they could relate to, feel me?"

"It's funny that you say that people are tired of the same old drug stories. What do you as an author think that you're doing differently from other urban fiction writers?"

"Crespo, I deal with reality. No super heroes, no unbelievable events, strictly reality. The reality of it is, every drug dealer isn't rich. All drug dealers don't live in mansions and drive Rolls Royces. I write about life from all perspectives. I vow to keep it True 2 Life forever."

"Where do you get your stories from? Do you interview prison inmates? How do you go about formulating your stories?"

"Interviews?" he laughs. "Nah Crespo. For a lot of years, I lived these books. Thanks to God, with the help of my family and friends, today I only write about that lifestyle."

"So, you're saying these are true stories?"

"True to some," he claims. "Somewhere on the globe, somebody is living these books out as we speak. From state to state, ghetto to

ghetto, it's all the same game, just different players, and different slang,"
the author explains.

"I've done several interviews with rappers and authors. No
disrespect, but every one of them claims to have been big time drug
dealers at one time or another. No offense."

"None taken, Crespo. No disrespect to you either, but I refuse
to sit here and talk about my past. I'll never blow myself up. That's a
closed chapter of my life. I have moved on. It's over. Besides, I let the
streets tell my story."

"Ooh, I like that!" Sha-Rock admits. "That was gangster. I
heard he's official. Mad niggas in Northern State vouch for him. They
speak real big about him. They say him and his brother are some good
niggas," Sha-Rock informs Miranda who isn't the slightest bit interested
in any of it.

"I respect that. Let me ask you this. Do you feel like you're
glorifying negativity by writing these books?" Crespo asks.

"Nah, I don't believe that," the author states. "Negative is what
I used to deal with. I don't knock the hustle. I just want to show the kids
a different way to eat. The same lil jacks who used to idolize us, when
we were doing negativity, are the same cats that seen us selling books
out of our trunks when we first started this publishing thing. We're still
hustlers, but now we're just hustling books. Hopefully we've shown them
that hustlers don't limit themselves to hustling crack or slinging guns.
If you're a true hustler, you can move anything that you get your hands
on. I consider myself a hustler to the fullest. If I have to sell pencils and
erasers, I'll be alright. People, we have to open our minds. Stop chasing
the illusion. I know you have heard this so many times before, but the
fact still remains. The majority of my dudes are either doing double digits
in the Fed Pen or they're covered with six feet of dirt. Right now, I'm
trying not to be in neither position. God forbid this book thing doesn't
work out, you'll probably catch me somewhere selling shoestrings," he
laughs. "Anything besides that crack," he adds.

"That's a precious jewel, Saadiq," Crespo says. "People, I'm
sorry but we're running out of time. Saadiq, is there anything you would
like to say to the audience?"

"Yes," he replies. "Ladies and Dudes, come party with me

tonight at Opium. It's the official release party of *Sincerely Yours*. I represent the hood, please come out and show me some love. Peace y'all, see you at the club!" he shouts.

"Alright people, that's," Crespo manages to utter before the author interrupts him.

"Hold up, Crespo. Let me give some shot outs! If I don't, my people will kill me," he laughs. "Shot out to my Mom Dukes, my daughter, E, my little sister, and my nephew! Big shot out to Friend or Foe Entertainment, Chaos, and O' Gully!"

"Alright, alright, that's enough, Saadiq. I hate to cut you off, but we're out of time. Miami, I almost forgot. Tomorrow at noon, I'll be giving Al-Saadiq and The True 2 Life Family the key to our lovely city. All of you are invited to join us. It's going to be big. Everyone will be there. It's an event you won't want to miss. Thanks for listening to WVCG radio. I'm Henry Crespo, and I'm out. Peace!"

"We wouldn't miss it for the world," Sha-Rock says demonically. "Ma, get your best dress ready. We're going author hunting."

Miranda and Sha-Rock have just finished eating at a fine Italian restaurant on Ocean Drive. They walk a few blocks back to view Versace's house. Miranda is so overwhelmed with the size of the mansion. She can't believe how one man lived in such an enormous house. She's speechless as she stands in the very spot where he was killed. The huge cement wall that surrounds it adds so much suspense to it, making it hard to actually see the house. She walks around the corner to get a better view of it. She still has no luck, but she can hear the water splash down the waterfalls. She can only imagine what the inside looks like. After taking a series of photos on the stoop, they proceed in the opposite direction.

They walk up the block, just enjoying the breeze. It's so crowded out there. People are dining on the sidewalk in front of the eateries. The sidewalks are so full that it's impossible to pass. They have to walk in the street.

A crowd on the corner catches Miranda's attention. She looks up at the bright sign that reads, Wet Willies. Her curiosity leads them to the center of the bar.

In one hour, Miranda consumes over four frozen margaritas, while Sha-Rock drinks virgin strawberry daiquiris.

Sha-Rock finally manages to pry Miranda away from the bar. "Excuse me," says Miranda, as she approaches a waiter. "Can you tell me, which way is Club Opium?" He replies by pointing.

They finally walk into the club. The party is jam packed already, and it's not even midnight yet. They had hell trying to get inside. The line wrapped around the corner. It took them forty-five minutes to get inside. Sha-Rock overheard some girls chatting in the line; the party is not only the author's release party. It's also comedian/actor Jamie Foxx's party. Rumor has it that P-Diddy, Timbaland, and even actor Tom Cruise are already in the party.

Miranda didn't come here to work and she told Sha-Rock that she no longer wants to deal like that, but he managed to persuade her into trying to get close to the author kid. Sha-Rock told her this is the opportunity of a lifetime, and he would hate to miss it.

Miranda disperses into the crowd. She combs the entire joint in search of Tom Cruise. She loves him with a passion. She refuses to go home without at least seeing him in person.

Sha-Rock looks at the VIP section. He spots a huge banner with three books on it. It's obvious that's the author's section. About twenty dudes lounging around on the couches and puffing ten-inch long cigars occupy that area. The table is full of yellow bottles in silver buckets. Sha-Rock counts a total of twenty buckets to be exact. Also, about fifty glasses of mixed drinks spread across the table. Sha-Rock has to admit to himself, they're doing it big. Twenty bottles at $500 apiece is $10,000 in champagne alone. Dollar signs flood Sha-Rock's eyes.

While Sha-Rock peers through the crowd, trying to figure out which one is the author, the music stops. Everyone stops dancing and turns their heads to the deejay's booth. "Sorry y'all," the deejay apologizes. "Right here to my left, I have two important people. First of all, y'all who don't know who this man right here is, let me tell you. This is my good friend Henry Crespo. He'll be running for Mayor soon. He's no stranger to politics. He's been at the mayor's office for the past seven years. He wants to have a few words with y'all," DJ Khaled says as he passes the microphone over.

"What up people? I'll keep this brief. I know y'all came to party. Like my man Khaled said. I'll be running for office soon, and I really need the support. I represent y'all. Trust me, I won't let you down! Also, please tune into my radio show, "Kicking it With Crespo," every Saturday between 9 and 10 P.M. I'm dealing with politics as well as hip-hop and culture. Every week I have several phone interviews with people all over the world with the most sought out answers to questions pertaining to any issue. If you have a beef with a politician and you need to air it out with him, or you just need to know how to go about starting your own record label, just call me, and I'll get the information you desire," he claims. "Now, this to my left is Al-Saadiq Banks. For those of you that tuned in tonight, you're already familiar with him. For those who are not, let me formally introduce him. This is my man, Al-Saadiq Banks, best selling author of *No Exit* and *Block Party*. He's here tonight to present his newest release, *Sincerely Yours*. There are boxes of books at the entrance of the club. Go and get your free copy. He'll be signing books from 2 A.M. to 3 A.M."

The author peeps the silence. He shakes his head negatively. "Please don't put me on the spot," he whispers.

Henry Crespo ignores his plea. "Saadiq, is there anything you would like to say? I know that you're a shy dude," he teases as he hands the microphone over, giving the author no choice but to talk.

He holds the microphone nervously. The look on his face shows that Crespo just put him on blast.

Sha-Rock looks him over from head to toe. He's definitely not what Sha-Rock expected. Judging by his name, Sha-Rock expected a big beard Muslim, but judging by the contents of his book, he expected some hood-type dude. Sha-Rock was wrong with both of his predictions. The six feet tall, slim framed dude stands there bashfully. He's wearing a black and white pin-striped custom-made button up shirt. His diamond fluttered cufflinks light up the deejay's booth. A white satin ascot covers his neck. His black denim jeans sag onto his black alligator and ostrich Lucchese cowboy boots. An oversized New York Yankees cap is pulled well over his eyes, revealing only his nose and his thin goatee. Sha-Rock admires his flavor but the average dude wouldn't be able to understand it.

"Peace," he says extremely low into the microphone. "Thanks for the support, and having me," he says quickly before handing the microphone back to the deejay, who blasts the music again.

The author and Henry Crespo walk over to the bar area. They are deep in conversation when Sha-Rock walks over and rudely interrupts them. "Pardon me, no disrespect but I had to come over here and let you know that I really respect what you do. I was down Northern State Prison with a couple of your peoples. They speak real big about you. They say you're a fly dude."

"Oh yeah?" he smiles. "You were down Northern? What are you doing all the way down here?"

"Oh, I'm from Camden," he lies. "I'm just down here on vacation."

As they're talking, a lot of tension is coming from a small group of men across the room. They've been staring for a while now. One kid looks the author up and down. He stares at his cowboy boots before busting out in laughter. The author continues to talk, paying no attention to the group. "Hey my man, what are you drinking?" the author asks Sha-Rock.

"Just cranberry juice."

"Excuse me," he says to the barmaid. "Get a cranberry juice for my man right here, and a Grand Marnier for him," he says as he points to Crespo.

Just as they're watching the barmaid mix the drinks, someone squeezes in between Crespo and the author. "Let me get a shot of 151!" the man shouts rudely while stretching his elbows out as if he's moving them out of the way to make room for himself.

"Hold up, Fam," the author says in a calm manner. The kid is using his weight aggressively as he nudges the author violently. "Take it easy, Fam."

"Take it easy, what?"

"You elbowing me. You'll get your drink. I'm saying, take it easy."

"Or what, Crocodile Dundee?" he says sarcastically, as he looks down at the author's cowboy boots.

Al-Saadiq realizes that the dude is part of the group from across the room. It's all a part of their plan. They've been waiting for this all night long. They must have finally built the courage up to make their move. "Fam, it's nothing," the author reasons with him. "Just get your drink on," he says.

By this time the barmaid is passing the drinks over to the author as he pays for them. He passes the first glass to Sha-Rock. As he's passing the second glass to Crespo, the kid smacks the drink out of his hand. The glass falls onto the countertop, before shattering into little pieces. The alcohol splashes in his eyes, temporarily blinding him. He rubs his eyes until he regains his vision.

Crespo looks over to the True 2 Life squad. He raises his hand in order to catch their attention. They notice his waving and run over.

Al-Saadiq pushes the kid using all of his might. The huge man barely budges. He swings two wild haymakers at Al-Saadiq's head. He slips both of them. His squad runs over just in time. In fact both entourages reach the scene simultaneously. The True 2 Life entourage has them outnumbered. They form a tight circle around the opposing dude.

"Ah ah, back up. I got him," says the author as everyone backs away giving him room. Al-Saadiq's face shows evidence that he doesn't want to fight, yet and still he stands there with his guard held up high, right hand in front. This could get ugly. He outweighs Al-Saadiq by at least ninety pounds, and he's four inches taller.

The man launches a huge bolo at Saadiq's head. Al-Saadiq ducks it, steps in closer and taps him with a four-piece combination to his face; right, left, right, left, before spinning around the man. He ends up behind the man. The punches were as light as a feather. He didn't exert any power in them. He swung them only to aggravate the man.

The man turns around to face him once again. He can't believe he just got played like that. He promises himself that'll never happen again in a million years. He immediately swings one more haymaker. Saadiq slips this one as well, stepping in closer and tapping him again. This time he increased it to an eight-piece combination; right, left, right, left, right, left, right, left. The kid gets frustrated and rushes in for the attack. What a mistake. Al-Saadiq gracefully steps six inches to his right while firing a neck snapping, right uppercut, followed by a quick left cross. He completes the combination with a short right hook that lands flush onto the chin of his opponent. His opponent stands there motionless for about ten seconds before falling face first onto the floor. The crowd goes wild.

George Dukes, the club promoter, leads five bouncers over to the area. The bouncers pick the man up from the floor and drag him away. "George," Al- Saadiq calls out. "It's alright. He just had a little too much to drink. Don't put him out," he begs. "Let him party." The bouncers release him and the crowd disperses. "Now what were you saying?" Al-Saadiq asks Sha-Rock.

"I forgot," Sha-Rock laughs. "I like your style," he admits.

Al-Saadiq walks over to his section and grabs a bottle of Cristal. He walks back to the area where his opponent is standing with his entourage. "Here Fam, no hard feelings," he says as he passes him the bottle of champagne. "Drink up. It's on me. Never judge a book by its cover!" he shouts as he walks away.

Sha-Rock eases away from the author. He moves far enough away that he's not clearly visible by them, yet he can still keep his eyes on them.

Sha-Rock spots Miranda making her way toward the bar. She struts gracefully, holding a large pina colada in her hand. The sundress, the flower in her silky hair, and the pineapple on her glass makes her look so tropical.

Miranda walks toward Al-Saadiq and Crespo. She looks in their direction as they both lock eyes with her. As she passes, her eyes are still glued to them.

"Got damn," they say simultaneously. She reads their lips. Got them, she thinks to herself. She walks to the far end of the club and blends into the corner. Her beauty catches the attention of everyone. She has to fight the men away.

2 a.m.

The book signing is in effect. The line runs deep. Not a single dude is standing in line. The author stands at the edge of the VIP section as his entourage surrounds him. They're not surrounding him for security purposes. They're busy trying to meet the beautiful women who are coming to get their books signed.

"How you doing, lady," Al-Saadiq asks as the blonde-haired, blue-eyed white woman hands her copy of the book over to him.

"Fine, and you?" she replies.

He notices a small piece of paper that reads "Morgan 818-419-5555" jammed in between pages. "Morgan, right?" he asks as he presses his pen onto the book, preparing to sign.

"Yes," she replies, wearing the prettiest smile. He signs the book quickly and takes the number from the book before passing it back to her. He recognizes her area code. She's from Cali. That explains her carrot colored tan. "My address is on the back. When you're in the California area, don't hesitate to call," she says as she confidently walks away.

Next in line is a frisky, younger black girl, who appears to be a few years too young to even be in the club. She stomps to the front. "What's good?" Al-Saadiq asks.

"Hey," she replies. "I read both of your other books. They was off the hook!" she shouts cheerfully.

"Thanks," he smiles bashfully, blushing from ear to ear.

"You signed them for me, too. You were at a bookstore in Baltimore a couple of months ago."

"Oh, okay," he says as he studies her face.

"I be showing you mad support, now you have to do me a favor?"

"What's that?" he questions.

"See your boy over there?" she asks as she points to his man who is standing in the back of the crowd. "Sign the book to Dana, and put his number in the back."

He laughs. "Oh that's M-Easy. Yo, Malik!" he shouts to his man. "Come here, real quick."

The girl and his man step to the side, making way for Miranda. He's at a loss of words. Her beauty intimidates him. "Ah, ah," he stutters embarrassingly, as he stares into her eyes. He then drops his eyes to the book with the pen pressed against it.

"Maria Sanchez," she says in a heavily accented Spanish voice.

He signs it. He finally finds some words. "Where are you from?" he asks as he stalls his writing just to get extra time to converse.

"No hablo ingles," (I don't speak English.) she lies.

"Oh, perdon." (I'm sorry.) "Donde Vives?" (Where do you live?)

"Vivo aqui en Miami," she lies.

"Cuantos anos tiene?" (How old are you?)

"Vente y dos,"(22) she replies before speaking to him in Spanish for approximately thirty seconds.

"Suave, suave Mami," (Slow, slow) he laughs. "Crespo," he calls. "Come here for a second." Crespo comes quickly. "Yo, tell her in Spanish not to leave. She doesn't speak English." Crespo says a few words to her before opening the hook on the end of the rope to allow her into the VIP section. He then leads her to the couch where they sit and talk while the author continues to sign his books.

Finally he's finished. The hour is up. He can't wait to make it over to Maria Sanchez/ Miranda. He steps to the couch where she's sitting. She's sipping on her pina colada. She has her legs crossed high. The long split of her dress exposes an extreme amount of thigh.

Henry Crespo stands up. "Yo kid, she's on you. Her name is Maria Sanchez. She's from right here in Miami. She's twenty-two with no kids and no husband. She doesn't speak a bit of English. I set it up for tomorrow morning. I told her to meet you in front of city hall at eleven for the ceremony. I did all the talking for you, kid. The rest is up to you," he smiles. "I don't know Fam, she might make the perfect wife," he says as he walks away smiling.

Al-Saadiq grabs a bucket of Cristal from the table and he sits right next to her. From across the room, Sha-Rock watches attentively, not missing a beat.

One hour passes and the author and Miranda are still sitting close sipping champagne. Their conversation is limited due to the phony language barrier. The majority of the time they have been just smiling and gazing into each other's eyes. When he looks into her eyes, he sees innocence and sincerity. Maybe, he should have brought his glasses?

Hundreds of people swarm Convention Drive in front of city hall. The *Miami Times* and Channel 7 have come out for the event.

Al-Saadiq and his whole entourage stand on the steps as Henry Crespo hands him the key to the city. To his left stands Miranda. She's such a pawn. She enhances his image tremendously. His multiflavored polo shirt hugs his tattoo-covered arms. The way he's dressed today gives Miranda a different perspective of him. His baggy sky-blue denim jeans and white Air Force Ones makes him look like a hood, but with a token like Miranda on his arm she gives him so much class.

Rehabilitated thug is the phrase that comes to Miranda's mind when looking at him. It's hard to read him because he sends off mixed messages. He doesn't speak much, but when he does he speaks modestly. His eyes show sincerity, and his swagger says cocky. She's come to the conclusion that she will have to read his books to fully understand him.

Meanwhile in New Jersey

Bree walks out of the projects and jumps in his Chevrolet hooptie. He sticks the key into the ignition and looks downward at his CD case, which is sitting across his lap. After fumbling through and locating his Jada Kiss CD, he sticks it into the CD player. He turns the steering wheel slightly to pull out of the parking spot, when the sound of screeching tires to his left startles him. A car with dark tinted windows pulls alongside of him. Seconds later, a second car zooms up the block toward him. Before he knows it, the block is covered with Ford Crown Victorias.

Four cops with their guns drawn surround his car. "Put your hands up, where I can see them!" says the six feet five inch, 300 pound redneck. "You move, you lose!" he adds. Another officer runs to the driver's side and drags Bree from his car. He falls flat onto his face. The asphalt scuffs his face as they drag him with no remorse. Bree tries to put up a fight but after a few stomps to his head, he gives in. They cuff him and slam him into the backseat of the Crown Victoria.

"What's going on?" he asks.

The detectives don't reply. They just continue to ride away as if he hasn't said a word.

Later That Night Back in Miami

It's 12 midnight Al-Saadiq Banks lays around in his hotel room awaiting Miranda's phone call. His entourage has gone to Club Rolex, but he decided to stay here and wait for her call. He isn't in the mood for watching go-go girls tonight. The only butt naked woman he wants to see tonight is Maria Sanchez.

A few miles away Miranda and her godfather are at Mangos having drinks. They finished eating dinner over two hours ago. He invited Sha-Rock but he declined. He's over at Club Rolex, hoping to keep an eye on the Al-Saadiq Banks, while Miranda is with Kiko. Miranda and Sha-Rock heard of his whereabouts over the radio.

Kiko has been sipping on Johnny Walker Black Label ever since dinner. She can tell he's drunk by his display of arrogance. He's usually quiet, but the drunker he gets, the faster his mouth yaps. Miranda has drunk at least three shots herself. She's feeling groovy as well.

They're sitting right next to each other. "Miranda, I missa your mother," he claims. Those words make her feel so uncomfortable. She wishes he wouldn't say that. Just sitting here with him makes her feel like she's betraying her father. "I care about her, but she no care about me the same. She only lova my money," he says. "You father giva her everything, but he no giva her no passion. That'sa what she miss."

His conversation is getting under her skin. She hopes it's only the alcohol talking, but they say a drunk person speaks a sober mind. "Me, I giva her little money anda much passion. You father he no know better. Too mucha time in the streets anda no time at home. You father, he like a brother to me. Today I still care about he, but he no like what I do."

Miranda is getting angrier by the minute.

"You father is a good man, but he too emotional. He put his heart into everything, his woman anda his business. He thinka with he heart and not he mind. That's why he no make it. He too emotional."

No motherfucker, she thinks to herself. He didn't make it because he chose to hold it down instead of snitching on you. You backstabbing bastard, she says to herself.

"Too emotional," he repeats. "Me move to Miami because of he. Me afraid he tell Feds who I am. Me no trusta nobody," he says. "Me no trusta nobody anda me no get too close to nobody. Me lova and trusta me only!"

Miranda is now enraged. Her father is doing a life sentence for a guy who openly admits that he doesn't love anyone but himself. On top of that he belittles her father by basically calling him a bitch ass snitch. Miranda feels sorry for her father right now. He was loyal to someone who had no loyalty or love for him.

The deejay changes the song. "Tu Con El" by Frankie Ruiz rips through the speakers. The dance floor fills up quickly. Kiko's eyes light up with joy. "Come on Miranda, let's dance." She's not in the mood for dancing. Before she can tell him no, he grabs her hand and drags her to the floor. When they finally make it to the center of the overcrowded dance floor, he pulls her close and dances away. Miranda has to admit, he dances very well. His moves are very smooth looking. She can actually see why her father said he was suave and debonaire. She's no match for him. She can barely dance salsa. Kiko senses her lack of confidence. He saves her by spinning her around and pulling her closer. His hands grip her tiny waist as she shifts her weight from side to side. He peeks his head over her shoulder and places his cheek on her cheek. The smell of Fahrenheit cologne greets her nostrils. The heat from her dancing increases her high. The music starts getting good to her. The liquor boosts her confidence. She starts to move a little more as her rhythm starts to flow. Her panty-less ass inside the silk dress, presses against Kiko's thin, tight dress slacks. The feeling excites him, giving him a full erection.

Miranda feels the bulge banging against her cheeks but the liquor makes her ignore it. Miranda has had one too many drinks. She's intoxicated. Suddenly, she loses focus of what's going on. She's so caught up in the music. She grinds harder on his bulge. The feeling gets good to Kiko. He spins her around to face him. He grabs hold of her waist, as he pushes his erection against her pelvic area. He can feel her naked cat through the silk. They grind away without shame like they're the only two people in the club.

All of a sudden Kiko kisses Miranda in the mouth, not sure of how she'll react. Surprisingly, she accepts the kiss and opens her mouth for him to transfer his tongue from his mouth to hers. Their tongues intertwine. Johnny Walker blankets both of their taste buds. Miranda is way past her drinking limit. She's never been this drunk in her life.

One hour later, Miranda wakes up groggy eyed in the basement of Kiko's house, lying across his huge waterbed. The slightest movement causes huge waves in the bed, giving her the queasiest feeling in her stomach.

The basement is fully furnished. Mirrors cover all the walls and the ceiling. Spanish music blares through the speakers. She tries to get up, but she can't. She's pissy drunk. The room is spinning before her eyes. She looks to her right, where she sees Kiko's image in the other room. She squints her eyes to adjust her view and block out the other three Kikos she sees. He's standing there counting money. He closes the briefcase and snatches it by the handle, before walking toward her. "Miranda, Miranda," he sings. He reaches to the nightstand and grabs a bottle of Johhny Walker. He lifts it to his lips and gulps it nonstop. After his guzzling session, he puts the bottle to Miranda's lips. She sucks away. She's so drunk that she can't even taste the alcohol. It's flowing down her throat like water flows in the river.

He then walks into the other room, holding his briefcase in one hand and his liquor in the other hand. That's the last thing Miranda sees before falling deep into sleep.

————————◆◆◆————————

In New Jersey

It's now three in the morning. Bree sits at the small table in between two detectives. They snatched him from his cell four hours ago.

"Okay," says the white detective. "Since you're playing like you have amnesia, let me see if I can refresh your memory? This woman," he says as he digs his hand inside a folder, pulling out a photo. He slams the photo down, face up. Kia stares at him from the picture. "This woman says you asked her to set up her baby's father, who is this man!" he shouts as he lays the mug shot of the man they robbed and killed, flat on the table. "On October eighteenth, this man was robbed at this woman's house. He sticks his hand inside the folder once again. "After the robbery, this is how he looked." He slams a picture of the dude laying on the pavement dead. The picture makes Bree nervous. "Weeks later, this woman looks like this," he shouts as he shows Bree a picture of Kia laying dead in her apartment. The picture looks gruesome. Bree can't believe that they really know everything. "This is the happy expecting couple before you," he says while showing a picture of the dude kissing Kia's pregnant belly. "And this is the happy expecting couple after you," he says as he shows Bree two pictures of them ass naked in the morgue with tags on their toes. The detective then pulls out two more pictures. One of them is of the dude laying in the casket dressed in a black suit on the day of his funeral. The other picture is of Kia laying in her coffin, dressed in a white gown, holding a beautiful baby girl in her arms. The baby looks like an angel, dressed in her little white gown. The picture breaks his heart.

"The day of the funeral was the first time that anyone had ever seen that baby. Kia never even got a chance to see her baby. This was her very first time holding her daughter," says the black detective.

"One live man, one dead man, one dead woman, and one dead baby," the white detective says. "Let me simplify that fraction for you. One man, three bodies equal one hundred years or the death penalty if you're lucky. Talk to me!"

The detective can't break it down any simpler than that. He even showed Bree the statement that they took from Kia in which she tells everything. Stinking bitch, Bree thinks to himself. He's sure they'll put him under the jail for this.

"Talk to me, Bree. Isn't that what Kia used to call you?" he asks sarcastically.

Bree's stone-cold face turns as soft as putty. "I admit that I set up the robbery. *We* didn't intend on killing him. And I didn't pull the trigger," he says with no remorse.

"Well, *you* may want to tell us who did pull the trigger?" the white detective asks.

-48-

In Miami

It's 4 A.M. and Sha-Rock hasn't heard from Miranda in hours. He's on his way leaving the club. She should have called him by now. He's been calling her phone but she hasn't been answering. The True 2 Life entourage is busy popping champagne. Their section is filled with so many gorgeous strippers, that it looks like a rap video shoot.

Al-Saadiq lays across the bed frustrated. His phone never rang. He's so mad because tonight is his last night in Miami and he spent it waiting around for Maria Sanchez. Who knows, maybe she'll find him in New Jersey somewhere? That would be a hell of a coincidence being that Maria Sanchez is from Miami. Maria may be from Miami, but Miranda is from Philly. If he knew what's best for him, he would hope and pray that they never see each other again in life.

5 A.M.

Miranda wakes up suddenly. She looks down. Her beautiful body is fully exposed. Her mother's silk dress lies across the bottom of the bed. She hears the water running in the bathroom one room away. Kiko, her godfather, is singing loudly. Miranda reaches over and grasps the bottle of Johnny Walker. She turns the bottle high in the air and gulps the remainder of it.

She's so drunk that she squats over and urinates right onto the carpet. After that she staggers upstairs to the kitchen to get a drink of water. It takes her forever to get back to the basement. Finally, she waddles back to the bed where she sits for approximately five minutes before dozing off again.

She awakens again. She sits on the edge of the bed and buries her face into the palms of her hands. Through the small space in between her hands, she can clearly view her twat. She's still drunk but it's starting to fade away. She slowly lifts her head up, only to find Kiko's manhood dangling in front of her. She slowly looks up into his eyes. "Miranda, kiss it," he says confidently. Miranda eases off of the bed and drops to her knees in a submissive position. He steps closer to her. She teases him by kissing him from his ankles on up to his thighs. The anxiety is killing him. "Miranda, please don't tease me. Kiss it?" he begs.

"Let me kiss it for you," says a male voice from behind Kiko's back. Kiko is startled. Who is that, he thinks to himself. He turns his head slowly. His face is greeted by his own nickel plated, white pearl handle, snub nose .38 revolver. Sha-Rock stands there with a smirk on his face. "Watch out, Ma. Let me kiss it for him," he says.

Miranda gets up quickly. "You dirty motherfucker," she says. "Did you actually think I was that damn trifling? You fucked my father. You fucked my mother. And now you thought you were about to fuck me, huh?" she asks in a surprised tone. "Go ahead baby. Kiss it for him," she says as she puts her dress and sandals on. "I don't believe this motherfucker!"

"Do you know where the dough at?" Sha-Rock asks.

"I sure do," she replies. "It's in that room back there."

"Get it girl," Sha-Rock says in the tone that a man would speak to a dog. Sha-Rock grabs Kiko by the neck and pushes him into the room, while Miranda walks to the closet where she saw him counting the money. She walks inside and in clear view there sits the briefcase and two plastic garbage bags filled with money. Both of their eyes light up. There's also a small cardboard box sitting next to the bags of money. "Bust that box open," Sha-Rock demands. Miranda busts the box open. "Paradise," Sha-Rock screams as he fixes his eyes on the box of kilos.

"Come on, let's take it and get it out of here," she says nervously.

"Slow down, Ma," Sha-Rock says. "I'm sure there's more. This is probably just the money he made off this flip. The motherload is in here somewhere."

"Sha, please let's just take it and go. I'm getting a funny feeling," she admits.

That's Sha-Rock's cue. He's going with her instincts. He refuses to allow this to slip out of his hands. Even though he's sure that there's plenty more stashed somewhere in here. It's difficult for him to say it, but he says it. "Alright Ma, show's over!" he shouts. She realizes this is her cue. Normally she would fly out of the room in fear of witnessing the murder. This one she wants to see. "Did you hear me?" he asks, wondering why she hasn't left yet. "Show over," he repeats.

"I heard you," she says. "I want to watch."

"Are you sure?" Sha-Rock asks.

"Miranda please?" Kiko begs. "Think about what you're doing. We're family," he claims.

"I'm positive," she utters.

"Miranda please?" Kiko begs. "What would your mother think of you? Your father and mother didn't raise you to steal."

"Stop being so emotional," she screams. "Sha, let me witness the honors?"

"My pleasure," Sha-Rock whispers.

"Let me say it?" says Miranda. Sha-Rock pushes Kiko to the floor and aims the gun at his head. "You slimeball ass nigga," Miranda cries. "This is for my father!" she sobs. "We caught you slippin'!"

Boom! Boom! Boom! Sha-Rock dumps three in his head. He then grabs the two bags of money while Miranda grabs the box of kilos. They run out of the house cautiously.

6:30 a.m.

In less than two hours Miranda and Sha-Rock have packed up their belongings, along with the kilos and the money into the car they just rented from Exotic Rental Company. They're zipping up highway I-95 north, doing a moderate speed of sixty miles per hour in the silver Bentley GT coupe. Miranda is driving. Sha-Rock feels that it's much safer to let her drive. If he's driving, the police will be more apt to pull them over. They had no choice but to drive home. There's no way they will be able to get the money and cocaine back on the airplane.

Their plane tickets will go to waste. That's $500 down the drain, but that's only a drop in the bucket compared to the bulk of cash they scored at Kiko's house. Sha-Rock still hates the fact that they didn't search the house for more.

It may take them forever to get home, but if they make it, Sha-Rock has it all planned out. While at the rental car place, Jimmy's number popped up in Sha-Rock's head. Sha-Rock called him and told him that it's imperative that they meet. He didn't tell what it's about, but Jimmy could tell by the sound of his voice that it was good news.

Never in a million years did Sha-Rock expect this sting. Just to think, he didn't even want to come. He owes it all to Miranda. She really came through. Her mind wasn't really on robbery. She did it for revenge of what Kiko did to her father. The money was a bonus. Now hopefully, Sha-Rock can do what he has to do, and leave her alone about Najee, she hopes. Who knows, he may even let her follow her dreams of modeling? She doubts it, but it doesn't hurt to dream.

10:30 p.m. Christmas Eve.

It's sixteen hours later and they're still zipping up the highway. They've switched positions though. Sha-Rock is now driving. He bops his head to the tune of Tupac's "Me and My Girlfriend." He's been behind the wheel for four hours now. Miranda held the road down for twelve long hours by herself. Right now, she leans back into the butter soft leather sound asleep. Sha-Rock is paying very little attention to the road. His mind is occupied with moves that he plans on making.

4:30 a.m.

It's six hours later, Christmas morning, and they're spending it driving on the road. Two more hours and they've been driving one full day, straight. This is the longest drive they've ever taken. Sha-Rock keeps himself motivated by thinking of the reward that awaits them at home.

Right now he's so tired that he can barely keep his eyes open. He realizes how dangerous that can be. He has to be on high alert for police. He would hate to doze off while driving and swerve. That will give them probable cause to stop him. Even worse than that, he could fall asleep, run off the road, and wake up in a hospital chained to a bed. He thinks of all the bad things that can happen to him. He looks over at Miranda. She's snoring loudly. She's been dozing on and off for the past three hours. He knows there is no way he will be able to get any more driving out of her. The twelve-hour stretch finished her off.

Sha-Rock can't take it anymore. His eyelids feel like weights and his eyeballs are as dry as sandpaper. He turns his right blinker on as he approaches a Motel 6. He merges to the right lane and pulls into the parking lot. He knows the more he rests, the longer it will take to put his plans in motion. As much as he hates to stop, he has to. He's in dire need for some shut-eye.

49

Two Days Later

Sha-Rock and Miranda made it home safe and sound, yesterday evening. It took them many hours but the most important thing is that they done it.

Miranda wonders how her father would feel if he knew what happened. She also thinks about her mother. Did her mother see her from heaven, she asks herself. She eases her conscience by telling herself over and over that she done it for her father.

They left Philadelphia two hours ago. They caught the attention of damn near every driver on the Garden State Parkway. Sha-Rock sped up the highway doing 110 miles an hour all the way up. He has fallen in love with the ride of the Bentley.

After finally making it to Route 46, Sha-Rock makes the right turn into the parking lot of the car dealership. Him and Miranda jump out looking like movie stars. Miranda has her full-length tan and brown chinchilla wide open. Underneath it, she's wearing the tiniest skirt and the skimpiest halter-top known to man. She's wearing more boot than anything else. Her ostrich riding boots zip up all the way to her knees. Sha-Rock is keeping it very simple. His full-length white mink coat drags across the ground. He's wearing sky blue denim jeans and three quarter black alligator boots. His thick cable knit horse neck sweater swallows his little bean-shaped head. His white, full-sized apple-jack mink hat, adds a ton of flavor to the outfit.

All the salesmen inside the dealership have their faces plastered against the glass window, admiring them. They look at the Bentley with the Florida tags. Then they look at Sha-Rock and Miranda, looking like old money. Three salesmen attack them as they're browsing around looking at cars.

Sha-Rock didn't come here to look. He came to cop. It's time to treat himself, he feels. He's been playing the sideline long enough. It's now time to get out of the old Porsche. He has a briefcase full of money in the trunk that's trying to bust its way up out of there.

The lot is full of exotic cars. They have everything from

Lamborghinis and Ferraris to Bentley Arnages.

So far nothing has really caught Sha-Rock's attention, but Miranda has her eyes glued on a candy apple red BMW Z4 convertible with custom white leather seats. "That's cute," she says as she slowly walks past it. Sha-Rock doesn't even cut his eye in that direction.

He quickens his step when he notices a white Aston Martin sitting in the corner. It's the exact same one that Kiko let them drive while they were in Miami. Sha-Rock walks around the car observing it from every angle. "She's a beauty," he says to Miranda. He looks at the small price tag on the windshield. When he sees $245,000, he quickly walks away.

Another vehicle parked way in the back catches his eye. He studies it from afar. He can't tell exactly what it is. It has a very unique look to it. It's a platinum colored coupe. The two doors say sports car, but the look says luxury. It seems like it takes him forever to make his way over to the automobile.

Finally he smashes his face against the window. The custom interior blows his mind. Everything is jet black. The trimming around the doors and all the detailing is of black and gray marble. It's love at first sight for Sha-Rock. "Isn't she beautiful?" the voice startles Sha-Rock.

"Y-yeah," Sha-Rock stutters.

"We just got her in yesterday," says the young white salesman. "It's the Maserati Coupe Cambiocorsa. Eight cylinder, eighteen-inch wheels, six speed, 4.2-liter engine, ABS brakes, and traction control. Consumer rating is 9.1. She's compared to the Jaguar XKR, the Mercedes CL class, and the Porsche 911. Price wise, she's a lot cheaper than the vehicle you're driving in, which I must say, I happen to love dearly, but the Maserati gives you more luxury for your money. Not to mention the unique design."

"I'll take it!" Sha-Rock shouts anxiously.

Miranda looks at him with a surprised look on her face. "Baby, think it over, she whispers.

"Wouldn't you like to know the price, first?" the salesman asks.

"It doesn't matter. I'll take it." Miranda thinks he's being foolish, but she doesn't know he's playing his hand. The salesman told him, it's cheaper than the Bentley and he knows the price of the Bentley. So with that in mind, he's sure the Maserati is in his price range.

"Follow me to my office please, sir?" the salesman says eagerly. He's in such a rush to make the deal.

Miranda and Sha-Rock pull their chairs close to his desk as he grabs his calculator. "Let me start off by asking you, around what ball-park figure are you trying to keep your payments at?" the salesman asks.

Sha-Rock looks at him like he just disrespected him. "Car payment? I'm looking to make no car payments," he says sarcastically. The verses of one of rapper Jay-Z's songs play in his mind as he repeats it silently. "We don't lease. We buy the whole car as you should." "I'm buying the whole car," he blurts out. "Cash!" he adds.

"Cash?" the salesman repeats. His eyes turn to dollar signs, just thinking of the commission he's going to make. "The car is $91,000. With the luxury tax and state tax, plates, etc. You're looking at somewhere near $108,000?" he says, fearing that Sha-Rock will change his mind.

Miranda looks at Sha-Rock. The foolish look on his face is pissing her off. She likes the car, but she doesn't want him to buy it. She just wants him to use the money wisely, to get on his feet. "Sha?"

"108,000?" Sha-Rock questions. "Tell you what. That cute little BMW in the corner, over there?"

"Which one? The red, Z4 Roadster?" the salesman asks.

"Yeah!" Sha-Rock shouts excitedly. "My lady loves it. What's the price on that?"

"No Sha," she whispers, as Sha-Rock stares straight ahead.

"The price of that one is about $40,000. Will that be cash as well?"

"Of course," Sha-Rock replies arrogantly. "It's the only way."

"With taxes and all, you're looking at $42,000."

Sha-Rock calculates in his head. 108 + 42 = 150. "That's 150, right?"

"Yes, sir."

"That's a bit high. Don't you think? Don't forget, I am paying cash." He reminds him.

"I know, but that's the best I can do. The price is not negotiable."

"Bullshit, Johnny," Sha-Rock says as he reads the name on his name tag, John Segal. "Everything is negotiable! Come on, Johnny, I'm willing to bet you that over eight thousand of that is for your pocket. Come on now Johnny, I sold cars for years," he lies. "I'm not trying to bust your balls Johnny, but please don't bust mine," he says mimicking the salesman's voice. "Beautiful ring," says Sha-Rock referring to the salesman's wedding ring. "I know you have a family to feed. Don't blow the deal because of greed. Your wife would hate you for that. You can eat off of me, but please don't feast," he laughs. "I'd hate to go over your head and call your manager. Better yet, I can take my money to any one of those salesmen on the floor. I guarantee they'll outbid you!"

The salesman thinks quickly, while punching keys on his calculator. He looks up with disgust written all over his face. "Alright, I told you 150. I'll take five off. Make it 145?"

"Wow!" Sha-Rock shouts. "Five whole thousand? Thanks Johnny" he says in a proper, preppy type voice. "I'm out," he threatens. "Let me go holler at the short black brother over there. I'm sure he'll take care of me," Sha-Rock says as he gets up from the table.

"Okay, okay," he shouts greedily. "Give me 142, deal?"

"One hundred forty-two, uhmm? I tell you what. I got 145, and I need chrome wheels for both cars. Give me the paperwork. Let me sign before my arthritis kicks in," he jokes.

One hour later, Miranda is signing the paperwork as the detail men clean the cars up. The salesman almost faints when Sha-Rock hands him the briefcase full of $100 bills.

"Sir, I have to inform you that this large sum of money has to be reported," the salesman games.

Whatever, Sha-Rock thinks to himself. He has to say this just to protect his own ass. "I know, I know. I got everything in order. My uncle will come fill out the papers tomorrow, then you can discard all the paperwork that she's signed, alright?"

"Alright, you're the man," says the salesman.

Miranda is sort of upset that he just blew 145 grand. The salesman takes the money into the accountant's office. "Sha, this is a waste of money. I thought you were going to use this money to get on your feet. We already have cars at home."

"Excuse me, did you say something, selfish?" he teases, remembering the time she called him selfish. "Don't ever call me selfish. I take care of my baby," he smiles.

"Sha, we already have cars."

"We sure do," he replies. "But those are automobiles we're getting. We're bringing both of those old ass cars here tomorrow. He's going to buy them off of us."

"I thought you were going to use that money to get right?"

"I am," he replies. "Don't worry, Ma, I got it all figured out," he claims.

Sha-Rock sits behind the wheel of his new ride. The loud aroma of the leather is so strong that it's giving him a headache. As he revs the engine up, he examines the interior. The leather doesn't have one single crack or blemish in it.

Miranda is parked parallel to him. Her behind sinks into the butter soft leather. Sha-Rock admires how beautiful she looks behind the wheel. It looks like that car was designed especially for her. Her chrome rims sparkle as the sun beams off of them. He can see the image of his car through her rims.

Sha-Rock is such a negotiator. He paid only $3,000 for two sets of rims that value at $5,000 per set. He saved an additional $7,000. That's the advantage of paying cash, he thinks to himself.

The Bentley is still parked on the lot. "Ay Johnny!" Sha-Rock yells.

The salesman walks over. "Yes, sir?"

Sha-Rock tosses the keys to the Bentley out of the window. "Here catch!" He also throws a stack of fifty $20 bills, in a rubber band. "Take the wife out for dinner. It's on me. I'll be back tomorrow to get the car and bring my other cars to you, alright? Don't be afraid to hurt her," he laughs.

"Thanks!" the salesman shouts joyfully.

Sha-Rock feels good. He just made a couple of people's dreams come true. He pulls a CD from his inside pocket and jams it into the CD player. Rapper Lloyd Banks' "I'm So Fly" rips through the speakers. He blasts the music. The bass makes the windows vibrate. He rolls the passenger's side window down to speak to Miranda. "Yo, ungrateful," he says in a joking manner. She smiles at him. "I'll race you home!" he shouts. "Go ahead, I'll give you a fifty car head start," he claims.

The tires screech loudly as Miranda burns out of the parking lot. She didn't even confirm the race before pulling off. Sha-Rock estimates fifty cars passing him before peeling out of the lot. He catches up with her in no time. He blows a kiss at her as he leaves her in his dust.

She reads his lips as he says, "Bye, bye."

50

Later that evening while Miranda is out with Tamara, showing off her new ride, Sha-Rock goes to his sister's house. As soon as he walks in, he hands his sister two bags of money. One is for her and one is for her to send to their mother. Each bag consists of $5,000. The large sum of money worried his sister, but she still didn't refuse it.

He has been spending the money rapidly. In total, they scored $300,000 in cash and twenty-five kilos. So far he spent $145,000 on the cars. He gave $5,000 apiece to his mother and sister. And he gave $10,000 to Miranda. That's $165,000, leaving him with $135,000 in cash. He still wishes they had searched the house for more. He's sure that couldn't have been everything. How could it be, when Kiko's cars value at close to $600,000? Sha-Rock truly believes that there were some millions stashed in there.

The money is halfway spent. He figures it's time to make some of it back. His first customer was his sister's husband. When Sha-Rock showed him the material it blew his mind. Never in his life did he see cocaine that pure. The kilos are snow white, and the powder is fluffy and light as a feather. It's not the cut up garbage that's sold in New York. It's evident that the work has never been touched. He didn't complain when Sha-Rock told him $25,000 for a bird. Sha-Rock had to tax him for the stunt he pulled on him when he sold him the kilos before, and he beat him.

His sister's husband went to the same closet and pulled out $100,000 cash for four pies. Sha-Rock threw him one on consignment. Being that he fronted it to him, he dragged a few extra thousand. Instead of twenty-five, he charged him twenty-eight. That makes them even now. Now Sha-Rock doesn't feel that stupid about him beating him before.

Right now Sha-Rock sits at McDonald's on West Market Street in Newark. He's waiting for Jimmy to pull up. He can't wait to see the look on Jimmy's face when he tells him the good news.

Jimmy pulls into the lot and parks around the other side. He then walks around and jumps into the van excitedly. "What's good, nigga? I was worried about you. You just fell off the face of the earth. Man, I had to get low!" Jimmy shouts. "Niggas tried to catch me slippin'. The wolves was standing right in front of my BM's house. Luckily, I had my dynamite on me. As soon as I saw them, I started cutting at them," he lies. "That shit was crazy, kid! You should have seen them fag ass niggas running for their lives! Somebody had to put them on me," he assumes.

"Oh yeah? What day did that happen?"

"Thanksgiving night."

"That wasn't stick-up. That was them fag ass Trauma Unit niggas."

"You think so?" Jimmy asks.

"I know so. Check, I'm over in New York at that Club Envy, and guess who the fuck I run into? Trauma," he answers before Jimmy could guess. "I don't know how long them niggas was watching me. I peeped them when I was walking out the door. To make a long story short, I'm trying to make it to the G-Ride, to get my thing, and them niggas parked in front of the parking lot. I ain't no fool! I take off and them niggas start ripping at him. Nigga, the cannon was sounding off, you hear me?" Sha-Rock asks in a high-pitched voice, while Jimmy is watching with his mouth stretched wide open, giving him his full attention.

"The nigga hit me in the leg, but that didn't slow me down. I'm still getting loose on him until he hit me in the back and flipped me. Man, I'm rolling over, trying to get up, that's when the little cat banged me again, hitting me in the stomach. All I could do is curl up with my eyes closed. Nigga standing over me with that thing aimed at my head. Click, click, then I hear boc, boc, boc. I think I'm hit, but I look up and see them hauling ass!" he shouts. "Word up, if it wasn't for my broad, I wouldn't be here today."

"Damn!" Jimmy shouts with a look of awe on his face. "Who shot you, Trauma?"

"Nah, that fag ass nigga ain't gone shoot nothing. I know his kind. Dude little brother popped me."

Jimmy is really scared now that he knows it was Trauma and not stick-up who were after him. Obviously they didn't believe his story. He's sure they won't stop until they find him. It's a good thing that he moved his family away, he thinks to himself. "So, he hit you three times with a .45, and you healed up already?"

"Yeah, except for this," Sha-Rock says as he lifts up his shirt and shows Jimmy the plastic bag of liquid shit that's attached to his stomach.

"Damn," Jimmy says as he squirms. The sight of it turns his stomach. "What do you want to do?" he bluffs.

"Oh, don't worry about that nigga, that's nothing. I'm going to handle that later. But right now, I got something else on my mind. You gone flip when you hear this!" Jimmy looks at him attentively. "What number are you paying for them things?"

"Why, what's good?" he asks defensively.

"Nigga, how much you pay?"

"Nineteen," he replies.

"How many you got left?"

"I'm out. I ain't got shit. I been banging them country boys for $25, 000 a joint. When I first went down there, I only took five with me. I sold them shits in two days. I been coming back and forth all month long. Altogether, I sold about twenty joints down there already," he brags.

"Oh yeah? Well I got twenty more for you. And I'm going to beat that price, too! Nigga, it's on! I told you we were going to take shit over when I came home! You didn't believe me! You thought it was a game! How seventeen sound to you?"

"Seventeen sound great, nigga. Tell me what happened," Jimmy pries.

"Nah Fam, just know I came through, and your worries are over. We about to come the fuck up!" he shouts. "When are you going back to VA?"

"As soon as possible," Jimmy replies, thinking of Trauma. The sooner the better, he thinks to himself.

"Alright, I tell you what. Follow me back to PA, and I'll break ten of them off for you? I don't care how much you sell them for, just give me $170,000 back."

"No question!"

"I was gone holler at the kid Bree to see what's good with him, but I'll wait until tomorrow. Jump in your joint and follow me," he instructs. "Let's make this happen!"

On the ride to Philly, the only thing on Jimmy's mind is the $70,000 profit he's about to make. He estimates the ten should take him two weeks at the longest. $70,000 in two weeks, what a come-up!

51

The Next Day

Sha-Rock, Killer Cal and Miranda drove to Teaneck, New Jersey, to take the old cars to the car dealership. They also have to pick up the Bentley.

Sha-Rock drove the Porsche, and Miranda drove her Nissan that she really doesn't want to get rid of. Actually she loves her Z more than the BMW, but she didn't tell Sha-Rock because she fears that he may tell her to keep that one too. She doesn't want to seem selfish, so she decided to go ahead and get rid of it; even if he breaks her heart parting with it.

Killer Cal beat the pavement down like a maniac. He truly enjoyed driving Sha-Rock's Maserati. Coming back, Sha-Rock rode in the passenger's seat of his car for the first time, while Miranda drove. Killer Cal abused the Bentley. He drove that car with no regard for the law. The speedometer stayed on 120 the entire ride, making it back to Philly in a little over an hour. He couldn't wait to make it home to his loving wife. She's been in the bed naked, waiting for him all day.

Once they got to Philly, Sha-Rock took Cal clothes shopping. He spent only a couple of hundred on him. He's so easy to please. A couple of Discus sweat suits and two pair of boots, and he was good to go. Sha-Rock also gave him $5,000 in cash. He didn't want to give him too much and lead him into temptation. Little does he know, Cal has been led into temptation for some time now. With the crack habit that he's acquired, he'll be lucky if that $5,000 lasts him two days. Some crack dealer is about to get every penny of that.

-52-

Two Days Later

Today is one of the happiest days of Sha-Rock's life. Him and Skip have just been reunited after three long years. Skip is still in the halfway house but they gave him a weekend furlough.

He was a little upset at Sha-Rock when he saw how Cal was living. He couldn't believe that Sha-Rock is riding in a Maserati, while Cal is living in an abandoned shack. Sha-Rock explained that Cal has made a pretty penny over the months. Sha-Rock thinks he just feels comfortable living like that. As long as he's known Cal, he's always been a down low, dingy type dude.

The three of them spent the early part of the afternoon shopping and go-go bar hopping.

Sha-Rock just dropped Cal off. Watching those go-go girls didn't do a thing for Cal but make him horny. The whole time he was in the bar his mind was on his wife lying in the bed waiting for him.

Sha-rock zips up the turnpike. Skip can't wait to see Bree. He really misses him. He has a great deal of respect for him. "I can't wait to see my little man," says Skip. "He gone be bugging when he see me."

"Yeah, that kid love you to death. I wasn't gone fuck with him at first, but I felt how much love you have for him," Sha-Rock admits.

"No doubt. I love that kid. Not like I love y'all, but I love him." Skip pauses for a minute. "Yo, what's up with Cal?"

"What you mean?"

"I mean, he don't act strange to you?"

"Cal always been acting strange," Sha laughs.

"Nah, he's strange as hell! You think he's getting on again?"

"Nah, I don't think so. It's that medicine. Sometimes he takes it. Sometimes he don't. Today, I don't think he took it. Did you see how he was sitting around all quiet and shit?" Sha-Rock asks. "Mouth all dry?"

"Yeah, his lips was chalky white," Skip replies.

"Yeah, that's how he looks and acts when he ain't taking his medicine. He just sits around like a zombie, dazing into space."

"We have to watch him. Something don't feel right," Skip says.

"He'll be alright. I don't let him take any guns home with him, so there's no way he can hurt anybody," Sha-Rock assumes.

"Oh, okay."

They finally make it to Jersey. Sha-Rock pulls up to Orange Projects. "This is where he be," says Sha-Rock as he cruises the block. At least thirty young boys crowd the front of the tall building. All of them have their eyes glued to the beautiful Maserati with the sparkling chrome rims. Sha-Rock can read their lips as they compliment his whip. Some admire the car as others hate from the sideline. " I don't see him out here," Sha-Rock says slowly. He stops in the middle of the street and looks at the crowd. "Nah, he ain't out here."

"Damn," Skip shouts in a discouraged tone. "I really wanted to see that lil nigga. When was the last time you seen him?"

"A couple of weeks before I got shot."

"So, the niggas that shot you, where they from?"

"They're from Newark. This is Orange," Sha-Rock replies.

"Oh, they from Newark? What did I tell you when you came to see me?" Skip asks sarcastically. "I told you they live!"

"Yeah, they alright, but I'm live too! On everything that's gone be handled!" Sha-Rock says in a frustrated manner.

"For sure, nigga!" Skip replies. "I'm just fucking with you," he claims. "You know we ain't letting it go like that!"

Sha-Rock pulls of slowly. "Yo!" someone screams from the crowd. Sha-Rock turns around. A young kid stands there with both of his arms in the air.

"Who is that?" Skip questions.

"I don't know, " Sha-Rock replies as he snatches his gun from his waist. The kid trots over to the car.

Skip has a nervous look on his face. All he needs is to get into some trouble up here, and he's going back to prison.

Sha-Rock squints his eyes tightly. "Oh, that's Bree's little cousin," Sha-Rock confirms as he sticks his gun back into his pants. "That's the one I told you about, remember?"

Skip exhales. "Oh yeah!"

He walks to the driver's side. "What's up, kid?"

"Nice ride, bee!" he compliments.

"Thanks, " Sha-Rock replies quickly. "What up?"

"Stressing, bee stressing," he sighs.

"Why, what's up?" Sha-Rock asks.

"Oh, you didn't hear?"

"Hear what?" Sha-Rock asks without a clue.

"About Bree."

Both of the hearts pump faster. "What about Bree?" Sha-Rock questions.

"He got knocked off a couple of days ago."

"With what?"

"With nothing. Jake blocked him in right on this block like fifteen cars deep. I heard they trying to put three bodies on him. Something about some robberies," he explains.

Sha-Rock sits quietly. Instantly, Kia comes to his mind. He hopes they didn't get him for that. "Nobody ain't bail him out yet?"

"Nah, I'm out here trying to get the money up, bee. His bail high as hell. They want fifty cash."

"How much you gotta get up?" Sha-Rock asks.

"Fifty," he replies with a stupid look on his face. "Shit fucked up, bee!"

"Fucked up? What happened to all that weed y'all had?"

"Bee, you know how shit be? Been taking mad losses," he claims.

Sha-Rock sighs with frustration. "Where he at?"

"He in the Incredible Hulk," he replies.

"Incredible Hulk?" Sha-Rock repeats. "What the fuck is that?"

"Oh my bad. That's the new County Jail they just built. That's what we call it. I talked to him the other day. That nigga sick! He told me to see if I could get in touch with you, to tell you to come snatch him?"

Fifty, damn, Sha-Rock thinks to himself. That's a lot to ask for, he says to himself. Skip looks at Sha-Rock. He's waiting to see what Sha-Rock will say. He can't say he doesn't have it because he just bragged to Skip about the big sting in Miami. He hates to say this, but he's only saying it to please Skip. "If y'all got somebody to bail him, I'll put the paper up."

"Oh, we got the name already. That's nothing, bee" he says joyfully.

Damn, Sha-Rock says to himself. "Alright, give me your number. I'll hit you tomorrow when I get my hands on the dough." The kid calls the number out and Sha-Rock pulls off angrily. "Damn!" he shouts. "I wonder if those bodies got anything to do with us? I hope not. I ain't trying to go back, Skip. Sorry to tell you but I'll mirk your little man before I go back. I have to bail him. If shit don't sound right, I ain't got no choice but to rock him," Sha-Rock says while looking in Skip's eyes, waiting for some type of confirmation.

"I feel you, if that's the case, but I seriously doubt it. The kid is way too thorough for that. He's a stand up dude. You don't have to worry about him telling. If anything he the kind of dude that will take the weight for everything and cut y'all loose," Skip says. "Just bail him and get him a lawyer? I'm sure he'll hold it down."

"I hope so!" Sha-Rock shouts. "I ain't going back to prison!"

Sha-Rock is on his way up to New Jersey to take the money to Bree's cousin. He couldn't sleep last night worrying if Bree would tell or not. Sha-Rock isn't trying to go back to prison. Especially with the way things have come together for him. He hopes and prays that Bree holds it down for his own sake.

Meanwhile in New York

Miranda and Tamara have just finished auditioning for the HBO series "The Wire." They both feel confident that they'll get the part. The people were practically falling at their feet. Of all the girls that were auditioning they were by far the best looking and the best dressed ones there. Everyone else wore the scampiest, little whorish outfits. While they were dressed conservatively, they still managed to outshine them.

They hop into the Bentley GT, and pull off slowly. All the other girls either walk to the train station or jump into little raggedy cars. They all watch them enviously, wondering who they are.

"Girl, I know we got that part," Tamara says confidently. "Did you see them busted ass bitches?"

"How could I miss them?" Miranda asks. "Ran down Uggz; shits leaned over to the side, black market Seven jeans, and Canal Street pocketbooks. They were a mess!"

"I'm serious! The way we walked in, they thought we were stars already!"

"I know that's right!" Miranda confirms.

"We're guaranteed to get those spots."

"Ungghh huh," Miranda agrees, but she really hopes they don't get the part. She snuck up here without telling Sha-Rock. They discussed modeling once again, and his answer still didn't change. She can picture it now; Sha-Rock flicking through the channels and spots her prancing around. He'll kill her. The only reason she came is because Tamara pestered her to come.

"This car rides lovely, says Tamara. "I would love to have one of these. I could see me now. You wouldn't be able to tell me shit!"

"Yeah, it is lovely. I really don't want to take it back."

"When are you taking it back?"

"Tomorrow."

"You're driving all the way back to Miami?"

"No, they have another company up here in New York somewhere."

"Oh, I thought you had to drive all the way back down to Florida?"

"I wish. Girl it was so beautiful down there. I'm ready to relocate," Miranda claims.

"Like that? You sound like Najee. That's all he talks about is MIA. He wants to move down there too.

"Go ahead," Miranda suggests. "I wish Sha wanted to leave. Girl, I would be gone in a heartbeat. I'm ready to get from up here."

"I mean, I'm ready to move too but I don't know if I want to go that far? Najee would leave right now if I told him I'm with it."

"What are you waiting for? Ain't nothing up here."

"I don't know. Maybe I need to take a vacation to see what y'all love so much about that place. Maybe I'll tell him I'm thinking of relocating, but I need to see how it is first. That way I can get a vacation out of him," she laughs. "Lord knows that I need one. I'm under so much pressure that I don't know what to do."

"About what?"

"About life. Girl, a bitch going through it right now," she admits.

"What happened?" Miranda asks.

"What didn't happen?" Tamara asks sarcastically. "For starters, I just found out yesterday that I'm eight weeks pregnant," she says sadly.

"Oh yeah?" Miranda shouts joyfully. "Congratulations! I'm glad you took my advice on locking him down," she teases. "Why do you look so sad? That's a good thing."

Tamara grins. "Trust me, it wasn't intentional. A baby is the last thing I need right now. I'm not trying to put myself out there like that." She pauses. "I'm thinking of getting an abortion."

"Abortion? What are you talking about?" Tamara already knows how Miranda feels about abortions. She's totally against them. "What did Najee say?"

"He doesn't know. I didn't tell him because I know he'll want me to keep it. Miranda, I know it's wrong but I have to look out for me," she explains. "I can't get stuck like that."

"Stuck how?" Miranda asks with a bit of fury in her voice.

"Stuck as a single mother," she replies.

"Tammy, I don't think Najee would get down like that."

"No, I don't think so either, but some things are beyond his control."

Miranda is confused. She doesn't have the slightest idea of where Tamara is going with this conversation. "What are you talking about?"

"Miranda, Najee may be going away for a very long time. His lawyer says if he loses trial he'll get life."

"But he's innocent, right?" Miranda asks, trying to pry.

"That's what he's telling everyone, but I know better."

Finally, Miranda says to herself. She always knew there was no way that Tamara could have been that gullible. She's just pissed that Tamara tried to hide it from her.

"He's guilty," Tammy informs. "His lawyer says they have informants and everything. It doesn't look good for him at all. He told Najee that he should consider taking the fifteen years they offered him."

"Fifteen years?" Miranda asks. "Damn, what a plea."

"Yeah, fifteen. If he loses he gets life," she informs. "I'm not with the visiting jail shit. The other day he told me he wish he had kids, just in case they finish him off, his kids could carry on his name. Girl, we got into the biggest argument over that. I told him that was the most selfish shit I ever heard him say," she shouts. "Girl, I refuse to take my child to visit his father in prison every week, giving him the impression that it's okay to go to prison; lying to him, telling him daddy is in school! I can't do it. Miranda, I'm not ready for this," she cries.

Miranda can feel her pain. "Tammy, you're my heart and I'll never steer you wrong. I'm with you, regardless of what you decide."

"Thank you," she whispers. "I don't want to seem selfish but I can't go through with the baby thing. I have to get an abortion. I knew everything was too good to be true. I swear, sometimes I feel like I'm cursed. All these years I've been getting shitted on by these no good niggas, just taking all my pussy and showing me off like I'm some kind of trophy or something. None of them ever really gave two shits about me. Then finally, I meet someone who I love and he shows me that he has feelings for me. And look what happens? The motherfucker is about to go to jail forever! Miranda, I'm done," she sighs. "I think I'm about to be a nun," she jokes.

"Shit, I think it's already too late for that. You got too much dick on that jacket," Miranda teases.

Tamara laughs while trying to sniff the sobs away. "He was just about to give it all up, too. I've been on him, telling him to invest his money, and plan for his future. He's a good man. He just got caught up. No one ever showed him that they cared for him. Girls have always used him for his money. His mother is a dope fiend. He dropped out in the eigth grade, for crying out loud. His education is scarce. He can barely spell, but he knows how to count that money. I'm sure with time, I could have shown him a better way," she claims. "Modeling was just starting to come together for him, too. Now that's over as well."

"You never know. God may save him," Miranda says to comfort her. "Maybe God is just trying to give him a wake up call, so he can stop running and focus more on his modeling career?"

"Some wake up call? Ever since the arrest, he's been running even harder. Ralph Lauren canceled his contract, too. They took all the billboards of him down," she says.

"How did they find out?"

"Who knows? The other day, he asked me would I hold him down if he has to go away. I lied to him and told him yeah. The truth is, I know I will never be able to do that. Yesterday would have been the happiest day of my life," she says as the tears well up in her eyes. "He proposed to me," she says as she pulls a small jewelry box from her purse.

She opens it and Miranda peeks at it while still driving. The huge rock blinds her. Miranda gasps for air. She has to adjust her eyes to get a clear view of it. A slight bit of jealousy forms in Miranda's heart as she looks at the glittering beauty. She tries hard to keep the jealousy concealed. This ring makes hers look like a ring out of the bubble gum machine. It's fluttered with so many sparkling diamonds that no one in their right mind would ever believe it's real. In fact, if Miranda hadn't seen the trunk of money with her own two eyes, she too would doubt the authenticity of it. "That's beautiful," she says with a phony smile on her face. Extreme jealousy lies within her heart.

"I know, but I have to give it back. It wouldn't be right if I take it. I would only be taking it for the beauty, and it wouldn't be sincere. I know he only wants to marry me just in case he goes to jail. Then I'll be obligated to do the time with him. The pressure is killing me."

"What are you going to do?" Miranda questions.

"I have to deal with this, one issue at a time. I set an appointment yesterday for my abortion. That's priority. I hate to do it, but I have no other choice," she sighs.

"Like I said before, I'm with you no matter what. Don't worry. Everything will be alright." Miranda can tell Tamara is fighting back the tears. "Tammy, it's alright to cry." Miranda says, giving her the green light to cry makes the tears flow. "Go ahead Tammy. Let it all out. You'll feel better."

January 6, 2005

Out with the old and in with the new, Sha-Rock screamed as him and Miranda brought the new year in together for the first time in three years. He gave Miranda the option to do whatever it is that she wanted to, but she chose to stay indoors. Just lying on her man's chest, watching the ball drop on Channel 9 was enough for her. Again, Tamara invited them to another function and Miranda refused. Najee and his crew gave a New Year's Eve Players Ball in Englewood, New Jersey. Miranda figured it was best to keep Sha away from that.

One week has passed since Sha-Rock gave Bree's family the money they needed to bail him out. Sha told Bree's cousin to tell him to call him as soon as he touches down. Sha hasn't heard a word from him yet. He wonders if they released him. He plans to go up to Jersey in a few days to check the status of the situation.

Business wise, things couldn't be going any better for Sha-Rock. His brother-in-law just bought four more kilos, and he also gave Sha-Rock the $28,000 that he owed him.

Jimmy breezed through his ten pies in record-breaking time. He caught a slight attitude when he came to re-up and found out that Sha-Rock had only six kilos for him. He claims that six birds are not enough to hold him. He says he'll be finished with those in about two days.

Sha can't believe that he ripped through nineteen pies that fast. He plans on blowing sky-high. He's already in a fairly decent position as it is, but he figures making a few powerful business moves will put him way ahead of the game. That's why he plans on making Jimmy a partner. He's going to put Jimmy in charge of the entire operation. Sha-Rock is sure that he can hold it down if he has to, but he just feels that Jimmy has a better business mind than he does.

Sha-Rock is going to give him full control of everything, just like he promised he would when they were in Northern State. Deep down inside, Sha-Rock knows he doesn't have the "hustle" in him any longer. He's all burned out. He'd just rather pass the torch to someone who still has the energy for it.

Sha-Rock and Miranda cruise through Cherry Hill, New Jersey. They're in Sha-Rock's car following a middle-aged Caucasian realtor. They're in search of Miranda's dream home. This is all part of his "out with the old and in with the new" concept.

Life has been going one hundred miles an hour for Miranda these past couple of weeks. She's so overwhelmed with everything. Right now she's living her dream life. The only thing missing is the fact that her mother and her father aren't here to share her happiness with her. Sha-Rock has been showering her with gift after gift. The best gift that he's given her out of all is not material. It's the quality time that she had been begging for. They've been together everyday faithfully except for the few times that he may have gone to Jersey. Even then he's back before she could miss him. They even sit at the table together eating breakfast, lunch and dinner, just like a family is supposed to. Nothing can compare to the way he makes her feel when he spends time with her.

Twenty houses later, they're finally done searching. The realtor claims she's shown them every available home in the Cherry Hill section. Miranda has viewed so many beautiful homes that it's extremely difficulty to decide which one she wants. Sha-Rock's impatience didn't help her any. After about the tenth house he stopped getting out of the car. At that point, he just wanted her to make up her mind. He acted as if it's just that simple. After all, this will be the home that they'll live happily ever after in. Miranda has it narrowed down to about four houses. She told the realtor to give her a few days to make up her mind.

One Week Later

Miranda and Tamara are shopping the afternoon away at King Of Prussia Mall in Philly. Today Miranda has been treating her. Miranda felt like it was the only thing she could do to cheer Tamara up. She has been so depressed lately.

Yesterday she had the abortion. Miranda can tell it's beating her down mentally. She cried to Miranda all day yesterday once they left the clinic. Miranda's heart goes out to her. She feels sorry for the situation that she's in.

Tamara has been very distant with Najee lately. They spend very little time together, wherein she used to spend night after night at his house.

Speaking of Najee, Tamara's phone rings. She looks at the display, and presses *no* immediately, sending the caller straight to her voice mail. Guilt fills her heart. She never believed this day would ever come. Her love for him hasn't changed but she's just so confused. "That was him again," she informs Miranda. "Tell the truth," she demands. "Do you think I'm wrong? What would you do?"

Miranda pauses for a second or two. "Do I think you're wrong? I can't answer that. I'm not the judge. I can't say what I would do in your situation. For one, when Sha went to jail, we had been together for years already. I was already madly in love with him," she admits.

Hearing Miranda say that makes Tamara feel terrible. Just to think, her and Sha-Rock were in the midst of creeping around while poor little Miranda was at home waiting faithfully. Who would have ever known they would meet and become such good friends? Is that coincidence or destiny, Tamara asks herself.

"Also, Sha didn't get sentenced to life either," Miranda adds.

"What if he did?" Tamara asks. "What would you have done?"

"Honestly?" Miranda asks.

"That's the best policy," Tamara replies.

"This is me. I told you before; you have to do what works for you. Again, I'm with you in whatever you decide, but if I were in that situation, being who I am, I would hold him down. My father always taught me to stand behind my man. I wouldn't be able to live with myself if I turned my back on him. I never told anyone this, but my mother turned her back on my father. When I talk to him I can feel his pain. I could never do that to any man that I love. I'm sorry. I just can't do it. I'm not going to sit here and lie to you like I won't do me. Life is a long time. I'm young and the coochie still gets wet," she jokes. "Life goes on and no matter who I decide to deal with, they would have to understand my situation or I couldn't fuck with him. That's plain and simple. He'll have to respect the fact that I am going to visit him, accept his phone calls, and take care of him. That's just me," Miranda utters.

Tamara starts to weep. "I'm sorry Miranda. I'm just not built like you. I wish I was but I'm not," she cries. "I think I'm calling it quits. I have to tell him. It's the least I can do. I can't lead him on like that. To my knowledge he's been up front with me. He treats me better than I've ever been treated in my life. I owe him the truth. How will he look at me? Will he think that I only used him?" she questions.

"On the real, he's definitely going to think that. That's for sure," Miranda adds. "He'll think that you're breaking out on him because shit is getting thick. You can't blame him for that."

"Thanks for making me feel worse," she jokes with tears in her eyes.

"I'm just keeping it real," Miranda says as her phone begins to ring. "Hold up," she whispers to Tamara. "Hello?"

"I'm going to the bathroom to get myself together," Tamara whispers before walking away.

"Yes, this is Miranda Benderas. Who is calling? Oh okay, I did?" she shouts cheerfully. "When? Okay, what about my sister? Yeah, Tamara Hill? No, why?" She pauses. "Yes, I'll be there for sure. Bye bye." That was the woman who auditioned them for the show. Miranda got the part. The woman said everyone fell in love with her at first sight. The bad part is, Tamara didn't get picked, and it was her idea to go there from the start. Her agent gave her all the details. How could they choose those busted bitches over Tamara, Miranda asks herself. Tamara was definitely looking forward to that part. She was banking on it. All she talked about is how doing this show will open so many doors for her. Miranda doesn't know how she's going to break the news to her. The last thing she needs right now is another disappointment.

Hours Later

Sha-Rock and Jimmy are just meeting. Jimmy jumps in the van holding a plastic shopping bag in his hand. "What's up, my dude?"

"You," Sha-Rock replies. "How shit looking?"

"Lovely! I got niggas lined up. They love me down there!"

"They supposed to."

"Here, here goes $102,000," Jimmy says as he hands the bag over to Sha-Rock.

"Nah, hold it," Sha refuses, while reaching behind his seat, retrieving a smaller plastic bag. "You said you pay nineteen, right?"

"With my peoples? Yeah!" he shouts.

"Alright check, here goes $88,000. Put that with the 102 and get ten joints from your people. You said you banging them at twenty-five right?"

"All day," Jimmy replies.

"So that's $6,000 profit off of each one, right? You keep $3,000 and I keep $3,000. How that sound? Fifty-fifty. We're partners. Is that cool with you?"

"No question," Jimmy replies quickly. He calculates mentally. Splitting the profit will hurt him drastically but he isn't risking any of his own money. That just about evens everything out.

"It's your call," Sha-Rock claims. "You're the boss. I'm turning everything over to you. You make the calls. You make the decisions. I'm just the silent partner. We start with those ten and end up where ever you take us. You can break me off by the week, month, or whatever. It ain't no pressure. I trust you one hundred percent."

Jimmy looks him in the eyes. His heart softens up. He can't believe that Sha-Rock has that much faith in him. "Damn, that's fly!"

"Hey, I told you how we were going to put it down, didn't I? You must didn't believe me? You thought I was just another one of those beat, ass lying ass niggas in the box, huh?"

Jimmy is speechless. He just smiles. At the conclusion of their meeting, Sha-Rock drops Jimmy off to his car. Now he's on his way to Orange to pay Bree a visit.

One Hour Later/ 10 p.m.

Sha-Rock sits in front of Orange Projects on the dark block. He's parked near the corner. His eyes are focused on Bree's hooptie Chevrolet.

Seeing his car pissed Sha-Rock off. Just to think that he's home and he still hasn't called really disturbs him. He can't understand why Bree hasn't called him yet. Someone bails you out for $50,000 and you don't have the decency to call and thank him? It's just not adding up.

Two men walk out of the building. Both of them are dressed in all black. The taller one fits Bree's description, but Sha-Rock isn't sure if it's him.

The men shake hands before going their separate ways. The shorter man walks toward a black Cadillac Escalade, and climbs in. He pulls off quickly, while the other man is still walking in the direction of Bree's car. Now Sha-Rock is sure that's him.

He stops at the Chevrolet and Sha-Rock pulls out of the parking space. He cruises toward him while honking the horn to catch Bree's attention.

Bree squints his eyes as the van approaches. He quickly reaches under his shirt for his gun. Sha-Rock pulls directly in front of him, while Bree is backing away from his hooptie, allowing himself space to move freely. He grips his black 9 millimeter at his side. He gun is fully loaded with the safety off. He's prepared to put in work.

Sha-Rock notices the gun. "Yo Bree! It's me!"

Bree finally recognizes the van. He slowly steps toward him, wearing a tough-guy face. He still holds his gun close to his side.

"Hold your fire, cowboy," Sha-Rock teases.

Bree still maintains his tough face. "Man I didn't know who the fuck you was, creeping up on me like that. Shit crazy around this motherfucker," he says while leaning on the van. His gun rests on the door. "The fact that he's still holding his gun after realizing who he is makes Sha feel uncomfortable. "What's good, homeboy? Why didn't you hit me when you checked in? I thought they still had you."

"Nah, I been home for a few days. I just been trying to get my money together. "I gotta get a lawyer," Bree says as his eyes wander up the block.

Sha-Rock looks in that direction to see what he's looking at. A police cruiser is riding in the opposite direction. "Get in, homeboy!" Sha offers.

Bree is hesitant until he spots another cop car with his left blinker on, coming in their direction. He jumps in quickly. "Pull off," he shouts. "I'm dirty as hell. I got the blammer on me and some smack!" he shouts as he tucks his gun inside his pants.

To their surprise, the police don't even follow behind them. Sha-Rock makes the right onto Central Avenue. They cruise down the block with no destination. Tension fills the van. Bree's silence makes Sha-Rock feel uncomfortable. Not to mention the fact that he has yet to release the gun from his grip. This tells Sha that Bree doesn't trust him. But why, Sha asks himself. Everything was fine between them the last time they saw each other. Sha-Rock speaks to break the tension. "So, what it look like?"

"Psst," he sucks his teeth in frustration. "It look crazy. Ol girl told everything. Raggedy ass bitch!" he shouts. "Them detectives was up my ass! They gone try and fry my ass," he says.

"Nah man, they ain't got shit. No witness, no weapon, no nothing. Get a good lawyer and you walk away clean," Sha-Rock says.

"The bitch signed statements!"

Sha-Rock decides to test him. "What did she say? Did she see anything? Did she mention anyone else?"

"Nah," Bree replies. "Y'all good. She didn't say shit about nobody else but me. I'm in this one by myself," he claims.

He sounds convincing but Sha-Rock doesn't trust anyone. "Yo, I had Skip with me the other day," Sha says, trying to remind him of how they met. Hopefully if he has any plans of snitching, he'll change his mind. Sha figures Bree will be less apt to tell if he knows Skip will be home to deal with him. "He couldn't wait to see you. He was hurt like motherfucker when your little cousin said you was bumped. That boy got a lot of love for you."

Hearing Skip's name loosens Bree up. He finally takes his hand from underneath his shirt. "Is he home?" Bree asks.

"Nah, he's in the halfway house. He might be coming out next weekend. He's dying to see you!"

"Yeah, I can't wait to see that nigga, either. I know he big as hell, ain't he?"

"No bullshit!" Sha-Rock confirms. "Yeah, he was saying you'll be alright 'cause you a stand up dude," Sha-Rock says to see how he reacts. "He told me you're strong. That's all you need in a situation like this. That and a good mouthpiece," Sha-Rock adds.

"No doubt," Bree agrees.

"You got a lawyer in mind?"

"Yeah, my dude turned me onto this Jew boy. He's supposed to be the best representation right now. All the big boys in this town use him. I called him already. He want twenty cent just to start the case."

"Twenty? Say no more. I got you. Don't even worry about it. I'll never leave you out in the cold like that. Not just because of Skip; me and you done things together, too. I got love for you," he claims. "On the real, you won my heart over that day when I first met you and you hit me with that grand. I didn't need it," he admits. "I just wanted to see where you were at. You fucked me up when you gave it to me. I'll never forget that," he says as he pulls up in front of the projects. Sha-Rock digs in his pocket and pulls out $2,000. "Here," he says as he passes the money to Bree. "This is a little something to keep the lint out of your pocket," Sha says, repeating the words Bree said to him the day when they first met. "I'll bring the twenty grand to you tomorrow night. We gone fight this one all the way out."

"Good looking out, bee," Bree mumbles.

"I'll hit you when I'm on my way up."

"That's what's up. Be safe, my dude," Bree says as he gets out of the car, remembering the day when they first met. He gave Sha-Rock that money from the kindness of his heart, never imagining a day like this would come. That may have been the smartest thing he has ever spent a grand on, he thinks to himself.

The Next Day

Miranda tossed and turned all night long. She couldn't sleep, thinking about the many homes that she viewed. She told the realtor to give her a couple of days, but she wants to get it over with. At the rate that Sha-Rock is spending the money, she fears he may go broke soon. At least if they get a house, they'll have an asset, she thinks.

Miranda picked Tamara up bright and early this morning. She needs her help in making her final decision. She has narrowed her selection down to only two homes. They already viewed the first one. Now they're touring the second one.

"This house is crazy," Tamara whispers, as the realtor leads them through the house. Tamara is right. It's a custom built two-story house with a remodeled gourmet kitchen and an adjacent playroom. Miranda admires that the most. While she's in the kitchen burning, she will be able to keep an eye on their future children. The family room has a traditonal old school feel to it. It even has a fireplace. The room overlooks the in-ground pool. It also has an office, a master suite, and three smaller bedrooms. The bathroom has a built in Jacuzzi. The luxurious house is surrounded by over two acres of land. To top it all off, in the backyard there is the biggest gazebo Miranda has ever seen.

"So what do you think? Do you like this one or the other one?" Miranda asks.

"Girl, go with this one!" Tamara shouts joyfully.

"Are you sure?"

"Girl, I'm positive. This is beautiful."

The realtor looks at Miranda awaiting her answer. "This is it," Miranda says. "I'm about to call my husband, right now," she says as she dials the numbers.

Sha-Rock picks up on the second ring. "Yo?"

"Babe, I made my decision."

"Oh yeah? Which one?"

"The one with the gazebo. You know that's my dream to have one of those," she replies.

Sha-Rock knows how indecisive she can be. "Are you sure?"
"Yes, I'm sure."

"That's what it is then. Tell the cracker chick, we'll be there
tomorrow with the money. How much is it again?"

"$580,000," she says, increasing the volume in her voice so that
Tamara is sure to hear her.

"Alright, tell her my uncle will be there to sign the papers and
bring the down payment. Sha-Rock is not paying cash for the house.
Sha-Rock has an uncle in Camden who owns a construction company
and a lot of property. Luckily his uncle has A-1 credit. The bank only
requires him to put down 7 percent of the price, which equals less than
$41,000. Sha-Rock is putting down $100,000, almost tripling the required
amount. He plans to pay the house off in no more than two years. His
uncle is more than willing to put the house in his name for a small fee.
Sha-Rock doesn't mind paying because he realizes that nothing in life is
free.

Miranda and Tamara fly out of the house. They're headed straight
for the Grange furniture dealer in Manhattan. Their furniture is quite
expensive but Miranda refuses to pack cheap furniture in her luxurious
home. She's living her dream out. She may as well go all the way out.

Hours Later in New Jersey

Sha-Rock pulls in front of Orange Projects. Bree stands alone out
front waiting for him. He steps toward the curb when he spots the van
pulling up. He jumps in the passenger's seat with no hesitation. "What's
good, my dude?"

"Chilling, chilling," Sha-Rock replies as he pulls off quickly.
"Here's the paper," says Sha-Rock as he passes the brown bag over to
him.

While Bree grabs the bag with both hands, Killer Cal raises up
from the back seat quietly. Suddenly he wraps a telephone cord around
Bree's neck. Bree sees his shadow. He tries to move but it's already too
late. The cord is cutting into his skin. He gasps as he tries to grab hold of
the extremely thin cord. He can't seem to pry his fingers in between his
neck and the cord. He's so nervous that he doesn't know what to do. He
has his gun on his waist but he's so busy trying to get the cord from his
neck that he's totally forgotten about it.

"Bree, I'm sorry to do this to you, but shit don't feel right," Sha-

Rock explains. "You acting too shady, lil bro. I want to give you the benefit of the doubt, but I can't afford to gamble like that. I refuse to let you jam us up. I don't have a choice. Better safe than sorry," he says as Cal tightens up his grip. Bree gasps louder and louder. His eyes are damn near popping out of his head.

Breathe, one and then the two. Two and then the three. Three and then the four. Then you gotta breathe. Killer Cal sings the verses of rapper Fabolous's new song in his head. The more Bree squirms the tighter he twists the cord.

They slowly approach the corner. Bree is no longer moving. Cal loosens the cord slightly to test the waters. As soon as Cal eases his grip, Bree's head crashes into the dashboard, causing a loud thumping noise. Sha-Rock pumps the brakes to see if he's faking. It's obvious that he's not because his upper body leans to the right before his head bangs into the passenger's window. "He's dead," Sha-Rock whispers.

"Damn, all he had to do is breathe," Cal says in a sarcastic manner, wearing a demonic smirk on his face.

Sha-Rock makes the quick right onto Route 280. They ride about a quarter of a mile before pulling over onto the shoulder. Sha-Rock peeks around cautiously. "Now!" he shouts as he snatches the plastic bag from Bree's lap.

Killer Cal slides the door open and hops out. He pulls the passenger's door open quickly. Bree's upper body hangs from the van, while his bottom half rests on the seat. Killer Cal spots Bree's gun tucked in his pants. He snatches it from his waist before dragging Bree out of the van by the telephone cord. Bree's body collapses onto the asphalt.

Sha-Rock continuously glances the area as Cal jumps in the passenger's seat and pulls the door shut. "Dead men can't talk!" Cal shouts as Sha-Rock pulls off at full speed. Sha-Rock looks in the rearview mirror once he gets a half a mile away. Bree's body lies curled up on the shoulder of the road like a hunk of garbage. He wonders how he's going to break the news to Skip?

---●◆●---

One Month Later/February 13

Things are going fine. Miranda picked out all the furniture for their new home. It's paid for and ready for delivery. Sha-Rock had a fit when Miranda showed him the furniture bill. She must have lost her mind in that place. Their bed alone costs $8,500, not including the rest of the set. The living room set came out to a quarter of the house down payment. He was highly pissed but he couldn't complain. Especially after she reminded him about spending $140,000 on cars. That was the tactic she used to keep him from chastising her.

Miranda and Tamara are just leaving the movie shoot. Miranda is so proud of herself. She really did her thing. Tamara took the news better than Miranda expected her to. She acted as if it didn't bother her, but Miranda saw differently in her eyes. Miranda knows how much she was really looking forward to being on that show. There's no way in the world that it means nothing to her.

Coming here today was a definite power move for Miranda. She met so many powerful people there. From the looks of things, she may be on the high road to success. There's only one problem though. If Sha-Rock finds out he'll kill her for sure. She knows that it's impossible to keep it a secret forever, but she plans to do it as long as she possibly can.

Miranda and Tamara just left the Dominican Doobie spot on Broadway. Now they're cruising through 125th Street in Sha-Rock's Maserati in search of Najee. Tamara is supposed to meet him here. She hasn't seen him in two weeks, and she misses him dearly. Her plan is to stay away from him, hoping he'll get tired of the cat and mouse chase and move on. In reality she doesn't want that but she knows that it's better that way for him and her. At the present she's in need of some body maintenance. She's trying not to deal with him like that. She wants to keep the sex at a minimum. She knows all it will take is one night with him and he'll blur her vision all over again, making it harder for her to cut him loose.

Miranda spots Najee's brother Najim's white BMW 645, on the opposite side of the street. "There they go!" Miranda shouts as she busts

286

a quick K-turn in the middle of the street. She rides in reverse, backing up to the crowd of boys that surround the BMW. The oncoming traffic honks at Miranda for rudely blocking up the lane. The group admires the car from afar, paying close attention to the chrome twenty-two-inch rims.

Najee runs to the passenger's side of the car quickly. Just looking at his face sends chills up Tamara's spine. She has already moistened the crotch of her jeans. "What's good, Tammy?" he asks in a confused tone. "Randy," he sings. "Hey baby!" he shouts while looking at Miranda, who is just smiling at him. "Tammy, what's the deal? If I didn't know no better, I would think you cut me off?" he teases.

Najim runs over to Miranda's side. She's so busy looking straight ahead that she doesn't notice him coming "Hey Mama," he shouts through the window, which she has rolled down halfway. She jumps from him startling her. "Damn, baby girl riding hard," he teases. "Somebody eating!" he shouts referring to the car. She bites down on her bottom lip to conceal her blushing.

"Boy, you scared me. What's up?"

"You," he replies. "Still playing hard to get?" he asks. The rainbow reflection from her sparkling diamond ring attracts his attention to her finger. "I see your status has changed, huh?"

"Not yet," she replies.

Najee whispers into Tamara's ear. Whatever he tells her leads her out of the car where they stand hugging and kissing. Miranda hasn't seen Tamara that happy in weeks. "You ask her," Tamara shouts joyfully.

Najee bends over and peeks inside the car at Miranda. "Randy, what are you about to get into?"

"I don't know, why?"

"I want to take Tammy out to eat, but she won't go unless you go. She on some high school shit. She acts like she scared of me or something? She must think I'm about to hold her hostage."

"Yeah, that's a good idea," Najim interrupts. "I'm hungry as hell."

"Who invited you?" Tamara asks in a joking manner.

"My brother don't move without me. I don't know what y'all might do to him," he smiles.

"Randy, what's up?" Najee asks. "Just give me an hour, that's it. You don't know how bad I miss my lady. Please?" he begs.

"Come on, do that for him?" Najim begs. "We can get a bite to eat, and y'all can be on y'all way," he whispers sexily.

"We?" Miranda asks. "This ain't got nothing to do with me and you. If I decide to go it's only because Najee is my nigga, that's it," she replies.

"Come on Miranda?" Najim begs. "It ain't a date. You can tell your dude it was a business meeting. You won't be lying to him. I really do have some shows in Atlanta I want to discuss with you."

"Randy, what's up? Time is running out. We could have been at the table eating already!" Najee shouts.

Miranda looks at Tamara, waiting for a signal if she really wants to go or not. Tamara gives her the eye and nods her head up and down indiscreetly. Miranda gives in. "Alright Tammy, but you're riding with me!" she shouts. Two coupes, no backseats, Miranda thinks to herself. Sha-Rock would put his foot up her ass if she were to put another nigga in his car. Tamara hops in immediately and they follow the 645 over a few blocks to Amy Ruth's soul food restaurant.

Meanwhile, twenty miles away, Sha-Rock is having a business meeting of his own. Him and Jimmy sit alongside Branch Brook Park in Sha-Rock's van. Jimmy passes him $30,000. "I ain't finished yet, but I'm close. Yo, I got the deal of a lifetime for you," he claims.

"Yeah?" Sha asks eagerly.

"Hell yeah!" Jimmy shouts. "Check, my connect's connect is about to pack it up and go back to his country. They done. The thing is, they got a lot of work left to move before they break. My connect ain't shit but a middle man, dragging a point off each brick, feel me? He's willing to turn us over to the main dude."

This sounds weird to Sha-Rock. "Why? I mean, I ain't second guessing your judgment, but I don't understand why he would do that. How does that benefit him?"

"It's like this, my connect ain't got no real money. He just got a mean connect. Once they gone, he'll be scrambling like the next motherfucker, feel me? They're leaving whether we cop the joints or somebody else cops them. At least if we buy them, he could still get his cut." Jimmy explains.

"Alright, now it makes more sense to me," Sha-Rock admits. "I didn't understand where you were coming from at first."

"Ol boy said he can get the price down to $15,000 a pie for us."

"Fifteen?"

"Yeah nigga, fifteen, but we have to buy everything he got. All in one shot, feel me?"

"How many he got?"

"Fifty," he replies, expecting a negative reply from Sha-Rock.

"Fifty? How much does that come out to?"

"$750,000," Jimmy mumbles. "Listen, before you flip, just hear me out first," Jimmy blurts out not even giving Sha-Rock a chance to reply. "I got 250. If you could just come up with the 500, we can put it down. I don't know what your bank looks like," Jimmy says, although he already calculated to the best of his knowledge. He knows he made Sha-Rock over $270,000 by himself, and he doesn't have a clue of how many Sha-rock may have sold on his own. "Hear me out, before you answer. As soon as I sell the first twenty joints, I'll give you straight money. I should have that for you in less than two weeks. You see how I do? I'm doing my numbers," he brags. "Altogether, it shouldn't take me no longer than four weeks to finish. This is a once in a lifetime offer. We'll score $500,000 profit. Half a M profit in four weeks. If that ain't playing like the big boys, I don't know what it is!" he shouts. "This will definitely put us at heavy hitter status. If you got the paper, you can't let this opportunity slide past us. You'll hate yourself forever. Trust me on this one?" he begs. "I won't steer you wrong. Sha, you have to be in it to win it, baby!"

Sha-Rock can see the excitement in his eyes, as well as hears it in his voice. "When do you need the money?"

"Huh?" Jimmy asks, not expecting that answer.

"When do you need the money?" he repeats.

"Let me finish the two birds I have left. Then it's on!"

"So, hit me when you're ready."

"That simple?" Jimmy asks.

"Yeah, I told you. You make the calls. I'm rolling with you. It's your people. I don't know them. If you trust him, I have no other choice but to trust him."

"Sha, don't worry. He's a good dude. He's harmless. Anyway, in the little time that I've dealt with him, he's never hid anything from me. I even ate dinner with his family a few times."

"Say no more Jimmy. I'm with you, baby."

Hours later, Sha-Rock makes it back to Philly. Miranda just called him. She's on her way home as well.

He pulls his suitcase from the closet. Before placing the $30,000 Jimmy just gave him into the suitcase, he counts what's there already. There's $630,000 in $100 bills. The addition of the $30,000 Jimmy gave him gives him a grand total of $660,000.

Tomorrow Sha-Rock has to meet with the realtor and give her the $100,000 down payment. His uncle is charging him $30,000 for putting the house in his name. Sha-Rock takes thirteen stacks from the suitcase for the house business. Now he's left with fifty-three stacks. Jimmy needs $525,000, so he takes the remaining $5,000 and zips the suitcase up. This move is all or nothing, he utters to himself as he looks at the stack of $5,000.

Tamara and Najee start their Valentine's Day off right. She sits up in his bed as he walks in butt naked with a tray of food in his hands. She deserves breakfast in bed for the next month, the way she performed last night. Najee really gave her the maintenance she needed. He unclogged her pipes and flushed all the backed up fluids from her system. She only planned to eat and go back to Philly but no matter how hard she tried, she couldn't deny him. His caressing and whispers in her ear at the table made a puddle in her panties. She knew there was no way in the world she could go home alone with her box on fire like it was.

Each time Najee would put out one fire, he'd set another one before she knew it. Love gushed from his hose and splashed against her interior walls at the conclusion of each session. She realizes how stupid it was to have sex without using protection, but in the heat of the moment it didn't seem to matter at all.

Miranda and Sha-Rock have just dropped the money off to the realtor. The house is officially theirs. Now they just have to wait for their closing date. Miranda is the happiest woman alive right now. She can't believe she has a home of her very own.

In Miranda's eyes, Sha-Rock has made up for all the arguments they've been having, and the three-year layoff, when he went away to jail. Right now, all that is so far behind her.

Yesterday she sat at the table with Tamara, Najee and Najim. Najim used every line in the book on her, and none of them fazed her. His charm and good looks didn't have the slightest effect on her. What Najim doesn't know is, Sha-Rock *nigga proofed* her many years ago. Sha-Rock made up the term *nigga proof*. It means teaching your woman the game. He prepared her for slick guys like Najim. Thanks to Sha-Rock she can spot game a mile away. Sha-Rock's *nigga proofing* tactic had nothing to do with it this time though. At this point in her relationship, she's completely satisfied. There's not one thing missing in their relationship. Miranda believes when a woman is satisfied with her man, no other man can get in between them. Her motto is why get the 500 Mercedes when you really want the 600? She's a firm believer that as long as there is a model out that you think may be better than the one you have, you'll never be able to appreciate the one you have. That's why she believes you should set your standards and stick to them. Get what you want the first time, and that way you won't have any regrets. From day one, Sha-Rock has always been the man of her dreams. She always knew that one day, he would make her the happiest woman in the world.

She just wishes her mother were alive to share her joy with her. She may not be here in the physical, but Miranda knows her mother's spirit is with her everyday. Miranda knows that her father will also be happy for her, except for the way they obtained everything. Miranda knows her father well. Even though Kiko crossed him severely, he still wouldn't have wished death on him. He would be so disappointed to know that she stole. That was another one of his famous golden rules. Never touch something that doesn't belong to you. He always told her, when you do dirt, you get dirt. She's sure if her father ever finds out, he'll cut her off forever.

In North Philly

Killer Cal's house is surrounded by commotion. City inspectors are snooping around the outside of the house. There are two of them to be exact. Killer Cal has barricaded all the doors and windows. He doesn't know why they're here, but he plans on finishing them off if they invade his territory.

He tiptoes through the apartment, wearing a camouflage fatigue outfit along with his helmet. His dagger is in its holster at his right side. On his left side, there is another holster. Inside it sits a 17 shot nine-millimeter. It's the gun he snatched from Bree the night he strangled him to death. Sha-Rock doesn't even know that Cal took it.

Cal runs over to his bed. He leans over and picks up his wife's corpse. Her lifeless body dangles freely. He places the body underneath his bed. In his mind, bombs and gunfire sounds off. He kisses her mouth. "Get low," he whispers to the corpse before pulling the covers over the edge of the bed to conceal the body. He then snatches the gun from his waist as he crawls toward the front door.

He scales up the wall until the window is at eye level. He peeks out sneakily. The two men are standing directly in front of the window. One of them is posting a paper on the door using a staple gun. After the posting is hung up, they jump in their car and pull off.

Killer Cal waits for twenty minutes before he cracks the door open, and snatches the paper from the door. After slamming the door shut, he reads the posting. It's a complaint about the horrendous smell that's coming from his house. They inform him that the neighbors have made several complaints. It states that he has a matter of weeks to handle the problem. His mind tells him it's the sewage system. No one could ever tell him that his beautiful wife is stinking the entire block up.

Later That Evening

Miranda and Sha-Rock lay up in their new home. They have no business in here until after the official closing date, but the realtor allowed them to stay the night in here. Although there's no furniture throughout the entire house, it still doesn't feel hollow. Love fills every square foot of the house.

Sha-Rock lies on his back, while Miranda curls up close to him, staring at the burning fireplace. They have been sipping wine in silence. Both of them are entertaining their own private thoughts.

The year couldn't have started out any better for Miranda. Something tells her this will be a memorable year. She plans her future mentally. She pictures herself walking the runway while Sha-Rock cheers her on. One day that dream will become reality, once she gets the courage to tell him. Until then she'll only be able to dream about it. She's also been considering having kids for him. Only after he marries her though. That would make their lives so complete. She realizes that time waits for no one, and neither one of them are getting any younger. She still has time, but Sha-Rock will be approaching his mid-thirties soon.

Sha-Rock's mind is not on the future. He's busy worrying about the past. After seeing the realtor, him and Miranda drove to Newark to meet with Jimmy. Sha-Rock hesitantly parted with the $525,000 Jimmy asked for. Jimmy promised him everything would be fine. He claims his plan is fool proof. Sha-Rock sure hopes so. In his pocket he holds a mere $5,000. Jimmy's plan has to work, or else it's back to the drawing board.

"Let's toast," Miranda whispers in his ear. They hold their glasses high. "To the good life," she shouts as they tap glasses.

———————◆◆◆———————

The Next Day

Jimmy anxiously parks his rental car in front of a Bronx apartment building. He dials his connect's phone number. "Poppo, I'm here," he shouts into the mouthpiece. He waits in the car as usual until he sees his man's face appear at the doorway.

The connect warned him never to get out of the car until he comes to the door and scopes the surroundings. He's not only worried about police; they're also on alert for stick-up. Stick-up kids lurk in the area plotting on out-of-towners. They drive around in search of out-of-town license plates. If they peep foreign plates, they'll follow them to the spot. Sometimes they rob them before they go in and sometimes they wait for them to come out.

Jimmy's connect gives him the okay, by the nod of his head. Jimmy then hops out of his car and walks toward the building. Jimmy stands in the doorway as his uncle drags the $750,000 pulley into the building.

His uncle not only cooks and tests the cocaine, he also transports it back for him. With his old wrinkled skin and his head full of gray hair, he's perfect for the job. He has transported many of kilos for Jimmy in his old customized van.

They all stand in front of the elevator along with an elderly Hispanic woman and a teenage Hispanic girl. The old woman looks Jimmy and his uncle up and down. She knows they're up to no good. They look so out of place because the entire building is populated with Hispanics. Jimmy gets an uncomfortable feeling as she stares at the large suitcase. She watches them indiscreetly until she gets to her floor. She rolls her eyes as she exits onto the ninth floor.

Jimmy and his connect shake hands as soon as she gets out of the elevator. "What up, Poppo?" Jimmy says.

"Chilling Papi," he replies. "Viejo, what's up?" Viejo means old. Poppo gave him that nickname.

"Hey como esta!" he says in a laughing manner.

The connect starts to yap away. "What took you so long, Papi?

He was ready to leave. He thought I was trying to set him up. He's very scary. Whatever you do, don't ask him too many questions. He'll cancel the deal. He think everybody is Fed. You sure you got all the money, right?"

"Yeah, yeah," Jimmy answers.

"My money too, right?"

"Poppo, it's all here. $525,000," Jimmy says with a frustrated tone.

"Ok, Papi. I just don't want to blow the deal. If all the money is not there, he'll think I play games with him. I just don't want any trouble."

The last floor is approaching. The number seventeen lights up. They step out of the elevator. Normally the last floor is the penthouse, but in this building it's the rat hole. This is the worst floor of the building. The hall is cluttered with junk, like old stoves and pissy mattresses.

Poppo is the superintendent of the building. Him and his family live on the second floor, but he also has an apartment on this floor. No one knows about the apartment up here, not even his wife. He uses this apartment to conduct his business and to trick off with the local prostitutes.

They walk into the shabby looking apartment. A stocky built man sits at the kitchen table. He stands up in a nervous manner as they enter. "Have a seat," Poppo suggests, while pointing to the raggedy looking living room set. Poppo walks to the cupboard and pulls one kilo from the shelf. He walks over and hands it to Jimmy. Jimmy's uncle watches greedily as Jimmy tears the tape. The man speaks softly in Spanish. "He said he wants to make sure all the money is here, before he brings the rest of them," Poppo translates. "He wants you to check it out before he sends for them."

Jimmy finally tears through the casing. He examines the material thoroughly. It's nothing like the ones Sha-Rock had, but it's beautiful. Jimmy breaks a piece from each corner. Then he cracks the block down the center. From the middle, he snatches two equal sized pieces. He places all six pieces onto the digital scale. The numbers read thirty-two. "Thirty-two grams," Jimmy says to his uncle as he passes him the rocks. His uncle anxiously walks toward the stove. Poppo has all the instruments ready for him. Unck slams the cocaine into the pot. He then adds the baking soda and water. The hotter the cocaine gets, the more fumes fill the room. Poppo has another pot of boiling hot water, on the back burner. Jimmy and Unck assume that it's potpourri to kill the aroma of the cocaine.

Poppo fans his hand past his nose. The smell alone is enough to get a person high.

Jimmy hears a tapping on the door. "Poppo," he whispers. "The door." Poppo tiptoes to the door and cracks it open. A trampy looking black female peeks her head through the cracked door. The aroma of cooked cocaine must be the bait that Poppo uses to reel his crack-addicted prostitutes in.

"Hold up. Wait a minute," Poppo says as he slams the door in her face.

"Wait," she manages to say before the door muffles her voice.

"You the man, Poppo," Jimmy teases. Poppo displays a cheesy looking smile.

"Finished finally," Jimmy's uncle says as he starts scraping the rock from the pot. He dumps the ready rock onto a paper towel to drain the water from it. Jimmy hauls the scale to the counter. The six rocks have magically formed into one solid flat rock. Unck dumps the rock onto the scale. "Thirty-seven!" Unck shouts. "It's still wet though. It didn't lose," he says. The loud noise of Unck's wet fart sounds off. This is tradition for him. Every time he sees cocaine or even thinks of smoking cocaine, he busts an uncontrollable fart.

The smell of rotten eggs fills the kitchen. "Ooh, Viejo," Poppo says as he fans his hand in front of his face.

"Go check it out," Jimmy instructs. Unck takes off like lightning, headed toward the bathroom.

Someone is tapping on the door again. "Damn," Poppo shouts as he quickly walks to the door. He snatches it open. "What?" he asks furiously. The run-down looking prostitute stands there bashfully. "Come in!" Poppo shouts. "Go and sit down."

The other man speaks furiously. Jimmy can't understand Spanish but judging by the anger in his voice, Jimmy can tell he's upset. "Okay, okay," Poppo says with reasoning. "Papi, go in the bedroom and count the money," he whispers so that the prostitute can't hear him. The man then opens the door to the bedroom and walks in.

Jimmy drags the suitcase on wheels toward the bedroom. "Unck!" he shouts. Unck doesn't respond. He's too busy blasting away.

By now, he's probably hanging out with Dr. Spock from "Star Trek."

"Viejo in outer space," Poppo teases.

Jimmy looks back at Poppo, laughing as he steps into the bedroom. He turns around as his first step lands in the room. Thump! Heavy impact crashes into his nose, blurring his vision. He tries to shake the blurriness away, but another blow drops onto the top of his dome, dropping him to his knees. As he's falling, he reaches in his pocket for his .40 caliber. Just as he grips it, the impact of a long nosed handgun bangs across his jawbone. Lights out! He falls backwards, dropping his gun from his hand.

Fifteen Minutes Later

Jimmy regains consciousness. He's propped up against the wall. The room is pitch-black. He looks downward. His hands and feet are tied together with rope. He doesn't quite remember what happened. The right side of his face is exploding with pain. Duct tape covers his mouth. It's all starting to come back to him.

Suddenly the lights come on. He looks to the right. His uncle's dead body lies about three feet away from him. A hole the size of a pool ball is in his forehead. His face is covered with so much blood that Jimmy can't see his facial features.

Jimmy's eyes comb the creepy looking room. Burning candles are lined up along the bottom borders of the walls. A huge picture of Jesus on the cross takes up the whole side of the wall. A table with several pictures and a bunch of burning candles sets in front of the that same wall.

How could Poppo set him up for a robbery, he asks himself. He can't believe that he fell for it. His greed led him right into the trap. He thinks of the money Sha-Rock gave him. His mind runs wild. Just as he asks himself why, the other man walks toward him and drags him by the rope that's tied around his ankles. Once he finally gets him in front of the table, he snatches Jimmy by the neck and pulls his head close to it. "Look at that picture," the man, says in clear English. "Do you know him?" he asks furiously.

Jimmy stares at the portrait. Fear takes over his body as he stares into Chulo's eyes.

"Do you know him?" he asks again. Jimmy shakes his head negatively, but his eyes say something different. The man commences to pistol-whipping Jimmy. Jimmy grunts after each blow. "Do you know him?" he repeats.

Jimmy looks over to Poppo, with his eyes crying desperately for help. Poppo's face shows no emotion.

The man holds a cellular phone in front of Jimmy's face. Jimmy's cell phone number along with his name is spelled out across the display. "Is that you?" he asks. Jimmy doesn't reply, until he strikes him again with the butt of the gun. "Is that you?" he repeats. Jimmy nods his head up and down in fear of being struck again. "So, what do you mean, you don't know Chulo? This is his phone. The police found it in his pocket the day he was murdered. The last time I talk to Chulo, he took five kilos to New Jersey to meet you. You don't remember me but I remember you. Look at me closely. The first day Chulo come to New Jersey, I was with him. Remember, Chulo and the driver were up front? Do you remember the man in the back seat?"

Jimmy looks at him closely. It's all coming back to him now. Jimmy is well aware that his life is about to be ended. There's no way they'll spare him.

"I knew I would catch up to you one day. This is a small world. You fell right into the trap. It wasn't hard. I got connections. A few phone calls here and there, bring me right to my man," he laughs as he walks out of the room, leaving Jimmy in suspense.

Jimmy fears what they're going to do to him. He looks at Poppo expecting mercy, but Poppo just lifts his hands in the air. "There's nothing I can do," he whispers.

The man walks back into the room. He has towels wrapped around a hot boiling pot with steam flowing from it. In fact it's the same pot that was on the stove. "Have you ever heard the saying, greedy people starve?" he asks Jimmy. "I'm sure you did," he says. "My cousin was greedy. I told him time after time, make him come to you. He didn't want to listen because he was scared you would buy your material from somebody else. He didn't listen and look what happened to him. But Jimmy, you're greedy too. Poppo made you an offer you couldn't refuse, huh?"

Jimmy watches the steaming pot, wondering what he's going to do with it.

"Bring me the pictures," he says to Poppo. Poppo walks over and lays the police photos on Jimmy's lap. They're the photos that were

298

taken at the crime scene. Chulo lies twisted underneath the dashboard console. "Look what you did to him! My cousin died in fear. The last thing he saw was you. You are his last memory; not his wife, not his kids, you!" he shouts. "I want these photos to be the last thing you see, so you can take his memory to your grave," he shouts as he tosses the boiling contents in Jimmy's face.

Jimmy cringes as the liquid splashes into his face. The scalding hot water burns like fire. He squints his eyes tight from agony. Heat swelters his eyeballs. He slowly opens one eye, then the other one. He sees darkness. He rolls his eyes around, still not able to see anything. He starts to panic. His hands are tied at his waist so all he can do is try and bear with the heat that scorches his face and eyes. Not being able to see leaves him in suspense.

"Jimmy, look at me, I'm over here!" he teases. "You can't see me can you? Of course you can't, the lye has stolen your vision," he laughs satanically. "Look, I'm over here now!" Pop, pop, pop! Three shots to the head take him out of misery.

—————◆◆◆—————

Three Days Later/February 18

Sha-Rock hasn't been able to sleep in days. He's been calling Jimmy all day, everyday, getting no answer. He has numerous thoughts running through his mind. He doesn't know if Jimmy got arrested or if he ran off with the money. He really doesn't believe Jimmy would do that, but a half a million dollars could bring out the worst in a man. The bad part is, Sha-Rock doesn't have the slightest idea of where to start looking for him. All he knows is Jimmy was scrambling in Virginia, that's it. He prays that Jimmy calls him soon. He hopes Jimmy is just so caught up in getting money that calling has slipped his mind. Sha-Rock doesn't believe that, but he just needs something to go on.

Miranda has noticed a change in his attitude over the past couple of days. He hasn't told her what happened and he doesn't have plans of telling her. He would hate to hear her mouth. She'll consider him to be the biggest fool of the century.

Sha-Rock walks into the doctor's office. If it wasn't for the situation with Jimmy, today would be one of the happiest days of his life. Today the doctor is going to remove the coloscopy bag from his stomach.

Meanwhile

Miranda and Tamara are at the old apartment packing. They've been at it since early this morning. They both look a mess, wearing their baggy sweatpants and filthy scarves tied around their heads.

They're just about done. Several boxes spread across the entire apartment. They saved the kitchen for last. Tamara stands on the stepladder passing the dishes down to Miranda when the doorbell rings. Miranda shuffles to the door and snatches it open, without even looking into the peephole.

To her surprise, two suit and tie wearing Caucasian men and a well-dressed, middle-aged Black woman crowd her doorstep. She assumes that they're Jehovah's Witness or members of the Church of Latter Day Saints.

"Miranda Benderas?" the white haired man asks. Hearing

her name come out of his mouth startles her. She can't find the words to answer him. He looks down at a picture he's holding in his hand. "Miranda Benderas?" he asks again.

What's going on, she asks herself. "Yes," she replies.

"Miami Police Department," the man says. Her heart drops. "Miranda Benderas, you are wanted for questioning in Miami, Florida, for connection to a murder."

"A murder?" she cries.

"You have the right to remain silent. Anything you say, can and will be held against you. You have the right to an attorney. If you can't afford an attorney, one will be appointed for you," he says.

Miranda's ears are still stuck on the words *Miami Police Department*. She pictures Kiko lying in his basement dead. She stands there with her mouth stretched wide open. She can see the detective's mouth moving, but she can't seem to hear the words coming out. It seems like everything is moving in slow motion.

She snaps back into reality when she sees the female detective pull her handcuffs from her pocket and walk toward her. Fear brings the beast out of Miranda. She kicks and screams like a wild woman. The next thing Miranda knows, she's laying ass up while the detectives pin her arms behind her back.

Tamara hears all of the commotion and runs to the front door. She stands there in disbelief. "Watch it, ma'am," the female detective instructs as they drag Miranda inside. She then pushes Miranda to the ground violently. "Where's your boyfriend?" Miranda sobs quietly as Tamara stands there dumbfounded. "Search the house. If he's not in here, she'll tell his whereabouts eventually."

Minutes later, they drag Miranda out of the apartment. "What's going on?" Tamara asks. "Where are you taking her?"

"Miami, Florida, ma'am," the male detective says in a very respectful tone. "Here's my card. Call me in two or three days, and I'll give you all the details of her whereabouts."

"Two or three days?" Tamara asks.

"Yes, ma'am."

Miranda screams at the top of her lungs. She fights to the best of her ability. She even falls onto the ground to prevent them from taking her. They literally have to drag her outside. Neighbors watch from their porch as it takes all three detectives to force her into the four door Chevy

Impala.

Tears bleed from Tamara's eyes as they cruise up McKean Street.

Sha-Rock jumps into his Maserati. He feels so relieved after getting the bag removed. He feels like himself again. Just as he starts to think about Jimmy, his phone rings. He looks at the display, which reads private. He prays aloud. "Please God, let this be Jimmy," he begs before answering it. "Hello? Who is this? Slow down, I can't hear nothing you're saying!" Tamara's words rip through his soul. "Meet me at your house," he suggests. "I'll be right there," he utters. "This can't be happening," he screams while banging his head on the steering wheel. He's confused and scared. Part of him wants to go to Tamara's and the other part wants to flee the country. How, he asks himself. Who could have told? How did they find our whereabouts? Are they looking for me? Will she tell on me? These questions pop up in his head one after the other.

-61-

Noon

Five days have passed and still no news about Miranda. Tamara has made several calls and she still hasn't received any answers. She's in the dark about the entire situation. When she asks Sha-Rock what's going on, he acts as if he knows less than she does.

These have been the worst days of Sha-Rock's life. He wishes he were dead. He feels so bad that he got his lady caught up in this terrible situation. It takes this terrible event to make him realize how disgraceful it was to get his woman involved in this mess. All day long, he envisions her in jail, crying hysterically. He knows that she's scared to no end. He can't stand the thought of how they may be treating her.

He sits around day in and day out, waiting for his phone to ring. It's been eight whole days since he's heard from Jimmy. Something tells him he might as well chalk it up as a loss. He promises himself that he'll find Jimmy and his family, and when he does it will be a bloody massacre. He just can't believe Jimmy would move out on him like that. He thought they had built a bond.

Sha-Rock spends most of his days thinking about the could have, would have, should haves. I could have just given him half of the money. Then I would have some money left. I should have just gone with him. The point is, he did none of the above, and now he has to pay for it.

Sha-Rock lays across the bed of the Days Inn on Routes 1 and 9 in Elizabeth, New Jersey. He's been staying here ever since that dreadful day. He could have stayed at the new house, but he doesn't trust it. He doesn't think Miranda will tell on him intentionally, but he's not sure what type of pressure they have put on her.

He has had thoughts of turning himself in, hoping they would let her go. He highly doubts that. He can't turn himself in. Then how will they get the money up to fight the case? Money is the keyword in this whole ordeal. Without money he can kiss their freedom goodbye.

His cell phone rings. It's Tamara. He answers it anxiously. His suspense heightens. "Yeah? How did she sound? Was she crying? Did she ask about me? What did she say they said about me? Alright call and find out what's up," he says. "Later!" Sha-Rock knows better than to talk on the phone like that, but right now he's not in his right state of mind. Tamara's call calms his nerves slightly. Just hearing Tamara say that Miranda sounds alright makes him stress a little bit less. Tamara also said that Miranda gave her a phone number to a lawyer in Miami. She instructed Tamara to call him. She claims that he'll handle everything from there.

Thirty Minutes Later

Sha-Rock's cellular phone rings again. "Hello?"

"Sha?" Tamara asks. "The lawyer just called me back. He said altogether we need $100,000 cash.

Sha-Rock's pulse stops. "How much?"

"$100,000," she repeats. "Her bail is $750,000. The lawyer is going to push for 10 percent but he needs $25,000 to start the process.

What worse situation could I be in, Sha-Rock asks himself. Just the other day, he was staring at almost $700, 000 and today he has a measly $4,500. All of a sudden, the cars, jewelry, and expensive shopping sprees seem so foolish. "$100,000? Alright," he says confidently as if it's attainable.

"So, what do you want me to tell him?" Tamara asks.

"Tell him to start the process. I'll be there in a day or two," he bluffs. "When Miranda calls you back, tell her not to stress. It's nothing," he says arrogantly, before hanging up.

Who says men don't cry? Sha-Rock sobs like a baby as he thinks about the $100,000 he needs. He needs it quick. He thinks of all his options. He can ski mask the money up but he doesn't have any leads, with Bree dead and Jimmy nowhere to be found.

He worries himself to sleep, wondering how he can get the money up.

6p.m.

Sha-Rock and Killer Cal cruise around North Philly brainstorming. "I could sell the car but that might take too long," says Sha-Rock. "Niggas on the street ain't got that type of money laying around. And the dealer will only pay me half of what I paid for it. I ain't trying to take a loss like that. If push comes to a shove I'll do it though. I swear if it wasn't for that nigga Jimmy, I wouldn't be under this pressure.

That nigga would rather be in jail for them fifty kilos than for me to catch him on the street. $525,000! I don't believe that shit!"

"No need to keep worrying about the past, Baby Boy. Think about the future. You have to hurry up and get her before she starts to get nervous. You don't think she'll tell on you, do you?"

"Who Miranda? Hell no!"

"Baby Boy, that's the same thing that wack ass nigga Bree thought."

"First of all, I ain't Bree and that chick ain't my broad. I schooled Miranda for days like this. She knows to keep her mouth shut."

"Alright," Cal whispers in disbelief. "Just hurry up and get her before she loses faith in you. She's dangerous on the other side. She's seen too much, and she knows too much. Baby Boy, they scored when they got her. They got the bookkeeper!"

Sha-Rock's phone rings. "Yo?" he answers. It's his sister. "Lisa, what's up?"

"Nothing," she replies. "Shonda is mad at you."

"Why?"

"You didn't even call her and wish her happy birthday. She said you never forgot her birthday."

"Oh shit. That's right. Damn, put her on the phone."

"Hello?" his niece, Shonda answers. "Ay girl. I didn't forget," he lies. "I was just trying to make you think I forgot. Happy birthday to you. Happy birthday to you. Happy birthday, my dear niece. Happy birthday to you!" he sings. "What are you doing for your special day?"

"Thank you, Uncle Turkey. Me, Mommy and Little Rahiem going to Red Lobster in a little while. My daddy was supposed to go but he sick. Do you want to go with us?"

"Nah, me and you will do something by ourselves. I promise, alright?"

"Yes."

"Put your mother on the phone."

"Hello," Lisa answers.

"Damn Lisa, I really forgot. I have to make it up to her. What time are y'all leaving?"

"At eight on the dot. I'm meeting up with two of my girlfriends and their bad ass kids. Oh, I forgot to tell you, Mommy called. She said tell you, she's been thinking about you and Miranda."

"Oh boy!" he shouts, trying to cut her off. He doesn't want to hear that.

"She says, she doesn't know what it is, but it can't be good. You and Miranda have been popping up in all her dreams."

"Yeah, yeah, yeah!" he shouts. "Tell Moses, I'm alright," he jokes. "Your mother be bugging! So, you said eight, right?" he changes the subject purposely.

"On the dot!" she shouts.

"Alright check, I'll be there at ten minutes to eight. I have to give my girl something before I go out of town. Don't leave, alright?" he shouts before hanging up.

7:50 PM

Sha-Rock and Killer Cal pull up in front of Sha-Rock's sister's house. He's driving his van. He didn't bring the car because he doesn't want to hear his sister's mouth. She counts every dollar that he spends.

He runs inside, leaving Cal in the van. His nephew and his niece tackle him as he enters. "Hey Uncle Turkey!"

"What's up y'all? Happy birthday, girl. Here," he says as he hands her two crisp $100 bills.

"Thanks!" she shouts cheerfully.

"What about me?" his sister asks. "You need to be giving something," she says sarcastically. "I'm the one who stayed in labor for seventy-two hours, giving birth to her," she says while holding her hand out.

"Psst, I got you, later. Where ol boy at?" he asks referring to her husband.

"He's in the back, playing that damn game as usual. Come on y'all! Let's go before I change my mind," she threatens. The kids hurry and they all walk out the door. "You said you're going out of town?" she asks Sha-Rock who is lagging behind her.

"Damn, you nosey," he teases. "Syke, yeah. I'm headed to Miami."

"Didn't you just come back from Miami?"

"And? I'm going back."

"Is Miranda going with you?"

"Nope! I'm going by myself. I got a little shorty down there," he lies.

"You know I'm telling, right?" she laughs.

"Nah, I'm bugging. She's going with me. I got business to handle. As soon as I leave here, I'm going to scoop her up and we're out," he lies.

"Okay, be safe!" she shouts as she opens her arms wide for a hug. Sha-Rock hops into his van, and Lisa and the kids pile up in her Honda.

At the corner, Lisa continues to go straight, while Sha-Rock makes the right, followed by three more rights. He ends up exactly where he started. He's directly in front of Lisa's house.

He rings the bell once. He stands there for approximately two minutes before he decides to ring it again. Seconds later, Lisa's husband peeks his head through the curtain, behind the glass window. He opens the door without hesitation. Sha-Rock walks right in. "Sha, what's the deal?" he asks as he closes the door behind him. "I started to holler at you before you left," he says as he approaches the door to his house.

Sha-Rock notices that he has so much conversation for him lately, wherein before he barely wanted to speak. "I'm glad you didn't. You know how nosey your wife is? Lisa is a trip," Sha-Rock says as he follows close behind. "How are you making out?" he asks as they enter the apartment.

"Lovely kid, lovely," he replies. "My phone ringing off the hook," he says as he walks into his bedroom and sits on the edge of the bed. "Yeah, I was about to call you last night, but I wanted to wait until I finished. I still got money in the street and I got about a half a joint left," he says slowly, as if he's trying to determine the exact amount. "Hold up," he says as he drops the game's controller on the carpet. He then walks toward the closet, where he always keeps his goods. "Let me see."

From the angle where Sha is standing, he can see straight into the closet.

"Yeah, I got a little over a half a brick," he shouts while holding it in the air.

"Yeah, I was trying to see if you was straight. I only got a few left. I don't want you to miss out, smell me?"

"No question."

"Yeah, and I'm breaking out of town, so I want to set you straight before I jet."

"Uhhmm," he says as if he's debating. "I got a little over a buck. I don't want to go without," he mumbles. "I'll take four now, unless you want to bring me five, and I hit you with the change when you come back from out of town?"

"No doubt about it nigga."

He places the half a brick into the shoe box and bends over to retrieve the money. Sha-Rock tiptoes over and stands close behind him. Rahiem sees Sha-Rock's silhouette against the wall. He turns around quickly, staring straight into the barrel of the .44 magnum. Rahiem laughs it off goofily. "Go ahead, Sha. Stop playing."

The seriousness in Sha's eyes tells Rahiem that it's not a game. "Make a sound and I'll spill yo ass right here. No bullshit," he whispers sternly.

"Sha, what's going on? What is this about?"

"Listen nigga, I didn't come here to talk. Turn it over." The doorbell rings. Sha-Rock pulls Rahiem up by his collar. "Come on," he whispers aggressively.

Sha-Rock opens the door for Cal, who rushes in like a madman. Cal pulls out the duct tape and rope. Rahiem is so scared that he doesn't put up the least bit of a fight.

After Cal performs the tying and taping procedure, he stands over Rahiem with Sha-Rock's gun aimed at his head. Oh, how Cal would love to pull the trigger, right now. He already has his target marked. He has a clear shot right in between Rahiem's eyes. Cal is like a dog. He can smell fear in the air. His trigger finger has an itch that needs scratching. He can't wait for Sha-Rock to give him the word. Sha-Rock enters the room with three shoe boxes in his hand. "Now boss?" Cal asks anxiously.

Rahiem looks up awaiting Sha's answer. "Nah, nah," Sha-Rock replies. Rahiem exhales a sigh of relief. "We can't do it in here. That will fuck my sister and the kids up for life." Rahiem looks at Sha-Rock for sympathy. "Don't look at me with the puppy dog eyes. You know I don't fuck with you like that. I never fucked with you from jump. My sister saved you. I been wanted to do this," he informs. "Killer, I'm going to pull the van up the alleyway. Bring him out the back door so nobody can see us." At this point, Rahiem realizes that his life is over.

Sha-Rock cruises for a matter of minutes, trying to determine where they're going to finish the job. Finally they pull in front of an abandoned house. "Take him in the alleyway," Sha-Rock demands.

Cal jumps out and snatches Rahiem from the van. Rahiem is

squirming like a fish out of water. After wrestling, Cal finally manages to drag him into the alleyway.

Sha-Rock opens one of the shoe boxes. He places one of the stacks to his mouth and kisses it. "Miranda, you're coming home to daddy," he whispers.

Boom, boom, boom, boom, boom, boom! Killer Cal empties the gun. You can always expect him to overdo it.

What a fucked up birthday this will turn out to be for Shonda, Sha-Rock thinks to himself. Unfortunately, this is one that she'll never forget. "Sorry baby," he says aloud.

───────◆◆◆───────

The Next Morning

Sha-Rock received Lisa's hysterical phone call last night at about 11 p.m. Too bad he wasn't in town to comfort her. Well at least, that's what he told her.

Lisa doesn't have the slightest idea of who could have done that to him. She claims that she doesn't know a soul who could have wanted him dead. She said as long as she's known him, she's never known him to have an argument, let alone a fight. Sha-Rock can believe that. He always knew that Rahiem was as soft as cotton. Sha-Rock knows his kind. Dudes like him never make enemies. They just want everybody to get along. Rahiem lived his life by the Dr. Martin Luther King Jr. speech. All he wanted to do was get money and skate through without beef.

Sha-Rock hates the fact that he caused his sister pain, but his back was against the wall. He doesn't know how he'll face her and the kids knowing what he's done. He's sure this will bother them forever.

In total, Rahiem has $117,000 stashed in the house. Sha-Rock broke Cal off with $2,000 and he kept the rest. Cal didn't have a problem with it because he understands what Sha is trying to do.

Cal has already smoked the bulk of his money away. At this very moment, he's higher than an astronaut. He's been smoking rock after rock, nonstop. He sits on his bed fully clothed with his glass pipe jammed in his mouth, while his loving wife's corpse lies underneath the bed collecting dust. What a way to treat the woman he loves.

12:00 Noon

Sha-Rock sits in the backseat of the cab as it pulls in front of the Clinton Hotel in South Beach Florida. They left Philadelphia over three hours ago. The cab just dropped Tamara off at the lawyer's office, downtown Miami.

Sha-Rock's uncle gave him a traveler's check to give to the lawyer. His uncle tried to charge him for using his name to post bail for Miranda, but Sha-Rock promised to pay him later. The lawyer said he could start the process without his uncle being present, but eventually he'll have to come to Miami. Sha-Rock can only imagine how much that will cost him.

Sha-Rock never told his uncle why Miranda had been arrested. His uncle really doesn't care either. He's so money hungry that his only concern is how much he'll be paid for his services. He's aware of what Sha-Rock used to be into, so he probably assumes that she's locked up for drugs.

Sha-Rock wanted to go to the lawyer's office with Tamara, but he's too paranoid. He's scared to be seen in Miami. He doesn't know how intense their search for him is. They may have a description of him, but he knows they don't know his name, unless Miranda has told them.

Sha-Rock places him and Tamara's carry-on bags in the closet of the room. He rented a room just to have somewhere to wait for Miranda's release. He's afraid to be walking around Miami for hours. As soon as he lies on the bed, he forces himself to sleep.

Three hours later, a tapping on the door awakens. He's startled until he creeps to the door, and peeks through the peephole. Tamara's face eases his fear. He lets her in immediately. "What up?" he asks anxiously.

"Sha, I don't know," she sighs. "The lawyer said it may take a day or two to put everything in motion. He told me to stay close and he'll call me in a few hours."

Five o'clock comes and both of them are still waiting for a phone call from either the lawyer or Miranda.

Another hour crawls by and Sha-Rock's patience is running out. "Yo, call that motherfucker and see what's going on," he says in a hasty manner.

Tamara picks up the phone and dials the lawyer's number. "Hello, Mr. Goldman? This is Tamara Hill. I'm calling about Miranda Benderas. Anything new?" She remains silent as the lawyer speaks. "Okay, I'm here. Bye."

"What did he say?"

She sighs before speaking. "He said there's nothing he can do today. He'll definitely have some news for us early tomorrow."

Sha-Rock plops into the recliner. He expected this to be a one-day process. Something tells him it's going to take a lot longer than that. He leans back, deep into the chair as he flicks through the channels with the remote.

Tamara begins whispering into her phone with the sexiest voice.

Sha-Rock assumes she must be talking to her boyfriend. He desperately tries to hear what she's saying. He lowers the volume as sneaky as he can, but the lower the volume goes the more she lowers her voice, unintentionally. Finally, he decides to give her some privacy by stepping out of the room.

Ten minutes later he returns holding two bottles of spring water, only to find Tamara stretched out across the bed. She's already deep into her sleep. The sound of her loud snoring bounces off of the walls. He sits back in the recliner and continues to watch the television.

Every now and then, he peeks over at Tamara. She's lying on her stomach. The devil is playing tricks with him. Her plump rear and her juicy thighs continuously catch his attention. He can barely keep his eyes off of her. He thinks back to the day when he first met her. Back then her body was nowhere near as developed as it is now, but she was still just as gorgeous. He often wonders what would have become of them if he had not gone to jail? Of course at that time, him and Miranda had years in already, but he remembers Tamara's exact words clearly. She said, "Your girl is not my concern. As long as you keep her under control, we're good." She was perfectly alright with being his mistress. At times he feels weird when he's around her, knowing that they had crept around. They never had sex, but he always wondered how it would be. "Tammy," he calls out. She peeks up slowly. "I'm about to step out and get something to eat. Are you hungry?" Hunger is not his reason for leaving. His lusting thoughts are starting to have an effect on him. He has to escape.

"Nah," she replies while half asleep. "I ate before I came in."

It's 9 p.m. and Sha-Rock is just getting back to the hotel. After eating, he walked around to clear his head. The fresh air really done him so good, but the fact still remains; Miranda is in a terrible situation and at worst case scenario, both of them will spend the rest of their lives in prison. He thought of a few ways to make some quick money, but only one seems easy to reach.

He walks into the hotel room. The smell of Irish Spring soap fills the air. Hearing the shower water running makes Sha-Rock picture Tamara in the nude. The actual thought excites him, forcing his imagination to run wild.

Sha-Rock leans back in the recliner. Seconds later, the water stops and Tamara walks out. He no longer has to use his imagination. He gets an eyeful. "Tammy, I'm in here," he shouts many seconds too late.

"Ooh!" she shouts, as she turns around and runs back into the bathroom. She gives him a round of applause as her ass cheeks clap after each step. She slams the door shut.

"Sorry Tammy," he lies. In all reality, he loved the peep show.

The room is filled with silence until she finally speaks. "Bring my clothes to the door?" she requests.

Sha-Rock grabs hold of her jeans and her T-shirt before walking to the bathroom door. "Here."

She cracks the door open and snatches the garments inside. Seconds later, she walks out with her head hanging low from shame. "I'm sorry," she pleads. "I didn't know you were back. I didn't hear you come in."

"Nah, that was my bad. I should have told you I was in here. Don't worry, I didn't see anything," he lies. Yeah right, he says to himself, while replaying the entire vision. Sha-Rock's eyes drop to Tamara's firm C cups. He can't help it. Her stiff nipples are staring at him through her tight fitted T-shirt.

He walks into the bathroom and closes the door behind him. As he's standing over the toilet taking a leak, he notices a satin and lace bra and thong set on the shower rod. She obviously took them off so she could wash them out. Just to think that Tamara is in there, wearing no underwear drags Sha-Rock's mind into the gutter. How convenient, he utters to himself.

He walks into the room, straight to the recliner. He sits down and tries to act as if he's tuned into the television, when in all reality, Tamara is the only thing on his mind. He shifts his eyes to the left, to see what she's doing. She's laying underneath the blanket with it pulled up past her neck, holding it tightly. From the looks of it, she appears to be uncomfortable. He speaks without taking his eyes off of the television. "Tammy, if you feel uncomfortable, I'll get another room? I didn't think we would have to stay overnight. That's why I only got one room."

"That cab driver told me a big convention just came into town today. All the money in the world couldn't get you a room right now. Anyway, it's alright," she claims.

"You look mad uncomfortable over there. Are you sure?"

"Yes, I'm sure," she replies.

Sha-Rock flicks through the channels. "Tammy?"

"Huh?"

"This is off the record, alright?" he asks in a low whisper. He pauses before speaking. "I always wanted to ask you this. How come you never told Miranda about us?"

She hesitates before speaking. "What was it to tell?" she snaps.

"Knock it off. You know what I mean."

"It wasn't anything to tell. We went on a few dates and that was it. It's not like something happened between us."

"If something would have happened, would shit have changed then?"

"I don't know. I didn't find out that you were her boyfriend until we got tight. If we had sex, I probably would have stopped communicating with her."

"When I first found out who you were, I didn't want her with you because I thought you would tell."

"I wouldn't do that," she claims. "What would that prove?"

"Nothing, I guess," he replies. "Can I ask you a question? Off the record of course?" he asks.

"Go ahead."

"Have you ever wondered how shit would have turned out if I didn't go to jail?"

"Never."

"What do you mean, never? You mean to tell me, it never crossed your mind?"

"Well maybe in the beginning. That's before I met Miranda. I take everything as a sign, though. If you had not gone to jail, I would have just been your mistress. Me and Miranda would have never become friends, and you would be just another nigga fucking me and going back home to his main girl."

"One more question. Keep it real," he insists. "Have you ever wondered what it would have been like?" He realizes that he's now reaching by asking this question.

"What?" she answers innocently.

"You know, *it*," he says childishly.

"Sha, say what you mean. I'm a grown ass woman. All the childish talk, I'm not with it," she snaps.

Her sassiness belittles him. "Alright, have you ever wondered what sex would have been like between me and you?" He sighs afterwards as if he's said a mouthful.

"Sha, right now all this is irrelevant. Even if it did cross my mind, it doesn't matter now."

"Why not?"

"Because it doesn't. That was the past. It didn't happen, so there's no need to wonder about it. If it was meant to happen, it would have happened."

"Can I tell you something, without you ever repeating it?" he asks.

"I didn't tell all this time. What makes you think I'll tell now? This entire conversation is off the record as far as I'm concerned."

Sha-Rock likes the sound of her last statement. He wonders if she's trying to give him a hint? There's only one way to find out, he thinks. "Every time I see you, I think about how it would be. I have to keep it real. I never lost it for you," he admits.

"Boy, please!"

"I swear Tammy!" he says as he holds his right hand high in the air. "Nobody ain't tell y'all to become best friends. You was my friend first," he jokes, sounding like a child.

"You're silly," she smiles.

"Tammy I swear, if I could have it my way, I would want both of y'all. You don't think that would be cool? Y'all are already friends," he jokes. "That's really my fantasy. No bullshit!"

Tamara smiles brightly, giving Sha-Rock the incentive to continue running his mouth. "Word up, I would get rid of pretty boy first. You know your little New York dude? Then I would move you right in with us."

She continues to blush. "My New York dude is almost out of the picture," she replies.

"Oh yeah? That ain't what I heard. Miranda says y'all are madly in love."

"Yeah, I love him, but ...."

"But what?"

"But, I want more out of life. The last thing I need in my life is stress."

"Are we still off the record?" he asks.

"Psst," she sucks her teeth, while smiling.

"Is there any way, I could help you relieve some stress?" he asks as he walks toward the bed where she's laying. Nervousness feels her body. "Tammy, have you ever had a big shiny apple that looks so sweet? Then when you bite into it, it's rotten on the inside?" Without giving her time to reply, he continues to speak. "I look at you all the time, and I wonder if you taste as good as you look?" Tamara melts away. "Listen Tammy, I love Miranda, and I'm sure your feelings for her are strong too, but what we had came first. I feel like we have unfinished business, and I won't be able to just leave it like that. If you can honestly tell me that you never wished it had happened, I'll erase this feeling that I have. Can you tell me that?" he asks. She doesn't reply, but the look on her face tells him she's too ashamed to admit that she feels the same way. "It feels like this was meant to be. Look, me and you all the way in Miami. I don't think that's coincidence. It's destiny." He pauses for a second. "Tammy, there's something that I've always wanted to do to you since the first time I saw you. For one night, let's just take it back in the day. We both know Miranda exists now, and we knew she existed back then. Please promise that whatever happens tonight will stay right here in Miami?" he begs. He leans his head close to hers as she lays flat on her back. His face is so close that she can feel the air coming from his nostrils. "Promise," he begs, as his lips touch hers.

"I promise," she sighs before grabbing the back of his head and kissing him passionately. He lies on top of her and they grind against each other like two teenagers. The grinding becomes more and more intense. Tamara's moans and sighs drive him crazy. He eases off of her and flips her onto her belly. He climbs aboard and slowly grinds against her butt, while cupping her firm breast. He gently pinches her erect nipples to heighten the pleasure. Tamara's insides get creamier by the second. "Sha, this is wrong," she utters.

"Shhh," he replies. "Just one time?" he begs. He unbuckles her jeans and slowly peels them off of her. They're so tight that he struggles to pull them down. He manages to roll one leg down. He then sits up for a second, just enjoying the view of her perfectly rounded rear. He leans over and slowly drags his tongue down her crack. He doesn't stop until he tastes the sweetness of her nectar.

A two-minute sister is what you may call her, because she reaches her peak before his first lick. He doesn't want to miss a drop. He lays on his back and props her directly on top of his face. He palms her cheeks and mashes her onto his face. She winds her hips in a circular motion, as she moans excessively. Chills shoot through her body every time her clit greets his tongue.

Sha-Rock lifts her off of him. He jumps up quickly and pulls off of his pants and underwear. His manhood stands at full attention. He pulls her toward him and bends her over the bed. She has one pant leg on and the other one drags the floor.

With no warning he drives himself deep inside her almost ripping her tiny opening. "Unghh," she grunts as he fills her insides.

Sha-Rock answers Miranda's question about who is bigger, him or Najee. Sha-Rock crashes into her walls as if he's trying to knock them down. She screams in a loud hoarse voice. The pain is too much. She tries to pull away from him but he hunches over and wraps his arms around her waist, giving her no way to escape his rapture. He pounds on her furiously. Suddenly, he slows down his pace. He pokes her slowly. She begs for more, as his anaconda swims through her ocean. Droplets of her love trickle down her legs.

His legs stiffen, and his cannon pulsates. He snatches himself out of her abruptly. He aims the cannon at the center of her back, and unloads. She sighs with relief as the buckshots explode all over her back. Warm pellets plaster her skin.

They go round after round, after round. They spend the entire night partaking in bone chilling, spine tingling, back breaking sex.

It's one hour and twenty minutes into round five and Tamara is winning. Not only has she gotten used to his size, but she's also managed to tire him out. After riding him for one whole hour, he doesn't have a bit of stamina left. She's drained him dry. She shows no mercy on him. She continues to bounce vibrantly. Suddenly a cold feeling zips through her body. She stops all movement. Finally she explodes and collapses on top of him. She falls asleep in his arms, just as the sun rises.

At 9 a.m. the ringing of the cellular phone awakens Tamara. While still layng on Sha-Rock's chest, she reaches over and answers the phone. "Hello?" She's shocked to hear Miranda's voice. If Miranda could only see through the telephone? "He's in his room down on the first floor," she lies. The sex is over and now the guilt sets in. "Alright, I'll call to his room and tell him. We'll be right there. I love you too," she claims before hanging the phone up.

One hour later, the lawyer drops Miranda off at the airport, where

Tamara and Sha-Rock await her. Tears drip down her face at the first sight of them. She's happy to be greeted by two of the people she loves the most in the whole wide world. She exhales. What a nightmare these past days have been.

Three Days Later/February 22

Miranda has been staying away from Tamara. She's sure Tamara is waiting for answers. She'll never admit to Tamara what happened. Tamara is making it difficult by calling her nonstop. Miranda doesn't know how long she can continue to avoid her. She's running out of excuses.

Miranda's lawyer found out that the chauffeur informed the police that Miranda and Sha-Rock had come to Miami. He also stated that Miranda was the last person seen with Kiko. They got hold of Miranda's name through her mother's records. The credit card that she used to rent the Bentley traced her back to Philadelphia. She also says that they know her boyfriend came along but they have no clue who he is. The description they have of him is so general. They're looking for a tall, muscular build, bald, black man.

Miranda said they drilled her over and over for hours at a time, but she claims that she stood her ground. When it was time to sign a statement, she supposedly wrote the words, "I wish to make no statements at this time." She then printed the actual time and signed her name on the form. Sha-Rock was so proud to know that she kept it gangster. He promised her she would make out alright. He told her if shit doesn't look right by the end of the trial, he would step in and take the weight for the murder. Sha-Rock's main concern is getting the money up to fight the case.

Sha-Rock, Lisa, and their mother are in the funeral director's office. The funeral is already in session. They're just paying off the balance of the funeral.

Lisa sits at the director's desk counting the money while Sha-Rock and his mother stand side by side near the door.

Mother Ford places a peppermint in her mouth after her dry coughing. "Uhhm, uhhmm," she clears her throat. She pulls a small bottle of oil from her pocketbook. She dabs a few drops onto her index finger and places her finger on the center of Sha-Rock's forehead. At first he fades away from her until she grabs hold of his hand. "Baby, I can feel the evil spirit's presence. They're lurking around you." As she anoints him, she prays silently.

A weird sensation runs through his body from his head to his toes. The feeling frightens him. He wonders if she knows that he killed Rahiem? Tears well up in his eyes as he watches the tears flow from her face. It hurts him so bad when he thinks of all the pain he's caused her. Through it all, she's never given up on him. He's so grateful to have her on his side. He knows that her prayers have kept him alive all these years. One day he hopes to make up for the heartaches he's caused her.

"Baby, the evil spirits have a hold on you. You pop up in my dreams. I don't know what's going on with you, but you have to be careful. You know my dreams come true. I dreamed about this funeral, but it wasn't Rahiem laying in the coffin. It was you," she sighs. "Everything that's happening, I saw it in my dreams. Only difference, Rahiem was standing here in your place."

"Ma, what did I tell you about telling me your dreams? Keep them to yourself," he pleads.

"Baby, I'm sorry. Please be safe?" she begs.

Lisa walks over to them. Her eyes are puffy and red. She hasn't stopped crying since the phone call. Sha-Rock hugs her tight. "Lil Sis, it's gonna be alright. I got y'all," he claims.

She can't speak, so she just nods her head up and down. Finally she finds the words to speak. "Sha, thank you for the money," she whispers.

"Lisa, that's nothing. Stop thanking me." The funeral price came out to $13,000. Rahiem had $8,000 in the bank, and Lisa had to get the other $5,000 from Sha-Rock.

Lisa and Mother Ford walk into the funeral room, while Sha-Rock walks outside. He doesn't have the heart to stand over the coffin, knowing that he put him there. Sure he maybe cold-hearted, but not that cold-hearted.

It broke his heart to hear what Lisa and the kids had to say about the incident. Lisa said she's been praying that they find Rahiem's murderer. The kids said they hope the murderer gets the death penalty. If they only knew, Big Bro, Uncle Turkey, is the culprit. He wonders if they would still feel the same way if they knew?

One Month Later

Miranda flew into Miami yesterday evening. Her feelings toward Miami have changed. She's really grown to hate it. At one time this was her dream place. Now just hearing the word tears her to pieces. She only came here to meet with her lawyer.

They sit across from each other in the lawyer's office. He sits there staring at the stack of papers that are piled up on his desk. She anxiously awaits the news. His long saddened face tells her the news can't be good. He finally looks up into her eyes, without saying a word. The suspense is ripping her apart. "Mr. Goldman, please! You're killing me," she shouts.

He pauses for another thirty seconds before finally speaking. "Miranda, Miranda," he utters slowly.

"Yes," she asks desperately.

"First of all let me start off by saying what I was hoping wouldn't happen, has happened," he says with a sympathetic look on his face. "You were indicted." He lowers his head while sighing.

"How?" she asks. "Do they have anything?"

"Honestly, they have enough to finish you. They have several witnesses that watched you and him leave Club Mangos together. The chauffeur states that he dropped you and him off a few hours before his murder. They have liquor bottles with your DNA all over them. One half hour after the murder, you checked out of your hotel room. In less than one hour later, you rented a car, when you already had a round trip airplane ticket. Not to mention, your return date was several days away." He shakes his head from side to side. "Gosh Miranda, you're asking me to perform a miracle. I have to be honest. This doesn't look good."

"Keep it real," she demands. "What are my chances?"

"Slim," he replies quickly. "I spoke with the prosecutor. They don't believe that you done it. Bottom line, somebody has to get charged. They really don't want you, but they'll charge you if they can't get anyone else. The chauffeur claims that you came with your fiancé. Your credit card only shows a purchase of one flight ticket? I need clarity. I'm your lawyer. I'm with you. We can bullshit them together, but please don't bullshit me. I need to know every detail, so I can go in there prepared for whatever they have in store. If you bullshit me, I'll go in there looking stupid and blow the entire case."

Miranda paid for her ticket using her credit card, but Sha-Rock paid cash only because he was debating going, so he paid at the very last minute.

"If there's no fiancé, we have a chance, but if a fiancé pops up, we fall right at their mercy," he warns her. "You look like a good girl, and I would hate to see you hurt yourself. I have seen so many young girls fall into this deadly trap. The case of the good girl falling in love with the wrong guy. I hate to say it like this, but if you didn't pull the trigger, you shouldn't be charged with murder. Right is right," he adds. "There's a huge gap in between murder and conspiracy. That individual is the key to your freedom, Miranda. With him in custody, I can almost guarantee you no more than five years at the worst case. Of course, I'm pushing for dismissal. I want to see you walk away from this, but it doesn't look good. I don't have room to breathe, let alone make a mistake. We can't go to trial. They'll burn us!"

Meanwhile in Philly

Sha-Rock and Tamara both agreed on leaving that skeleton in the closet back in Miami, but one of them must have packed the skeleton in their luggage by mistake. Tonight marks their tenth sexual engagement this month. Pulling that off has been easy, being that Miranda has been staying away from Tamara.

Sha-Rock's excuse has been the fact of him laying low, hiding from the police. Every time he gets the urge to see Tamara, he tells Miranda how he feels uncomfortable and something is telling him not to stay home that night. She ignorantly falls for it every time.

The hot water gushes through the shower head and sprinkles onto Sha-Rock's muscular back. Tamara buries her face into his chest, to keep the water out of her eyes. He has her pinned against the wall. Her arms wrap around his neck, while her legs are crossed around his waist. He holds her in the air by cupping her buttocks. His fingers sink into her fluffy cheeks. He balances himself on the tips of his toes, while digging into her, using short, deep pumps. She's so hot and wet that she's trying to forget about the uncomfortable feeling that's inside of her.

The slightest stroke of his wand causes her intense pain, but as the saying goes, "pain is pleasure" and she's enjoying every inch of it. He lifts her higher, while standing flat on his feet. He draws himself back, only giving her the tip. The teasing drives her wild. She's tired of the teasing. Her need to feel all of him increases. She tightens her grip on his neck and bounces down on him consuming him in entirety. "Aghh," she sighs as her juices pour from within.

Back in Miami

"Think about it, Miranda. Life is a long time," the lawyer says. "Ask yourself, will he still love you thirty years from now?"

A Few Days Later

Miranda lays curled up in the same bed that her man and her best friend have been betraying her in. Tamara sits on the edge of the bed, patting Miranda's back, trying to comfort her. Up until now Miranda has been holding up extremely well. Tonight she could no longer hold it in. Her lawyer laid it out plain and simple for her. She can tell and walk away with a smack on the wrist or she can keep her mouth shut and take a lifelong ass whipping. Either way she loses. If she goes to jail, she loses her life, but if Sha-Rock goes to jail, a part of her will die. She can't imagine how life would be either way. Tamara suggested that she might have to tell on Sha-Rock in order to free herself from the madness.

"Let it all out," says Tamara, as she strokes Miranda's hair. Miranda still hasn't admitted the truth to Tamara. She told Tamara some off the wall story and she bought it without disbelief.

"Thanks for your support," says Miranda as she sits up in the bed, wiping her eyes dry.

"You're more than welcome. That's what sisters are for," Tamara says as she opens her arms wide. Miranda falls into her arms in search of comfort.

A Few Miles Away

Killer Cal sits in the passenger's seat of Sha-Rock's van. They're parked in front of some condominiums in Center City. Skip turned them onto a kid from West Philly who supposedly is holding onto a fortune. This is his place of residence. They've been watching him for two days already. Sha-Rock knows he shouldn't be working in Philly, where he lives. He never makes it a habit of shitting where he eats, but right now this is his last resort.

Sha-Rock sits in the driver's seat entertaining several thoughts. His primary concern is Miranda. No matter what he's doing, the situation constantly interrupts his thoughts. He also thinks of all the successful robberies that he's had in this short time. No one would ever believe that he's dead broke after all the money he's had in his grip. It all boils down to a bunch of meaningless murders.

He only has true remorse for one murder and that's his brother in law. He can't believe he actually killed Lisa's first love. He's the reason his nephew and niece will grow up without a father. Sha-Rock always hated him but he has to admit, he couldn't have chosen a better husband for his sister or a better father for the kids. His mother always told him that you would reap what you sow. He can't help but wonder what his payback will be. He'll consider himself lucky if it's only death.

He thinks of all the people's lives that he's altered. He went against all the rules by killing hustlers for money. It's hard for him to believe that he's turned into the hater that would kill a hustler for doing what he's supposed to do, which is getting money. Back in the day, Sha-Rock wished death on all dudes who were like that. His code has always been hustlers against the stick-up kids. His lack of motivation made him look for a shortcut. His shortcut led him to the quick road to destruction. An old head that was down prison with him told him something that he never forgot. He said, "Never go against the grain. Stick to doing what you do. The dudes in here with the murder charges are drug dealers, and the dudes in here with drug charges are stick-up kids. You very seldom go to jail for doing what you do because you know that game and you respect it. Every time you step out of your element it results in big trouble." It made sense to Sha-Rock then and it makes even more sense now. The bad part is that he has both feet in and there's no stopping now.

For once, Killer Cal is actually thinking sane. "Baby Boy, shit can get real ugly. I know you love Miranda and you prepped her for shit like this but you have to remember she's still a woman. She can only take but so much pressure. I love you like a little brother, and I hate to say this, but either you gone have to bounce to Miami and cut her loose or you gone have to do the next best thing," he says, while looking straight ahead.

Sha-Rock knows exactly what he's saying. He hates the fact that this thought would even cross Cal's mind. "Cal, what are you saying?"

"Baby Boy, she's the only link to you. I love you. I deal with Miranda because you love her. I don't want to see the girl in that position, but I would hate to see you there. There's only one way to fix all of it. Baby Boy, say the word and it's done; no more worrying."

Sha-Rock evaluates Cal's statements. He feels even more terrible that those same thoughts had crossed his mind. Nothing in the world could make him harm her. His poisoned thoughts make him feel so guilty. "Big Bro, I love that girl, you hear me? I would never do that.We gone get the paper we need to fight the case. She'll be alright. I got some things brewing. If all else fails, I'll sell the cars back to the dealer. Please don't ever make that suggestion again?"

Killer Cal gives him a head nod, letting him know he hears him, but no way does he agree with him. Not only is Sha-Rock gambling with his own freedom, he's also putting Cal's freedom in jeopardy as well. Miranda knows enough information to get both of them the death penalty. He realizes that Sha-Rock is thinking with his heart and not his mind. Hopefully it will all work out for the better.

Two Weeks Later

Sha-Rock watched the kid from West Philly close for two weeks, and he hadn't gotten the smallest lead. That gave him no other alternative but to do the one thing he didn't want to do. Yesterday he swallowed his pride and took his car back to the dealership. He literally begged them to buy the car back. After seeing how desperate he was, they made him a lousy offer of $45,000. He wanted to spit in their faces and drive off but he couldn't. Miranda's lawyer called pressuring her for more money. He told her a payment of $40,000 was well overdue, and if she didn't hurry up and pay, he would be forced to drop the case.

This morning, Sha-Rock took $40,000 from the $45,000 and gave it to Miranda so she could overnight it to the lawyer.

Sha-Rock still hasn't admitted to Miranda that he's broke. She thinks he sold the car out of fear of drawing attention to himself.

Miranda has been standing in the long line at the post office for thirty minutes already. She's sending her father underwear and socks. If he didn't tell her he needed them badly, she would have stepped out of the line. Just as she steps up two baby steps, her cell phone rings. "Hello?" she whispers. No one replies. "Hello?" she repeats. Still no one answers. "Hello," she whispers again. Suddenly, she hears a muffling sound in the phone. Seconds later, she can hear voices faintly. She can't make out what they're saying though. She listens closely. Someone is giggling in the background. It's obvious that it's at least two voices. Sha-Rock's phone must be on without him knowing it?

Sha-Rock's voice echoes in the phone as clear as day. "I'm sorry, Ma," he says before busting out in laughter. Then the muffling sound starts up again, with goofy giggling in the background. Miranda assumes that Sha-Rock and whomever he's with must be play fighting. Her heart drops. She would love to believe that what she's hearing isn't really true, but it's so clear that she can't deny it. "Sha!" she shouts, disregarding the fact that the post office is jammed pack. Everyone turns their heads toward her after the outburst. "Sha," she repeats with no embarrassment. He's still not responding. She storms out of the post office, still holding the phone to her ear. "Sha!" she shouts as the tears pour from her eyes.

It all comes together. She feels so stupid. All the nights that he's been in Jersey, she thought he was working. Now she believes that he has a girl up there. He left the house today claiming that he was going to Jersey for work. How could he do this to me, she asks herself.

Two Days Later

Miranda hasn't said a word to Sha-Rock about hearing him on the phone. It's been killing her trying to refrain from mentioning it. She just wants to observe him and get her facts straight before bringing it to his attention. That way he can't deny it. She doesn't want to alert him so he'll stop doing what he's doing. She plans to give him enough room to hang himself.

Hatred fills her heart when she looks at him. No one could have ever told her he was cheating. It was so unsuspected to her. She continuously asks herself how could he cross her when she's in the position that she's in? Just to think, she thought about giving up her freedom for him. She's so disgusted with him that when he calls her *Boo* or *Ma* it irks her to no end. Before she found that sexy, but now she realizes those words mean nothing to him. He uses them as a figure of speech.

She almost couldn't refrain when he came in last night and reached over to sex her. The thought of it made her stomach turn, but she gave in just so he wouldn't suspect anything. While having sex with him, she felt dirty and disgusting. He couldn't imagine why she wouldn't get wet for him. Sha-Rock could never imagine the damage that he's done to their relationship.

Miranda can no longer hold it in. She has to tell someone. Where else better to go to for comfort than her good friend, Tamara?

Tamara opens the door and sees Miranda standing there looking a mess. She knows it must be something serious, because Miranda would never leave her house wearing a head scarf on her head. "What's wrong?" Tamara questions.

Miranda storms into the apartment without replying. As soon as she gets in the living room, she collapses onto the carpet, crying loud and hard. She bangs on the floor and kicks like a baby who is having a temper tantrum.

Tamara kneels down beside her. "It's alright baby. Let it all out," she says just as they always do when the other one is in need of a good *boo hoo.*

"Aghh," Miranda screams, looking ugly. "I can't take it no more," she cries. "I just can't take it no more!"

"Girl, it's going to be alright. God knows you're innocent. He's not going to let you spend the rest of your life in jail for a crime you didn't commit."

"It's not just that," she yells. "All this that I'm going through and now he goes and cheats on me."

The word *cheat* sends a chill up Tamara's spine. "Cheat?" she asks hesitantly.

"Yeah, cheat. I've been faithful to him all these years,' she cries. "Tammy, you know I have been loyal to him?"

"I know," she confirms. "How do you know that he's cheating on you?"

"I got proof," Miranda says as she dials numbers on her phone. She then hands the phone over to Tamara. "Here, listen." Tamara reaches for the phone slowly. Her jaw drops as she hears messages that she left Sha-Rock. Miranda figured out his security code and broke into his voice mail. Tamara drops the phone. She stands up and backpedals away from Miranda. Miranda's tears of hurt turn to tears of rage.

Miranda stands up. "You dirty bitch!" she shouts. "I don't believe you!" she hollers as she snatches Sha-Rock's long-nosed .357 from under her blouse. Tamara yells for her life. "Bitch if you don't shut up, I'll kill your trifling ass in here," Miranda whispers as she aims the gun at Tamara's head. Tears drop from Miranda's eyes. After all they have been through, Miranda would have never suspected her to backstab her like this. Miranda has done so much for her. She's supported her mentally as well as financially. All she wanted in return was for Tamara to be happy. She thinks back to all the times she saved Najee by lying to Sha-Rock, telling him she didn't know anything about him.

"Come here!" Miranda demands. Tamara's feet are glued to the floor. Miranda grabs her by her hair and slings her around like a rag doll. "You dirty, trifling bitch," she cries. After a series of knees to Tamara's face, Miranda drags her around the room by her hair.

"Oww, oww," Tamara screams. "Miranda, please?"

"Miranda, my ass, bitch!" The more Miranda thinks of the disrespect, the harder she pulls her hair, and knees her to the face. Miranda manhandles her furiously, using only her left hand. Her right hand grips the .357. Miranda and Tamara's blouses are both ripped open, causing their enormous tits to bounce all over the place. Drops of blood fall onto Miranda's sneakers. The sight of the blood increases Miranda's adrenaline. She tugs her hair even harder as if she's trying to pull it from the roots.

Tamara squirms away, causing Miranda to lose her grip. In the palm of Miranda's hand is a bunch of thick hair that Miranda managed to snatch from Tamara's scalp. Tamara lifts her head up and looks around for an escape route. Before she can get away, Miranda kicks her in the chest. Tamara falls backwards, landing into a corner of the wall. Miranda quickly corners her and proceeds to stomp her without sympathy. Tamara tries to defend herself, by grabbing hold of Miranda's foot. This enrages Miranda even more. Miranda grabs her by the hair with her left hand. "Oh, you want to fight back, bitch?" she says. Without realizing it, she swings the .357 with her right hand. The gun crashes into Tamara's skull. Boom! One shot releases from the chamber.

"Owww!" Tamara screams. The glass coffee table shatters into pieces. This scares Miranda just as much as it scares Tamara. Miranda lets go of her hair. Tamara covers her head and curls up into a ball. Miranda steps back, looking to see if either one of them has been hit. Tamara is scared out of her mind. She thinks Miranda tried to shoot her purposely. Her muscles are frozen stiff. Miranda tugs her hair, pulling her upward. She rests the gun on her forehead. "Bitch, all that I have done for you? I've been a real friend to your hoe, no man-keeping ass! I supported you through everything; the hundred abortions, the syphilis, and the gonorrhea! You gave my man that sick pussy!"

"I'm sorry, Miranda. I'm so sorry."

"Bitch, sorry ain't gone save your sorry ass today!" she shouts. "Where did y'all fuck? How many times did y'all fuck? And, did y'all use protection? Three questions, and you only got three seconds to answer all of them," she states. "Starting now, one!" she counts. Tamara answers all three questions using only two seconds.

"Bitch, don't you ever as long as you live say another word to me. If I catch you anywhere near him, you got a problem," she shouts. "If you call and warn him, I swear on my mother, I'm coming back and I won't miss next time."

Several Hours Later

Sha-Rock is just coming home. He's been gone all day. He jumps into the bed and crawls up close to Miranda. She lies there as if she's still asleep. As soon as Sha-Rock's head hits the pillow, he falls asleep. The tugging of Sha-Rock's wood awakens him. He peeks downward with one eye and sees Miranda's head underneath the covers. Expecting a blowjob, he spreads his legs wide. Miranda jams his tip into her mouth and bites down until her teeth breaks the skin. "Aghh!" he screams from excruciating pain. "Bitch," he calls out, as he attempts to jump up. He tries to back away from her but he feels the sharp blade of the huge steak knife pressed against his pulsating head. He looks down and sees the teeth marks that she left. The sight of it brings tears to his eyes. Numbness replaces the pain that he felt.

"My best friend?" she cries while still holding the knife against him. "My best friend?" she repeats. "All the bitches in the world and you had to fuck my best friend?"

"Miranda, let's talk," he pleads. "L-let's talk," he stutters. He wonders how she knows. Did Tamara reveal their secret? How could she cross him like that?

"Ain't shit to talk about, nigga."

"Miranda, think about what you're doing," he says in fear of losing his pride and joy.

"Think? Did you think?" she shouts. "I swear, I don't believe y'all. My best friend and my man! Ain't that a motherfucker? I never thought you would do that. And just to think, my lawyer told me to tell on you," she informs him. "I didn't even make it to jail yet, and you already fucking my friend. I was about to spend the rest of my life in jail for your cheating ass. Thank you," she shouts sarcastically. "I asked God to show me a sign to help me make my decision, and now I got it!"

"Miranda, please take the knife off my shit," he begs. "I want to talk."

"Talk!" she demands. "If you lie to me, I swear to God you gone be dickless," she cries.

"Listen Ma?"

"Ma, my ass!" She drags the point of the knife across his shaft, slightly cutting into his flesh. "Don't you ever call me that! I heard you call that bitch, Ma!"

"Aghh," he screams. He's not screaming from pain. He's

screaming out of fear. "Please listen," he begs. "It's all business."

"Business?" she repeats after him. "Business? You fucking my friend is business? You must really think I'm stupid? What fucking kind of business is that?"

"Hold up, hold up, listen. I'll explain it to you," he reasons with her. "You know how long I've been trying to get you to turn me onto that Harlem model nigga, right? You didn't do it, so I had to do it myself. It's all business," he claims.

"Motherfucker, all the niggas I brought in and I didn't fuck not one of them and the first one you do, you gotta fuck?" she asks in a high-pitched voice. "Business my ass!"

"Listen Miranda, please?' he pleads.

"I'm not listening to shit!" she shouts as she stands up and lets his prize loose. He sighs with relief. He runs toward her, but she backs up and pulls the .357 from her sweatpants. She aims it high. "Back up off me. Don't touch me," she says sternly.

He breaks down. "Miranda, what's going on? I told you it's business. You don't even care what's going on with me. Fuck me, right? Just fuck me? Jimmy ran away with $525,000 of our money. Our money," he repeats. "I'm dead broke, Miranda. I had to do something."

Miranda backpedals toward the door, still aiming the gun at him. "Tell it to the judge!"

"Huh? What does that supposed to mean, Miranda? Huh?" he questions. "What about us?" he asks in a high-pitched voice.

She finally makes him way to the doorway. "There is no us. When you crossed me, you lost me," she whispers, as she exits the house. He starts to run toward her until she stops and gently taps the trigger, threatening to shoot. He stops in his tracks. She backpedals all the way to her car. She hops in and pulls off recklessly, causing her tires to screech. She leaves Sha-Rock with the taste of burned rubber in his mouth.

He stands there wearing the most stupid look on his face. He thinks she's only speaking out of anger. He's sure that she's coming back until he runs to her closet and finds out that are her clothes have been removed. He then runs to the dresser drawers. She hasn't left one pair of panties behind. Suspense fills his heart, while pain fills his manhood. He drops to the floor holding both heads.

-68-

-----◆◆◆-----

One Month Later

Sha-Rock has been living in suspense for the entire month. He hasn't been staying at home. The words *tell it to the judge*, replays in his head over and over. He doesn't want to believe that she was warning him, that she's about to snitch on him. He hopes she was speaking out of anger.

Killer Cal has been making matters worse by constantly telling him that she'll definitely tell on him now because she's brokenhearted. At first Sha-Rock didn't believe it, but now he's sort of convinced. He now realizes how much of a bad decision that was. A few orgasms is going to cost him his life.

He can't imagine where she could be staying. He even called Lo Jack and told them his car had been stolen, but they wouldn't give up any information because the car isn't in his name. They switched the cars out of his uncle's name soon after they bought them.

Miranda has instilled a great deal of fear into Tamara. Sha-Rock managed to see her only one time since the incident. He had to black mail her to get inside her house that particular time. He told her that he got word that Miranda was on her way over to kill her. He gave her two hours of his best sex and he hasn't heard from her since. He drives past her house on a regular basis. He assumes she must be staying in Fort Lee. Yeah, Fort Lee. Sha-Rock knows everything. He has fucked every small detail out of her. It's amazing how informative pillow talk could be after explosive sex!

Najee pulls into the tight parking space. The bright lights of his Mercedes illuminate the dark block. At four in the morning, China town looks more like a ghost town.

Najee diddy bops to the brick-faced warehouse looking building. A bum wrapped up in a bunch of blankets lays curled up in front of the doorway. A pushcart that's full of cans sits about ten feet in front of him.

The sight of the bum makes Najee angry. He runs over and slams the cart over aggressively. He then walks toward the bum. Najee greets him with five solid kicks to the back. "What the fuck did I tell you about sleeping here?" he asks. "You stinking motherfucker! I pay $7,000 a month for this spot, and bums crowding the doorstep!" The bum absorbs the abuse and crawls a few feet out of the way. Najee then sticks his key in the door. "I been telling you this all week!" he adds.

While Najee is turning the key in the lock, the bum gets up and tiptoes quietly behind him. Once he gets within reach, he throws a pillowcase over Najee's head. Najee squirms, trying to put up a fight until he feels the painful blow of the cold steel bang against his dome.

Sha-Rock runs over and pushes the door open. Once they're inside the building, they escort Najee over to the elevator and press number five.

Once they reach the fifth floor, they lead Najee to the door of his loft. Sha-Rock opens the door without hesitation, and they all step inside. Killer Cal stands there holding the pillowcase over Najee's head with one hand, while he holds the gun to his head with the other hand.

Sha-Rock runs directly to the back of the loft. He retrieves the duffle bags full of dope and runs back to the door. Sha-Rock has to give him credit for this. No one would ever suspect him to use a loft that cost $7,000 a month to rent, just to stash his dope.

Killer Cal whispers in Najee's ear. "You got caught slippin', Baby Boy." He then fires three consecutive shots to the back of Najee's head. Najee's body collapses onto the floor. Killer Cal bends over and snatches the pillowcase off of his head to make sure he's dead. The blood that's leaking from his head and mouth seal the deal. Killer Cal hog spits on his forehead before they flee the scene.

They hop in the van and pull off at a moderate speed. It's a clean getaway. Tamara made everything so simple, and she doesn't even know it. When she receives the news, she'll never think her big mouth put Najee in this position.

"Duffle bags of dope!" Sha-Rock shouts. "We're back on board, baby!"

-69-

———◆◆◆———

Another month passes and Sha-Rock still hasn't heard from Miranda. This is going a lot further than he expected. He's been moving with extreme caution because he doesn't know what to expect.

He hasn't heard from Tamara either. He surely thought she would have called him to tell him about Najee's murder. Thanks to her, Sha-Rock is now ahead of the game. In the loft, Najee had a total of six hundred bricks of heroin. It only took Sha-Rock one week to get rid of all of it. He hooked up with two dudes from North Philly that he used to deal business with before he went to jail. They bought 150 bricks every other day until they bought him out. Selling each brick to them at $300 made him a total of $180,000.

As soon as he was done he called up an old friend of his who turned him onto a cocaine connect. His first flip was five kilos. The connect charged him $20,000 a bird. The other $80,000 he stashed. That situation taught him to put something away for a rainy day.

Sha-Rock has been taking care of Cal, just like he did back in the day. He's been giving him $2,500 a week. He's also been putting $2,500 away for Skip. He has to feed his team.

Things are moving slowly but that's fine with him. It's better for him that way. He buys five kilos for the week and he slow walks through them, dealing with only four or five customers. He profits a clean $10,000 a week. He lays in the cut in a secret location. The only time he comes out is when he's making a sell.

Killer Cal is moving throughout the streets of North Philly. In his pocket, he holds ten vials of crack that he just bought a few blocks away. As he walks, he can actually taste the crack. He can't wait to get home and take a hit. The crack is calling him. There's no way he can make it to the house. He peeks around to make sure no one is watching before dipping in the alleyway of two abandoned houses. He stands close to the building as he drops the pellets of crack into his stem. His hands tremble as he lights it. He sucks the glass like a human vacuum cleaner. As he's blasting, his eyes comb his surrounding area, watching for pedestrians.

It can't be, he says to himself. The crack is playing tricks with his mind. After taking one final pull, he puts the blazing stem into his pocket and proceeds up the block.

As he gets closer, he realizes it's not the crack. It's real life, and his eyes are not misleading him. He stops in his tracks watching Miranda get out of her BMW. She peeks around nervously as she walks into the pawn shop. Now is the perfect time, he tells himself. Sha-Rock will never know. He loves the girl so much that he refuses to believe that she'll snitch on him. Cal fears that Sha-Rock's ignorance will cost both of them dearly. Cal thinks back to the murders they've done while she was there. He never agreed with her presence from the start. He knew how dangerous that was, but he didn't put up much argument because he was just so excited to be working again. Something always told him the bad decision would haunt them.

He has to get home to get his gun. He can't afford to let her get away. If she gets away this time, he's sure he'll never get another opportunity.

He takes off in the opposite direction. "Sha-Rock, I'm about to ease your pain," he utters as he races up the block.

When Miranda walks into the shop, a crackhead is at the counter showing the owner a small gold bracelet. The owner takes the bracelet and in return he hands him a $20 bill. The man then hurries out of the store. Miranda waits for him to disappear from the front of the store before pulling her engagement ring from her purse. She hates to part with it but she has no choice. The little modeling jobs have been keeping her alive, but things are so tight. She barely makes enough money to feed herself and keep a roof over her head. The agent that she met at the filming of "The Wire" has helped her a great deal. He placed her in an apartment in the Soho section. She shares the apartment with another model. The rent alone is $2,400 a month. They split all the bills down the middle. The girl pays her part of the bills with ease but Miranda has to struggle. The other girl stays busy. Miranda on the other hand only gets a job here and there, and when she is lucky enough to get a gig, her agent makes the bigger percentage. He's more like a pimp than an agent.

Miranda is in the process of selling her car. She's already placed the ad in the paper. She has a few potential buyers, but nothing solid yet. She's asking $30,000 for the car but she already has plans of taking anything close to that. She has no choice. Her lawyer is down her back, and she needs the money ASAP. Anyway, getting rid of the car will relieve her of some stress. She can't afford it anyway. Her insurance was cancelled a few weeks ago, and there are times when she doesn't even have gas money.

Without saying a word, Miranda passes the ring through the small opening of the bulletproof glass. The ring sparkles brightly as the Italian man turns it over examining it. He places his instrument up to his eyeglasses and zooms in on it. His face shows pure greed as he studies the ring from every angle. Finally he lifts his head up and says, "I'll give you $800."

"$800!" she shouts. She feels disrespected. "You better look at me again. I ain't no fucking crackhead! My shoes cost more than $800."

"Take it or leave it," he says arrogantly. "I'm being nice by offering that much."

"Give me my fucking ring," she demands. "I don't know who the fuck you think I am? I got the appraisal from my insurance company. I know what it's worth. Give me my shit! This is a $40,000 ring and you talking about $800. He passes her ring back to her and she walks away hastily. "Fuck you!" she shouts as she approaches the door.

Just before she grabs hold of the doorknob, he yells. "Okay, okay! Wait, Miss." She turns around slowly. "The best I can give you is six grand."

"Six grand? Ain't nothing," she replies while snatching the door open.

"Alright, $7,500? That's my final offer."

"Give me $10,000 and you can take it." She realizes that she's selling herself short, but she's terribly desperate right now.

"Alright, deal," he confirms. She closes the door and walks back up to the window. "You have to wait here until I get the money from the bank. Just give me about twenty minutes?"

Killer Cal races inside his apartment. He runs straight to his bed and lifts the mattress up. His wife's corpse shifts to the middle of the bed. Yeah, she finally made it back into the bed. The foul treatment made Cal feel terrible.

He grabs hold of Bree's old gun. He immediately slides one bullet into the chamber. He then tucks the gun inside his pants. Before walking out of the door, he blazes his stem one more time.

After taking the hit, he immediately dashes out of the house.

Miranda's pretty face bounces around in his deranged head. One day Baby Boy will thank me for this, he says to himself.

He steps outside, closing the door behind him. The presence of an unmarked police car parked across the street startles him. He stops short. His mind tells him to turn around and go back inside the apartment but he doesn't want to draw attention to himself. He's sure they already saw him because they locked eyes. The sound of engines racing followed by screeching tires sound off.

The cops jump out of the unmarked car. Ten other detectives accompany them. They all crowd the street. "Freeze! Police!" the detective shouts from across the street. All the cops stand still, not sure of what Cal's next move will be.

Cal attempts to sneak away by backing into the alleyway. "Don't move," the detective shouts as they all draw their guns and aim at him. Cal disregards their threats. He continues to back away. As he's backing up, he bumps into a row of garbage cans, causing him to stumble. He ducks down behind them and peeks over the lids. He snatches his gun from his waist, while paying close attention to the detectives who are standing there in awe.

The Marine comes from within him. His mind takes him back to the war. The bombs are bursting. Explosions echo in his head. Fire and smoke cover the field in front of him. Two officers run toward the alley with their guns drawn. "Enemy approaching," Cal warns the platoon. He rests his gun on top of the garbage can. "Aim, fire," he utters. Boc, boc! The first shot hits the lead detective in the chest. Luckily he has his bulletproof vest on. The impact knocks him back to the curb, tumbling backwards. The detective fires back recklessly. Pop, pop, pop, pop! The second detective squeezes as he backs out of the alleyway. Pop, pop! Cal fires back, letting them know that he means business. Boc! The bullet passes the detective's head, missing him by less than in inch. The detective ducks down real low and hides behind the car for cover.

By now, the streets are covered with police. Cal stands up quickly and aims. Boc, boc! The detectives disperse as the shots ring off. Just as he lowers himself to safety, a series of shots come back at him from every angle. Pop! Pop, pop! Pop, pop! Three shots rip through the side of the house, close to Cal's head. The other two crashes into the aluminum can and ricochets into the window of the house next door. Close, he thinks to himself. He looks around in search of a better shield. On the house next door, a refrigerator and an old washing machine set against it. He has to get to the other side.

A matter of minutes pass and neither Cal nor the police have fired any more shots. Cal leans against the house peeking in between the cans. He realizes that the police have him outnumbered thirty to one, but he still doesn't show the slightest bit of fear.

"Calvin Collins, drop your weapon," says the officer who is holding the bullhorn to his mouth. Never, Cal says to himself. Hold up, he utters. How do they know my name? "Calvin, you'll never make it out of here!" Cal rises up unsuspectingly. He fires while running across the alleyway to get to the other side. Boc! He makes it over successfully. Just before ducking behind the sink, he fires again. Boc! The bullet shatters the window of the cop car. The officer with the bullhorn ducks in the nick of time. One second later, he would have been labeled a hero. Cal hears the loud noise of a helicopter approaching high over his head.

Meanwhile

Sha-Rock's cell phone rings. "Hello?" he answers.

"Sha, turn to Channel 6!" Lisa yells. They're showing a big shoot-out on the news." Lisa is yelling so loud that he can barely understand what she's saying. The only thing he heard clearly was Channel 6. He flicks the stations until he reaches the exact channel.

"People Channel 6 live," the anchorman says. "Folks, we're hovering over the home of a murder suspect. Sha-Rock looks at the house they're showing. It looks familiar but he can't place it due to the angle. They're filming the house from the helicopter. "Philadelphia man, Calvin Collins, a.k.a. Calvin the Albino, exchanges fire with police as they attempt to take him into custody for questioning of a quadruple murder."

Sha-Rock can't believe his ears. He sure hopes he's hearing wrong, but as sure as day, that is Cal's house. He listens closely as the anchorman continues to speak.

"Police have reason to believe that this man is a suspect for a triple murder in New Jersey." Cal's mugshot flashes across the screen. "After his alleged accomplice turned states evidence, he was strangled to death a few days later." Damn, they know everything, Sha-Rock says to himself. He's sure Bree has snitched.

"Sha!" Lisa screams into the phone. "They're talking about your friend, Calvin!" He ignores her as the anchorman speaks again.

"One more suspect is at large. Police believe that he's somewhere in Philadelphia." Sha-Rock's heart skips a beat, after hearing that last statement. He knows that they're talking about him. He hangs up on his sister, so he can listen attentively.

At the Scene

The noisy helicopter frightens Cal. He looks up at the copter. His mind runs wild. He sees the enemy paratroopers preparing to jump from the copter. He raises his gun in the air and fires. Boc! After firing, he rolls over, laying flat on his stomach. His plan is to stay low to make it difficult for them to hit him.

"Folks, the suspect has fired at our news copter!" the anchorman shouts. Sha-Rock fears for Cal's life. There's no way he'll be able to make it out. Cal has always told him he would never give himself up for anything in the world. Sha-Rock didn't know he really meant it.

Killer Cal, pops up firing recklessly. Boc, boc, boc! He crawls onto his knees and pulls the sink closer to him. Now he has the perfect shield surrounding him.

"People, an officer is down!" the anchorman shouts. "Calvin Collins just fired three consecutive shots. From the looks of it, the officer has been hit in the head."

The anchorman has Sha-Rock's full attention. The whole ordeal is playing like a movie, only his partner is the star actor. "Come on baby. You fucking up." Sha-Rock is scared shitless. Cal is fighting a losing battle. He can't believe this is really happening. He's sure there is no way Cal can make it out. He knows they'll kill him now that he's shot a cop.

Cal backs up against the wall so that he can see the street and the backyard at the same time. He switches his eyes from side to side. His adrenaline is pumping. The bombs explode loudly. Oh no, he cries as his bunkee steps into the land mine. Cal looks to his left and spots three

341

enemy soldiers climbing into his backyard. He aims and fires without hesitation. Boc, boc! They dive onto the ground. He then looks to his right and spots two more enemy soldiers approaching the alleyway. He aims at them. Boc, boc! After firing, he crouches real low to the ground. He releases his clip to count how many rounds he has left. "Damn," he utters. The odds are against him. Police are in the backyard and the street. They're cornering in on him. He slams the clip back into the butt of the gun. It's all or nothing, he says to himself.

Sha-Rock's heart goes out to Cal. He wishes he would stop, but he also knows it's too late. Cal has already caused too much damage to stop now. He has to go out blazing.

"Folks, they finally have him cornered from both sides and snipers have set up on the roofs of the neighboring houses!" the anchorman shouts enthusiastically.

Sha-Rock looks closely at the snipers that are aiming at Cal from the roof. He already knows how this movie is going to end. "I can't watch it," Sha-Rock admits to himself, as he shuts the power off.

"It's all or nothing," Cal repeats, psyching himself up. "They'll never take me alive!" he shouts, while standing up and firing one shot in each direction. Boc! Boc!

Boom! Boom! Boom! Snipers from every roof fire consecutively. Killer Cal falls flat onto his face.

Sha-Rock's phone rings. "Yo?"

"Sha did you see it?" Lisa asks.

"They killed him?" he asks, already knowing the answer to his question.

"Yeah, the snipers," she replies sadly.

Sha-Rock turns the television back on. The copter's camera zooms in on the alleyway. Cal's body lays twisted on the concrete. Tears dribble down Sha-Rock's face. He watches all of the police crowd the alleyway. He can't even think straight. His life is one nightmare. He realizes there's no fixing this situation. There are too many odds. He has to face four bodies in Jersey, one in Miami and the loss of one of his soldiers, and his wife. This is too much for a man to deal with.

An hour later, he's still watching the television. Right now the cops are searching Cal's apartment. The anchorman speaks. "Folks, we've just received shocking news. As the police are searching Calvin Collins apartment, they've found a number of dead bodies. Sha-Rock listens closely to the alarming news. "Yes, people. Police have located the body of a missing woman who was found lying nude and dead in his bed. Police believe that it's the corpse of his ex-wife, Sharon Jenkins-Collins, who was kidnapped from her home some time ago. Also at her home at the time of the crime was her long-time boyfriend Charles Brown, whose body was found dead in their home from over forty stab wounds."

"Also in Collin's apartment they've found five other nude, severely mutilated female bodies stashed in his closet. All the women have the same complexion and hair color as his ex-wife," the anchorman informs. "Officials say that judging by the smell of the apartment, the bodies have been here for months. Sha-Rock remembers the stomach turning smell of the apartment. He then envisions the woman laying in Cal's bed that day. The thought of it all makes him shiver. A serial killer, Sha tells himself.

Twenty minutes later, Sha-Rock watches as police drag six body bags from Killer Cal's apartment. He can't understand how all that passed by him. He never had a clue. Sha-Rock finally admits that Cal really had a serious mental problem.

Sha-Rock's phone rings again. It hasn't stopped since the incident aired. He turns the power off and lies onto the bed. Everything happened so fast. It may take him a while to digest what he just witnessed.

Two Months Later

A distraught Miranda has just been escorted to her cell. Dressed in her orange jumpsuit and shower slippers, she in no way looks like the fashionable Miranda that had men falling at her feet.

Earlier today, she got the shock of a lifetime while in court. Today she lost the trial. Her lawyer told her all the odds were against them. He begged her to tell on Sha-Rock, but she refused. In return she was sentenced to life without parole. She stood there with a cement face and a jello heart as the judge sentenced her. In actuality, she never thought this would happen. She truly believed that God would make it alright.

She has been in custody for ten hours already, and she still hasn't shed a tear yet. Maybe it hasn't hit her yet. She's could still be in a state of shock. It may take her ten years to really realize that she'll die in prison.

Her lawyer pressured her so badly about snitching on Sha-Rock after admitting to him what really took place. She considered it, but for the life of her, she couldn't make herself do it. Even though he crossed her dearly, she just couldn't do it. Love didn't blur her vision because his betrayal overpowered it. The first couple of weeks away from him was hell on her, but eventually she learned to live without him. Without him in her life, she felt free. She was actually pursuing her dream career without sneaking around. It's just too bad that it took all of that just to finally follow her dreams.

As soon as she situates herself in the cell, she begins to write a letter to her father.

Papi, by the time you receive this scribe, I hope you are in the best of health and spirits.

Today, Miranda Benderas died and 0540-972 was born. At 12:45 p.m. I was sentenced to life in prison without parole. Although, I did create the atmosphere, I didn't commit the actual crime. The prosecutors and the judge all knew that I was innocent of the murder. Just like you, I could have been freed today, but I chose not to. You always taught me not to tattletale.

I stood there wearing the same game face you taught me to wear. Remember what you told me? You said never let them see you sweat. I was scared out of my mind, but they couldn't tell. In fact, my look was so cold that the judge threatened to increase my sentence.

Another thing you taught me was to stand behind my man. I can whole-heartedly say that I done that. He may not have been the ideal man that you wanted for me, but he was my man. I supported him in all his endeavors. I stood by his side through every battle, just like the trooper you told me to be. You said, behind every successful man, there's a good woman. I forgot your clause to that statement, when you say, "that doesn't mean she can't be just as successful." Papi, I put my dreams on hold to be the obedient woman that he wanted me to be.

You were the very first man that I fell in love with. The pain that you left me with when you walked out of my life made me realize I couldn't lose another lover, ever. That's why I did any and everything he asked me to do. My biggest fear was losing him.

Don't blame yourself for my destruction. My actions got me here. I'm a big girl and I take full responsibility for my actions. Remember you said if you had it to do again, you would do it the exact same way? Well, I feel the same way. Papi, I have no regrets. I took this one for the home team. He slandered our family name. You always said, a person that doesn't stand for something will fall for anything. I have no regrets because I stood for something and that's our family dignity. Although I'll pay for this forever, at least I can live with myself for not rolling over. My pride is everything. Like father like daughter.

I guess this is the beginning of my ending.

Love always,

Your Little Princess, Miranda.

One Year Later

Sha-Rock walks out of the shower wearing only a towel tied around his waist. He steps into his bedroom and stops at the doorway. He smiles as he enjoys the view of his bed. It's not the bed that he's admiring. It's the beautiful Tamara who's lying in it.

Sha-Rock searched high and low for her. Having no success in locating her he eventually gave up. He was forced to erase her from his mind. He thought he would never see her again in life. It was a blessing in disguise when she showed up at his doorstep early this morning.

Tamara's naked body lays curled up in the corner of the bed. Her complexion bounces off of his black silk sheets.

Tamara helped Miranda pick out the bed but never did she expect to be laying up in it.

He climbs behind her and pulls her close. Her body feels so comforting to him. He begins to plant kisses on the back of her neck. The noise of her sniffling catches his attention. He turns her over, laying her flat onto her back. The tears run down her face. "What's the matter?" he asks, as he dries each tear with his fingertip.

"Nothing," she replies

"Nothing? You don't cry like a baby for nothing. What's the matter?" he asks again.

All of a sudden, a familiar voice comes from the speakers of the television. He lifts his head up quickly. What he sees blows his mind. Miranda is acting out a scene on "The Wire." He sits there dumbfounded as she does her thing, like a seasoned actress. He tries to play it cool, but jealousy burns him up inside. Seeing her face makes him miss her dearly. He often thinks of her. After several months of looking for her, he gave up on that search as well. He was so worried about her telling on him that he ordered a subscription of the *Miami Herald*, just to keep in tune with her trial. His fear was eased the day he opened the paper and found out that she didn't tell on him.

As he's staring at the television, he wonders when Miranda managed to do this without him knowing. He's shocked to find out that she can actually act. He feels saddened because he never gave her a chance to carry out her dreams.

Miranda's brief scene is over with. The camera flashes to another scene. Tamara is still crying. "What?" he asks.

"Nothing, I just miss her so much." Tamara can't help but envy Miranda for getting that role. Being on that show would have been a dream come true for her.

"Listen Tammy, Miranda walked out on us. Nobody told her to disappear without keeping us informed on what was happening with her. It's not our fault!" he says before leaning his head close and kissing her mouth. She's crying so hard that she's barely returning his kiss. "I missed you so much," he utters while planting kisses all over her face. "Why did you leave me alone like that?"

The kissing builds up his excitement. He climbs aboard anxiously. Getting the privilege to make love to her once again is like a dream come true. "Tammy, I miss this pussy so much," he states while entering her. She stops crying long enough to hold her breath as he thrusts himself inside her. He makes love to her passionately as she stares at the ceiling crying.

Her lack of movement makes him feel uncomfortable. He's had sex with her enough times to know that she doesn't operate like this. Normally, she's a beast in bed.

He digs deeper and pounds harder trying to get some type of emotion out of her. Expecting moans of pleasure, all he receives from her are short grunts of pain. Her insides are as dry as cotton. She would normally be drenched by now.

He looks up into her tearing eyes. "What the fuck is wrong with you?" Suddenly, he feels someone's presence standing over him. He looks back over his shoulder. Three men stand over him. Only one of the men has his gun aimed at Sha-Rock

"Don't stop. It was just getting good to her," the gunman says sarcastically while the other two men laugh. "Turn over," he demands. "Nice and slow."

Sha-Rock does as he says. He's baffled. Many thoughts are racing through his mind. As soon as he gets off of Tamara, she jumps up quickly, clearing herself away from the bed. She immediately runs for her clothes and puts them on in record-breaking time.

The gunman speaks. "Let me introduce myself. My name is

Najim. You never met me, but you knew my twin brother quite well. His name was Najee."

Sha-Rock is looking him directly in the eyes. He already knows how this story is about to end. They caught me slippin', he says to himself as he closes his eyes, waiting for the shots to ring out.

"Ah ah," Najim says. "I can't let you get off that easy. Say it out loud," he says as if he's reading Sha-Rock's mind. "Let me hear you say it," he says while staring at Sha-Rock down the barrel of the gun.

Sha-Rock opens his eyes. He looks around the room at each person individually. He feels like he's been violated. Dudes standing in the bedroom of his house aiming guns at him while he's butt naked.

He can't believe that he fell for the same trick that he's used on so many dudes. They say a man's strong point is also his weakness. Sha-Rock proves the myth to be correct.

His mother always told him, he'd reap what he sowed. She was absolutely correct. He really hates to say it, but his respect for the game makes him. "You caught me slippin," he utters, before Najim lets the cannon loose. Five shots to the dome leaves him splattered in a bed of silk, bloody sheets.

Tamara stands there with her eyes covered up, not wanting to witness the murder. "Tammy," Najim calls to her. She takes her hands away from her eyes. She's shocked to see the barrel aimed in between her eyes.

"Please Najim, please?" she begs. "You promised me you wouldn't kill me if I did it," she pleads.

"Shut up, you trifling bitch," Najim shouts before dumping one shot into her forehead. She collapses onto the floor lifelessly.

Two Days Later

Miranda places the collect call. "Yes?" the receiving caller accepts her call. "Miranda, what's good?"

"Nothing much, Najim," she replies. "What's up with you?"

"Everything is everything," he replies. "Miranda, thanks for everything."

"No, thank you!"

THE END

ACKNOWLEDGEMENTS

First and foremost I have to thank God for showing me a different way. I prayed to you for years, asking you to show me a way out. Just when I was starting to lose hope, you answered my prayers. Me an author? Who would have ever known?

I know you don't agree with the books that I'm writing, but please continue to be patient with me. Change takes time. Please continue to bestow your mercy and blessings upon me? Ameen!

I'm back once again. A few people think I went soft with my last one. Well, I dumped 10 Viagras before I wrote this one. How hard is that? Ha ha ha!

I have to thank my loyal readers all across the globe; New York, Realadelphia, Baltimore, Florida, Texas, and New Orleans. Y'all definitely showing the kid mad love. Crystal Gamble from Chi-Town, thanks for the synopsis. Angie, and family from Camden, what's good? Tracey Hamilton, Annette Foster and Joanie Smith what up?

Mom Dukes, look up the block. Your boys ain't on them corners no more. Ain't you happy? I see you blushing from here. I love you. Telly, keep doing that little step thing. One day I'll be sitting at the Nets game, and halftime you'll come out cheering. Do your thing!

Fajr, sky is the limit. You can do whatever you choose to do. I'm living proof of that. There are 2 words that I will not tolerate from you. "I can't." Eliminate them from your vocabulary. Always remember; Think big, you get big. As-Salaamu Alaikum!

To my entire family and all my friends thank you. Y'all have been a ton of support to me. Each of you has supported me in your own special way. It's greatly appreciated.

To my trainer, Charlie Thomas, thanks for taking the time out with me. The same combinations that you taught me to use in the ring are the same combos I use to fight my way through life. I've been hit with every combo life has to offer. I've been hit straight up. I've been sucker punched. Life has even hit me below the belt. But guess what? My legs may have wobbled, but my back never touched the canvas. I refuse to lay down. Charlie, I still remember that time I was fighting, and you screamed out "8 piece." I thought to myself, only a fool will stand there and let me hit him with 8 punches? I fired away. Either he was a fool, or my hands were just that got damn fast! Middleweights beware! I've been in my basement going hard. I got 12 good rounds in me. Y'all better hope this book thing works for me. If it doesn't, I'll have to pull the Ponys out of the closet. And the winner is!

Rafii, As Salaamu Alaikum! You've acted as a straight jacket to me. Thanks for keeping me focused.

To my other good friend Rafii, keep bumping your head, and Allah will handle the rest. As Salaamu Alaikum!

To my Big brother Bas, I feel you with all that you're going through, but you better pick up a pen or a phone and holler at me. One Love, One God, As-Salaamu Alaikum!

Special shot out to all the barber shops and beauty salons that allowed me to pump my books in their establishments; Youngers, Cut Creators, Showtime Unisex, La Mazyk's, Flawless Creations, Kleen Kutz, and any other shop that I may have forgotten.

All the brothers in TLE Variety, As Salaamu Alaikum! Friend Or Foe Entertainment, it's time to turn it up. The streets are waiting. Shareef from Blue Print Entertainment, what up! Nitty and 5 Star Entertainment, y'all showed us mad love at that Cricket Club. Big shot out to DJ. Til. Born from Planet Earth, what's the deal Homie! Savoor Clothing, keep pushing. It's all a hustle. Tonisha hold your head up. You have always been a trooper. Lil OE from G.K.V. How could I forget you? Special thanks to Adila Francis and Fahiem from the Source Magazine, Laura Lubrano from Vibe Magazine, Antione and Artie from FEDS Magazine, Cavario from Don Diva Magazine, and also my people over at XXL Magazine. Tiffany from Dubrow Management, what's happening? Mecca, it's time to turn the Heat up! Tracy and Rakib, from Creative Impressions, thanks for blasting my joints! Source of Knowledge y'all showing the kid crazy love, too. I can't forget about Gateway Books, y'all definitely keep me in mind. Thanks so much.

I've met some fly people throughout my travels. Mikell Davis (Black Mafia Series) As-Salaamu Alaikum, Homie! Shannon Holmes (B-More Careful) Congratulations on making that big step. That's a beautiful look! Treasure E. Blue (Harlem Girl Lost) They're loving you, kid! Keep hustling. Sean Timberlake (Second Chance) Holla at a gangster! Crystal Winslow (Criss Cross) You are so focused! Keep your mind right. Deborah Smith (Robbed Without a Gun) Keep your circle tight and you'll be able to work out the kinks. Moody Holiday (Wild Innocence)

Your name is buzzing in the bricks. TN Baker (Still Sheisty) I knew you had it in you. They're screaming your name. Tracy Brown (Dime piece) keep blazin them bestsellers list. Kashamba Williams (Driven) I have to give you the female hustler of the year award. Keep doing what you do! Wahida Clark (Every Thug Needs A Lady) I haven't heard from you in a while, but I'm sure you're in the lab brewing something. As Salaamu Alaikum! December, don't let all that knowledge of the business go to waste.

Much respect for my people who have been repping me from day one. On a different vibe; I have been hearing rumors of a certain individual whom is still questioning my credibility. I'm not going to say your name and blow you up, but you know exactly who you are. In fact, as you're reading this, you're probably burning up inside. Please don't get it twisted. I am not an industry dude. I'm an in- da-street dude. The only thing that has changed about me is my eating habits. Check my resume. I'm from the Audi 4000, Benz 190-E era. I'm not new to this. I'm True 2 this. Stop wasting time running around town inquiring about me. That's not gangster at all. Don't pick and choose. If you want it, come get it. You know exactly where I'm at. I'm not hard to find!

Oh, one more thing. This book wasn't made to disrespect my town. Out-of-towners please don't get any ideas. If this book was based on a true story, the main character wouldn't have made it past the first twenty pages. Also, no disrespect to any other towns that I have mentioned in this book. Please don't email me talking about; your brother was one of my characters. This book is all fiction! Love is Love! Thanks for all the support.

To my graphics team, Porfirio, what would I do without y'all? This cover alone should get me on all the bestsellers list. Y'all outdone yourselves with this one.

Sha- Sheldon, RIP. Homey, you're gone but not forgotten. You got called back three books ago, but the team still holds you close. Your team jersey is still in the plastic. Yo, I still have your phone number locked in my jack. When I get to the gates of heaven, I'll call you so you can bust the gates and let me in. Until then, Rest In Peace, my dude!

Any reader that I have had the pleasure of meeting knows my motto; Real People Do Real Things. You all have been so Real with me, and that's a beautiful thing. In return, I vow to keep it True 2 Life forever. Peace, and I'm out!

True 2 Life Productions
P.O.BOX 8722, Newark, N.J. 07108

E-mail: true2lifeproductions@verizon.net
Website: www.true2lifeproductions.com

Also by the Author:

Sincerely Yours?
ISBN # 0-974-0610-2-6 $13.95
Sales Tax (6% NJ)   .83
Shipping/ Handling
Via U.S. Priority Mail $ 3.85
Total $18.63

Block Party
ISBN # 0-974-0610-1-8 $14.95
Sales Tax (6% NJ)   .89
Shipping/Handling
Via U.S. Priority Mail $3.85
Total $19.69

No Exit
ISBN # 0-974-0610-0-X $13.95
Sales Tax (6% NJ)   .83
Shipping/ Handling
Via U.S. Priority Mail $ 3.85
Total $18.63

Caught 'Em Slippin'
ISBN # 0-974-0610-3-4 $14.95
Sales Tax (6% NJ)   .89
Shipping/ Handling
Via U.S. Priority Mail $ 3.85
Total $19.69

PURCHASER INFORMATION

Name: _____

Address: _____

City: _____ State: _____ Zip Code: _____

Sincerely Yours? ___

Block Party ___

No Exit ___

Caught 'Em Slippin' ___

HOW MANY BOOKS? _____

Make checks/money orders payable to:
True 2 Life Productions

**COMING
FALL
2005**

Made in the USA
Monee, IL
23 April 2020